CW00816124

THE
MISSING
HOUR

Robert Rutherford is a founding member of the Northern Crime Syndicate crime writers' group and has been shortlisted twice for the CWA Short Story Daggers. *The Missing Hour* is Robert's second novel after his debut thriller, *Seven Days*. He lives in Newcastle with his family.

Also by Robert Rutherford

Seven Days

THE
MISSING
HOUR

ROBERT
RUTHERFORD

HODDER &
STOUGHTON

First published in Great Britain in 2025 by Hodder & Stoughton Limited
An Hachette UK company

The authorised representative in the EEA is Hachette Ireland, 8 Castlecourt
Centre, Dublin 15, D15 XTP3, Ireland (email: info@hbgi.ie)

1

A CIP catalogue record for this title is available from the British Library

Hardback ISBN 978 1 399 72644 3
Trade Paperback ISBN 978 1 399 72645 0
ebook ISBN 978 1 399 72646 7

Typeset in Plantin Light by Manipal Technologies Limited

Printed and bound in Great Britain by Clays Ltd, Elcograf S.p.A.

Hodder & Stoughton policy is to use papers that are natural, renewable
and recyclable products and made from wood grown in sustainable forests.
The logging and manufacturing processes are expected to conform to the
environmental regulations of the country of origin.

Hodder & Stoughton Limited
Carmelite House
50 Victoria Embankment
London EC4Y 0DZ

www.hodder.co.uk

To Nic,
In the words of McFly, it's all about you

Chapter One

They come for him in the stillness of the early hours, rubber-soled boots muted as they sink into the thick pile carpet of the hallway. No splintering door frame to announce their arrival. One swipe of key card against touch-plate grants access with a soft click. They move inside the darkened hotel room, four-strong, tasers drawn. Red dots dart across the sleeping figures like mosquitoes. Shadows retreat as their eyes adjust, helped by the shaft of light that follows them through the door.

Two peel off, moving towards the man who's snoring up a storm. A third stays in the short corridor, blocking the exit, while the fourth pads around to the woman's side of the bed. The other three look to him, tensing as he holds up three fingers. Two. One.

Silence explodes into noise. Hands rip back covers, grabbing wrists, wrenching them together. Snores transition into grunts. Grunts become shouts. More noises than words, trying to make sense of the half-formed shapes trussing him, dragging him up from his dreams and into a waking nightmare. He bellows like a wounded animal as the cuffs bite into his wrists. He's huge. A bear of a man, but his size is no help as the two men by his side heave him over the edge of the mattress. He struggles, twisting away from their grasp. One of them bears down on Grant with his full weight, forcing Grant's head down at a rate of knots until his head catches the bedside table corner. The sound is somewhere between a thud and a crunch, cutting off his protests like he's landed on a mute button.

The woman had woken a split second after her husband, and she twists now, struggling to sit up, but she's pushed back against the mattress by a gloved hand. She opens her mouth to scream, a dark black oval amongst half-lit shades of grey, but the same hand clamps over her mouth.

'Police. Stay put. Do. Not. Move. Understand?'

Her eyes dart like flies looking for a place to land, head wrenching to the side, looking for her husband. A second attempt to rise meets more resistance. Her mouth is suddenly uncovered, but only for the time it takes the arm to slide six inches lower, pinning her neck to the pillow. Her eyes widen, panic clearly visible even in the gloom.

'Understand?'

She tries to nod, but that just makes the forearm across her windpipe roll in deeper.

His spare hand goes back to her mouth now, releasing just enough pressure with his arm that she can suck hungry breaths, air whistling through his fingers on the way in. Her eyes roll so far right as to practically disappear, as she seeks out her husband. A single silent tear makes a break down her cheek as he is dragged to his knees.

The motion rouses him, and the noise he makes as he comes to is primal as his brain reboots. On instinct he slides one leg forward, pushing up. It takes the man either side of him by surprise, and for a split second she pictures Grant rising to his feet, the smaller men scattering in retreat.

But it's a parallel universe that never snaps into existence. Instead she hears the metallic snick of a baton extending, and can only watch as one of the men swings it in a deadly arc. It connects on the side of Grant's knee. Sounds like a jockey whipping a horse, and his leg crumples beneath him. Grant falls towards the bed, towards her, his face a mask of pain.

But the angle is all wrong. Instead of falling onto the mattress, his head whistles past the edge, continuing down to the floor. She hears rather than sees the impact. Even on the carpeted floor, the solid thunk sends a sickening shockwave to her core. This time when they lift him up, it's as if someone has hit his off switch, head lolling forward like a puppet with strings cut.

It takes three of them to hoist the barely conscious man to his feet, and they part-walk, part-stagger under his weight back towards the door, one of them reciting his rights as they move. The fourth man waits until they've cleared the entrance, and have disappeared into the hallway before he removes his hands from the woman.

She stares at him as he backs away, and something in her eyes makes him wonder if she's about to leap out of bed, go for him against all odds. Instead, she pushes up to a sitting position, hugging knees to her chest.

'My husband,' she says in a voice that sounds almost childlike. Soft, vulnerable. 'Where are you taking him?'

'Your husband is under arrest Mrs Brewer.'

'Arrest? That's ridiculous. Arrest for what?'

'Murder.'

He sees the word strike home, stunning her like a sucker punch. Watches her try and process the blow he's just dealt to her perfectly ordered world.

'That's ... murder? That's ridiculous. I'm coming with you. Where are you taking him?'

'He'll be interviewed at Patchway, but you need to stay here Mrs Brewer,' he tells her. 'We'll be in touch when you can speak to him.'

'But—' she starts, and he holds up a hand to cut her off.

'Stay here,' he repeats, edge to his words like a teacher scolding a naughty child. 'You can speak to him when we're done with him.'

'Well how long will that be?' she asks, but his back has turned before she's finished her sentence. Her voice is heavy with hope, but he heads out, following his team without even acknowledging the question.

Chapter Two

And just like that, I'm in the eye of the storm. The men who swept over the room like a wave have retreated now, like a riptide dragging Grant off out to sea. In the silence left behind, I hear my own voice screaming in my head to move. Throw on my clothes and follow them to wherever they're taking him. But my body doesn't respond, limbs made of concrete, bonded to the bed, as I suck in a succession of shallow breaths.

Move!

I glance across at the concave impression where Grant had lain, literally sixty seconds ago. See the curve where his hip has dug deep into the memory foam. In spite of it all, I have to stifle a laugh at the stupid notion that I could cast a mould of him from it. But then my eyes fix on the bedside table. On the dark wet smudge that hadn't been there when we'd slipped between the sheets. Blood. Grant's blood.

Move! Now!

Seeing the trace of him is like a starter's pistol. I leap up and zip around the room, snatching items of clothing like it's a supermarket trolley dash. Stepping into rumpled jeans, slipping on flats. The briefest of pauses when my foot catches one of Grant's leather brogues, sending it spinning away under the bed.

I have a ridiculous moment of worry about him having nothing on his feet, as if he hasn't got bigger problems right now. Then I'm off down the corridor, patting my pockets in a panic, feeling for my car keys and phone.

I jog to the bank of elevators, jabbing an impatient finger at the button and check my phone. Just gone six a.m.

'Murder?'

Even though it comes out as barely a whisper, I look around, worried that someone might have overheard me. Stupid of course, there's nobody there. It's six o'clock in the bloody morning.

The downward arrow above the doors glows with an eternity's worth of promise before they finally slide open, and I slip sideways through the widening gap, as if the fraction of a second will get me to Grant faster.

Murder!

Here, now, in the cool calm box of the lift, the word seems so abstract. For it to be in the same sentence as Grant's name just does not compute. Questions flit around my head, ones I can't allow to land just yet. Can't believe they're actually ones I need answers to. Murdered? Who? Why? When? I shake them away. It's a mistake. Has to be. They have the wrong man. The lift pings and doors slide slowly open, revealing the ghost town that is the lobby. The receptionist on nightshift is only visible from the eyes up, rest of her hiding behind a raised Kindle, making no effort to engage. As I breeze past, I catch a furtive glance that suggests she knows exactly why I'm rushing out into the night like the place is on fire.

As I run outside, leaving the warmth of the lobby, a fine rain jewels the air, lit up by spotlights that illuminate the front of the hotel. Even as I reach my car, my eyes are drawn to a pair of retreating red brake lights moving away at a pace along the tree-lined road, winking at me in the gloom. Wheels spin as I stamp on the accelerator, and I power down the half-mile stretch after them, catching the soft glow of headlights swinging left onto the main road as I try to make up ground.

I keep my eyes fixed ahead as I follow them along largely empty roads, alone with my thoughts. This is a horrible mistake. There can't be any other explanation. We'll get to whatever station they're taking him to, and straighten all this out. It'll make for one hell of a story at dinner parties. I try and convince myself that we might even laugh about it when it's in the rear-view mirror, but that does little to soothe the savage seas churning in my stomach.

The journey seems to stretch out beyond all sense of time. I keep a respectful distance behind the unmarked car, fearful that the very presence of headlights behind them at this hour might provoke a confrontation, but they simply wind their way out of the countryside, dragging me in their undertow. They edge towards Bristol, but break west at Bishopsworth, and do no more than flirt with the outskirts of Bristol itself. The road hugs the River Avon, matching it twist for twist. The officer had said something about Patchway. Is that a station or a town? My sense of geography here is sketchy at best, and the thought of losing the police car is a black fog, flooding me with a sense of dread I can't shake. The Clifton Suspension Bridge sweeps across the sky above me, and a lump grows in my throat. Grant and his stupid tour guide skit. No matter where we travel, he makes up stories about the history, the landmarks. Stupid tales, not an ounce of truth in them, but ones that always tease a smile from me.

Grant isn't perfect, but he's not capable of this – of murder. In all the years we've been together, I've never seen him so much as raise a hand let alone swing a punch or wield a weapon. His size is usually enough to make anyone think twice. Big enough that people move around him on a night out, like moons around a planet.

The cloudbank up ahead starts to glow around the edges, trimmed with fire. My eyes feel grainy, like I've had sand kicked in them at the beach. The radio cycles through a playlist, punctuated by soundbites from a DJ with far too much enthusiasm for the early hour, but the chatter barely registers over the carousel of thoughts filling every corner of my mind. Should I call someone? A solicitor? The *Manchester Standard* has its own legal counsel, but they deal in contracts, in libel and slander. As far as I know none of the staff have ever been charged with a criminal offence to test the boundaries of their expertise, at least not in the nine years Grant and I have worked there.

'One thing at a time,' I mutter to myself.

Find out where they're taking him. Call Rose, my editor at the paper. She'll know what to do, or know who to speak to at least.

Breathe, Maggie. Breathe. I recite the mantra in my mind. Signs advertising the approach of the M5 motorway flash past, and I merge onto it, wondering if they're making a straight run back to Manchester. That notion lasts less than ten minutes, though, as they peel off, looping back across the motorway, onto Gloucester Road, passing through Patchway, finally leaving the dual carriageway to pull up alongside a blocky two-storey pair of buildings. I watch as a black metal gate slides closed behind them, and I park in a visitor space out front.

I switch the engine off, stare at the clock, wonder if it's worth a call to wake Rose up. I know they can hold him for twenty-four hours, no matter how trumped up the charges.

I let out a loud sigh, realise I'm gripping the wheel hard enough to blanche my knuckles and let go, hands hovering an inch above it. The tremor is slight, but it's there all the same, fingertips quivering like divining rods. I fight the urge to leap out, forcing myself to close my eyes for a three count, before snapping open, looking in the rear-view mirror. The eyes staring back look startled, exhausted. Far from the fire that Grant would bring if roles were reversed.

I hold one last deep breath, blowing a noisy exhale through my nose, get out and head inside. A young female PC, hair pulled back into a tight bun, looking way too alert for this time of day, greets me with a smile from behind a Perspex screen as I walk into reception.

'Morning, how can I help you?' she asks, in a rolling Bristolian lilt.

'My husband. I'd like to see my husband, please.'

The words feel clumsy on the way out, a combination of emotion and exhaustion.

'And you are?'

'Maggie. Maggie Brewer. My husband, Grant, they brought him in just now. They hurt him, he's hurt, I mean he hit his head while they were, you know…'

It's as if the hour-long silence on the way here has brought me to the boil, words tumbling out at pace now.

The constable fixes me with a patient smile. 'Mrs Brewer, slow down. You said he's just come in? What makes you think your husband is here?'

'The officers, the ones who took him, arrested him I mean, I followed them here. Just now.'

'Okay, one thing at a time, talk me through what's happened, and let's see if he's here.'

'I've just told you he's here,' I snap. It comes out harsher than I intend and the edges of the PC's smile harden. 'Sorry, I'm sorry, it's just ...' I punctuate it with a sigh. 'I'm just worried about him. He hit his head, you see, and I just need to know he's okay.'

The constable nods, accepting the apology, and taps at her keyboard. I crane my neck, trying to see what's on screen, but the angle is too tight. Instead I stare at the young constable's face, looking for a shift in expression that might tell me something, anything, but the poker face doesn't crack. After the longest wait, she finally speaks.

'So, what I can tell you Mrs Brewer, is that your husband isn't here. I can—'

'Sorry, sorry' I interrupt. 'What do you mean he's not here? I just watched them drive him in.'

'Watched who exactly?'

'The ones who arrested him. Their car ... I followed them here... they drove in here, through the gate at the side. They—'

'If you'll let me finish Mrs Brewer, he's not here, but I can see there was an arrest warrant for him ... carried out this morning ...' Her voice tails off as she goes back to reading from her screen. 'But he's not been booked into the custody suite. Let me just ...'

The smallest flash of a reaction ripples across the constable's features, something I can't quite read, but the couple of seconds of silence that follows hangs heavy.

'What is it? What does it say?'

'Bear with me, while I check something,' she says, standing up and heading towards a door behind her.

'Check what?' I hear the desperation in my voice now, pleading for a straight answer.

'Take a seat and I'll be right back,' the constable says, and vanishes into the depths of the station. I'm left staring at the slowly closing door, heart pounding so loudly in my own ears, that I fancy it would be audible if there was anyone left here to hear it.

A minute turns into two. Two become five. I eye the seats, hard plastic buckets that couldn't look less appealing if they were lined with drawing pins. Instead I pace back and forth around reception. A quick glance at my phone. I'll call Rose at seven. Should I ring anybody else? That brings a fresh mist to my eyes. Grant. He's the one I'd call if I was in trouble. My go-to. The one person I know is guaranteed to *not* pick up if I called now.

Grant's sister, Izzy, pops to mind. The other half of the least identical twins ever born. One of the calmest in a crisis I've ever known. I make a mental note to call her right after I speak to Rose. Get her help to sort a solicitor first.

Finally, a little over ten minutes since she disappeared, the constable reappears. At the same time, a second door set in the wall to the right opens, and an older woman steps out. I look from one to the other, unsure of what's happening here. Is it my imagination or does the constable look uncomfortable? The older woman approaches me now, hand outstretched. Smart trouser-suit, face framed by jet-black hair.

'Mrs Brewer, I'm Detective Inspector Fatima Ansari. If you'd like to follow me please,' she says, gesturing back through the door.

'Have you found my husband? Can I see him now?'

'Let's have a chat about this in my office.'

'Where is he?'

'Please, Mrs Brewer. It'll be easier if we can chat through here.'

Why won't she just answer my bloody questions? The sterile-looking corridor stretches out behind Ansari, disappearing into the bowels of the building. An image flashes to mind of Grant in a cell, white-washed walls closing in, and a wave of claustrophobia washes over me, the corridor seeming to shrink as I stare at it.

'I just want to know what's going on.'

'And I'm happy to talk to you Mrs Brewer, but maybe somewhere more private?'

I look around the reception area again, empty save for the two of us, plus the constable, whose eyes flick my way again now, in a way that screams something isn't right. Why is getting a straight answer so bloody hard? Anger starts to simmer, steaming away enough of my worry to give my voice some snap.

'Here's fine, thank you.'

Ansari stares for a beat, then nods.

'Let's have a sit down at least, eh?'

I frown, but allow myself to be guided towards the seats, and Ansari settles into the one next to me.

'As my colleague said, Mrs Brewer, your husband is not at this station.'

'Then she must be mistaken,' I say before Ansari can get another word out. 'I followed them from the hotel where they arrested him. And while we're on that, they were way too rough with him. I'll be speaking to our solicitor about that. And murder?' I throw up my hands in exasperation. 'It's ridiculous. Grant wouldn't hurt a fly. Who's he supposed to have killed?'

'I can't get into that yet Mrs Brewer, but I can assure you, I've checked myself and he's not here.'

I open my mouth to speak, but Ansari holds up a palm to buy a few more seconds. 'Bear with me. He's not here, but I do know where he is.'

I go to stand, the need to go to Grant a physical thing, dragging me upwards. but Ansari places a hand on my shoulder, gentle pressure encouraging me to stay put.

'I need to go,' I say, taking it up an octave. 'Where can I find him?'

'I'm being told he hit his head during the arrest. There were two cars. One that came back here, and the other that took him to Southmead hospital.'

My hand flies to my mouth, everything dissolving into soft focus as tears prickle my eyes. Bastards. Someone will pay for this, for hurting him. My Grant, who doesn't even squash spiders let alone hurt people. I blink, and a pair of teardrops make a break for freedom down both cheeks.

'Hospital?' I echo the last word, as if unsure what Ansari has just told me. 'How bad is he hurt?' I don't give Ansari time to answer. 'I need to go now. Which way is Southmead?'

'Mrs Brewer, I've just spoken to one of the officers at the hospital. I'm so sorry ...'

The rest is white noise.

Chapter Three

When he sees who's calling his heart sinks. The voice on the other end is clipped and to the point.

'Did you get what we needed?'

'Sir, there were complications. I—'

'Yes or no?' Direct. Simple. A man used to getting his way.

A pause. 'No, Mr Osgood.'

'And now he's dead.'

Statement, not question.

'Yes, but we have his phone, his laptop. We'll find it.'

'We?'

'I mean I. I'll handle it.'

'And if it's not there? What then?'

There's a pause again, and he feels the pop of perspiration across the base of his back. He's faced down murderers, thieves and drug lords, but there's something about the voice on the other end of the line. Cold, detached. Supremely confident in the knowledge that if orders aren't carried out to the letter, secrets can be aired that will wreck his life, never mind career. A plan B pops to mind, and he grasps it with both hands.

'His wife. She's at the station now. He could have confided in her. Might have told her something.'

Two seconds of silence.

'Could have. Might have. I deal in absolutes. I pay you for absolutes.'

Silence again, save for measured breathing on the other end.

'Find out what she knows.'

'And if she knows anything?'

He asks the question, even though he dreads the answer.

'Like I said, I pay you for absolutes. If she knows, then you know absolutely what to do.'

Chapter Four

Once the recording starts, they take turns, like actors reciting lines.

'Present in the room are Detective Inspector Oliver Hermannson.' This new face comes with a hint of an accent around the edges. Could be Scandinavian with a name like that. He's the definition of clean-cut. Thirty-something. Short blond hair, no hint of a five-o'clock shadow, and a jaw you could use as a ruler.

'Detective Inspector Fatima Ansari.'

Hermannson nods at me, signalling my turn.

'Maggie Brewer,' I say, hearing the tension in my voice, tightly strung. I'm rattling through the curve of emotions at a rate of knots. This morning's shock and denial has evaporated, for now at least, replaced by a slow burning anger. If I close my eyes, I can still hear the noise Grant's head made as it connected with the side-table. I look across at Ansari, echoes of this morning's conversation on replay in my mind like a macabre highlight reel I can't switch off.

Bleed on the brain … Hairline skull fracture … Seizure … Dead on arrival.

'Monty Dobson, representing Mrs Brewer,' the solicitor rounds off the roll call.

Ansari takes the lead. 'Let me start off by saying Mrs Brewer, that I'm so sorry for your loss, and we really appreciate you taking the time to speak to us. If you need to take a break at any time, you just let me know, alright? Any questions before we start?'

I nod, gaze flicking between Ansari and Hermannson. 'Which of you can tell me why my husband was killed?'

Even saying the words feels like an out-of-body experience, but the nausea in the pit of my stomach anchors me to this reality I can't quite accept.

Hermannson shifts in his seat, breaking eye contact, but Ansari holds my gaze.

'Mrs Brewer, what happened to your husband was a terrible accident, but I can assure you it'll be thoroughly investigated.'

'An accident?' I ask incredulously. 'An accident? Spilling a glass of water is an accident. Tripping over a shoelace is an accident. You weren't there. The way those officers manhandled him, that wasn't right. He hadn't done anything wrong.'

'Mrs Brewer,' Hermannson interjects. 'The officers were there to execute an arrest warrant, and we had reasonable belief that your husband had committed a very serious offence. As my colleague says, this was an accident. Nobody went in there looking for this, but our officers have to take reasonable precautions when dealing with someone they believe could be a violent individual.'

'Violent?' I say, feeling somewhere between baffled and amused. 'Grant? That's the stupidest thing I've ever heard.'

'And yet we have enough evidence to satisfy the Crown Prosecution Service for a warrant.'

I shake my head, wearing a bemused smile on my face. 'This is all a joke. Has to be. You've got him mixed up with someone else.'

'That's not possible Mrs Brewer,' Ansari says firmly. 'The evidence is as compelling as it gets.'

'Who is he supposed to have killed?' I ask, leaning back, folding my arms, daring them to state their case.

Hermannson looks at Ansari, who shrugs, and he clearly takes that as a green light. 'Does the name Paul Cosgrove mean anything to you?'

Grant was an open book when it came to his work, trusting in my discretion both as his wife, and a fellow journalist. I let the name rattle around in my mind a moment, but I'm drawing a blank, making me all the more convinced this is all a colossal mistake.

'No. Who is he?'

'He *was*,' Hermannson emphasises the past tense, 'a medical researcher at Luminosity, a bio-engineering firm based up in your neck of the woods just outside of Manchester. He was found dead in the early hours of yesterday morning in some woods around thirty miles from your hotel.'

I say nothing, just stare back at him, waiting for him to try and join dots that lead to Grant so I can pour scorn on their crackpot theories. Patience has never been my strong point, though, and Hermannson's matter of fact tone is grating on me. These people have ripped the heart out of my world. Maybe not these two sat in front of me now, but in the bubble of the interview room, I can only think of the police as a single entity. A collective force that did this to Grant. To us.

I'm used to being the interviewer, not interviewee. Smiling across a latte at celebrities selling their latest film, recounting a failed relationship. It's all a game. They have their story to peddle. My readers want it all with a slice of the salacious. Both sides playing their part with saccharine sweetness.

'And?' I say finally. 'I still don't see what that has to do with Grant.'

'We have reason to believe your husband killed him, Mrs Brewer,' Hermannson says with the tired patience of a grown-up explaining something to a child.

A laugh bursts out before I can stop it, and I slap a hand over my mouth to bottle up any more that might follow.

'That's ridiculous. What possible reason would Grant have to kill a man I've never even heard of?'

Hermannson shrugs. 'To be honest, we were hoping you could help us out with that part.'

'You what … you think I had something to do with this now?' I gasp, eyes widening.

The solicitor, quiet up until this point, comes to life now. 'Detective, do you have anything that links my client to the crime you're alleging her husband committed?'

Ansari steps in, soothing voice in contrast to Hermannson's brusque tone. 'We're not suggesting that you're involved Mrs Brewer, just looking for any insight you can share. How your husband knew Mr Cosgrove? What the nature of their relationship was?'

'And Mrs Brewer has already confirmed she doesn't know anyone by that name,' Monty Dobson says, flashing me a reassuring smile. 'So, might I suggest we move on?'

Hermannson looks far from happy at the suggestion, but Ansari takes it on the chin and pivots her questioning.

'I understand your husband was an investigative journalist Mrs Brewer. *Manchester Standard.*'

'We both work there.'

'Ah yes' Ansari consults the pad in front of her. 'You do the gossip column, I believe. *After-party?* Your husband was an investigative journalist. Broke that big story about organised crime in Manchester a few years back?'

I wonder if it's a flash of condescension I see, comparing my work to Grant's. Equivalent to putting a Nobel scientist and a kid with a chemistry set in the same sentence. Same disregard for what I do that lurks beneath the surface of most conversations with my own dad. Never Grant, though. He had gone to great pains to make me feel like an equal, even though others go out of their way to do the opposite. I nod, but say nothing.

'I understand he spent some time undercover back in those days?' Ansari continues.

Hermannson butts in. 'There were rumours that he crossed a few lines to get the really juicy stuff.'

'Don't you dare,' I hiss, feeling my hackles rise. 'Don't. You. Dare. My husband was a good man. Better than any of those who killed him. You can ask all the questions you like but you do not get to drag his integrity through the mud, not unless you want to add slander to the suit I'll be filing against you.'

'What I think Detective Hermannson is getting at,' says Ansari, trying to stick a plaster over an open wound, shooting her co-interviewer a steely glance, 'is that Mr Brewer had mixed with some nasty people in his time, and we're wondering what he was working on at the moment? Could there be a story linked to Mr Cosgrove, or to Luminosity? Something he was investigating that could have made them cross paths?'

'No,' I say, very matter of fact.

'You sound pretty certain,' Hermannson counters.

'Grant and I didn't have any secrets.'

'Really?' he says, raising an eyebrow. 'I thought you journos were all about protecting your sources, keeping your secrets?'

'From the likes of you maybe,' I say, screwing my face into an ironic smile. 'But we both played for the same team. It helped to have someone who understood the job to bounce things off.'

'What was he working on at the moment then?'

I puff out a loud breath. 'Nothing to do with bio-engineering.'

Hermannson narrows his eyes, seeing it for the evasive answer that it is.

'Can you share what it is?' Ansari asks.

'Not without speaking to Rose Evans at the *Standard*.'

'I understand you wanting to protect your husband's reputation Mrs Brewer—' Hermannson starts, but I cut right through him.

'Really? I don't think you do, bearing in mind you're the one who wants to drag it through the dirt. You can't just ...' I stop mid-sentence, as something clicks into place. 'This man who died, you said he was killed the night before your officers murdered Grant?'

Hermannson lets my attack slide. 'We estimate he died between ten p.m. the night before and two a.m. Saturday, give or take,' he confirms, then adds with a smirk, 'only half an hour away from your location.'

I feel the smile spread across my face, warm like a sunrise. 'Then it can't have been Grant. He was with me from Friday morning.'

'Mrs Brewer, you don't understand. We—'

'No,' I say, feeling the righteous anger welling up, colouring my cheeks. 'You're the one who doesn't understand. He was literally with me the whole time. No way could he have done this.'

'If you'll let me finish, Mrs Brewer,' Hermannson says, and there's something in his face, a poker player about to drop a royal flush on the table. 'We didn't arrest him on a whim. We have his DNA.'

I open my mouth to speak, but the words won't come. I try a second time, but now the fire has gone out in my belly, replaced with cold confusion.

'What do you mean you have his DNA?'

'Exactly that Mrs Brewer. We found his DNA at the scene.'

My mouth is as dry as sandpaper. I look to Dobson for help, but his face is a placid mask. My brain scrambles to make sense of two conflicting realities. One in which a supposedly infallible science has made a mistake, and another in which Grant, my Grant, has hidden something this shocking.

'But he was with me the whole time,' I say weakly. 'He couldn't have—'

'We have his DNA,' Hermannson repeats, tone softer now, even as he replays his trump card.

The room starts to spin, Hermannson's words like waves eroding the foundations of my world. My unshakable belief in my husband, cracking, crumbling, like badly fired clay.

Grant. My husband. A murderer?

Chapter Five

Funerals are a celebration of a person's life. Grant would have loved the lack of black. How about that time when he…

If anyone else throws a well-meaning platitude my way today, I can't guarantee I'll be able to stop myself from grinding one of the tiny triangle sandwiches from the buffet into their open mouths to shut them up. One thing I do know is that Grant would have loved how uncomfortable my dad looks. He and Grant tolerated each other for my sake.

He stands ramrod straight, like there's a broom up his backside and a coat hanger in his jacket. That's how Grant used to describe him.

There it is again. Past tense. Everything about him has changed from is to was. Seven days, and still, it all feels like a terrible practical joke waiting for the big reveal. As if I'll walk through the door and see Grant waiting on the other side, throwing that smile of his my way, all teeth, with crinkles that stretched from eyes to temples.

It's not a joke, though. This is real. My new reality. Life stripped back to the wood, with none of the niceties. A week of interview rooms and intrusions. Of questions and condolences. Most of all, though, it's what isn't here that stands out the most. Everything about Grant was larger than life. Wasn't just the fact he is – was – six foot six. It was everything else that came with him. The cheesy dad jokes he would have embarrassed the two point four kids we'd planned somewhere down the line. His *let's drop everything and do this instead* whims. The stupid facts he would quote as gospel, making me believe all sorts of ridiculous made-up trivia for his own amusement.

My mind leaps tracks like a runaway train, across to the version of him I don't want to think about. The one the police have pegged as a murderer. Still can't quite make sense of a world where he could be capable of what they're saying. The scientist, the one they're saying he killed, died from repeated blows to the head, according to news reports. Grant was certainly big and strong enough to do that, but violence just wasn't in his DNA.

A sad smile creeps up on me at the unfortunate play on words. There has to be room for error. Mistake in the lab maybe? I've tried telling them he never left my side

Dad looks around and catches me staring at him, twitch of a smile, slightest of nods, but he stays rooted to the spot. He's never been good at the emotional stuff. At least he hasn't mentioned work, today of all days. He's travelled light to Manchester this time, leaving the massive chip usually in residence on his shoulder back home in Newcastle. He has always wrinkled his nose up at celebrity gossip, much less acknowledged the reporting of it as any kind of career. Mam, by contrast, praises me to the hilt for every word I write.

My two sisters, Julie and Moya, flit around like sprites, topping up drinks, tidying paper plates, producing an endless river of tea. They check in every time they pass, gentle squeeze on my shoulder in place of words. Brothers are a different breed, though. Davey and Freddie are more cut from Dad's cloth when it comes to showing feelings. They're here, though, that's all that matters.

Thank God I agreed for Grant's parents to arrange the wake. The beauty of it being at their house is that

I don't feel overwhelming guilt at the fact I'm planning to slip away in the next five minutes. There'll come a time, I hope, when I can picture Grant without swallowing down a lump the size of a cricket ball. That possibility feels a lifetime away right now.

I've been dreading the spectacle of the funeral for a fortnight, but at least it's done now. Monty Dobson, the solicitor, has done a good job of fending off attempts by the police to interview me, but they've made it clear they expect me to give a statement sometime in the next week. The thought of reliving any of it again makes me squirm but I owe it to Grant, to hold those responsible for his death to account. Then there will be the small stuff, inconsequential, but painful nonetheless. Notifying banks, utility companies and the like. Davey said he'd take care of it but I can't shake the sense of obligation that it needs to be me. That, and it might bring enough of a sense of purpose to see me through. Maybe.

I catch a waft of Mam's perfume before I feel the light touch on my shoulder.

'Hey Mags. Get you anything?'

'How about a good excuse to leave?'

Mam's face creases into a kind smile. One that I've seen a thousand times before, and the familiarity is a warm blanket.

'You want to get out of here? Go. I'll cover for you.'

'I can't just leave, Mam.'

'Sweetheart,' she says, leaning in to whisper. 'You can do whatever the hell you want. You honestly think anyone's going to have a go at the grieving widow?'

I toy with arguing, but the throng of mourners, the never-ending sympathetic smiles – it's oppressive, borderline claustrophobic. The lure of home is growing stronger with every passing second. North Pole to my needle, and after a moment, I nod.

'Anyone asks, I'll tell them you've got a migraine. And don't worry about your brothers and sisters, I'll give you a call before we head back home.'

Thoughts of escape bring such a flood of relief that I feel myself tear up as Mam leans in for a quick squeeze. As she pulls back, her eyes look full up too, but only for a second, then she's off, heading back into the fray. I slide my half-drunk cup onto the table, and make a break for it before anyone else starts smothering me with kindness.

Only takes a few smiles and a brisk pace to deflect any would-be words of comfort and I'm out the front door seconds later. I haven't quite made it to my car before I hear a voice.

'You leaving or just heading to the shop for more booze?'

I recognise the peculiar mix of accents before I even turn. Manchester born and bred, but edged with an American twang. Subtle, not strong. The product of five years bouncing between Harrogate and the Big Apple. I look over my shoulder and see Grant's sister, Izzy, leaning against the wall that leads to the back lane, vape pen in hand.

'Maybe both,' I say, with a tired smile.

'Don't blame you. Depressing as fuck these things. He'd have hated it,' she says, very matter of fact, like Grant has just taken a rain check for a better offer.

She's been mistaken for Grant's girlfriend more times than for being his sister, never mind his twin. Looks-wise they're poles apart. Izzy is almost a foot and a half shorter than Grant, with hair that's a different shade every time I see her. Grant used to joke that she changed colour more often than a traffic light.

Today it's a pale cornflower blue, like her eyes. She takes a draw on her vape, puffing out a cloud that would make a dragon proud. Of all his relatives, I'm glad it's her who has caught me escaping. She's always made me feel like part of the family, right from day one. Izzy's one of those people who connects effortlessly with those around her. She and I grew pretty close when she split up with her husband a few years back. Turns out we have a lot in common, like both having dads who barely manage to hide their disappointment in their kids.

'Yeah, I'm not too keen on this particular one either,' I say, walking slowly back towards her. She wafts away the smoke and opens her arms. I walk into the embrace and feel the hitch in my breath as she folds them around me.

'You're still family,' she says softly. Always will be. None of this shit changes that.'

I nod, not trusting myself to speak. Instead I just cling tighter to the only person I think truly loved Grant as much as I did. Do. Death doesn't change that.

'Don't believe that rubbish you read in the papers,' she goes on. 'You know as well as I do, he could never be that person.'

I sniff loudly, pulling away, and nod.

'I know,' I say. 'But he's not here to defend himself. They're going to try and pin it on him, and I don't know how to stop them.'

'Me neither,' Izzy says, taking a fresh puff on her pen now I've retreated a few paces. 'Shouldn't stop us from trying, though.'

'You're right,' I say. 'I just need to get today over with, and I'll figure out the rest later.'

Izzy nods, glancing towards the house, then back at me. 'I still expect him to walk out here and slag me off for smoking this fruity rubbish you know.'

That's the phrase he used to use, and a laugh bubbles out as I hear his voice inside my head repeating her words.

'Feels like I've been sliced clean in half,' Izzy says, eyes misting over, lost in her own thoughts. She snaps back a second later. 'None of this sister-in-law rubbish any-more,' she says nodding firmly. 'You've been promoted to full sister as of right now.'

I move before I think, lurching forwards, latching onto her again. We stand like that for an age. I'm sure I feel a tremble in her shoulders, like she's finally letting the tears out, but when I pull back, her cheeks are dry, although her eyes are pools ready to spill over.

'Whatever you say, Sis.'

I snap a salute, and she grins.

'I mean it,' she says. 'You need anything, I'm here.'

'Same,' I tell her. She's the closest connection I have now to Grant, and it's an effort to peel myself away, but I do, promising to call her to meet up for a cuppa next week. One more hug for the road, and I head off to find my car.

The journey home, like the week that has preceded it, is autopilot, muscle memory. One minute I'm climbing into the car, the next I'm staring up the short path that leads to our front door. Correction, just my front door now. My heels tap out a sad solo beat on the hard wood floor, and the door closes with a solid thunk that echoes deep into the flat. I stand for a moment, soaking in the silence. These past two weeks, alone here, it's felt oppressive. The exact opposite of when Grant was here. It's as if the soul of the place, and his, have departed together.

'What do I do Grant?' I whisper the words, scared to ask, knowing there'll be no reply. Then, impossibly, as ludicrous as it seems, it comes to me. A decade together, ten years of childish humour on his part, and it has rubbed off. I start humming 'The Sound of Silence', remembering Grant doing his best rendition of the Disturbed version at the Christmas party.

The first smile in a week flickers, bittersweet. Gone again a second later, but no denying it had been there. Even now, he can still reach me. I head into the bedroom, shaking my head, still humming, marginally less melancholic for the brief connection to a happier time.

I slip out of my dress, letting it puddle on the floor, switching to jogging bottoms and a hoodie. I'm about to head downstairs, when something catches my eye. Grant's black Ted Baker case that had made the journey back from our weekend away without him pokes out from the foot of the bed where I'd slung it a fortnight earlier.

It's been daring me to open it for days, but the thought of sorting through his things feels like another step along the road to moving on, and that's not something I'm sure I'm up to yet. I stare at it, psyching myself up to the task. Not as if anyone else will do it if I don't.

'Oh, for God's sake,' I mutter, and stride over to it, lifting it up and onto the bed in one movement. Before I can think of a reason not to, I'm unzipping it, flipping the lid back, reaching in to flick open the clasp that holds the fabric strips across his shirts, but once that's done, I pause. Stare down at the time capsule of socks and T-shirts. Items folded and packed by hands I will never hold again. Fingers I'll never feel running through my hair. I blink, and for a moment, I'm fired over two weeks into the past, standing in the same room watching him pack for our trip down to Somerset. A weekend in Wells was meant to be something of a reset after a tough six months at work for both of us.

Blink. Back in the here and now. I start lifting things out, draping shirts back over hangers, stacking socks in a drawer, making neat piles I know will end up in a charity shop, but one step at a time. I've just scooped up a pair of jeans when my ring finger snags against the lining, and as I use my right hand to free it, careful to not tear the fabric, I feel it. Something solid, not the shell of the case itself. Something separate from that. Something that moves.

I frown, feeling the edges of it. Hard, rectangular. I look for a zip to open the lining, but instead I spot a stray thread on the seam. Not quite the neat stitching of the rest. I work a nail under a loop of thread and unpick it, stitch by stitch, until it's big enough to slip a thumb and forefinger through. What I pull out makes no sense. A phone. Not one I've seen before. Certainly not Grant's. The police still have that. Whose then? I shrug the stupidity of that question away with the slightest of head shakes, chewing on my bottom lip. Not his iPhone, but who else could have put it there if not him.

Why would a man have a second phone he hides from his wife?

'Don't do this to me Grant,' I mutter as my heart tap-dances a rhythm in my chest. 'Not this. Not now.'

Chapter Six

The man sits hunkered down in his car, watching as Maggie Brewer comes bustling back out. She's barely been inside five minutes, and there's something different about her on the way out. The way she bustles down the path, and into her car. More of a sense of purpose than he saw when he tailed her back here.

For now, his brief is to wait and watch, making do with monitoring her phone and emails. Not through official channels. His paymaster can be resourceful when it comes to side-stepping legalities. What he's seen has been pretty one-sided. Family and friends checking in on her. Short, polite replies. Nothing to suggest she's anything other than the grieving widow.

He follows at a discrete distance, through stop-start traffic, until she pulls into a retail park. Whatever she's doing, it doesn't allow for her attention to wander enough to worry him about being spotted. She disappears into Curry's, and by the time he finds a space and follows her inside, she's already heading to the checkout, clutching a small box. He makes a loop around an aisle full of laptops, and comes up behind her, glancing down as he walks past. Spots the phone charger in her hand. Once he's outside again, he positions himself where he can see her in the line of people.

No indication that she even looks at anyone else, let alone attempts a conversation. Sometimes a trip to the shops is just that, nothing more. In his line of work, it pays to be certain, and he waits until she starts to turn away from the cashier, before he scurries back to his vehicle.

The stakes are too high, for him, and those who control him, to leave anything to chance. There are ways to get information from someone. Means of extracting what's needed. Lines he's crossed before, had been ready to cross again with Grant Brewer. He hopes for the widow's sake that's a road he doesn't need to go down with her. That won't end well.

Chapter Seven

I stare at the logo glowing on screen as it powers up. My breathing sounds unfeasibly loud in the silence of her kitchen. Losing Grant has hit me like a truck, appearing out of nowhere, T-boning my life. I've told myself for a week now that life can't get any worse. Yet here I am, faced with the possibility that even from beyond the grave, Grant may have one final secret that would slam that truck into reverse, backing over me one more time for good measure.

Looking at the phone on the counter, heart thudding with the possibility of what I might find on it. I've never had reason to doubt him, but my mind flashes to an argument, one we had a year ago. Pictures from the work night out. A young intern from the *Standard* sitting on Grant's knee, arms draped around his neck. Grant laughing it off when I made snide remarks after a few too many glasses of wine. How I'd felt foolish the morning after. But now? Had I been right all along? Is this why he's gone to these lengths to hide the second handset?

And if he's hiding something like this, what else could he be hiding? There's a niggle at the back of my mind. One that I didn't mention to the police because it felt preposterous. But now? Now it's a seed germinating, roots spreading, squeezing the breath from my body. The night that man was murdered, Grant and I hit the sack around ten. I had drunk way too much and woke up for the loo just after midnight. Didn't spot it till I shuffled back to bed, but where Grant should have been, there was only rumpled sheets.

He has always been a borderline insomniac so I'd just assumed he'd slipped out for a cigarette or whatever. I didn't hear the door go, but remember feeling the bed dip when he climbed back in. The coolness of his arm that slipped around my waist. The soft glow of my Apple watch lighting up as I slid an arm up to scratch my nose. Five past one. An hour since I returned to an empty bed. More maybe. Who knows what time he snuck out? At least sixty minutes unaccounted for, though. More than enough time to drive thirty something miles to a dark patch of woodland and …

I shake my head, sending intrusive thoughts scattering like snow in a globe, snapping back to the here and now; to the phone in my hand.

One betrayal at a time. Deal with what's in front of you, I tell myself, not wanting to ask myself the questions about a missing hour that I know the police will ask if I tell them.

My stomach feels hollowed out, like someone had taken an ice-cream scoop to my insides. The home screen pops into view with a chirp, various apps littering the screen. I hover a finger over the screen for a second, opting for the contacts first. Empty. Text app next. A single thread. No name, just a number. All that's visible in the preview pane is a single word.

OK

I open it, afraid what I might read, but I couldn't stop myself now even if I tried. I stare for a second, scrolling down. The rest of the conversation, whoever it's with, is a series of equally as brief exchanges, going back around six weeks, giving very little away. No sense of who they're to, or what they relate to, but it's enough to make my fears flare up, burning all the brighter. A second phone. Secret meetings. None of this translates into a story I can sell to myself. The most recent is dated a little over a week before his death.

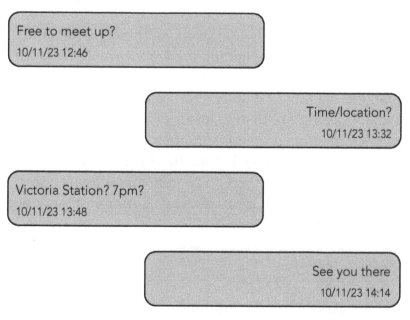

Free to meet up?
10/11/23 12:46

Time/location?
10/11/23 13:32

Victoria Station? 7pm?
10/11/23 13:48

See you there
10/11/23 14:14

The date triggers a memory. Last-minute tickets falling onto my desk to a gig at the Manchester Arena. Grant looking sheepish as he tells me he has to work late. I'd gone with a friend instead, but I'd still beaten Grant back home. He hadn't slunk in until the early hours. I'd still been miffed, and pretended to be asleep. Hadn't thought anything of it at the time other than being second choice to a job he seemed to love more than me at times. Now, though, I ask myself if he'd crawled out of somebody else's bed, back into ours.

The notion takes form, gathers substance around it, anger and betrayal mixing into a coarse cocktail.

'Don't do this to me Grant,' I mutter under my breath. It's easier, in this moment, to hate him rather than mourn him, and before I can give it too much thought, I'm tapping the number, lifting the phone to my ear, psyching myself up to tear a strip off whoever had sunk their claws into my husband.

As a standard network voicemail greeting kicks in, I exhale a loud breath, getting ready to leave a verbal barrage, but think better of it. If I was on the other end of that, the last thing I'd do is return the call for more of the same. I need more than to just leave a stinging voicemail for closure. I need to look into their eyes.

I cut the call short before the beep, and tap out a text instead. There's every chance that whoever she is won't even know Grant is dead. I mimic a previous message.

> Free to meet up?

I stare expectantly at the message, at the blank space beneath it, willing bouncing dots to appear to signify a reply. When they pop seconds later, I almost drop the phone in surprise.

> Can't talk now. Victoria station – Beer House 7pm?

I spot the tremor in my fingers as I type the reply. A meeting I don't want, but have to make.

> See you there.

Chapter Eight

Rush hour has been and gone, but there's still a steady flow through the station. A dozen destinations flicker across displays. I sip nervously on a Diet Coke, pretending to scroll on my phone, glancing up every few seconds at the doors that lead out to the platforms. Every time they swish open, I expect to see the intern, or a version of her, sashay through, unaware that the man she thinks she's meeting is just a memory now.

I'm not even sure I'll know them when I see them, and, not for the first time, question my own sanity for doing this. What does it matter, now that he's gone? For all I know, the other woman, whoever she is, might not even know Grant is … was married. I could end up venting to someone just as innocent as I am. Not too late to get up and leave, but stubbornness sticks me to my seat.

It's four minutes past the hour, and no likely candidates have entered the bar. All I've seen are steady streams of fans flocking to see yet another Spice Girls reunion. A mix of girl's nights out, and mothers dragging daughters along for a glimpse of their own teenage years. At one point, there are that many Spice Girl's T-shirts in the room, I begin to feel like I'm breaking a dress code.

Watching the ebb and flow as gig-goers and commuters mingle, I give a wry smile at the thought of being stood up by Grant's mistress. Oh, the irony. I slide the phone out from my bag, checking for any messages, but the last one on the thread is my own.

Another minute ticks by. Two. Three, and I'm about to write it off as a bad call when the doors open and a throng of people walk in. Not one big group. They split off into three. Four young girls, university age, bustle across to the bar lost in conversation. In front of them is a timid looking Asian man in a rumpled suit and grey overcoat. But it's the woman bringing up the rear that sets the jackpot signals dinging. She could be cloned from the same lab as the intern. Black pencil skirt clinging to hips. White blouse with one button too many popped. Chestnut hair cascading over her shoulders. The woman glides over to the bar, coming away a minute later with a white wine, and takes up residence twenty feet away.

I fail miserably in my efforts not to stare. The answers I need are within touching distance now, but I have to be sure. Have to know it's the right woman, before I drop the emotional hammer on her. I unlock the phone, open the messaging app, and tap on the number, lifting the handset to my ear as the woman takes a sip of her wine.

It rings once. Twice. A third time. Still no reaction. I stare so hard at the woman, willing her to pick up, that I'm almost unaware of the voice in my ear.

'Hello?'

What throws me, though, making my brow knit in confusion, is the fact it's a man's voice on the line.

'Hello, Mr Brewer?'

My eyes dart around the room, scanning faces.

'Mr Brewer?' This time with a touch of urgency. Seconds tick away, buzz of the bar going on around me, almost drowning out the shallow breathing on the other end of the call.

My heart is beating so hard now, it's practically pulsing through my jacket, but still I say nothing. Then, just as I'm gearing up to reply, I see him. The Asian man in the suit, phone to his ear, stock still but eyes darting around the bar like flies. When he finally notices me staring, his mouth drops open a fraction, and before I can say a word, he's off out through the door.

'Wait,' I say, but he's already out of sight.

I ditch the dregs of my drink, torn between the confusion of his exit and relief that Grant hasn't betrayed me. I hurry after the mystery man, pushing past a couple on their way in. I see him again, exiting the station to the right, and I trot after him, craning to see over commuters' heads, looking down the line of black cabs stretching off up the road like shiny dark beetles. I worry for a second that he's already ducked into one, but finally spy him bustling towards Todd Street, glancing back towards the station. Who the hell is he? Why is he running away? What connection does he have to Grant?

I pick up the pace, closing the gap, glad I wore flats. By the time he reaches the junction with Corporation Street, I'm only twenty feet back, and call out.

'Wait, please.'

His head whips around at the sound of my voice, and I see a worried look on his face. Why is he scared? He doesn't even know who I am.

'Please,' I try again. 'I'm Grant's wife. I just want to talk.'

He's doing a slow jog now, a stiff gait that doesn't speak of regular exercise. I put on a spurt and get close enough to reach out, touching his shoulder.

'He's dead. Grant is dead.'

That stops him like he's hit a brick wall, and now I'm up close I can see the undiluted fear etched into his face, light sheen glistening on his forehead. I'd say he's late thirties. Slight build bordering on skeletal. Nerdy wire-rimmed glasses and hair that is long overdue a good barber.

'He's dead?'

The man is gently spoken, almost a whisper, but I put that down to the shock of the news as much as anything. Barely a trace of any accent, not enough around the edges to give much away. I nod, noticing he's looking past me, as if expecting someone.

'I'm so sorry for your loss, but I have to go,' he says and takes a step backwards.

'Wait!'

I reach out again, grabbing a handful of lapel this time. 'Who are you?'

'Let me go,' he says, swatting ineffectively at my hand.

'Not until you tell me who you are, and how you knew my husband.'

'Get off me. Please!' he says, practically begging now.

'I'm not letting you go until you answer me.' I see his eyes roving behind me again, and I chance a glance, seeing nothing but a flow of people, breaking around us like a river around rock. I take a stab in the dark that this was work-related.

'I can help,' I say, 'I work at the *Standard* too.'

Something flickers in his eyes. Wheels turning, decisions being made.

'You said he was your husband?' he asks, words still laced with mistrust.

I nod emphatically, pulling out my own phone, holding out the screensaver for him to see. Grant and I, taken on my birthday last year, suited up and ready for a skydive. Both grinning ear to ear. The man stares a few seconds longer, finally nodding towards Starbucks on the corner.

'We need to get off the street. It's not safe.'

Chapter Nine

He watches Maggie Brewer disappear into Starbucks, wondering at the identity of the man she'd just chased down. He had been in two minds as he skirted around them, giving them a good six-foot berth. In the end, he opted for holding his phone at waist height, preferring footage rather than still shots, hoping he might pick up some audio as a bonus.

He doubles back, sees through the window that they head straight to a table, no pretence of ordering coffee. Too risky to go in. He retreats over the road, taking up residence outside the large branch of NEXT, enough footfall to act as a smokescreen when they come back out. Leaning against the plate glass window, he scrolls through the short clip he's just taken, scrubbing a finger back and forward slowly as he reaches the point where the man comes into shot. Pauses it at the clearest frame, screenshots and sends it to an unnamed number on WhatsApp.

He flicks it back to the start now, and holds it up to his ear, straining to hear it above the migrating herds of late-night shoppers and early-evening drinkers. His own footsteps tap in his ear. A tram glides past. He listens intently now, closing his eyes, willing the background noise to fall away. Sounds of the city are a constant base note, but above it all, just for a split second, words filter through. Just a handful, before the rest of the conversation is swallowed up by the drone of a bus engine pulling out of Withy Grove.

Only three words make it through the haze of sound. It's enough, though.

I can help.

Chapter Ten

'What did you mean, it's not safe?'

I wait him out, watching as he plays with a discarded sugar packet on the table. Glancing at the door as a young couple walk in, tracking them as they approach the counter. Finally, satisfied they're of no interest, he speaks.

'Exactly that. You said your husband had passed away?'

I nod. Say nothing. Wonder again how this man's life and Grant's intersect.

'I'm truly sorry for your loss,' he says, tongue darting out to wet cracked lips. 'How much do you know?'

I debate how to play this. Too stand-offish and it'll be obvious I'm fishing. Could always bluff, but after the day I've had, I simply don't have the energy.

'I buried my husband today. He was arrested on some trumped-up bullshit that he couldn't have done. I know he didn't because he was with me, but they arrested him anyway. They arrested him and he died. Then I found this.' I spin the phone on the table. 'And yours is the only number in it. Honestly? I thought he was having an affair.'

That makes him look up, puzzled. 'Then you know nothing?'

'I know you were scared enough to sprint from that bar,' I say. 'I know you were happy to meet Grant, but scared of anybody else, which tells me whatever you two are involved in, it must be something pretty heavy.'

'That's between me and your husband.'

Something else occurs to me. Something I've never even considered, and I lean in. 'You weren't, were you?'

'Weren't what?'

'Having an affair?'

'What? No!'

His denial comes out louder than he obviously intended, attracting glances from a few of the customers.

'I just, you know, didn't want to assume that ... never mind.'

'You said he died after they arrested him. What happened?'

The constant deflection is getting annoying, but I take a deep breath and run him through the previous week's events.

'And they had his DNA you say?'

'That's what they tell me. But they can't can they? I mean this just makes no sense. None of it makes any sense.'

'And you're absolutely positive there's no way he could have slipped away without you noticing?'

'We were miles away,' I say, patience wearing paper thin. 'He was with me all night, apart from ...' I stop short, not wanting to mention the sixty-minute window. The thought of seeing any kind of judgement on a stranger's face is too much to bear right now. That, plus it's a Pandora's box that I can't allow myself to open in case something inside takes root. 'We've even asked for the CCTV from the hotel to show he never left.'

'With you apart from ...?' He isn't about to let it lie, so I decide to share what I've kept back from the police.

'Not long, can't be more than an hour, but I woke up and he wasn't there. He came back around an hour later.

'And you say he was arrested early Sunday morning. So this missing hour would have been on the Friday night?'

'Yes, that's right.'

'I can tell you one thing. I owe him that much. He and I spoke on the phone at length that night. Around midnight if I recall. Does that account for your missing time?'

The relief that floods through me is a cleansing tide, washing away the residue of doubt. Restoring the version of the world that makes sense.

'It does,' I say. 'But apart from that, you've told me nothing. I still don't even know your name, and why are you so interested in why he was arrested?'

He purses his lips, clearly still uncomfortable about being here at all, let alone giving up any information of his own.

'Mrs Brewer, it might be better for you if you didn't know what your husband and I spoke about.'

I narrow my eyes at this, the last evasive straw, my already short fuse fizzling, as something else, something previously not considered, occurs to me.

'Is this the reason he got arrested?' I snap. 'Whatever *this* is.' I jab a finger at Grant's secret phone again. 'Do you know something that can help clear his name?' I pick it up, and before he realises what I'm doing, I snap a picture of his face, all ovals of surprise, eyes and mouth.

'Give me that!'

He reaches across the table, but I scoot my chair back a foot. Holding the handset well out of range.

'You either tell me how you know my husband, or I go to the police with your picture, and tell them you know something about that man they say he murdered.'

If he had looked scared earlier, the threat seems to push him to the edge of an emotional cliff.

'You can't. They'll…'

'They'll what? They'll kill you too?' I say, no attempt to hide the sarcasm, but see curiously that my words seem to have hit home in some way.

'Keep your voice down,' he hisses, looking over both shoulders.

'If you don't tell me what's going on, I swear to God, I'm walking out of here right now and into the nearest police station. Your choice.'

When he just stares back, I push back my chair and start to stand up.

'No,' he implores. 'Wait. I'll tell you, alright. I'll tell you.'

I lower myself back into the seat, fold my arms, and fix him with a stare that dares him to stall again.

'My name,' he begins, 'is Christopher Xiang, and I don't believe your husband's death was an accident.'

Not what I'd expected. It catches me unawares, and as much as I want to ask what he means by that, the words are stuck in my throat. All I can manage is the slightest of headshakes as he continues.

'Tell me, Mrs Brewer, have you ever heard the name HELIX?'

Chapter Eleven

They've been in there almost an hour now. Safe to say whatever they're chatting about, it isn't the weather. Not good. Maggie Brewer and her solicitor have made a lot of noise this past week, and there'll almost certainly be consequences for those that had entered the hotel room.

A WhatsApp notification pings, replying to the pic he'd fired off. Positive identification. Christopher Xiang. Senior Research Technician at Luminosity. Can't be a coincidence that the widow is with him now. Has to be him. Grant Brewer's source. The man has no idea of the exact nature of the problem, only that it matters to those who can make his life very difficult if he doesn't fix this. If he doesn't sort it, and soon, it'll be out of his hands. There has already been a not-so-veiled threat to send in Mr Clay. He has only met Clay once, but with a man like that, once is enough. Once is all that most people ever meet him.

A glance back over the road confirms they are still at the table. Looks like Xiang is doing most of the talking. What does that say about how much she knew walking in there? The fact that Grant Brewer's death had been sanctioned, albeit not quite in the way it went down, makes him nervous about what it is exactly he's being paid to nip in the bud. Will he be equally as expendable once he knows what Brewer and Xiang have been colluding on? No, he's a useful asset, he tells himself, almost believing it enough to stop worrying.

When they eventually leave, his orders are to stick with Xiang. The widow isn't going anywhere. He thinks, not for the first time, about the man he used to be, back before his one error of judgement that set him on this downward spiral. He's still hopeful there could be a way out of this, clean, a path back to the side of the street with fewer shadows. Far away from the likes of Mr Clay.

He tells himself he's not a bad man. That what they have over him, many might have done the same. He took a bad man off the streets. Kept them from hurting others. The fact he had to plant evidence to do it is the stick Clay keeps beating him with. How the Irishman even found that out is a mystery he has yet to unravel. Hermannson has toyed a thousand times with calling his bluff, telling him where to shove his threats. But he has seen first-hand what happens to people who cross Clay, and the men who pay him. Not even his warrant card could save him. And it wouldn't just be him they'd target. Family and friends wouldn't be safe either. Collateral damage too great to consider.

He's distracted by daydreams, and almost misses her as she emerges. She's alone, no sign of Xiang, either with her, or at the table they had been occupying. Shit. How would he explain this? Nervous perspiration pops, blotting his shirt. Maggie Brewer is crossing the street, heading his way. There are other people around. But not enough to lose himself in. Not close enough to the door to dodge inside NEXT either. She's checking both ways for approaching trams, and he's about to turn his back, and hope for the best, when their eyes meet.

There's a moment when he wonders if she's noticed him, sensing the danger somehow. Her eyes flick past him, and he takes the chance to stare down at his phone as if it's the most interesting thing he's ever seen. He catches himself holding his breath, letting it trickle out nice and slow through his nose, counting off the seconds in his head. Should be safe when he hits ten. Enough time for her to be well past him. Shapes drift past on the periphery, footsteps. He's just hit six in his head when he knows he's busted.

Chapter Twelve

I shake my head. 'HELIX? No. What's that?'

'It's not just a what, it's a who,' Xiang says, enigmatically. 'HELIX is part of it, but so is IQ. They're my employer, at least I think they are. Not directly,' he shrugs, 'but they're the spider at the centre of the web.'

'What is it you do?'

'I work for a genetics research company.'

'You're a doctor?'

He shakes his head. 'Research Scientist. Spend most of my time stuck in a lab.'

'So how did you and my husband meet?'

'I reached out to him. The work I do is very specialised. I don't make headlines, but I do save lives. What we do now could save thousands in years to come.'

'Who is *we*. You said you don't work for HELIX, so who do you work for?'

'A company called Luminosity, or at least that's who I thought I worked for. They're just one of a wider network of companies that all lead back to the parent one, IQ.'

It's as if he's talking in riddles, and I huff out a loud breath in frustration. 'Then who the hell are they, and what the hell is HELIX?'

Xiang gives a wry smile. 'I'm still figuring that out as I go.' My impatience must be scrawled across my face, because he holds out a palm to placate. 'Your husband was going to help me expose corruption on a national scale, Mrs Brewer. We don't know the full extent of it yet, but Grant was going to help us.'

'Us?' I say, narrowing my eyes. 'Who else is involved?'

'There are three of us. A colleague of mine, and a friend of his, someone from outside Luminosity, who has a way with computers.'

'A hacker?'

'He's not a fan of the name, but yes, I suppose you could call him that. My work colleague, you don't know, but you will recognise the name.'

When he tells me, I have to get him to repeat it to be sure. Paul Cosgrove. The man the police say Grant has killed. It sends my head spinning like I've walked off a fairground ride.

'I don't understand,' I say finally.

'This is what they do. They manipulate reality to suit their own ends.'

'So, you're saying you believe me, that Grant is innocent?'

'Not just innocent, Mrs Brewer. A scapegoat.'

'But his DNA?' I say, wrestling again with the contradiction of heart and head.

'You'd be surprised how easily reality can be shaped to suit a story.'

'We have to go to the police,' but even as I say it, the hotel room scene echoes in my mind. Grant being manhandled in the half-light. Dull thud of head against table. All carried out by the people I want to put my trust in. And what does he mean *shape reality*? Is he suggesting evidence has been planted?

'There's no guarantee they're not part of this,' Xiang says.

'Who then?'

52

Xiang sighs. 'That's why I went to your husband. He has a reputation for protecting his sources, and for exposing that which does not want to be exposed, does he not?'

A dozen questions swirl in my mind, as if the connection to Grant has pulled a plug. 'You said they manipulate reality. How can they manipulate DNA? They said his was at the scene. Everyone says DNA is never wrong, but I know, I just know in my heart, he can't have done what they say.'

The words tumble out, leaving an emptiness. One in which questions echo. If DNA is never wrong, then could it be that my memories of that night are? I squash down the doubt.

'My work involves finding ways to fix certain conditions before they occur. Working at a molecular level, to understand the reasons behind genetic mutations that cause any number of conditions. Did you know over half a million people in the UK have some form of underlying faulty gene that can put them at risk of anything from high cholesterol to abnormal heart rhythms? Usually people in my field, we are limited to working with a small number of subjects, especially when we're looking for something so specific to study. Luminosity has given me access to the largest subject pool I've ever known. Too wide.'

I'm thankful that he's keeping it high level, avoiding the temptation to get lost in the detail of what is clearly his passion.

'I still don't get what this has to do with Grant, though,' I say, and frown as he does another check of the café's customers. 'And who exactly do you keep looking for?'

'I've not been to work for over a week now,' he says, strain threaded through every word. 'The people who set your husband up, they will only have done that because he got too close. Who do you think they'll come for next? He assured me my name would be kept out of it, but …'

'Then do what you were going to do with Grant. Expose them, then it's too late. There'd be no point hurting you.'

'What would you have me do? Update my Face-book status with it? Best case I get laughed out of a job, worst case I end up like Paul. I needed the platform your husband had to tell my story. My work is my life, Mrs Brewer,' he says, shadow of sadness weighing him down. 'Do you have any idea how it feels to know that everything you've been doing is based on a lie.'

I almost tell him about Dad. That he thinks most of what I write is half-true at best. He said, she said. That he'd hoped I'd do better. Like I haven't tried. Haven't been forced to watch the last few opportunities at serious journalism go to less capable men with better connec-tions than mine. How he should just be proud that I refuse to give up. Won't give up till I get where I want to be. Almost, but instead I leave him to his monologue.

'I wish I didn't know what I do. That I could go back to being just another geek in a lab. But I can't. I can't let them get away with what they're doing, Mrs Brewer. I'm a Christian, and I couldn't look my priest, or my God, in the eye, if I do nothing. But I don't have the proof. Not yet anyway.'

'Proof of what?' I snap, fed up of running around in circles.

'Proof of what HELIX is. I told you that I had access to a large subject pool for my work. It's not just a few hundred people. It's everyone. You asked what HELIX is? I believe HELIX is a DNA catalogue of every man, woman and child in the United Kingdom.'

Chapter Thirteen

'That's impossible' I say, screwing my face up in disbelief. 'How would you even collect that? We're talking tens of millions of people.'

'I assure you it's not only possible, it's an absolute fact,' Xiang says, sitting upright, giving off *how dare you doubt me* vibes.

'And what? They've got a sample of Grant's that they planted on your friends' body?'

'Not exactly. The truth is more…nuanced.'

I'm starting to recognise his rhythms, how he approaches sharing anything substantial with caution. Patience is the key. Getting information out of him is like unpicking a knot. Rush it, and you risk it cinching tighter.

'They will have a sample, yes, but there's every chance your husband knew nothing about it.'

'How is that even possible?'

'There are layers to this, far more than I can talk you through today, some I'm still peeling back myself, and some I suspect, but can't prove yet. What I can tell you, though, is that through HELIX, Luminosity and IQ have access to the DNA of anyone and everyone in the UK, and I fear their motivations are far from altruistic.'

What he's suggesting is on such a scale that I can't quite wrap my head around it, like trying to hug a mountain.

'But why kill Grant?'

'These are dangerous people Mrs Brewer. The work that companies like Luminosity do, and all the others that sit under the IQ umbrella, it's worth billions. People have been killed for far less. I can only imagine that whatever questions your husband had been asking had reached the right ears, or the wrong ones for him as it turned out. You said you can help. You are a journalist also?'

'Yes,' I say, nodding enthusiastically, even as the voice in my head screams warnings. This isn't reporting who was seen with their arms wrapped around the wrong person at a VIP party, or interviews on a red carpet. People have died, plural. I tell myself I can handle this. My editor, Rose Evans, has contacts at Greater Manchester Police. She'll have someone she trusts.

'Yes, I can help.'

This is becoming about so much more than clearing Grant's name. It isn't just that I want to do it. I need to do it. If what this man says is true, this is violation of human rights on a colossal scale, all in the name of profit, and that's before I factor in what happened to Grant. Personal investment aside, it's the serious journalism I've hungered after for years. The kind even Dad couldn't look down his nose at. The kind I envied Grant for, even if I'd never told him outright. Rose will have my back. Give me the opportunity I know I deserve rather than dish out work based on the old boys club network like the editors before her. I'm sure of it.

The look on his face isn't one of immediate gratitude, and I wonder if I've misread him.

'You've just lost your husband. I can't expect you to get mixed up in this. Especially knowing how dangerous it is.'

'That's exactly why I need to. If what you're saying is true, these people killed my husband. I can't just walk away from that. I owe it to him to finish what he started.'

Even though I say the words with conviction, my confidence is on shifting sands. What if Rose doesn't green-light me on this, even if every word is true. The *Standard* has a dozen or more who could be ahead of me in the queue. A story this size, the decision might not be in Rose's hands. If I can take this to her as a *fait accompli*, though, there might be a chance.

Xiang's face softens. 'Your husband was passionate about bringing this to light. I see some of that in you.'

'Then give me what you gave Grant, and I'll help you finish what he started.'

'Your husband spoke of you,' he says after a pause. 'You are what I imagined you to be. You have a kind soul. That's how he described you, in fact. He said you were his soulmate.'

'I can do this' I implore him. 'I need to do it, for Grant.'

We lock eyes, and I fancy there's sadness in there, mingled with the fear. Whatever it is, melts away into resignation, and he nods.

'I don't wish to drag you in, but if I do nothing, they'll come for me soon enough anyway. Besides I have a feeling you wouldn't let this drop now.'

I feel the corners of my mouth crease. 'That's decided then,' I say. 'Where do we start?'

My smile fades, though, as his forehead furrows. He's looking beyond me, through the window at something, or someone.

'We should leave,' he says, standing up. 'You have the phone. I need to speak to my friend, the computer expert.

I'll call you and we can talk some more. I'm going to the bathroom. Best you're not here when I get back.'

He whirls away without waiting for a reply, and I stare after him, bemused. I twist, peering out at the street outside, but whatever spooked him has gone. I slip Grant's phone back into my bag, and head out into the cool evening air.

No trams trundling towards me, so I dart across the road, head swimming with Xiang's revelations. Feels like I'm dipping a toe into a bottomless dark pool, but Xiang is right. There's as much chance of walking away from this now as there is of finding Grant waiting for me when I get home. I catch a split second of a man's face over by the shop window. See the briefest flicker of recognition before he drops his gaze, and something pings in my mind, casting me back a week.

It's one of the officers who interviewed me the day Grant died. Hermannson, wasn't it? I have a follow-up interview scheduled for tomorrow, but that's not until the afternoon.

'Detective Hermannson? What are you doing here?'

He looks up at the sound of his name, face like a kid caught with a broken ornament at his feet.

'Mrs Brewer' he says, squeezing out a smile that doesn't quite touch the eyes. 'Hello, I um, I thought I'd save myself an early morning start and head up tonight. You doing some late-night shopping?'

'Hmm? Oh, no. I just...It was my husband's funeral today. I just needed some air.'

He nods, as if he can relate, and an uncomfortable silence follows.

'I guess I'll see you tomorrow then,' I say, giving him a cursory smile.

'Yes, tomorrow.' He shuffles a half-step back. 'Unless, if you wanted to save time, we could always have a chat now. Doesn't have to be formal. Maybe a coffee over the road?'

He gestures towards Starbucks, and the hairs on my neck prickle. Xiang will be heading out of the bathroom any time soon. Seeing me walking back in with a policeman, I may as well lay charges along whatever brief bridge we've built. His nerves were on enough of a hair trigger without that. I mentally scroll through acceptable excuses that don't make me sound as evasive as a politician talking about expenses. I force a few degrees of warmth into my smile.

'I'd love to, Detective, but my solicitor would have kittens if I told them we had a nice chat over a cuppa without him. He's quite protective, especially with how strong a case he thinks we have.'

I square my shoulders, stretching my five-two frame as much as it'll allow. Inside, I feel battered, both by Xiang's claims, and the emotional slash and burn of the funeral. Hermannson makes a half-hearted shrug, but doesn't look too disappointed. If anything, he seems distracted. A glance at his phone, as it chirps in his clenched hand, followed by the briefest of glances over my shoulder.

'Okay, we do it your way.'

A second glance, and something flares in his eyes, barely long enough to register, before he resets. My subconscious is a split second ahead of me, cranking my pulse up a notch before the possibility registers. What's behind me that's so interesting?

Starbucks.

The word pops into mind like a firecracker, making the mental leap from that to Xiang. Did Hermannson see me in there with him? Is that why he's lurking out here now? If there's a shred of proof in the pictures Xiang is painting, could Hermannson be part of the same machine that chewed Grant up and spat him out? If he is, how deep could this go within the police?

I remind myself that everything Xiang has shared, however worrying, is unsubstantiated. If Hermannson was here for Xiang, he'd hardly be trying to buy me a latte, would he? My anxiety starts to level out. I remind myself that I'm perfectly safe, here amongst a street full of people. Of course the Detective looks nervous. I want heads to roll for Grant. His may well be one of them, and he knows it.

'Goodnight then,' I say, walking past him towards the entrance to NEXT.

'Night,' he replies, as I pass him and enter the store.

The urge to turn and see if he's watching is irresistible, a magnetic pull that wins out after a dozen more steps. The pane he had been resting against is empty. I frown, taking a couple of steps back towards the entrance, almost disappointed to be proved wrong.

That doesn't last long, as I squint against the store lights, seeing Xiang having exited the coffee shop, heading away down Fennel Street. Any disappointment is wiped clear from my mind, replaced with a rising sense of dread, as Hermannson crosses the street at a trot, phone to his ear, picking up his pace the moment Xiang disappears from view.

Any other day, any other circumstances, I'd not give a coincidence like this a second thought, but after what I've heard in the last hour and seeing how uncomfortable Hermannson looked when I clocked him, something inside screams that I need to act. To warn Xiang. If I'm wrong, then Xiang won't hold an abundance of caution against me. If I'm right, though…

I start back through the door, and it isn't the transition from heated store to autumn chill that makes me shudder, goose bumps popping on my arms like braille. What if I'm right?

Chapter Fourteen

He's wondering whether to switch tack and follow the widow as the only target left, when Xiang emerges, cautious as a mouse poking it's head out from a skirting board, sniffing the air. The scientist doesn't hang about, darting left and disappearing along Fennel Street. Hermannson pushes off the window and trots across, sliding through a group of shoppers, breath fogging out ahead of him like he's puffing on an e-cigarette.

An uneasy feeling descends on him, heavy like a cloak, as he skirts the corner by Starbucks, catching a glimpse of Xiang. Fennel Street is pedestrianised, less crowded than the main drag and it won't be hard to keep tabs on him here. The challenge will be staying concealed if Xiang turns around.

Every step takes him further down the rabbit hole. He has done plenty of things he isn't proud of these last few years, but he's always been careful, a planner. Whatever happens tonight will be pure improv. This trip was about Maggie Brewer, learning what she knows, or doesn't. Stumbling across her meeting with Xiang could be the break he needs. If the scientist is taken off the board, everything else could follow like a house of cards, provided Maggie Brewer is no threat.

He's already taking a chance by arranging to speak to the widow tomorrow. His Superintendent has allowed him to take leave rather than be chained to a desk while Grant Brewer's death is investigated. If it comes out that he's been up to Manchester, spoken with Maggie Brewer, questions will be asked. Ones he won't be able to answer without setting off a chain of events that will pull him under.

What choice does he have, though? It's been made quite clear that if he doesn't deliver, that's what awaits him anyway. Not so much rock and hard place as between a landslide and a cliff edge.

Up ahead, Xiang's pace seems to stutter, only half a dozen steps, slowing down as if he's looking at the ground. Practically slows to a halt, and Hermannson gets ready to veer left, seeking the cover of a doorway, should Xiang look like he's turning around. A split second later, and Xiang is off again. Hermannson flicks a glance left and right as he goes. Can't shake the feeling, an itch between his shoulder blades, that Xiang isn't the only one in the crosshairs tonight.

The silhouette of Manchester Cathedral looms large up ahead, and Hermannson's eye is drawn to the rows of spires, spiking upwards into the gloom, soft lighting filtering through stained glass windows. He almost misses the glance from Xiang as he rounds the corner. The briefest of moments, and he's gone.

Shit. No idea how, but Xiang has made him. Hermannson throws caution to the wind, jogging the hundred yards to the same spot. There's something else bothering him. A flash of something in Xiang's hand. Glow of a screen maybe? Had someone warned him? If they have, if it was the widow, that can only mean one thing. She knows.

He skitters around the corner, gearing up for a sprint to catch his target, but slows to a walk. The road ahead is empty, save for an elderly couple walking away from him, linked arm in crook of elbow, as if they're stepping onto a dancefloor, and a man in a suit hurtling towards him on a bike.

63

Hermannson side steps, letting the cyclist whistle past, and scans the doorways to his left. Nothing. The Cathedral looks shut up tight too. Xiang would have to have set a time of Usain Bolt proportions to clear the length of Cathedral Street, so the entrance to the Corn Exchange to the left seems the only remaining logical option.

Hermannson ducks inside, and as intent as he is on locating Xiang, he can't help but waste a few seconds taking in the cavernous interior. Not what he was expecting. Curved glass panels soaring several stories above, punctuated by a glass dome that must sit atop the exterior like a cherry on a cake. Beneath a rolling wave of arches, a dozen restaurants peep out, softly lit interiors clashing with neon logos.

Dozens of diners drift in and out, but no sign of his scurrying scientist. Hermannson curses under his breath as his task grows arms and legs, multiplying in scale. He works his way from one restaurant to the next, giving the briefest flash of his warrant card to front of house staff, quick lap of each, even checking toilets. Twelve swings, twelve strikes. Each one seems to add weight to the feeling in his stomach, like setting concrete.

When he emerges back onto Cathedral Street fifteen minutes later, the temperature feels like it's dropped five degrees. Could just be the nervous sweat that's sticking his shirt to shoulder blades. He pulls out his phone, knowing he'll be expected to report in this evening, mind racing to create a better version of events, something that doesn't make him look quite as amateurish. Back to basics. He's got an address now, but whether Xiang is daft enough to go back to it is another matter. Worst case, he'll sit on the widow again. They've met once, and he'd stake his reputation on them meeting again.

Hermannson goes to retrace his steps back to the main street, resolving to stop off at the first bar he sees. Just one to smooth him out. He's almost around the corner before the figure sat on the low cathedral wall speaks his name.

'Oliver.'

It's raspy, a half-whisper, but stops him in his tracks. He knows that voice. Declan Clay. He wonders how long Clay has been trailing him? The very fact he's here speaks volumes as to levels of confidence in his own ability to carry out his orders. It still makes him nervous at how little he knows himself. His remit is simply to find out what Xiang knows, who he's shared it with, and hold him somewhere secure while decisions are taken. The fact he has no inkling what that might be, makes him wonder how expendable he becomes once Xiang shares anything with him.

'Mr Clay, what are you doing here?'

He's rarely heard anybody use anything other than the formal address for Clay. On those few occasions, it's been met with a stare with all the warmth of a snowball. Clay is one of those men whose reputation casts an image far larger than his actual stature, like someone standing up in front of a projector at a cinema. Hermannson has heard stories, some so outlandish as to defy belief. He might not believe them if he hadn't seen what Clay is capable of first hand.

Snapshots of a warehouse flash up in his mind, a scene he has tried to forget. What's left of a man, tied to a chair. Clay advancing towards them, vegetable peeler in hand. Hermannson can still hear the screams that echoed that day. He suspects he was made to attend as a warning of what happens to those who step out of line.

'Come now, Oliver. You know why I'm here. When was the last time you saw me show my face when things were going well?'

The softest of Irish lilts might fool others as to what this man is capable of, but Hermannson knows that his warrant card won't buy him an ounce of mercy if it ever comes down to a straight-up one-on-one.

'What makes you think things aren't going well?'

Clay pushes up from his perch. Hermannson has five inches on him, but takes a half step back as the smaller man approaches.

'Let's call it an educated guess, but the fact you're sweating like a paedo in a playground makes me think I might be right. Where is he?'

A split-second glance back towards the Corn Exchange. Rock and a hard place. Screwed whatever answer he gives.

'In there,' he says with a flick of his head.

'Show me.'

Hermannson hesitates, and knows it's a pointless bluff. 'I saw him go in. Just haven't found where he's holed up yet.'

'Do yourself a favour, Oliver; don't ever play poker with a face like that,' Clay says, closing the remaining gap between them, placing a hand on Hermannson's shoulder. Fingers like pincers clamp on, digging in to the meaty part by the neck. Pale blue eyes fix onto his, and there's a sense of controlled chaos oozing from Clay. A genie looking for an excuse to come out of the bottle.

'Now, I'm going to ask you once, and once only Oliver. Tell me what happened?'

Hermannson sucks in a lungful, nods. Hates himself for what he's become. Wasn't that long ago he'd have stood up to the likes of Clay, consequences be damned. They pay well, but more and more these days the money doesn't buy peace of mind for what he does to earn it.

His own greed has woven a noose around his neck he isn't sure he'll ever slip out of.

They slow-walk towards the building, and Hermannson takes Clay through what he's seen and heard. The Irishman listens in silence. Hermannson debates leaving out the part where he's pretty sure Xiang made him, but thinks better of it.

When he's done, Clay says nothing at first. Just stares up at the Cathedral.

'Do you believe in God, Oliver?'

'What? Um, I … no, my parents were atheists.'

'Some of us are long past redemption,' Clay says. 'The things I've seen and done, I just got to keep rolling the dice, double or quits, and hope there's no big fella in the clouds. Helps that you don't believe. Means you won't have to ask for forgiveness for what comes next.'

'What? What the hell's that supposed to mean?'

Clay tells him. Lays out exactly what will be required of him, and in such detail, that it makes the vegetable peeler seem humane.

Chapter Fifteen

I don't go straight home. Instead I walk slowly back towards the station, letting events of the last hour percolate. Xiang had texted a thank you, with assurances he was safe and that he'd be in touch. My head spins at the enormity of his allegations. He hasn't divulged yet how he uncovered all that he claims to know, but I know in my heart that I believe him already, or at least that there's some truth to it. Enough to clear Grant's name.

Hermannson is a worry, though. We're all drilled from an early age that the police are our protectors, that we have a duty to report wrongdoing to them. If he's somehow involved, how far does it stretch? I wonder about the other officer, the one I'd spoken to first that day. Ansari. Is she part of this too, whatever this is? Where do I even begin to unpick a conspiracy this large?

The entire population catalogued? The notion is of such a scale that it defies belief. How is it even possible? The enormity of the logistics needed feels incalculable. And to do it all right under people's noses? This dwarfs anything Grant has ever worked on before, and the idea of taking it on, of picking up where he left off, scares me half to death.

There's a slew of missed calls and texts, mostly from Julie and Moya, asking where I disappeared to. Is it really still the same day that I buried my husband? Time feels elastic, stretched out of proportion, enough that it might never snap back into place. The notion of a present that doesn't include Grant is surreal enough, but to think he could have been targeted?

My car is at the NCP Arena car park, and I'm thankful that the meeting with Xiang hadn't been later. The prospect of battling it out with twenty-thousand Spice Girl wannabes is about as appealing as tomorrow's meeting with Detective Hermannson. I've just climbed in the car when there's a buzzing from my bag. Not my phone. Grant's. A text from Xiang. No message, just a link.

> Christopher Xiang is inviting you to a scheduled Zoom meeting
> Time: December 4th 2023, 11:00 PM, GMT

Under that is a Zoom link, meeting ID and passcode for a session only a few hours from now. A chance to brace Xiang for more answers sooner than I'd bargained for. This must mean he's spoken to his pet hacker. I have a cliché vision of a surly teenager in a hoodie, surrounded by junk food wrappers, hiding in a dark room, bashing away furiously at their keyboard.

This gives me a few hours, plenty of time to make it home and join the call from the comfort of the sofa. I start the engine, but sit there for a minute, letting it idle. Could Hermannson have doubled back and trailed me here? No, I dismiss the notion. I've got an appointment with him tomorrow. He's hardly going to struggle to track me down when he knows exactly where I'm going to be.

The rows of cars stretch off into the distance either side, bright neon strips doing nothing to alleviate the sense of the low-slung roof closing in. Nobody jumps out from the shadows, though. Traffic is sluggish, and it's

more of a crawl than a drive home. I catch my eyes drifting to the rear-view mirror more than usual, and shake
my head, trying to loosen the notion of a shadowy figure
tailing me home. I don't quite manage to slough it off,
though, and the uneasy feeling persists, like a muscle that
won't stop twitching.

Closest parking spot is a good fifty yards away from
the front door. Sums up my life at the moment. As I pull
up, it's as if the world is conspiring to feed me paranoia.
The streetlight two doors down is out, leaving the path
cloaked in shadow. I look both ways up and down the
street, but there's not so much as a car headlight, let alone
any people, and I bustle inside, locking the door, leaving
the key in for good measure.

The next hour is a stream of half-bitten nails, and
furious Googling. Christopher Xiang's social media is
a closed book. If you're not a friend or follower, it's a
total shut-out. The only other references, and there are
precious few, relate to academic papers he has written,
dating back a decade. I try reading excerpts but it might
as well be in Latin.

Instead I turn my attention next to IQ. Try a dozen
variations on it, adding the word *company*, expanding
to *Intelligence Quotient*, linking it to genetics. Google
spits out everything from clothing lines to scuba gear.
Nothing that looks even vaguely linked to a genetics
research company or a DNA database.

"Cos of course, they'd just advertise it on Google,
wouldn't they?' I mutter to myself. I even try searching for the two police officers, Hermannson and Ansari.
Nothing more than name drops in local newspapers for
Ansari. Hermannson gets more hits, though. All linked
to a case from four years back, where he had taken down

several members of a high-profile crime family. This one made a few of the nationals thanks to the amount of contraband seized. Nothing of any note since.

I hope I'm judging him unfairly, that he isn't part of whatever this is. There's something that bothers me about him, though. An aura of intensity, nervousness even, more body language than words. As if there's a constant vibration to him, never settling.

A glance at the clock and it's fifteen minutes until the Zoom meeting opens. I close down browser windows, and slip my phone into my pocket. The kitchen is a mess. Day-to-day tasks like housework have shrunk down so small against the backdrop of everything else going on that I've barely noticed the accumulation of cups and plates encroaching on the counter like a slowly creeping sand dune. I busy myself now, relishing the sting of hot soapy water. Wash, rinse, repeat. I move onto drying, going through the motions, mechanical, thankful for the distraction. I'm almost done when the tea towel slips from my grasp, landing square in the still-full sink like a pool cover.

'Shit,' I snatch it up, wringing it out even though it's a lost cause. Plenty of spares in the cupboard next to the washer, but as I open the door, a memory ghosts past me. Reaching behind a neatly folded stack of towels, my fingers close around the box I had placed there two months back. It feels heavier than I remember.

As the lid lifts, the watch face inside catches the light, making me squint. I take it out, laying it on one flat palm. Turn it over, and read the inscription engraved on the back, lips moving along with the words.

For All Time.

Only three words, but enough to prise open the lid on everything I've been suppressing, as I stare at the gift that will never be given. I've tried so hard to hold it together this past week, but seeing Grant's Christmas present makes me feel like I'm slipping my moorings, light-headed, floating. Then the watch blurs, along with the rest of the room, as the tears come.

Before I realise what's happening, the box is clattering onto the counter, and I snatch up my car keys, heading out the door, no idea where, except that it can't be here.

I bowl down the path and into the car, door slamming shut. Fire up the ignition, gritting my teeth together, gripping the wheel so tight my knuckles ache. Focus on my breathing with eyes screwed shut, as if that can stop the twin tracks that trickle down my cheeks. I sit like that for what seems like an age, then finally open my eyes, scanning the street, half expecting someone to be staring at the crazy lady sobbing in her car, but it's only closed doors and drawn curtains that stare back at me. I shut off the engine. Where would I even go?

The dashboard clock catches my eye. The call with Xiang. It's one minute past. One hand reaches for the door, but I stop, not ready to go back inside just yet. I pat a hand against my pocket, relieved to feel the reassuring shape of a phone, and slide it out. Not a soul in sight still. Here's as private as anywhere.

My mouth is as dry as a cat's litter tray, as I open up the Zoom app, finger poised to tap the join button, and a single question fixes me in place.

What will be worse? Xiang being right about everything, and knowing that Grant was murdered by people who have already shown how far they're willing to go? Or what if it's all a fabrication, and Grant's death goes back to being a meaningless, avoidable tragedy? There's a third option. One that puts Grant miles away in a park when he should have been tucked up with me. Either way, he's still gone. I'm still here, with no Grant to protect me. He couldn't even protect himself, so what chance do I stand? A chill ripples through me as the answer is whispered in my mind.

None.

Chapter Sixteen

The first face I see is Xiang. He looks paler than when we parted earlier, like someone has applied a filter over his webcam. He's sat in a small boxy room, top half of an opaque glass door peeking over the crown of his head, framed either side by bookshelves. He blinks owlishly behind his glasses, and nudges them a fraction back up his nose with a poke of his index finger.

'Mrs Brewer. Thank you for joining us,' he says, fidgeting nervously in his seat.

My own face fills the window beside his, but there's a third below them. No video feed, just a picture, an animated GIF to be precise. A ticking clock, but not the conventional kind. Silhouettes of the continents are etched in the background, and it's not a complete clock face. Four fat round dots where numbers nine through twelve should be, rest of the dial empty. The hour hand is almost vertical, minute hand set only a few degrees to the left, twitching towards striking twelve, but never making it, as if held back by an invisible hand.

'Us?' I ask.

'Excuse my colleague. He's a little camera shy,' Xiang says with a shrug.

'Does he at least speak?'

There's a sound. A short, sharp exhale, borderline snort, and the border of the third window highlights yellow to show the source.

'What's with the clock?' I ask, noting the speakers name as *Tick Tock*.

'It's the Doomsday clock. You know, the one the scientists set that tells us how far away humans are from wrecking the planet for good?'

The voice has a peculiar pitch, like it's not long been broken in. Somewhere between teenage boy and young man.

'Doomsday clock?'

'What, is there an echo in here?'

'Layton, let's try not to be quite so prickly,' Xiang implores.

'You used my name man. We talked about this!'

'She's as much of a friend to us as Mr Brewer was, and she's got every bit as much to lose as we have now. Turn your camera on. You didn't hide your face from her husband, so I think she deserves the same respect.'

'I don't think that's a good idea Chris, I mean she...'

'She's been through enough Layton. Lost enough. More than us.'

'Hmm? Oh, yeah. Sorry, I forgot.'

It slips out so casually, that I can't help the barbed reply that boils up from the bubbling mess of grief that's an ever-present knot in my stomach.

'Easily done, unless you're me of course,' I say, taking sadistic pride in seeing Xiang flinch at the retort.

Only a few seconds of uneasy silence before Xiang steps back in as peacemaker.

'Camera, please,' he says, voice soft like velvet.

A second later the clock flicks off screen, replaced by a face. Layton isn't quite what I expected. Too many Hollywood movies showing hackers as weedy teenage nerds, thick glasses and acne you could play join the dots with. He looks young. Early twenties, buzz-cut hair military style, with a hint of puppy fat around the edges. Too much time spent in front of a screen.

'I owe you Mrs Brewer,' Xiang continues. 'Your warning about the policeman. I don't know what role he plays in this, but I'm glad I didn't find out tonight.'

I shake my head. 'Might have been nothing. I could have it all wrong. We all could.'

Another snort from the third window.

'Sorry, did I say something funny?' My annoyance peels away layers of nerves.

'Chris, I thought you said you laid it all out in Starbucks?'

Xiang puts me in mind of a flighty professor struggling to control squabbling students.

'Not all of it. The coffee shop felt too exposed.'

Layton rolls his eyes, less than impressed. I need this immature posturing like I need a hole in the head, so I step in before he can poke any more holes in how or why Dr Xiang has allowed me down their own personal rabbit hole.

'Look, today has been ... a bit of a mindfuck to say the least. First, I bury my husband, now I'm told he was murdered, and it's all part of a huge conspiracy. If that's true, I want to help. How about you give me a chance to catch my bloody breath, and fill in whatever blanks you need to fill in?'

Xiang steps in before Layton can send any more zingers back her way. 'I'll tell you what we know Mrs Brewer. We both will. There is still work to do, but what I can tell you, is that your husband isn't the only one who has suffered at their hands. There are others.'

'Please, call me Maggie. And what do you mean, others? How many others?'

'Fine, and it's just Layt. Only person that calls me Layton is my dad. As for how many, we're still counting,' he says, then after a pause 'but at least a dozen.'

Chapter Seventeen

'A dozen?' I say in disbelief, voice sounding too loud in the stillness of the car. 'What do you mean a dozen?'

'That we know of,' Xiang says, a sadness emanating from him like an aura. 'And if we don't do something soon, I fear that number will go up, at least by one, if not more.'

He leaves that notion hanging for all to see. Not just one. Three is the unspoken number. Everyone on this call.

'I mentioned earlier that I am a research scientist. Did you know there are almost twenty different congenital defects in the heart alone that you can be born with? Could be a hole in the heart, atrial or ventricular septal defects. I won't bore you with the full list. Through studying people with such conditions, we hope to understand why certain mutations occur, and some day, to be able to prevent them before they occur. I love my work, but it can be challenging at times. Funding, access to subjects, regulations governing what we can and cannot do in the name of science.'

'He means like cloning sheep, or growing an ear on the back of a mouse,' says Layt, ghost of a grin around the corners of his mouth. ''Cept he doesn't get to do any of the really cool stuff, do you Chris?'

Xiang gives a patient, if weary smile. 'I joined Luminosity five years ago. We did some good work in those first few years. The finest team of people I've had the privilege of sharing a lab with. Nothing ground-breaking you understand, but often my job is about the incremental gains. Then I stumbled across something a little under a year ago. It wasn't something I was even looking for at the time, but it was like lightning in a bottle. You are familiar with Alzheimer's, yes?'

'As much as anyone is I suppose,' I shrug.

'One of the causes is a mutation in certain genes. Once they mutate, they release a toxic protein fragment called amyloid beta peptide, that gathers in the brain. These deposits are thought to be a major factor in the onset of Alzheimer's, and I practically tripped over the answer, almost without realising.'

'You found a cure for Alzheimer's?' I ask, eyes widening. Talk about dropping a casual bomb into the conversation. Xiang has done it with all the nonchalance as if he's just shared what he had for lunch.

'Not exactly.' He beams a smile, the first I've seen from him. 'Not yet anyway, but with the right testing...'

'And these people at IQ, they want to what? Stop you? I don't understand?'

'Chris here is one of the good guys,' Layt slips back into the conversation. 'He's in it for the glory not the gold. Those fuckers at IQ are all about the cash.'

'But wouldn't a cure be worth a fortune?' I ask.

'Yep,' he shoots back, 'but not as much as all the drugs they can pump out there that do half the job. Why cure your customer base, when you can keep 'em coming back for more, right?'

He talks about it like it's no more than withholding dessert from a naughty kid, but I'm getting a feel for his level now, and don't react.

'So, what did you find then?' I ask, directing my attention back to Xiang.

'I had been allocated several dozen samples from the Luminosity database to study this protein, understand why it does what it does. One of these samples showed me something quite remarkable.'

'Wait, you say samples. Where do they come from? Are these people in your lab?'

'No, no,' he shakes his head. 'A number of sources. We sometimes ask for volunteers as part of clinical trials. Other times people leave their bodies to medical research. But Luminosity has access to … other subjects.'

'What kind of other subjects?'

Feels like he's building up to something. The lines etched in his forehead haven't been carved there by happiness. Whatever this is, it's been a heavy cross to bear. All the same, I want to reach through the screen and shake answers loose instead of what feels like glacial progress.

'I usually submit a request through our admin team, and get allocated a batch of DNA samples to work with. All anonymous, you understand. This time, though, this time was different. I needed to know who one particular sample belonged to. It's the key to everything.'

'Dude,' Layt butts in, 'she doesn't need your life story. Just spit it out.'

Xiang gives an apologetic smile. 'Of course, sorry. This sample showed all the hallmark genetic mutations that produce those toxic proteins, but there was something else. A mutation I've never seen before. This one produces a second set of protein fragments. One that coats the toxic proteins. Smothers them like a blanket, and chokes the life out of them.'

'Jesus,' I breathe out, impatience and frustration giving way to the enormity of what Xiang is laying out. 'You have to take this public,' I say, questions swirling around my head, words weaving into the beginnings of a story. My pulse quickens to the point I feel a little dizzy. 'They won't dare touch you once it's out there.'

Layt half-coughs, half-laughs, as if he's been caught mid-snacking.

'What's so bloody funny about that?' I snap, irritated by his teenage tics. 'These bastards killed my husband. It's all very well and good you sat there sniggering, but we can't just let them get away with this. And where does he even come into this?'

That last comment is meant for Xiang, but after a few seconds, it's the young hacker who fields it.

'You're not the only one who's lost someone.'

Layt's voice has flatlined, from borderline mocking to morose in a heartbeat. It's like someone has opened a window on my irritation, cool air quenching the fire in my chest. I open my mouth to speak, but Layt gets there first.

'He was my friend. Paul, I mean. It's my fault he's dead. They killed him because of me.'

I'm punch-drunk hearing the name. Paul Cosgrove. The man Grant supposedly killed.

Chapter Eighteen

Xiang steps back in. 'It's a matter of proof Maggie. We had it. Paul had it, and they killed him to get it back.'

'Proof? What proof?'

'The sample I told you about, when I saw what I had, I immediately tried to find out more about the subject, who they were, where we'd got the sample from, and I was told to back off. Well, first I was ignored, then told it wasn't possible and to leave it be. I couldn't understand. What I had discovered could profoundly change the way we treat the disease. I tried contacting our CEO. No way could I walk away from something so huge. Next thing I know, I'm moved off the project onto something else. Shut out, just like that.'

Xiang snaps his fingers. A thought tugs at me, as to whether I should be making notes, but I'm too transfixed by what I'm hearing.

'But you said Paul had proof?'

'He and I go way back,' says Layt, making it sound like years even though he looks like he has barely left school, let alone made friends with a thirty-something-year-old scientist.

'How did you know him?' I ask.

'We ran in the same gaming circles. *Call of Duty*. Played against each other at first, then teamed up. Turned out he went to the same uni as me. Both did Computer Science at Northumbria, so we bonded over a shared hatred of a couple of lecturers.'

'Gaming? Did you ever meet up in real life, or was he just an online friend?'

He glares at me, 'I might not have lost a husband, but yes, he was more than just an online mate. He and me have … well let's just say we've been through a lot of similar stuff. He helped me square off some shit I had going on at home. A good enough mate that I'll do whatever it takes to nail these fuckers for what they did to him.'

'Sorry,' I apologise on autopilot. 'I didn't mean anything by it. So how did your friend get involved in all of this then?'

'After Chris was moved off, he asked Paul for help, and he brought me in.'

'And what exactly is it you do?' I ask.

'Whatever needs doing,' he says, and I can practically hear the shrug. 'The samples Chris and Paul get are all stored digitally. They wouldn't tell him where the samples came from, so I found a way to trace back to the source.'

'All Luminosity employees submit a sample of their own DNA for research purposes,' Xiang says, taking up the thread. 'Both mine and Paul's are already part of the same database. When we get volunteers to donate samples, we have access to upload those to our database, even if we can't then download them again ourselves. Very much a one-way street. Layt suggested Paul upload another sample of his own, except this time, Layt had a way to piggy-back on it, trace it to the source.'

'Pretty basic to be honest,' Layt says. 'Bit like a trojan virus. Once it reaches where it's going, it unpacks a bit of code, sticks its foot in the door, and pings me back.'

'Back from where?' I ask.

'From HELIX. They've got a data centre housed underneath an IQ site, just outside Milton Keynes,' Layt continues. 'Did it remotely from G's laptop, and once we were in...' he huffs out a breath like he's seen something beyond words, 'what they have, it's insane man. Literally tens of millions of samples. Way more than what's on the National Database. Trouble is, we could look, but not touch, or not much anyway. They've got mad levels of encryption. I could only do one at a time, and the few I got took a week. There's gotta be a better way to get the lot. Not that it can't be done, just takes time.'

'Time we didn't have,' says Xiang, with a sad shake of his head. 'I reached out to your husband that same day. One week later, Paul disappeared ... both he and your husband ...' He trails off, leaving it unfinished.

'How did they find out?'

''Cos I wasn't careful enough' says Layt with a loud sigh. 'Thought I'd covered my tracks, but they traced it back to his machine somehow.'

There's a hitch in his voice, one that cuts through teenage swagger and speaks of an ocean of regret. A friend who blames himself for setting a chain of events in motion that smashed into Cosgrove with all the force of a runaway train. Grant too, if we're splitting hairs, but all I see is a teenager who looks out of his depth, and I can't help but pity him. Whatever guilt he's feeling, he'll wear that albatross around his neck for a long time yet by the sounds of it.

'Can't you just go back in the same wa, though?' I ask. 'Figure out a way to download the evidence?'

'They took his laptop. The code I wrote was on there.'

'What about your access?' I ask Xiang, but he shakes his head.

'They've tightened up since Paul was taken. Any sample requests go through a gatekeeper, upload as well as download now.'

'So, where the hell does that leave us?' My frustration rises like water in a sinking ship. 'What had Grant done so far? He must have done something to get on their radar other than talk to you, otherwise why kill him and not you?'

The bluntness of my own question takes me by surprise, and it's enough to insert a heavy few seconds of silence.

'Paul could have given them his name. He was missing for a week before his body turned up. A lot could have happened in that time,' says Layt, voice drifting off at the end, and I wonder what horrors he's imagining his friend going through.

'Last time we spoke, your husband mentioned he had plans to approach the PR arm of Luminosity, although I don't know if he managed that before they ...'

It's like nobody wants to finish any sentences that end with a death, as if saying it out loud makes it more real.

Where to even begin? The scale of the task dwarfs me, filling my field of vision like an approaching truck, smothering me with self-doubt. Grant was one of the best investigative journalists around. If he couldn't unpick it, what chance would I stand? Feels like I'm sinking in quicksand, but I can't just do nothing. Involving the police feels like the equivalent of sticking a foot in a bear trap, if my suspicions about Hermannson are right there's no way of knowing if others like him are compromised. Only other options are to follow the path Grant had set off down, or rope in Rose Evans.

The thought of Grant shakes something loose, a thought I can't believe hadn't occurred before.

'Back at the coffee shop, you said they have access to the whole country's DNA. The officer I spoke with, they said that Grant's DNA had been found where your friend was killed. Was that them? Was that their doing?'

Xiang nods. 'One way or the other I suspect so, yes. Your husband's DNA will be in HELIX, just like the rest of us. Once they have that, it's possible to construct a sample of DNA to match that profile without obtaining any tissue from him. That, or they somehow obtained another sample from him, maybe hair or saliva, and planted it at the scene.'

Anger wells up inside like a geyser, at the thought of anyone smearing Grant's name in such a way. An echo of the doubt I'd felt bounces around my brain, hot and searing like a tracer round. Doubt that I now know was a false positive thanks to whichever bastard at HELIX decided to put a target on Grant's head.

'If we don't have the original proof anymore, do we have anything else to go on?' I ask in desperation. 'Anything at all?'

'We know where the data centre is,' Layt says. 'But that shit is locked up tight man.'

I'm about to ask the location, when the screen seems to flicker. A blink and you miss it effect. I frown, wondering if Xiang's image has frozen, but then he blinks, mirroring my own expression of puzzlement.

'Are you okay Maggie?' he asks. 'I know it's a lot to take in, and I won't blame you if you want to walk away. After all, you...'

His words blur, sliding past without sinking in, as I narrow my eyes, studying the screen.

'I'm fine,' I murmur. 'Christopher, I think there's...'

That's all I manage to get out before the dots in my head don't so much join, as smash together. Not a flicker. A shadow, winking in and out of shot from behind Xiang's head. There one minute, gone the next. Then it's just there, only for a split second, before it, and the glass door pane, explode into a thousand glittering grenades.

Chapter Nineteen

It's a paralysis of sorts. My eyes flick back and forward across the screen, but the rest of me sits rigid, statue-still. I watch Xiang half-cower, half-twist, as the glass panel implodes, hands over his head, duck-and-cover style. But it's not just the glass that's gone. The entire door has burst in, hanging off one hinge now like a punch-drunk boxer.

A figure clad all in black, face obscured by a matching balaclava, double-times it into the room, making a bee-line for Xiang. Two more follow, fanning left and right. The first, I assume a man from the build, is on Xiang, before the scientist has time to even leave his seat, gloved hand grabbing his slender neck, pinning it to the desk. The gun appears in the spare hand as if by magic, its long, silencer barrel pushed hard enough against Xiang's head to make him cry out in pain.

Off screen, the sound of a room being ripped apart. Furniture toppling, drawers slamming open and closed. One side of Xiang's face is mushed against the desk, but the other is all too visible, one eye rolling around like livestock that knows it's next in line at the abattoir. He's trying to speak now, but it's hard to make out, what with half of his face embedded in his desk, as well as the sound of his room being torn apart. Sounds like …

'Pleesh, pleesh…'

His begging unlocks me, hands fluttering to my mouth. I hear another voice. Realise it's my own.

'Oh my God, oh my God, oh my God.'

The whispered mantra seems amplified by the chamber of my hands.

It hits with sickening force that if I can see them, they'll see me too. I tap the screen to turn my camera off, missing the first time in haste, but second time lucky.

'Where is it?'

The figure in black speaks for the first time, and the voice is all wrong. No gruff bark or bellow. No angry yell. The softly spoken words, almost whispered, pepper my arms with goose bumps.

'Where is it Christopher?'

The gentle way he speaks has no place in the maelstrom that is Xiang's room right now. Soft Irish edges sound immeasurably patient, though that's no guarantee of goodness.

'Whaa? I dunno wha oo mean?' Xiang is breathing hard now, flecks of spittle bubbling at the corner of his mouth. One of his hands moves, trembling fingers snaking towards the screen. My picture starts to wobble, and I realise Xiang is trying to close his laptop. His face suddenly pops to twice its size, and takes a beat to realise that it's because his is the only window left open now. Layt has left.

'Ah ah ah' the masked figure wags a finger. 'I'd like Mrs Brewer to stay with us if it's all the same.'

The screen tilts again, and the balaclavaed face seems to grow to fill it. Feels like he's about to pop out of my laptop, crawl out like something from *The Ring*. A thought crashes through the sea of panic I'm drowning in. My name. He said my name. How does he know who I am if he can't see me? Then it hits. My username in the corner of the now black screen. I whip my head around, looking out into the dimly lit street, half-expecting another trio of men in black to burst from the nearest hedge, but the only sound comes from my phone speakers.

'Ah what's the matter Maggie? Feeling left out? Don't you worry. We'll have a chat soon enough.'

All I can see are his eyes. They match the voice. Calm blue pools. Even though he can't see me, they seem to bore into my soul like drill bits for a second longer before glancing back down at Xiang.

'I'll only ask once more Christopher. Where is it?'

As he asks the question he grabs a fistful of hair, pulling Xiang up, and I barely stifle a squeal. A trickle of blood winds its way from one nostril to his top lip, and he's breathing hard like a sprinter post-race. The gun barrel is pushed tight into his temple now.

'I have no idea what...'

The sentence stays unfinished, punctuated by a single silenced gunshot. Soft, more like a cough. This time I don't even try and hold back the scream.

Chapter Twenty

Xiang's head is thrown to the left like he's been shunted by a car, catching the edge of the desk on the way down, rest of his body a fraction of a second behind, flopping out of his chair and out of sight onto the floor. There's a swooping sickness in my stomach, as if I'm falling in time with him.

The gunman slides into the empty seat like it's just been vacated on the Tube, folded arms resting on the desk just shy of the keyboard, gun still clutched in one hand. Those eyes latch onto mine again, pinning me in place, even though they can't actually see me.

'Quiet a second, would you?'

That quiet voice again, but it's an order, not a request. One finger goes to his ear, eyes narrowing, seeming to lose focus, before they snap back to me. Looks like he's smiling through the narrow slit of the mask.

'Who's a clever girl, eh?'

I frown. Whatever he's getting at is lost on me. In the background, the destruction of the room restarts. Are these the same men who framed Grant? What the hell are they looking for? Xiang had said Cosgrove was the one who'd had the proof.

Something catches my eye in the rear-view mirror. Movement along the street. A pair of matching silhouettes peel away from the patch of shadow by the end of the path. Two figures dressed in black. Breath catches in my throat, and I instinctively shrink down into my seat. A third shadow emerges another hundred yards ahead up the street from the entrance to my back lane.

'Maggie.' The man's voice splits my name into two sing-song syllables. 'Come out, come out wherever you are.'

They're here. In my street. Looking for me. Those men have just come from my house. What would have happened if I'd been inside? An image of Xiang's head bouncing off the desk flashes to mind again, bringing a fresh adrenaline spike. I know the answer to that question. I drag the phone out of sight under the dash to hide the illumination, sliding as far down as the space will allow.

'We're not here for you Maggie. We just want what's ours, and you never have to see these handsome features again. Just tell us what the good doctor shared with you, and we'll...'

The rest of his words are lost as I end the call, eyes flicking between the man up ahead, and the two in the mirror, still the only figures on the street. What if they come this way? How do they even know where I live? The policeman, Hermannson. He's the only one who could know that I'd met with Xiang. He must have seen us in the coffee shop before I came out, and sent these men here. To Xiang's place as well.

That thought spawns another equally as terrifying. If these men are with Hermannson, then Xiang was right. The police cannot be trusted. I try to process what that might mean, but my mind is still short-circuited by what I've just seen. What I'm seeing unfold outside my house.

Twisting and peering over my shoulder, they're hard to make out against the backdrop of the hedge, shadows within a shadow. Short, ragged breaths escape as I watch, unfeasibly loud in the silence of the car. They move now, flowing along the street, peeling off, heading this way. The third man makes his way to join them. My car is smack bang in the middle. If they meet anywhere near me, they'll spot me for sure. Fear turns to blind panic, shocking me into action like I've just been hit with a few hundred volts from a defibrillator. I toss the phone into the passenger seat, slipping the car into first gear and easing off the handbrake before starting the engine.

It sounds like the roar of a drag racer cutting through the quiet street. Thank God I didn't park too close to the car in front, so there's no manoeuvring, and I pull straight out and tear down the road, glancing at the third man as I pass him. See an arm rising up, what could be a long dark gun barrel separating from the black outline, and I brace myself for the impact of a shot that never comes.

I power the car around the first bend like I'm auditioning for Formula One, taking the next three in the same fashion. No sense of where to, just an unstoppable urge to put as much distance between me and them as possible. No lights powering out of the street, chasing me down. Doesn't mean they aren't coming.

I'd kept the headlights off so as not to warn the men, but flick them on now. Tonight, of all nights, it wouldn't do to get pulled over for a traffic offence. What the hell am I meant to do now? Where do I go? I haven't asked for any of this, but know instinctively it isn't something I can outrun. Can't just drive forever, though. It's a full twenty minutes of twisting and turning, before I pull off the main road, parking up in a back alley.

There's still a slight catch to my breathing, and the hand that reaches for my phone trembles like a drunk craving their first of the day. I can't do this alone. Who can I trust? Xiang is dead. Layt is gone, no clue where to start looking for him. I scroll through my contacts and tap to dial. The voice that answers sounds sluggish, sleepy.

'Maggie? What time is it?'

The adrenaline has long since flushed from my system, and now I just feel drained, heavy limbed like I've over-done it at the gym. The wave of weariness washing over me wrings out a few more tears, and the words catch in my throat.

'Maggie? Are you okay?'

'No,' I half sniff, half sob. 'I need help.'

Chapter Twenty-One

Declan Clay is a man accustomed to getting what he wants, and failure does not sit well with him. Especially not when he has to report it back in. He makes the call to Mr Osgood, watching with a bored expression on his face as his men give Xiang's flat a second going over.

'It's done?'

'Your whistle-blower won't be blowing any more whistles.'

'Have you retrieved it?'

'We're busy looking,' Clay says, half-distracted still by Maggie Brewer, and why she wasn't there when his team went calling. This was supposed to end tonight, and Clay can feel their collective failure draped over his mood like a wet blanket. He likes things to be neat, ordered. Ironic, for a man who creates chaos wherever he goes, but it dates back to his Army days. Old habits.

'And the woman?'

'She … wasn't quite where she was supposed to be,' Clay concedes. 'She won't get far, though.'

'How much does she know?'

'Like I said, she wasn't there. They were all on a Zoom call. She didn't hang around.'

'What about Xiang? Did he say what he's told her?'

Clay pulls off his balaclava, glancing down at his feet, and taps a boot against Xiang's leg. 'The orders for him were quite,' – he pauses, searching for the word – 'explicit.'

'I know what you were told to do. It was me that bloody told you. Don't tell me you didn't squeeze him a little before you finished with him?'

'Like I said, I'll find her. Don't you worry about that?'

'You're telling me not to worry? Do you have any idea what's at stake here? The bigger picture?'

Clay does. No doubt there will be levels to it, though, ones that are kept from him, but he knows enough of the scale and scope to know this is one Jack that can never be allowed out of the box.

'We've a lot still to do here Mr Osgood,' he says, the inference being *bugger off and let me do it.*

The other man grumbles something that Clay can't quite make out, before eventually agreeing.

'Well go on then, get on with it. You'll call me as soon as you find something?'

'Of course.'

Clay signs off, and surveys the carnage that Xiang's room has become. Looks about as tidy as it would if a hurricane had torn through it. He signals for his men to start wrapping the body up in the tarpaulin they've brought, but then thinks better of it as an alternate plan presents itself while he's staring at the body of the scientist. He claps a hand on the shoulder of the man to his left.

'Leave him be. I've got other plans for him.' The man goes to turn away, but Clay's grip keeps him in place. 'Plans for you too. I need you to find the woman.'

DI Oliver Hermannson peels off his own balaclava. 'Thought your men were there already?'

Clay shakes his head. 'They are but she wasn't inside. She was sat in her car the whole time. Drove off when they came out. Track her phone, there's a good lad.'

He sees the flash of anger in the policeman's eyes. He's pretty sure the copper would take a swing at him if he thought he could get away with it. There are consequences to that, though, beyond any beating Clay would dish out. Invisible ties that keep Hermannson in check and on the leash.

'What about him then? We can't just leave him here?' Hermannson says, nodding towards Xiang.

'Oh, that's exactly what we're going to do, my friend. I've got big plans for Dr Xiang here.'

Chapter Twenty-Two

Rose Evans might have sounded half asleep on the phone earlier, but even though it's almost one a.m., she looks as switched on as she does every morning.

'And you're saying these men killed Grant too?'

I nod, staring blankly at the wall of Rose's living room, right through it to seven days ago when life made more sense.

'Has to be,' I say with a shrug. 'They were going to kill me, Rose.'

'You don't know that.'

I snap into focus, giving her a glare that could peel paint.

'You're right. I'm probably over-reacting. They'd just popped round to make sure I wasn't too upset after watching a man have his brains blown out.'

Rose leans forward, folding a hand over mine.

'Sorry. I'm sorry. I didn't mean—'

I exhale loud and long, hunching over, deflating like a balloon. 'No, I'm ... I've come here for help. I shouldn't have snapped. I'm sorry.'

'Jesus, Maggie. What you've been through this past week, last thing you need to be doing is apologising to anybody.'

I look up at Rose, smiling through a fresh blur of tears triggered by her empathy.

'What do I do, Rose? I didn't ask for this. Any of it. All I want to do is eat ice cream, drink wine and grieve my husband, and instead I get this.' I throw my hands up in the air, letting them drop limply back into my lap.

'What you're going to do is get a good night's sleep, and let me make a few calls.' She pauses a beat. 'It'd really help if you'd tell me why you think they came after you. What Grant was working on.'

I shake my head with conviction. 'Christopher said there was proof, on a laptop but they took it back. There might be something else, something maybe Grant had. Until I get that, the less you know, the safer you are.' Rose shoots me a look, but I ignore it. 'You said make some calls. Who to?'

'People I trust.'

'Like who?' I press her, feeling a tingle of anxiety at the thought of this fast-diminishing circle of trust opening up to someone I've never met.

'My ex is a copper. A DI. He'll know if anyone has reported your guy getting shot. And this copper from Bristol, Hermannson, I'll ask him what he can find out there too. In the meantime, you're going to stay here, and take the day off tomorrow.'

'And you trust this ex of yours?' I ask, thinking about Hermannson. How he's up to his neck in this.

Rose wrinkles her nose, half-smiling. 'Of course, I'd trust him with my life.'

'And mine?'

The question hangs heavy for a second. Rose's smile broadens. 'He's a good guy. I trust him completely.'

The wattage on the smile is turned up a little too much, and I wonder why he's an ex if he's such a great guy. Rose's over-eager manner suggests she's still holding a candle for him.

'Relax,' Rose says, standing up, starting to clear empty wine glasses from the table. 'You're safe here. Nobody knows where you are. Come on, I'll show you the spare room.'

I wish I had the strength to argue, but I'm flat, like a car with its lights left on overnight, and let myself be shepherded along a narrow hallway into a boxy bedroom. Doesn't look like it's been slept in since the place was built. Bedcovers and assortment of pillows arranged with military precision, like a showroom. Seems like sacrilege to spoil it by actually lying on the duvet, but after Rose leaves the room, I walk over to it, and sink onto the oatmeal-coloured bedding like it's a cloud.

They won't stop. Won't keep coming, until they find whatever they're looking for. Until they find me.

The voice in my head is an incessant whisper, trying its level best to keep me awake, but I'm exhausted. Not just tired, but wiped. Drained. When I close my eyes, Xiang's face starts to appear, wild eyed, looking for a way out. Did he know, I wonder, that they were always going to kill him?

The image only lasts for a few seconds, though, replaced by one of Grant. My big beautiful man. I see him on the beach, back in the summertime. Our trip to Cornwall. Faded red shorts, doing his best impression of The Hoff, pretending to save me as I wade through two feet of water, waves lapping at his feet. Can almost feel his arms around me as he hoists me up and onto his shoulder in a fireman's lift.

I'm aware of my breathing deepening, of the scene in my mind starting to fade like old pictures, colours running. Feels like they've literally just disappeared when I wake with a start. Takes a few seconds to reorientate. Remember where I am. Why I'm here. Why Grant isn't. It hits hardest in the mornings.

Echoing voices coming from somewhere in the flat pull me back to the here and now. Rose's is one but the second voice is male, someone I don't recognise. There's a tinny, fuzzy edge to it, like it's coming through on speaker phone. I swing my legs off the bed, still fully clothed, and open the door quietly.

'You should have seen her last night, though, Liam. She was terrified when she got here.'

'I'm not saying she wasn't,' the voice replied. Liam is the ex, she presumes. 'Is she still there with you now?'

'Mmm-hmm,' says Rose, sounding like she's sipping a mouthful of something.

I open the door wide enough to step out into the corridor, and pad towards the kitchen.

'I'll come over. Be there in twenty minutes. Don't let her leave.'

'Don't think there's any danger of that. She's still asleep.'

'All the same, I'll be as quick as I can.'

'What is it?' Rose asks, and I can see her from the corner of the corridor now, pacing back and forward in the kitchen, cup in hand. 'What are you not telling me?'

'Eh? What you on about?'

'Liam, you're a shit liar. What's going on? What are you not telling me?'

Silence, apart from breathing coming down the line.

'Look, he begins, 'I shouldn't say owt, right. Not till I get there, but we're already looking for her.'

Hairs stand up on the back of my neck like hackles. My heartbeat ratchets up, like someone has just slipped a shock paddle under my jumper.

'What do mean looking for her?' Rose says, sounding as confused as I feel. 'Did someone else see those men at her place?'

'It's got nothing to do with her place,' he says. 'This guy she says she saw killed on her phone, we found him a couple of hours ago.'

'Oh my God,' Rose is out of sight now, half-open door blocking the view. 'So, she's telling the truth.'

That almost pisses me off enough to march in and confront her. Of course, I'm telling the truth. Does Rose think I'd make this stuff up for fun? I hold my position, though, waiting her out to hear the rest of the conversation uninterrupted.

'Have you arrested anyone yet?'

'That's what I'm trying to tell you, Rose. We want to speak to Maggie Brewer in connection with it.'

'Of course, you do. She's your star witness.'

'Not as a witness. Look, I shouldn't be telling you this, and if you print a word of it, we'll never speak again, but we found her bank card at the scene.'

'What do you...? Wait, what? What do you mean at the scene?'

'I mean as in four feet from the bloody body, at the scene.'

It's like someone has dropped an ice cube down my back. I stiffen, quick intake of breath, and take an involuntary step back, hand tapping against the wall.'

'But she wasn't actually there, she saw it on Zoom, so ... ohhh.'

'Yes, ohhh. She's not a witness, Rose. She's a suspect.'

Chapter Twenty-Three

I don't hang around to hear the rest of it, backing away and into the room I've just slept in to collect my phone and keys from the bedside table. I don't put my shoes on yet for fear of announcing my exit, and glide across the laminate hallway in stockinged feet.

My head spins like a centrifuge with the weight of those words. History repeating itself. They're doing to me what they did to Grant. Weaving a web of lies to suit the story they need. A suspect? How is that even possible? My bank card at Xiang's place. I don't even know where he lives. Even if I did, he was a cautious man. Could have been broadcasting from anywhere. Those men at my place. It has to be. They must have taken the card from my flat and planted it next to his body. Either that, or Hermannson has friends on the force up here. That thought strengthens my resolve to steer clear of the authorities until I have breathing space to think.

I ease the handle down on the front door, hoping for silence, getting it, and close it behind me with the same care. Rose lives in a first floor flat, and I hustle down the staircase now, slipping shoes on when I get to the bottom. Quick glance back up. Not even the creak of a door, let alone anything noisier to suggest Rose is following.

It's not that I don't trust Rose, but all the same, I can't be here. Rose's ex had said twenty minutes. A decent head start. Where to is another question entirely. As I slide into the driver's seat of the car, a voice in my head pipes up, one preconditioned to follow the rules. It's telling me to trust Rose, to trust her ex. Bank card or no bank card, I did not kill Xiang. Running will almost certainly make me appear guilty, but I can't face turning around and waiting for Rose's ex. Look at Xiang. He stayed put and look what happened to him. I start the car, and pull away.

I only drive for a couple of minutes, guilt coursing through me at running out on Rose. I hope the ex-boyfriend won't give her too much of a hard time. I fire off a quick text to her.

> Sorry to cut and run, but feeling a bit iffy and needed some fresh air. Thanks for the bed though. I owe you.

The call that comes through from Rose is almost instantaneous. I let it ring, glancing guiltily across as it vibrates across the passenger seat. When I was freaking out last night, Rose was who I gravitated to. Would have been Grant a week ago, but now there's nobody else. Is it really less than twenty-four hours since I watched his coffin disappear behind a curtain? I might have over a thousand friends on Facebook, but I've never felt more alone.

Doesn't leave much in the way of options. I can't involve my family. Couldn't forgive myself if they got dragged in and anything happened. That leaves me with precisely zero people I trust enough to reach out to.

Around me, the morning traffic crawls along, flowing like clogged arteries. I trundle alongside Monday morning commuters, eyes fixed forward, focusing on making it through the week. Some are chatting, some singing silent solos in time to breakfast radio. Will the police be looking for my car, I wonder? Can't stop nervously checking my mirrors, expecting a splash of blue strobing through the traffic towards me.

On the odd occasion I catch someone's eye, I look away so fast I practically flinch, as if they'll see it written all over my face. Fugitive. I almost laugh at my own melodrama, but this is no joke. I just need time to think. To decompress, and decide what my options are, if I even have any.

Just me at home last night, so nobody to corroborate. No idea whether I was picked up on any CCTV along the trip home to help out. The other big problem, though, is the fact I don't know where Xiang lived. He could have been shot in the next street over, and I wouldn't know, so hard to build a defence of 'I was miles away officer.'

Another thought pushes past all of these, squatting low and heavy, making me swallow hard. If they've planted my bank card, what else might the police find? Will my DNA be there just like Grant's was a week ago? No way of knowing without turning myself in. No guarantees I'd be handing myself over to the good guys even if I did.

The only person I can think of who is even remotely on the same side of the fence as me now is Xiang's young hacker friend, Layt. If I could reach him, maybe he would know what to do. I haven't the first clue where to start, though. Apart from his name and what he looks like I know literally nothing about him. Don't even have a picture I could run through a reverse Google images search. Even if I could reach him, he might want nothing to do with me after seeing the body count rise. First Cosgrove and Grant, now Xiang. Not a list he'll want to join.

A low persistent gurgle, followed by a fizzing sensation bubbling up from the depths of my stomach reminds me

I haven't eaten since the wake yesterday. I'm not hungry as such, but my body won't let me forget that it's long overdue a top up, and I pull off at the next junction.

There's only one car ahead in the Starbucks drive-through queue. I order a latte and a pack of caramel wafers to tide me over, hoping a sugar rush will pull me round. I pull into a parking space, dump three sweeteners in, and rip open the wafers. When the first bite hits my taste buds, I close my eyes in appreciation. The first wafer is gone in four bites. The second is done in three.

I reach over and pick up my phone, jumping as it pings in my hand. Message from Mam:

> Hope you managed some sleep. Sending you hugs from me and your Dad. Call you later?

I sit, finger poised to tap out a reply, wondering if any of what happened last night has made the news. Whether my parents know the police are looking for me. Whether there's an officer there with them now, waiting to see what I send back. I debate what to say, and settle on a bland reply:

> Slept ok thx. Speak to you later.

The silence in the car is an oppressive blanket, trapping me in a bubble with my thoughts, and a thousand questions I can't answer. I switch on the radio, cranking up the volume, hoping that the tunes will help drown out the voice in my head that's constantly telling me I'm screwed. I know I can't sit here forever. Can't go home. Not yet at least, but I need somewhere to breathe, collect my thoughts. Feels like I'm skiing down a black run blindfolded.

I look back at my phone. Four more missed calls from Rose, couple of voicemails and WhatsApps too. Texts from Moya and Julie as well. It's too much. I haven't had an anxiety attack in over a year, but it's there, lurking beneath the surface like an iceberg, waiting for me to sail straight into it. Grant was always the crutch to get me through the others. The hole he has left behind is huge, bigger than I can wrap my head around.

I close my eyes, picturing him again, the night they ripped him away from me. The perfect few days that had preceded it. Try to recapture the hopeful feeling, the lightness I'd felt, but without him here it's just a two-dimensional memory, a cardboard cut-out without depth of feeling.

Songs segue into news bulletin, and I open my eyes, staring at the display, waiting for the newsreader to mention my name, almost willing them to. That at least would be something. If they go public with it, feels like that turns a spotlight on me that would drive away any sinister intent from Hermannson, for now at least. What if I could work out a way to turn myself in with maximum exposure, put myself in a spotlight he wouldn't dare step into.

Headlines make way for lighter stuff, entertainment, a big film premiere due this weekend, sport, and weather. I don't hear the last sixty seconds, though. My mind is whirring like a hamster wheel.

A song drifts through the speakers. Annie Lennox singing about sisters doing it for themselves. It sparks a thought, breathing a little life back in, even if it's probably just temporary. I know exactly where to go now.

Who to call on. I pull a pair of old sunglasses from the glovebox, jump back on the motorway, heading east, towards someone I know will fight as hard to clear Grant's name as I'm prepared to. Maybe even harder.

Chapter Twenty-Four

Clay only comes into the office when shit has gone badly wrong. This doesn't fall into that category in his book, but he's been summoned, and it doesn't pay to bite the hand that feeds you.

Hermannson isn't a bad copper at heart, but on this side of the fence, he's like someone trying to make the leap from Christmas panto to Hollywood block-buster. He can learn his lines, but when it comes to it, he chokes. Clay had seen the look on his face as Christopher Xiang slumped to the floor. No stomach for it when it matters.

The lift doors open up straight into the boardroom, and Clay steps out onto carpet with a pile deep enough to feel the spring in it. They're only a half-dozen floors up, but the view is impressive. Huge plate glass windows in place of walls give a three-sixty view of the surrounding countryside, looking out over two reservoirs to the east. Back west, towards the motorway the village of Frankley Green, its residents blissfully unaware of what goes on barely half a kilometre away within these four walls, as well as directly under them. A dozen shades of green blend together into the kind of Middle England canvas the Yanks scramble over themselves to visit.

Clay takes a deep breath. Nothing to do with nerves. More to centre himself, find his level and keep it, despite being more than a little annoyed at being dragged ninety miles south of where he should be, fixing other people's messes.

Two other men share the room with him. No mistaking who's in charge. An anxious-looking dogsbody turns to him, jam-jar thick wire-rimmed specs magnify the eyes, giving him an owlish appearance. Whatever he was scrawling in his notebook, the pen stops, hovers above the page. The man Clay is here to see sits silhouetted against the glare of the morning winter sun. He, like it, should never be mistaken for warm. The minion is dismissed with a flick of a hand, and Clay waits until the nervous underling has scuttled past him before he approaches.

Clay strolls across, sliding into the vacated seat without waiting to be asked, mainly because he knows it annoys Osgood.

'You wanted to see me?'

Osgood turns to face him now, and Clay is struck by how different he looks from this time just a couple of weeks ago. The changes are miniscule, but Clay is a man who notices things on a micro scale. The faintest hint of shadow under the eyes, and a smile as convincing as a politician promising no tax hikes. To anyone else, though, he'd look like what he is. A man of power.

'You were supposed to be here half an hour ago.'

'You pay me to do things the best way, not the fastest. Things needed taking care of in Manchester first.'

Plenty more up there that still does, he thinks to himself, but keeps his mouth shut.

'You still don't have it.' He's stating a fact, not asking, so Clay waits him out. 'The policeman, what's his name again?'

'Hermannson.'

'Yes, Hermannson. You've reminded him what's at stake for him if this doesn't get fixed?'

Clay inclines his head. Says nothing.

'And the woman? Brewer's wife?'

'It's all in hand, Mr Osgood.'

'In hand as in…?'

'As in she'll turn up. Not as if she has many places to go. My money is she reaches out to her family, and we'll have that covered in the next few hours. That, and she's in the frame for Dr Xiang. Either way she's not a threat. Police pick her up, she's arrested and charged, just like the husband should have been. We pick her up,' he shrugs, 'even less of a problem.'

'Until you retrieve what Cosgrove stole, don't tell me it's not a problem.'

Clay grits his teeth, inwardly assessing how much damage he could do to Osgood using only the biro sat on the table between them.

'You've made the necessary arrangements with HELIX?'

'I went to see Dr Myers before I came up here.'

Clay can't quite decide who HELIX belongs to. Myers is the brains to Osgood's wallet, and a formidable force for a man who should be enjoying retirement somewhere warm. Osgood's bark is louder, but Clay sees a cunning in Myers that warrants wariness.

'Was there anything else Mr Osgood? Only I've got a long drive back, and like you say, we've got problems that still need fixing.'

Osgood pulls a face like he's just smelled a bad fart.

'That's precisely why I needed you here. Some things are best not discussed over the phone, no matter how secure you think the line is. I have this place swept twice a day to make sure nobody's listening.'

Clay raises his eyebrows. Must be something fairly meaty then. 'More problems need fixing?'

'Not more. Just one. I don't like disappointments. Hermannson has become one. He's let us down once too often. Once he helps you find the woman, he's of no more use.'

Hadn't seen that one coming. Even for a man of power, moving against a police officer is still a big deal. It'll take a little more thought, more planning. That's what Clay is good at, though. He'll do what he's paid for, and not lose a second of sleep over it. A lifetime of giving and taking orders conditions you to it. Still, having eyes and ears on the legal side of the thin blue line will be a miss.

'He's the only copper we have on payroll,' Clay ventures. 'You ask me, he's more use to us alive.'

'Except I didn't,' Osgood's reply is pure ice.

'Didn't what?'

'Ask you.'

The Irishman opens his mouth to reply, but clearly thinks better of it and glares like a scolded child as he rises to leave. Osgood turns his chair to gaze out through the window to the east, talking from behind the high back like a wannabe Bond villain.

'Oh, and Mr Clay? Our friend Detective Hermannson might be a disappointment, but see that you don't join him.'

As threats go, Clay has had worse, but after years of working with Osgood, he knows that this man has both the resources and the inclination to make good on his, or at least make an attempt that can't be ignored. Doesn't scare him, the notion of dying. He's faced it too many times. He'd far rather keep breathing, though, and not for the first time, wonders who would come out on top if it came down to it. Osgood and the army he could call upon, or himself, and the knowledge accumulated over a very long career, of exactly what it takes to carry out those kinds of orders.

If he can't find what Cosgrove stole, the little voice in his head that's served him so well all these years, all those tours of duty, tells him it might be time to start thinking about a plan B. He has seen lesser men than Osgood crumble under pressure, lose perspective, and with it everything else. If this ship is indeed sinking, Clay has no intention of going down with it out of any sense of duty. Not without a fight.

Chapter Twenty-Five

Duchy Road has been called Yorkshire's millionaires' row, and I can see why. This stretch of it is plot after plot of well-spaced out, detached houses. Behind me sits St Wilfrid's church, in all its listed building glory, the front resembling more of a castle keep than house of God.

The house is set back from the road, surrounded by a sandy gravelled drive that loops around both sides like a moat. I can only imagine how much this would set me back. The kind of house that doesn't get sold on the open market. Passes down through the family, rather than fall into the hands of strangers.

My feet crunch across the gravel like I'm walking on cereal, and I climb the half dozen stone steps to the front door. When I press the bell, it chimes through what sounds like an empty mansion. Wouldn't surprise me if a butler came to the door in full get up. But when the door finally opens, Izzy's face peers out, surprise shifting to smiles within a nanosecond.

'Maggie,' she says, beaming, 'come in, come in.' She stands aside, waving me through.

I wait a few feet inside, feeling awkward in the narrow hallway as Izzy closes the door. She places a hand across my shoulders, guiding me into a kitchen that looks like it belongs in a showroom. Huge black American style fridge freezer big enough to hide a body in, matching black Aga, all wrapped around a central island big enough to stick a mattress on and sleep four.

'Get you anything? Coffee, tea?'

'Coffee would be lovely, thanks.'

I perch on one of the black leather stools by the island.

'I've got Costa Rican, Ethiopian, Colombian. What's your poison?'

Slight shake of the head. 'Whatever you're having is fine.'

'Sorry,' she says, looking a little abashed. 'I can get a bit carried away with it.'

'I always thought you might sell this place you know, after the divorce,' I say, looking around the kitchen.

She chuckles, her back to me, popping Nespresso pods into the machine. 'Tempting, even just as an *up yours* to Dylan, but better to rise above it, eh? Besides, every roll of wallpaper and lick of paint in here is down to me, so would have hurt me just as much as him to sell it.'

'Is he still in Harrogate?'

'No,' she says, turning around, two cups in hand, smile fixed front and centre like a bayonet. 'He went back to the States,' before adding 'thank God.'

I know I'm not here for small talk, but the everyday-ness of it all is an escape that I can't bring myself to break just yet.

'How's the business doing?' I ask.

'Good,' she says with a satisfied smile. 'Got a way to go, but it's been my best year so far.'

Izzy is the artistic one in the Brewer family. Grant once joked that she came out of the womb clutching a sketch pad. Some of her work adorns the walls back at home. It's one of the reasons she and Dylan, her ex, didn't work out. He comes from old money and made it clear he didn't expect his wife to work. She let herself be dazzled by the family fortune, and his porcelain veneers that cost more than my car.

One thing she refused to compromise on, though, were her morals, and when she found him in bed with a naive young thing after coming home unexpectedly, she walked away and never looked back. Not before she poured half a tin of gloss paint into the naive young thing's handbag. The other half went over Dylan's Hugo Boss suit.

I remember the look of innocence on her face when she first told me.

'What can I say darling,' she had said in a haughty faux upper-class lilt. 'We artists are just a little temperamental.'

Since then she's rediscovered her love of art, and sells originals and prints of her work online, much to her dad's disapproval. He's old school. Doesn't trust online stores and businesses you can't see or touch. Her prints sell well. They make money, just not as much as she had at her disposal when she was with her ex.

'Wish I had half your talent,' I say, taking the mug she offers me. 'A five-year-old draws better than me.'

'You shush your face,' she lectures me with a pointing finger. 'You're a bloody good journalist. Better than most of those other hacks they give the big stories to from what Grant said.'

A warm flush of imposter syndrome spreads across my cheeks at the compliment. Guess I'm just so used to being kept in my box by previous editors that I've wondered at times if there might be some merit in Dad pushing for me to try something else. Hearing Izzy echo Grant, though, knowing that he had my back even when I wasn't in the room, makes me smile, even if I do look away as I do it.

The mention of his name forces me to confront the real reason for my visit, lurking like an unseen shadow. Izzy must see it written all over my face because she puts her own mug down now, and slides into the seat beside me.

'Anyway, enough about me. How are you doing?' she asks.

I pause, weighing up how to approach this. A dozen rehearsed lines from the drive over fall away like autumn leaves. Instead, I lead with honesty.

'I'm in trouble, Izzy.'

'You're telling me. You've come to me for help, you must be desperate.'

She starts to laugh at her own joke, but sees my face, and hers drops to match it.

'Sorry,' she says, any trace of humour sliding away.

I had planned to be sparing in the detail, not because I don't trust her, but because I don't want to drag anyone else fully into this whirlpool I seem to be spiralling down into. But the drip feed I'd prepared gives way to a gush of words, telling her almost everything, as I stare down into coffee. Almost everything. I draw the line at what it was Grant was investigating. No mention of HELIX, or IQ by name. When I get to the part about the police wanting to speak to me, I glance up, seeing deep lines carved into Izzy's head as she listens in, gaze locked onto me.

'Jesus, Maggie. What are you going to do?'

'I don't know,' I say, feeling strangely lighter for having unburdened myself, for now at least. 'I just need somewhere to stay for a night or two, while I work that part out.'

'And you're sure you can't go to a different police station with any of this? Maybe one around here?' she asks. 'If these guys have planted your stuff, they might be able to tell that straight off. And they can't prove you were somewhere you weren't.'

'He was in custody when he died, and that Detective, Hermannson, if he's involved, how do I know others aren't? I could end up just like Grant.'

'Fuuuuuck,' she lets it out low and slow. 'What do we do then?'

The fact she's talking about *we*, like she's already involved, brings fresh tears to my eyes, it takes everything I have not to give in and let them run free.

'Honestly,' I say after a pause, 'I haven't a clue. I just need somewhere I can stay for a few days till I figure things out. I'd go back home or up North, but those'll be the first places I'd look if I were them. I'll totally understand if you'd—'

'You're staying,' she cuts me off. 'End of discussion.'

I let out a breath I didn't realise I'd been holding, feeling a weight off already even though I know this is a long way from over.

'Pull your car into the garage,' she says, standing. 'I'll go and get the spare room ready for you.'

'Thank you, Izzy,' I say quietly. 'I owe you.'

'No you don't,' she says, and leaves me in the silence of the kitchen as she heads upstairs. I feel safe for the first time since I found that bloody phone, but I know it's an illusion. They're coming, and they won't stop. Ever.

Chapter Twenty-Six

I stare at the lifeless iPhone screen, turned off since the Starbucks car park earlier this morning. Am I being too paranoid, too easily influenced by shows like *Line of Duty*, to think they might be tracking it? Next to it on the bed is a freshly unboxed, bargain basement handset, complete with pay as you go SIM, purchased at the same motorway services. As much as I don't want to drag my family into this, the last thing I want is for Mam to see my name on the news without talking to her first.

I power it up, dialling from memory a number I've called enough times that it's tattooed somewhere deep in my brain. Seven rings, and I'm about to hang up when there's the click of the call connecting. Not Mam's voice, but one equally as familiar.

'Stephenson residence, how may I direct your call?'

My youngest brother, Davey. Class clown, and responsible for at least half of my top-ten belly laughs of all time. His accent, unlike mine that's been dulled from years of absence, is pure Geordie.

'Davey, it's me. Is Mam there?'

'Hey Mags. Yeah. You okay? You left canny sharpish yesterday?'

'I've had better days.'

'What's up?' he says, with a casual bluntness that only he gets away with. 'Apart from the obvious of course?'

'It's not ... I can't get into it now, Davey. I just need a word with her. Can you give her a shout for me please?'

'Nah, she's just popped to the corner shop to get some milk.'

I sigh, and Davey cuts back in.

'Is my craic really that bad then?'

I smile despite myself. 'No, it's just...'

'Come on, Sis, spill.'

'Honestly, Davey, I'm fine, I'll just call her back in a bit.'

'Listen Mags, I know you got the brains and I got the looks, but I'm not that daft.' He pauses, and when he speaks again, it's more hushed. 'You're not the first call I took since we got back. Some idiot from Manchester Police called ten minutes ago, asking if I knew how to get in touch with you. What's up? And don't tell me you forgot to pay a parking ticket.'

No love lost between Davey and anyone in uniform. He's been the black sheep of the family practically since he took his first steps. Two years served of a five-year sentence for assault, but knowing the kind of people he hangs around with, chances are there's far more he hasn't done time for that I don't know about.

'What did you tell him?' I ask, heart beating like a frightened rabbit.

'What did I tell him? Nowt. What's going on like, Mags? Whatever it is, I can help.'

'Not with this you can't, Davey.'

'Try me,' he says, with that cocky boyish confidence that I both love and find infuriating at times.

From somewhere outside the bedroom door, I hear footsteps, then a gentle tap-tap-tap at the door.

'Look, Davey, I've gotta go. I'll call you back, yeah?'

I end the call without waiting for a response, just as Izzy enters, carrying a tray. She places it on the foot of the bed, and takes a step back, like hired help, not wanting to encroach.

'Thought you could do with a bite to eat,' she says, pointing at a ham and cheese sandwich, bread so thick it could pass for breezeblocks. 'Listen, I've got to pop out. I'm meeting a friend for drinks in York, but I'll be back by six. Make yourself at home. Unless of course you need me to stay?'

'I'll be fine,' I say with a tired smile.

Izzy retreats back downstairs without much more small talk, and a few minutes later, I hear the whirring of her garage door and the purr of an engine over gravel crunching beneath tyres. I go to the window, peering out from the side of the curtains as Izzy's Range Rover disappears out onto the main road.

The sight of carbs on a plate elicits a gurgle from my stomach, and I alternate between bites of sandwich and tapping away at my new phone. I log into Gmail, and read through the notes I'd saved in the drafts folder. Recollections of the two meetings with Xiang. I told Izzy I don't know what to do, but when I break it down to basics, there are only two doors to choose from really.

Door one is to crash here for the foreseeable, but men like those who came for Christopher don't strike me as the sort to give up. They'll widen the search eventually. Come looking at Grant's family too. Nowhere near a long-term option. Door number two is to turn myself in, and hope I'm either wrong about Hermannson, or that he's acting alone. After all, it's GMP who want to talk to me, not Avon and Somerset. Maybe even the latter option, coupled with a rough and ready version of Xiang's story ready to email to Rose. To hell with it, I'll send it to the nationals if I have to. They'll probably get one of their own to write it up, but what matters is that the story breaks, not who breaks it. And once it's out there, surely it's harder for them to come after me in a way that makes it look like I've made it all up?

I just wish I knew the faces behind those balaclavas, those that had to pay for Xiang. A flash of memory again. Xiang's face, a mask of terror. That thought gives way to a third door. One I'd thought of briefly earlier and discounted. Layt. He'd got inside once, found some sort of proof. If I could somehow reach him, find out exactly what he had, who it implicated. If I have that, they'd all clamber over each other to print what I have to say, tabloids and broadsheets alike.

I open up a browser window and Google various search strings. Doomsday and Layt. Doomsday Layt Clock. Same results keep popping up, all about the clock itself. Not something I've heard of before. Wikipedia says it represents how close we are to some sort of man-made global catastrophe, by showing how close to midnight we are. As of January, this year, it's one hundred seconds away. Any other time, that would land as quite a sobering thought, but I'm way too preoccupied with my own mess to worry about the rest of the world for now.

All about the clock. No hits that include a reference to anyone called Layt, or Layton. I flip my phone across the bed in frustration, wincing as it bounces off the edge, rattling hard on the polished wooden floorboards.

Think, Maggie, think. Has to be a way to do this. Treat it like a story for the paper. If this was for an article, how would I track it to the source? Takes a minute but an idea flickers to life like a misfiring lightbulb. I scramble across the bed and onto the floor, scooping it back up and opening a browser window.

Can't believe it's been staring me in the face this whole time. Layt has already given me the key that could unlock his identity back when we spoke on Zoom. Time to give it a twist.

Chapter Twenty-Seven

Rose Evans tries to swallow, but the balled-up tea towel in her mouth is making it nigh on impossible. Two men carry out what can only be described as controlled destruction of her living room. She sits at her own kitchen table, arms bound behind her, a third man sitting opposite her, glacial blue eyes boring into her from slits in his black balaclava.

'Honestly, Rose – you don't mind if I call you Rose, do ya? You answer my questions honestly, and this goes smoother than a Michael Bublé concert. My Grandma was called Rose.'

His voice seems to soften at the memory, and she says a silent prayer that such a tenuous link might mellow him.

'Hated that woman. Miserable old bag,' he says, leaning forward with a dry chuckle. 'All I need to know, is what your girl told you, and where she went next. Now I'm gonna take that out so you can talk, and talk's all I expect. Anything louder than a nice chatty voice, and we're gonna have ourselves a problem. You with me?'

Rose blinks, squeezing out twin tears that track down her cheeks. She manages a nod, flinching as he extends a hand, wiping her tears with the back of his glove, before pulling out her makeshift gag.

'There you go. Your turn for the talking.'

She sniffs loudly, eyes itching like bad hay fever from all the crying. Swallows hard.

'She just ...' Another loud sniff. 'She just said that Grant's death wasn't an accident. That he was working on something that got him killed, but she wouldn't say what.'

'Oh, come on now, Rose. We know she was here all night. You two had plenty of time to chat. You publish her stories for God's sake. You're telling me she just breezed out of here without so much as a word?'

'Yes, I didn't even hear her get up, never mind leave. I took her a cup of tea around nine and she was gone. I swear, that's all I know.'

Rose feels panic bubbling up, like a saucepan left on the hob. She's babbling now, hoping for the right combination of words that gives this man what he wants, makes him leave.

He shakes his head. 'I want to believe you, Rose, really I do. Here's the thing, though. I'm an all or nothing kind of fella. It's not enough for me to want it, I need certainty. Need to be sure in *here*, you know?' He pats a palm to his heart. 'Truth of the matter is, most people will tell you what they think will get rid of you, and the people I work for, they don't pay me to take chances.'

'W-what do you want with Maggie?'

'Oh, that's between me and her. Just a little misunderstanding to clear up.'

'Please, I've told you everything I know. Please, just let me go, and it'll be like you were never here.'

He tuts. 'Ah Rose, if only it were that easy. I'm gonna spell this out for you nice and simple. If Maggie had told you why that nosy husband of hers had to die, you wouldn't have been swanning around here drinking coffee when we came calling. Trust me, you'd have already had the headlines planned out.'

Rose's eyes widen. Maggie's story. It's true. Are these the same men who came for her last night? Were they part of what happened to Grant?

'Now you might not think you know anything, but you'd be surprised what you can remember with a little encouragement.'

He stuffs the tea towel back in her mouth, jumps up from his seat and disappears into her bedroom. When he returns a minute later, she sees what he's holding and instantly bucks in the seat like she's been hit with a cattle prod. This is insane. Conflicting emotions swamp her. Desperate need to escape, knowing it's hopeless to think she could overpower three men. The chords in her neck strain, as she tries to bellow out a cry for help, but it barely makes it over the music that still drifts from her Sonos speaker.

He drags her chair closer to the bench, plugging in the hair straighteners he found in her bedroom. A quick tilt of the chin brings one of the other men across, and strong hands clamp onto her shoulders like twin vices, pushing the legs of her chair into the tile. She looks up at the first man, pleading with her eyes, shaking her head, every fibre of her telling him he doesn't have to do this.

'Oh, don't you worry, Rose. I'm not going to use that on you.'

Breath catches. She's not sure what's coming, but is sure, even behind the mask, that he's smiling. She can hear it in his words, sick bastard.

'He is.'

He nods at the man holding her in place, reaching forward, yanking off the balaclava, revealing a startled face underneath.

'Jesus, what the hell?'

The grip on her shoulders is released as he tries in vain to catch the mask before it tumbles to the floor.

'Rose, I'd like you to meet Detective Inspector Oliver Hermannson of Somerset and Avon Police.'

'Are you fucking nuts?' the newly unmasked blond man yells. 'She's seen my face now. She's seen my fucking face, and you give her my name as well?'

'Quiet down now, Olly. It's about time you earned your keep.'

'But she knows who I am!'

Hermannson's face is twisted into a mask of anger and desperation. Clay has doubts as to whether the copper has what it takes to do it, but self-preservation is one of the strongest instincts there is. Hermannson knows he can't very well have Rose Evans give his name to anyone who turns up to investigate. Clay knows that forcing his hand will bind the panicking policeman to their cause even tighter. For now, anyway. Osgood's orders were pretty clear on the longer-term picture. That in itself feels like a test for Clay.

'Then you'd better make sure she can't tell anyone when you've finished with her then, hadn't you?'

Chapter Twenty-Eight

It all starts with Cosgrove. Layt has already given me a way in. Just hadn't seen it till now. He and Cosgrove share a university. They'll hold records on all alumni. I just need to work back from Cosgrove to find a second name for Layt. That's the easy part. The tricky bit will be finding a way to get my hands on his address.

Easier said than done. It isn't like I can just call up and expect them to blindly hand over personal info to a random stranger. As the Northumbria Uni logo pops onto the screen, I start to plot out the running order. First things first, I need Layt's surname.

A quick scan of an article about Cosgrove's murder that says he was twenty-seven. From the brief time on screen with Xiang, I'd place Layt anywhere between twenty and twenty-five. If he's as good as he claims to be, though, he could have attended uni a year or more earlier.

I flick across to a new tab and open up LinkedIn. His career history has his degree at the bottom like a footnote. Says he graduated in 2019, so that gives me anything up to a six-year window, if I allow for the possibility that Layt could have been there as late as this year.

Using a search string of his name and Northumbria yields nothing of any use. Same if I add in Cosgrove's name or the course title. As if it'd be that easy. I change tack and start wading my way through a sequence of graduation photos I find on Facebook and Instagram.

My eyes flick over faces so fast that I almost miss him. The hair is different. More of a perm that seems all the rage with kids his age, and chubbier than the face from Zoom, but it's him alright. Larger than life on Facebook. Class of 2024. A few faces are tagged, but nobody with the right first name. Now I have a date, I narrow the search, and a few minutes later hit the jackpot.

'Hello Layton Brown,' I mutter as I save the image to my camera roll. 'Now how the hell do I get the nice folks at Northumbria to give me what I need?'

Asking nicely won't cut it. There is a way, but it's one that I know will leave a bad taste in my mouth. The kind of subterfuge that gives journalists a bad name.

Unless I can think of a better one before I get there, though, it's the only way I can find the kid who could be my only route to clearing my name as well as Grant's.

Don't know what makes me more nervous. The fact I'm going to have to lie about a dead man, or that I need to go to one of the few places they'll almost certainly be looking for me. Either way, I'm going home. But how the hell do I do that, knowing the reception that's likely awaiting me? No choice, though. The only way is forwards, although into what, I have no idea.

Chapter Twenty-Nine

Izzy has been gone an hour, and I wonder again how fair this is to involve her. The sense of injustice, of being ground in the cogs of a machine far bigger than I can get my head around, is oppressive. The thought of her being dragged into it doesn't sit well, and makes me all the more determined to work out my next steps and put a safe distance between us, for now at least.

How long should I stay here? Twenty-four hours, I decide. Enough time to bash out the bones of the story on the Notes app, then try and track down Layt. If that doesn't work, I'll head back to Manchester, share it with Rose, warts and all, maybe even get Rose to accompany me to the station.

Was it really only yesterday that I found that bloody phone? Less than twenty-four hours since I watched armed men come for me. I find myself staring at the cartoonish chickens on his profile picture, edges of the room blurring around me. It's the calmest I've felt in days, almost trance-like. Doesn't last, though. An insistent buzzing. I blink and I'm back in the room. Incoming video call. Davey's number flashes up on screen.

When his face pops on screen, I recognise the backdrop of our parents' back garden. Twin cherry blossoms lean against the wall behind him, and off to one side, the swing from my childhood that's as old as I am, back in service now the first few grandkids have appeared.

His expression is that of a disapproving parent tinged with concern. Although he's younger than me, he's trod a much harder path, and it shows in his face. His stint inside at Her Majesty's pleasure added lines to his forehead, and a scar to his cheek, although he's never spoken about how he got it. Still can't get used to seeing him with a beard, like he's a kid playing dressing-up.

'Thought you were calling back?' he says.

'Davey,' I say, lowering my voice, even though I know Izzy is still out. 'Sorry, I … I'm just in the middle of something.'

'Let me help you.'

'Uh-uh. I'm fine, honestly.'

'Stop telling me you're bloody fine. I don't even have to be in the same room as you to know you're not. Come on, this is me you're talking to. Where are you?'

'Trust me, Davey, you're better off out of it.'

'Where are you?' he repeats.

'Staying with a friend,' I say after a pause.

'Look, Maggie, that copper, he's called back once more already. This isn't going away.'

'I can handle it.'

'Really? Maybe you can handle this then' he says, 'Have a look at what I've just sent you, and don't worry, Mam doesn't know. Not yet anyway.'

The phone purrs against my cheek, and I pull it away, switching him to speaker, while I check out what he has sent. It's a URL. BBC Manchester news page. I frown as I click it. As the page snaps into focus, everything else in the room fades away into insignificance. Two faces stare back. On the left, Christopher Xiang. Next to him, my own face. It's the one I use as a Facebook profile picture.

More than the picture, the words leap out of the screen, embedding in my head. A wave of nausea slaps into me like a wave against a ship, rocking me back against the headboard.

Journalist sought in connection with two murders ...
   Signs of a struggle ...
   Reason to suspect Maggie Brewer was the last person to see him alive ...

The hand holding the phone drops into my lap. Davey's voice still echoes from the speaker.
   'Sis? Sis, you there?'
   They're coming for me. I don't know exactly when or where, or even who they are, but they're coming, just like they did for Grant.

Chapter Thirty

'Of course, I don't think you bloody did it,' Davey says when I finally pick the phone back up.'

It's like my thoughts are wading through treacle, synapses misfiring like a badly tuned engine.

'Davey, I … I don't …'

'Look, the day you cross a line like that, there's no hope for any of us. Whatever this is, we can fix it.'

'This,' I say, shaking my head, 'this isn't something you can just fix, Davey. You can't bring Grant back to life, or Christopher.'

'Christopher, is it?' I hear the first note of surprise in his voice. 'First name terms?'

Where do I even begin explaining the past twenty-four hours? Should I even try? The thought of anyone else getting dragged into this, getting hurt, is more than I can bear. I don't get a chance to decide, though, as Davey speaks again, and I realise I've slipped up.

'Wait, you said Grant. What's Grant got to do with this guy?'

'Nothing,' I say after a pause, but it had evidently been too long and Davey isn't buying it one bit.

'You forget who you're talking to? You've always been a crap liar, Mags.'

'Just leave it, Davey.'

'Leave my big sis swinging in the breeze so someone can hang her out to dry?' he says. 'Not a bloody chance. Look, unless you turn around and tell me you killed this guy, I'll do anything I can to help you get out from under it. To be fair, even if you did do it, I'd still have your back. Just tell me what's going on, and we'll work it out together.'

'I can't,' I say, a touch of conviction creeping back into my voice as the shock of seeing the article recedes a fraction. 'You don't know these people.'

'The police? You forgetting I've got a solicitor on speed dial, Sis?'

'Not the police. Well, not just them. And not all of them, least I think not anyway.'

'Who then?'

I huff out a loud sigh, every inch of me committing to holding the line, not dragging him down with me, but my own words bounce back. Not just the police. Those masked men hadn't come knocking with a warrant and handcuffs. The prospect of people like that, with the likes of Hermannson on their side feels like a snowy overhang about to drop onto the slopes, an avalanche in waiting, heading my way. It will catch up, it will bury me unless I change course.

Before I can stop myself, I'm talking, telling him everything, starting from the night they came for Grant. Barely pause for breath until my story reaches Harrogate. We're both silent for a few seconds.

'Wow,' Davey says finally. 'That's fucking insane.'

'Understatement,' I say, feeling a little shaky.

'If you weren't there, though, they can't pin a bloody murder on you just 'cos they say you dropped your debit card.'

'That's exactly what they were going to do with Grant. Xiang told me it's possible to synthesise someone's DNA if you already have a sample. If they've done that with mine too, I'm dead in the water unless I can prove it, and the only people who can help me are all dead.'

'Not all of them,' Davey says. 'What about that Layt kid you mentioned? He from your neck of the woods?'

'Maybe,' I say, propping the phone against a spare pillow and leaning back against the headboard. 'Think I have a way to find out, but I need to come up north to know for sure.'

'How long you staying in Harrogate?'

'I dunno,' I say truthfully. 'Couple more days tops.'

'Let me come and get you, Maggie. I can help.'

'How can you help, Davey? This isn't some scrap outside a pub. These people kill anyone who gets in their way.'

'I can help you find your young lad for starters.'

'Uh-uh,' I say. 'Trust me it's easier if I do that myself.'

'I can at least have your back while you do, then. I can keep you safe up here. I can rope in a few of Gregor's lads to help if needs be.'

'You're still working for Gregor?'

My tone leaves little to the imagination as to my opinion of Price. He and his family have been top dogs in the North East for as long as I can remember. The whole family traded on fear, even when we were at school with Gregor, back when he was a scrawny kid with join-the-dots acne. He dined out on the family, coasting through at times, but handy with his fists even back then when he needed to be.

'He's a legitimate businessman now, Mags.'

'And what exactly is it you do for him these days?'

Davey shrugs, and I fancy I spot faint patches of pink glowing in his cheeks, uncomfortable under questioning.

'Security Consultant,' he says, squaring shoulders and tilting his chin up a half-inch, as if the posturing comes with the title.

'Are you even allowed to mix with the likes of him, you know, people with criminal records, with the terms of your probation and everything?'

'He's never done any time, Maggie. It's all good.'

'Not yet,' I shoot back.

'Look, d'you want my help or not?'

'I still don't think this is a good idea, Davey,' I say, but feel my resolve weakening.

'Let me tell you what's not a good idea,' he snaps, stabbing a finger towards the camera. 'Me, visiting you in prison, and that's best case if these fuckers are even half as bad as you say.'

He's right. I know he is. Doesn't stop me feeling protective towards my baby brother, but the pull of familiar faces, streets and surroundings is so strong right now that I make a snap decision.

'Fine, you're right. I can't do this alone. You can't tell anyone else, though. You have to promise me that. Not Gregor, and especially not the rest of our lot. Dad'll have a heart attack if he finds out.'

He shakes his head. 'You're a stubborn bugger, aren't you?'

'I learned from the best,' I say, smiling for what feels like the first time in weeks. 'What now then?'

'You can't drive your motor up here. They'll clock you on the cameras. Text me an address,' he says, checking his watch, 'and I'll leave now.'

'And then what?'

'Then we find your boy.'

Chapter Thirty-One

I settle for a Post-it note on the kitchen table, thanking Izzy, saying I'll be back for my car when I can. It's just shy of two hours since I ended the call with Davey when I hear the crackle and crunch of tire on gravel from out front.

Even though it's a private drive, hedges shielding it from the road, I can't help but glance both ways as I peek out the door. I hate the nervous wreck this is turning me into, a pale imitation of myself.

Davey grins from ear to ear as he steps out from his Range Rover. It's not brand new, from the plates, but still way more than he should be able to afford. I'm afraid to ask where he gets his money from. Apart from his failed attempt to be a world-class burglar, his only real skill set is his ability to believe he can crash through anyone and anything that gets in his way. Used to work on the doors in Tynemouth for a spell, and he's still got his doorman's physique, as well as the look that goes with it. Short buzz cut, biceps that threaten to pop the seams on the fitted white shirt he's wearing. He wraps arms like mini-tree trunks around me, picking me up like I'm a kid.

'I've been thinking on the way down, and there is one good thing to come out of all of this.'

I give him a puzzled look as he sets me down.

'It means I'm not the black sheep of the family anymore.'

He finishes with a wink, and leans back to avoid my playful slap to his chest.

'You're a dick, you know that?'

'Maybe, but I'm also your ride home. Come on, let's hit the road.'

I slide into the warmth of his car, and before we've even left the city limits, I can feel my eyes growing heavy. I haven't had a full night's sleep since the one before the hotel room, and feel drained, like a marathon runner about to collapse at the finish line. Davey is prattling on about a girl he's been seeing, and how she'd been in the year behind them at school, but the gentle rocking of the car, combined with the whispered droning lullaby of tires on tarmac means I'm gone before we hit the motorway.

I jerk awake, confused, forgetting for a split second where I am. Davey glances across as I clock him, and hits me with a hundred-watt smile.

'Afternoon sleeping beauty. Not long to go.'

I yawn so wide my jaw clicks, and stretch as I sit up.

'I know you said you didn't want the others involved. We can go straight to mine if you like. We don't have anywhere to be till eight.'

'Where are we going at eight?'

'Oh, sorry, I made a few calls while you were asleep. Gregor has somewhere safe, somewhere you can keep your head down while we work this out.

'How much did you tell him?'

'Don't worry, I just told him it's a private family matter. That there's some folk you'd rather avoid while you're dealing with ... well you know ... losing Grant.'

I breathe the smallest sigh of relief. The circle has already grown bigger than I'm comfortable with just by including my brother. I know Gregor Price from old, know him by reputation now. No guarantees he wouldn't look to spin this his way somehow, profit from it even.

'Davey, I don't want you in anyone's debt over this.'

'Told you already,' he says with a wink. 'He owes me.'

I settle back into my seat, staring out at the endless rumpled white blanket of cloud, stretching out as far north as I can see.

'So do I, after this.'

'Nah.'

'Yes, I do. You've just dropped everything and come running, even after what I told you.'

'Part of the brotherly job description, innit? Besides, your credit's good.'

I smile, reaching forward to switch the radio on, but Davey beats me to it, covering the power button with one hand.

'Reception's shit here, you'll not get much, I could stick a CD on instead if you like?'

'What you got, Justin Bieber's *Best of* album? No thanks You're a fab brother, but you're tone deaf. Besides, it's bang on the hour. I want to hear the news.'

I wiggle my fingers past his, tapping it on. He gives me a look I can't quite read, like something's troubling him on top of my current situation, and as the news jingle kicks in, I find out what.

'Look, Sis, I didn't want you to find out like this, but you're about to hear something on the news headlines. It was on when you were dozing before. It's not your fault, okay?'

I turn to him, puzzled, studying his face. I don't have to wait long to understand. The newsreader leads with it.

'Bodies are mounting up in Manchester today, as police were called to the home of Rose Evans, assistant editor at the Manchester Standard, *after a neighbour reported hearing sounds of a struggle. They found Miss Evans' body inside, but have yet to release any details as to cause of death. Police say they would like to speak to Maggie Brewer, a fellow journalist at the* Standard. *Mrs Brewer is believed to have been the last person to see Miss Evans alive. They're also interested to speak to her in relation to a second murder earlier yesterday, that of a Doctor Christopher Xiang, who was found shot in his flat yesterday morning.'*

Feels like I've been sucker punched, unable to draw breath. Of all of it so far, this one is on me. I brought this to Rose's door. I might not have committed the act, but if I'd never made the call, never turned up at her door, she'd still be alive. How the hell had they even tracked her to there anyway? My phone? My car?

Nausea bubbles up, hot and visceral, my mouth flooding with saliva, warning me it's not going to be pretty.

'Stop the car,' I say one hand going to my stomach, the other resting on the door handle.

'What? Sis, you alright?'

'Stop the car.'

He nods. 'Washington Services are only five miles away.'

'Now.' I shake my head, and hope he just does it without question. One way or the other, the sandwich from Izzy's house is making its second appearance.

Davey hits the hazards, taps the brakes, and nips in behind the eighteen-wheeler he's just overtaken. It's not quite an emergency stop, but it's hard enough for the seatbelt to dig hard, squeezing an already delicate stomach, and I know I only have seconds.

I spill out onto the hard shoulder, managing to put a few feet between me and Davey's car before the scalding heat of bile rises in my throat, shooting out like a geyser. A car door opens and closes behind me, and seconds later, Davey's arm is around me, his other hand holding my hair back. Three more retches, until there's nothing left. After that, the only thing still flowing are fresh tears.

Davey folds me into him, holds me as I sob. Partly for Rose, but mostly still for Grant. For what I've lost. What more I could still lose. For the sheer bloody injustice of it all. For the fact I'm dragging my brother into the same mess that could be the end of me. Feels like an eternity, before I extricate myself, wiping tears on the sleeve of my sweater.

'I'm alright,' I say, the look on his face suggesting he's far from convinced. 'Honestly, I'm fine. Let's just get back on the road.'

He stands his ground, watching as I walk past him, but by the time I'm clicking my seatbelt back in, he's sliding back into the driver's seat. He starts the engine but doesn't pull away immediately. When I look at him, I see the worry in his face, and hate the fact that I'm the one who has put it there.

'They can't pin this one on you. No matter what they say. You were with Izzy, miles away. She can vouch for that. Doesn't matter what they drop on the floor this time.'

'That's just it, though, Davey, they can do pretty much whatever they want. I'm in that bloody database, just like everybody else. Christ, you'll be in as well. All they've got to do, is whip up another batch that matches my sample from what they have, and I'm a goner.'

'This is fucking nuts. Like something out of *Black Mirror*, man.'

'Shit,' I say, the implication of Davey's words sinking in. 'Izzy. I have to warn her. I can't let them do to her what they did to Rose.'

I reach into the footwell for my bag, scrabbling around for my phone, pull it out, and go to power it up. My actual phone, not the more recent acquisition. Davey reaches across, pulls my thumbs away from the power button.

'Wait, what you doing?' he says.

'Calling Izzy. I don't have her number in that one,' I say, gesturing to the burner phone.

'If the police are after you, that's the first thing they'll check. When they see your phone ping twenty miles from home, how long you think it's gonna take before they come knocking with a warrant at everyone's houses.'

I stare at the handset, a reminder that I led those men to Rose's house. A peculiar mixture of revulsion and relief washes over me. I never had this switched on at Izzy's house. That's something at least. I'm pretty sure it can't be tracked as long as it stays off. The thought of having to ditch it tugs at my heartstrings. Grant was forever nagging me to upload my pictures to the cloud, but I always found something else to distract myself with. The photos on it are a catalogue of the last few years of our lives. Some duplicated on social media, but most are only on here. Irreplaceable.

'I'll find a way to call her for you,' Davey says. 'Pop that in the glovebox so you don't get tempted and end up getting caught all for the sake of ten minutes on *Candy Crush*.'

I manage to dig out a smile I didn't know was there. 'Never had you pegged as a player.'

'What can I say, when you've got as many nieces and nephews as we do, it pays to be able to pass for a big kid sometimes.' He lets a few seconds of silence soak in before he continues.

'This will go away,' he says, taking my hand in his. 'I may be your baby brother, but if anyone comes at you, it won't be just me they have to get through. I know I don't talk about work, with good reason, but let's just say I don't exactly do flower arranging or manicures.'

I squeeze his hand. I love my not-so-little, little brother. He's no angel, and has had his fair share of scraps, but this is a different level altogether. For now, though, I feel as safe as I have in a long time. Protected.

We pull back into traffic, and within minutes, I see the Angel of the North peeking its head over the treeline, rusty brown wings reflecting the last shade of autumn in the leaves. No sooner have we sped past it, then we're leaving the motorway, winding around into the Tees Valley industrial estate.

'Where are we going?' I ask, confused, as I realise we should have left the motorway long before the Angel. Should have peeled off right after the services towards the Tyne Tunnel, a far quicker route back to the coast.

'Just got to see a man about a dog,' says Davey, as they pull up outside a slate grey warehouse. Looks closed up, whatever it is, the main roller door all the way down. 'Back in two,' and before I can ask where to, or why, he's out of the car, trotting across to a side door.

I lean forwards, watching with suspicion as he raps on the door. A moment later, it opens, and an older man somewhere in his sixties peers out. Must know Davey because he smiles, offers a hand, and ushers him in. I could swear there's a glance in my direction that lingers longer than it should. Davey is only inside for a couple of minutes, and when he emerges, he's zipping up his jacket. I see a hand go to his breast. Looks like he's patting something, adjusting its position maybe. What has he just collected? He climbs back in, smile as wide as the River Tyne.

'Who was that?'

'Hmm?'

'That man you just met.'

'Oh,' he says with a dismissive shrug. 'Just a mate I met at flower arranging class.'

I tap him with a playful jab to the shoulder, but he resists any further attempt to prise the information from him.

'One thing, while I think on,' he says as they rejoin the motorway. 'The place Gregor is loaning us, he's going to be there.'

I react instantly, shaking my head, and twist sideways to look at my brother.

'We can't bring anyone else into this, Davey.'

'He won't be stopping long. He's just swinging by to say hello, pay his respects.'

'Davey, no. It's too dangerous.'

The unspoken undertone being that Gregor is too dangerous full stop.

'He's coming, Maggie. We don't have to tell him anything, but he's gonna be there.'

This isn't part of the plan. I've not seen Gregor in years, but we have history, albeit very one-sided. He had tried and failed to fill the vacant slot of boyfriend when we were in sixth form and hadn't taken too kindly to the rejection. Not that it stopped him from trying it on whenever our paths crossed over the years that followed.

Nothing about him has ever appealed to me. He's a bully, a misogynist, and a general all-round idiot. Trouble is, he and Davey have been tight all those years, and my brother thinks the sun shines out of Gregor Price's arse.

If I change my mind, refuse the help, who's to say I'll stay safe long enough to find Layt? Might as well take a long walk off the end of Tynemouth pier for all the hope I'd have of coming through this alone.

Davey absentmindedly touches a hand to his chest again, and I can make out the smallest of lumps under his jacket. We speed up the A19, towards a meeting that feels like it will make or break me, and for the first time since before the funeral, I'm not thinking of Grant. Instead, it's a silent prayer. Gregor used to deal, even back then in sixth form.

Please don't let it be drugs.

I recite the words over and over in my head, praying my baby brother isn't like the man he calls his friend-slash-boss. Not sure how I'll react if that's who he has become. Either way, tonight, I will come face to face with him for the first time in years, and put my safety, my life, in the hands of a man I don't trust to tell the time, never mind the truth.

Chapter Thirty-Two

Declan Clay pulls into the Shell service station, tops up his tank, and heads inside to pay. The bored teenager behind Perspex doesn't even make eye contact, and Clay imagines what it would be like to reach through the slot in the barrier, grab a handful of their slightly stained polo shirt, and smash their head off it until they acknowledged his presence. It plays out so clearly inside his head, that he can practically hear the crunch of cartilage their nose would make as it hammered against the screen, the red spatter smeared like a hundred bugs on a windscreen.

Instead, he beams an overly friendly smile that isn't even acknowledged, and heads back out to his car. As he starts the engine, a call comes through the speakers. It's him again. Can't leave well fucking alone. Micromanaging for the millionth time. Clay gives a weary smile, and clicks a button on the wheel to answer.

'Mr Osgood.'

'I told you to call me on the hour, every hour,' Osgood's voice oozes through the car's sound system. 'It's five past.'

'There are a lot of moving parts here, sir,' he says through gritted teeth.

'What the hell am I paying you for if it's not to do as you're told?'

'I needed to take care of something. Took a little longer than expected.'

'And?'

'And we're working through a number of leads.'

Truth be told, the trail has gone cold, at least for now. Turns out Maggie Brewer genuinely hadn't told Rose where she was going.

'The newspaper editor. Was that necessary? We don't need any more attention on this.'

'I'm afraid it was,' Clay answers. 'We know Mrs Brewer was there overnight thanks to Hermannson coming through with the mobile trace. Miss Evans wasn't any the wiser about where she went after that, though.'

'You're sure?'

Clay nods, remembering the sizzle and scream, sizzle and scream. 'I'm sure.'

There were other ways it could have gone, easier ways. But what Clay doesn't share with Osgood, or anyone for that matter, is why he chooses that way every chance he gets. How it's a purer hit than anything you can shoot in a vein. That singular feeling of omnipotence. Of teasing out answers with the finesse of a conductor wafting his baton. Of choosing when and how it ends. Before Osgood can fire another question at him, his phone purrs as a text arrives. He keeps talking as he reads it.

'It won't blow back on you,' he says, wondering if Osgood picks up on, or even cares about the use of *you* instead of *us*. 'When the police get their crime scene reports back, it all leads back to Maggie Brewer. Just like it did for her husband.'

'As long as you're sure.'

Of course, I'm bloody sure, he thinks, but stays quiet, waiting the other man out.

'What next then?'

Clay is about to spin a general line about following up leads, but the text throws him a lifeline as he finishes it.

'I know where she went next,' he says. 'I'm headed there now.'

He ends the call with promises to update Osgood the moment he has her. He's about to pull away when he notices the low battery notification pop up on his phone. He lifts the lid of the armrest storage, looking for his charger, remembering he hadn't taken it back out of his bag after last night's hotel stopover.

Clay pulls away from the pump, coasting to a stop by the side of the carwash. He slides back out, waiting until he's directly behind the car before he pops the boot open. He catches it as it rises. Holds it a few inches open as he does a quick sweep of the forecourt. No one within fifty feet. He keeps his hand in place, but lets it rise to open up a gap of a few feet.

The strap of his hold-all pokes out from under the corner of a dark-blue travel blanket. He reaches in, tugging it towards him, but it's caught on something. He yanks a little harder, but it isn't budging. A glance over both shoulders shows nothing different to five seconds ago, so he lets the boot rise to the top of its arc, reaching in with both hands. He lifts the corner of the blanket up, muttering to himself as he sees the problem. It's managed to get snagged under the heel of a foot that pokes out from beneath the heavy blanket.

As Clay reaches in, lifting the calf attached to the foot to free his bag, the movement dislodges a heavy fold of material to his left. It falls away like a shroud, giving Oliver Hermannson's sightless eyes a glimpse of a freedom he can never grasp. The dark hole punched into his forehead is bang centre, the third point of a triangle with his eyes, like a bindi. Its angry red circumference looks drawn on. He's served his purpose but now he needs to disappear. Wouldn't do to have another body connected to the Brewers turn up.

'Sorry about that, Olly,' Clay says, tucking the blanket back over his face. 'Nothing personal.'

Chapter Thirty-Three

'I don't like this, Mags,' Davey says, scanning the street ahead. 'Not one bit. At least let me come in with you. Promise I won't say a word. He draws a pinched finger and thumb across his lips.

'It's not that I don't want you there,' I reassure him, 'but this only works if I'm in there alone.'

He nods but the concerned creases carved into his forehead tell me what he really thinks of the idea. I lean in for a hug, and feel as safe in his arms as I have since this whole mess began.

'You got this, and I've got you,' he whispers as he lets me go, and steps back.

I turn and look up at the building in front of me. A stunning red brick and terracotta combination that's stood for a century and a half. Must have walked past it dozens of times back when I lived up here, but I never truly saw it, least not the way I do now.

The address I have for the university admin office puts it somewhere inside, and as I head up the steps towards the door, I can't help but think it looks more of a mini-stately home than a place of learning. Inside is even more impressive. A stone archway frames an impressive staircase leading up to the first floor, before it sweeps off in both directions. Reminds me of the ones in Hogwarts that slide around, and send you off to God only knows where.

I catch the eye of a student scurrying past and ask for directions to the office, which is mercifully only one twist of a corridor away. When I get there, the door is a few inches open so I make do with a polite double tap and walk in, praying to God this throw of the dice works. There's a moment of panic as the door creaks when the unhelpful thought pops to mind that if Davey saw my face in the news, whoever is behind this door might have as well. But this isn't just my best shot, it's my only one, so that's just a bridge to cross if it comes to that.

The face that greets me from behind a raised counter is one big warm smile. Sixty-something, rain-cloud grey hair tied back in a bun, and I swallow down the pang of guilt I feel for the lies I'm about to tell.

'Afternoon,' she beams. 'How can I help you?'

There's a split second when I open my mouth that I don't trust myself to say the right words, as if the pressure will squeeze the truth from me like toothpaste from a tube, but I try my best to match her smile with a shy one of my own, and instinct takes over.

'I hope you can,' I say. 'I … ahm … if you can't then I don't know where else to try.'

'Ooh, sounds serious,' she widens her eyes, like we're sharing a joke, but she drops the faux-friendliness when she sees my face change. I let the tip of the emotional iceberg take over, and lower my eyes.

'I'm here about my brother. He was a student here.'

'We've got a few of 'em,' she tries her best to keep a light-hearted edge to the conversation. 'What's his name, and what do you need?'

'Paul,' I say. 'And it's complicated.' I pause for effect, placing the takeout coffee cup I brought with me on the desk. It's a delicate drip feed, steering her towards Layt without giving Cosgrove's full name. What if she knows it from the news?

'Complicated how?'

'I need to reach a friend of his that he studied with, Layt Brown, but they'd lost touch and I don't have Layt's details.'

She purses her lips, head tilting like a teacher about to tell off the naughty kid.

'Don't think I'll be able to help there my lovely. One thing I can't do is give out personal details like addresses, least not without permission. Does your brother not have any other friends who might know how to reach Layt?'

Now, the voice in my head whispers, and I lift my defences, picturing Grant's face. Only inches, just enough to let the grief waiting to smother me seep in. The speed with which the first tear falls surprises even me, and I swallow hard to keep the others in check.

'My brother died,' I say, staring at the carpet between my feet for a beat, before looking back up at the stunned woman. 'There's a lot I wish I could ask him, but …'

There's no need to fake anything I'm feeling right now. I see her sympathetic smile, and like a magician pulling a rabbit from a hat, she produces a paper hankie from nowhere for me.

'Oh my God,' she says, 'I'm so sorry to hear that.'

'Thank you,' I say between loud sniffs, hating myself for the show I'm putting on, even if the tears *are* real – albeit for the wrong man. 'It's still a lot, you know, to wrap my head around.'

She nods, reaching down beside her for a second hankie.

'And my brother and Layt were close. Paul was a few years older, but Layt was like a younger brother, you know?'

She nods again, like she can relate, but in reality, I've likely made her feel too awkward to say a word.

'I don't even know if Layt knows,' I say wiping another stray tear from my cheek. 'And when I found out Paul left him something in his will, I tried all sorts to track him down, I really did, and then I thought of the uni connection,' I add building up to the ask, but she beats me to the punch.

'I feel for you, I really do,' and even from the tone of her voice I can tell I'm going to need plan B. 'But I still can't give out another student's details, not without speaking to them first.'

Not that it helps me, but she does look genuinely sorry. Time to stick a foot in the door she's trying to tactfully close on me.

'Oh, no, I didn't mean …,' I smile through a sniff, like she's said something funny. 'Course you can't. I just thought seeing as you'll have his details on file, maybe you could, you know, call him for me. Maybe that way I can speak to him without you having to give me anything. Surely that doesn't break any rules, does it?'

That stops her, and she tilts her head a few degrees, like she's trying to work out a puzzle. I see her thinking it through, looking for a reason to say no, but after a few seconds she shrugs.

'I … don't see any reason why not,' she says finally, and starts tapping away at her keyboard. 'Layt Brown you said? Let … me … see, ah yes, here we go.'

She picks up her phone, punching in numbers. The smile is back, but it's not full beam this time, like she's not entirely comfortable. I hope it's not obvious, but I lean into the counter, and even though the numbers read upside down, the first few digits are like a defib to the chest. Zero one nine one. North Tyneside area code.

He didn't just go to uni here, he lives up here too. Least he did when he studied. Might not even be the right number anymore, I tell myself, steeling myself for failure, when her face changes, and she starts to speak.

I hold my breath as she introduces herself, feeling sick to my stomach, hoping I can pass it off as an extension of the grieving sister act if it shows on my face. She explains the reason for her call, followed by the longest silence as she listens.

'Do you know when he'll be back in?' I hear her ask, and my heart sinks like a stone. 'Okay ... yes ... yes, yes ... if you're sure? Will do. Thank you, and sorry to trouble you Mr Brown.'

She scratches out something on a piece of paper, lets the handset fall into place with a soft click, and I'm literally hanging on her next words, like they'll be a crutch that keeps me up or batters me to the ground.

'That was his dad I just spoke to. I'm afraid Layt isn't in at the moment.'

I daren't speak. Don't trust myself not to blurt out the truth in desperation if it'll make her call back. To tell his dad just how badly I need to speak to his son. That my life could literally depend on it. His too.

'But he did say that under the circumstances, he's happy for me to pass on his son's mobile number.'

I grip the edge of the counter, thankful for the high top hiding my Bambi legs. It's a lifeline. All I have to do now is convince Layt that he needs one just as much as me.

Chapter Thirty-Four

The world keeps turning around me while mine stands still. I sit on a low stone seat outside the Sutherland building. Davey paces nervously past me as I count the rings in my ear. He answers on the fifth one.

'Hello?'

Any hint of brashness from the Zoom call is gone. Watching a friend getting shot in the head will do that for you, I guess.

'Layt? It's me. Maggie.'

The silence sits thick like clouds waiting to burst. Breathing on the other end of the line.

'How did you get my number?'

'We need to meet up,' I say, ignoring his question.

'You've seen what they do when they find you. Far as I know, they don't know I exist, and I plan on keeping it that way,' he says, voice rising a notch. 'I'm hanging up now, Maggie. My advice? Disappear.'

'You really think they won't find you?' I fight to keep my voice level, mindful of people around me. 'How hard can it be if I managed it?'

'How did you?' he asks again after a pause.

'Meet me later and I'll tell you.' Seconds tick by. 'You said it yourself, you've seen what they do. We're in the same boat, you and me. Only two choices. Wait for them to come, or find a way to stop them.'

That gets a laugh. ''Cos of course it's that easy, isn't it?'

'Tell me I'm wrong.'

Another silence. Must be eating him up not knowing how I got his number, wondering how long it'll take the Irishman with the pale blue eyes to do the same. Eventually he sighs.

'What do you want, Maggie?' He sounds irritated to even be on the call with me.

'What do I want? I want my husband to not be dead. I want to have not been dragged into this in the first place, but seeing as I can't have that, I want the next best thing. I want to not join him just yet. I want my life back. And I don't know where to start without you. You and Christopher got me into this, so—'

'That was Chris, not me,' he snaps back. 'I'd have left you out of it.'

'Well that's bloody marvellous, but here I am. People keep dying around both of us, and unless we bloody well do something we're both going to join them.'

I know I've raised my voice too loud when I see Davey's face flashing a stern warning, but I'm past caring.

'Fine,' he sulks. "I'll meet you for all the good it'll do.'

I let a long slow breath out, and read out the address on Davey's phone of the house Gregor is letting us use. One small victory in the sea of shit I'm sailing through. He promises to be there for nine tonight, and when I end the call I see the tremors in my hand as I pass Davey his phone back.

'Sorted?' he asks.

'Says he'll be there,' I say, then lean forwards and bury my face in my hands like I'm counting in a game of hide-and-seek, except I'm not the one doing the seeking, and nowhere feels safe to hunker down.

'Well if he doesn't there's other ways to find him,' Davey says, but a moment later, he shifts uncomfortably, as if I'm not going to like what he says next. 'So, I'm thinking, we've got time to kill. I know Mam would love to see you.'

I'm torn, and I know he can see it. After what I've been through, I'd love nothing more. The prospect of being with her now exerts such a strong pull. I'm a moon to Mam's planet, forever circling, disappearing off in my own orbit, but never too far away. Leaving Mam behind when I moved away was one of the hardest things I've ever done, and now, more than ever, I need that familiarity. The sense of serene calm only a mother can bring.

What if they've tracked me here, though? A picture flashes to mind of masked men, splintering doors as they charge into Mam's living room. Davey must see the conflict.

'We can go around the back, across the field and in through the utility room. No one would even know we were there.'

I don't answer, staring past him, losing myself in the ever-darkening skies. Davey moves to rest his hands lightly on my shoulders.

'It's okay, Sis. Nobody knows you're even up here, never mind where you are.'

He gives a gentle squeeze, and it massages my doubts away. I smile, nod, and we walk to his car. One hour. I owe myself that much. So much the better if it's just Mam. Dad is a creature of habit, so he'll probably be propping up the bar at the local. He was uncharacteristically quiet at the wake, so there's every chance if he's in he might even feel too awkward to sneak in his usual passive-aggressive opinions of how he thinks I've wasted my life so far.

I shiver as I climb into Davey's car. It's been a long time since I've been back. Too long, but then again, it hasn't felt like home for a long time. Not since Davey's arrest. Things had happened that night, words said that landed like body blows, making out like it was my fault. I don't know what's worse. The fact that my own father blamed me for his favourite child getting dragged out of their house by four coppers, or the fact that it was true. Davey smiles across at me, and I squirm at the memory. He can never know. It would break part of him that couldn't be patched up, and that, I couldn't live with.

Chapter Thirty-Five

Memories batter me from all sides as we head inland. Landmarks from childhood drift past. Tynemouth swimming pool squatting behind trees at the roundabout on Beach Road. Monkseaton High School, roof studded with multi-coloured blocks, like oversized Lego bricks. Past the Beacon pub, scene of countless pre-drinks before hitting Whitley Bay, or Newcastle city centre. Finally into Wellfield estate itself. We park up on Burnbank Avenue, and waves of nostalgia wash over me.

It's been a slow dawdle here, via a sandwich shop to stop the growling in my gut. Nights draw in fast this time of year and the field at the end of the road is a carpet of dark grass, outline of trees jabbing up into the sky. My parents' house is less than five hundred yards away, and this feels like overkill in the extreme, but I force myself to remember the feeling of pure panic as those men left my flat. To imagine them hiding in the dark corners that street lights on my parent's road can't reach.

We trudge across the field, not saying much, and I see Davey tense as a figure breaks away from the tree line. It passes in seconds, though, as I spy the glowing collar of a dog as it tears past. Just a guy out for an evening stroll who pays us no attention, heading for the east gate that leads back into the estate. The field is damp with the remnants of this afternoon's rain, and it soaks through my socks and shoes as I swish through the grass. Over in the far corner, a path leads off north, skirting the edge of a farmer's field. My parents' house backs onto this, half-way between here and where the track joins back onto the main road. I see the dent in the hedgerow where a gate is recessed. I've trodden this path enough times over the years to wear away the grass all on my own. Davey pushes the gate open, and we step into the garden. The contrast is immediate, me shrouded in shadow, rooms of the house lit up like Blackpool illuminations, goldfish bowls of light in the deepening darkness.

As familiar as it feels, something is different. It's homely, but not home. Not anymore. Not the house anyway. Mam stands framed in the kitchen window, yellow Marigolds pulled high up her forearms. Davey and Freddie used to wind her up, saying with gloves like that she could pass for a customs officer ready to do a cavity search.

I'm close enough to see my own reflection in the window when Mam looks up, suspicious first at what-ever sound alerted her, shifting to a beaming smile when she realises who her visitors are. Her expression never quite hit the right notes for out and out surprise, though, and I suspect Davey may have given her a heads up, of our visit at least, if not the reason for it.

She throws her arms around me the second we step inside, Marigolds and all, and for as long as it lasts, I feel safe. Totally and utterly. As if the last couple of weeks haven't happened. So complete is the feeling that I feel a prickle of tears, almost like my body is seizing the moment to let the tension seep out.

It's Mam who breaks away eventually, after the long-est of moments, stepping back, her warm smile washing over me, triggering a breakaway tear down one of my cheeks.

'Oh, love. Come here,' and she pulls me back in.

I feel a squeeze on my shoulder as Davey walks past, leaving us to it. When we finally step back from one another, I fancy I see my mam's eyes swimming ever so slightly too but before I can speak, Mam has turned away busying herself. The kettle is flicked on, cups clatter on the bench, as she goes into her usual over-drive whenever anyone arrives. Tea and biscuits are her go-to in any situation, regardless of whether it's crisis or celebration.

I try to protest, but before I can blink, half a dozen types of biscuits are stacked up on a plate beside the cups.

'Your dad'll be sorry he missed you,' Mam says. 'He's just popped down to the Beacon for a quick one.'

The concept of quick one isn't in Dad's vocabulary. For a man who seems to take delight in pointing out other people's shortcomings, he's remarkably quiet on his own. At a guess he'll be at least four pints in by now, and as for sorry to miss me, I'm pretty sure he won't lose too much sleep.

'You go on through to the front room. I'll bring these through.'

As I wander down the corridor, I hear voices, and for the first time, the number of cups on the tray Mam is preparing registers. Five cups. Three voices coming from behind the closed door. One of them Davey, the other two female.

When I open the door, I worry for a split second that this is some kind of intervention. My sisters, Moya and Julie sit at either end of the couch, bookending Davey between them. Age-wise I'm nestled between the pair of them. Julie, two years younger than me, sits with her legs tucked up under her, hair scraped back into a ponytail. Moya, two years older than me, and only a year behind Fred junior, looks like an advert for perfect posture, shoulders squared against the high back of the couch. Over by the window, Dad's armchair stands empty. It'd be borderline sacrilegious, even now we're all grown up and he's a ten-minute walk away, to slide into his spot.

Julie jumps up, legs uncoiling like a spring propelling her up and off the couch, wrapping arms around me. Moya is a little slower off the mark, greeting a shade more reserved. Something's lurking beneath the surface, and I'm itching to probe, but don't want to fall head first into whatever mess Moya has going on right now, not in a group setting anyway.

Mam shuffles in, tray laden with cups and biscuits, balanced with skill that would be the envy of circus performers. Everyone has their own cups. One of those homely little quirks she has. Even Grant has one. I wonder if it's still in the cupboard.

'What are you two doing here?' I say narrowing my eyes at both sisters.

Julie shrugs. 'Just popped in to see Mam.'

There's a look that passes between them that makes me think the intervention could still be an option, but I see an even more obvious tell in Davey, as his cheeks flush and he meets my eye for a second, before looking away, guilty as a kid with their hand in the cookie jar.

'Why do I get the feeling you were all here waiting for me?' I ask.

'What? No, we were just …' Julie begins, but Mam blows any attempt at subterfuge out of the water.

'We were just worried, pet. When Davey called, he said you weren't coping that well. It's only natural you know, you only buried him yesterday love. These things take time.'

I don't know whether to be angry that Davey called ahead at all, or glad that he's respecting my wishes about confidentiality. No sign that they're aware of the fact I'm wanted by the police, not yet anyway.

'How long are you taking off work?' Moya asks, ever the practical one.

I may well be on the verge of the story of the century, but I haven't even thought about my actual job for days. No B list posing as A list celebs to interview, when in fact even B is a generous label for some. No pandering to their supposedly hectic schedules, and hour-long waits for people to turn up on time. Thoughts of work bring Rose's face flashing to the forefront, setting my heart racing, reminding me of what happens to people I …

'Uhm, I dunno yet really. Few weeks maybe.'

'Take as long as you need, Sis,' says Julie. 'And if they try and force you back before you're ready, you tell 'em to talk to me.'

Julie drags me over to the couch, pulling me into the gap between herself and Moya, slipping an arm through mine, and pulling me in closer as we cosy up. Moya reaches over, placing a hand on my knee, giving a gentle squeeze, and there in that moment, I'm part of something bigger, something that can take on anything. Stupid, I know, but the thought of my siblings standing side by side with me makes me swell with optimism, belief that I can ride this out, slide from underneath it.

We fall into an easy routine of conversation, cuppas and chocolate digestives, so familiar, that I don't even hear the front door open. The first I know of anyone else in the house is my father's face appearing at the doorway. I register the briefest flash of surprise on his face, before it's replaced with something sadder. He's never been one to wear his heart on his sleeve, but these last few times I've seen him, he has an air of melancholy about him.

'Hallo, love,' he says, and I can smell the booze coming off him in waves as he saunters into the room. He moves in that way people do when they know they've had one too many, but are trying desperately not to broadcast it. Slightest of wobble to his step. An attempt at a dreamy smile as he reaches down to give me a hug where I sit.

'Hiya, Dad.'

'Well this is a surprise. Didn't know you were coming up so soon.'

'That makes two of us,' I say, hearing Julie mutter something under her breath that I can't quite catch.

'What's that, love?' he says, turning to Julie.

'Nothing, Dad,' she says, but the terse smile on her face says otherwise.

'You had a good evening, love?' Mam asks.

'Hardly an evening, it's barely gone tea time. Only had a couple of pints.'

Pints of what, I think, but keep to myself. Whiskey? I could smell the malty base notes when he leaned in.

'Anyway,' he says, straightening up. 'Who's up for a real drink, then?'

Shaking heads and murmured thanks but no thanks all round. Even Davey, who'd normally be first in line. I wonder if he's abstaining out of some inbuilt brotherly drive to protect, keeping his wits about him.

'Son? You'll have one, won't you?'

'Nah, Dad, I'm good thanks. I'm driving.'

Dad screws his face up as if Davey's just answered him in Russian.

'Howay man, one won't hurt you.'

'Honestly, Dad, I'm fine.'

'I'll just get you a single.'

'Jesus, Dad man. I'm fine. We're not stopping long anyway.'

'Oh aye, where you disappearing off to so soon?'

Davey glances over at me, and I see Dad clock it.

''Sgoing on? What are you two up to?'

'Nothing, Dad. Davey's just running me to see some friends later, that's all.'

'Where's your own car?'

Davey cuts in before I can answer. 'Knackered. I had to go and fetch her.'

'Well why didn't you just come back with us yesterday?'

'I hadn't planned on coming back,' I say.

'So why are you?'

It's starting to feel like an interrogation, and I feel the shift in the room. Julie's body language all closed off, Moya sitting up even straighter if that's possible.

'I dunno, I just … it's all just been a bit much, you know. Yesterday threw me good and proper, and I just …'

I hear the hoarse edge to my words, emotion starting to clog up my airways. It's so bloody typical of the man. His superpower of turning conversation into confrontation. I try and fail to stifle a sniff, and it's as if the sound pierces through the fog of drink, letting him see how close I am to the edge.

'I'm sorry, love,' he says, squatting down beside me, patting my knee. 'It's lovely to have you home. I didn't mean anything by it.'

I look up into his eyes, first hints of bloodshot blush around his pupils, looking at me like I'm still his little girl. I'm about to reach out and give his hand a squeeze, when he manages to ruin it in the space of a few seconds.

'You can stop here as long as you want you know. Might not be a bad thing to be home. You know, time away from work. Won't be easy going back there after what's happened. Maybe you need a fresh start to help you get through this.'

I glare at him, irritation burning away any softness in my words. 'And how is a new job going to make me forget my husband was murdered, Dad? Hmm?'

'No, no, I didn't mean—'

'You just can't help yourself, can you?' Heat blooms in my cheeks, and I feel the words tumbling out now. This past week, I've felt like a stick in a stream, getting tossed about, no sense of being in control, but I'm channelling control now. 'Any chance you get to poke fun at what I do. To make out like it's the shittest job going. And now, you're trying to use Grant's death, to make it sound like it's the best thing for me?'

'Maggie, I—'

'I need some fresh air,' I say, rising abruptly.

I'm up and past him, the rest of the room disapproving of him as I move. Loud tuts from Julie, Moya shaking her head.

'Fred,' Mam snaps in a tone that leaves little room for interpretation.

'What? What'd I say?'

I don't hear anything else after that, pushing out through the front door, powering down the path in long angry strides, and out onto Waterloo Road. The night has well and truly closed in now, wrapping a cloak around the streets, quiet save for the distant hum of traffic coming from the dual carriageway a little way north that cuts down towards Shiremoor.

I've pounded these pavements so many times over the years, but tonight, familiarity definitely breeds contempt. Dad's clumsy way with whiskey-fuelled words has knocked the top off a scab that dates back decades, and I'm slapped with a sudden pang of home-sickness for our place in Manchester. As descriptions go, that one hits hard. It's not *our* place anymore, just mine.

I wonder if this seemingly constant barrage of emotions will ever quieten down these ridiculously ordinary reminders of an extraordinary event. In a masochistic kind of way, I welcome it at times. Any moments where I'm wallowing in waves of grief, I lose sight of what lies ahead. Doesn't last, though, and reality crashes back in like a tsunami, leaving me panicking about my precarious position. Pursue it and possibly perish. Don't, and spend God knows how long running from faceless pursuers.

I power down street after empty street, hands thrust deep in pockets. It's a surreal silence, as if the whole estate is holding its breath. Before long I realise I've come almost full circle, and bear right, round on to the beginning of Burbank Avenue. I contemplate calling Davey, asking him to meet me here rather than go back to the house. Can't leave without going to say goodbye to Mam, though.

I'm so lost in my own thoughts that the sound of the approaching engine barely registers. It isn't until the headlights round the corner from Tarset Avenue, dazzling me like an interrogator's spotlight, that I realise what a mistake it was to disappear like that. In that moment the car bumps up on the curb, cutting off my way forwards, and it dawns on me just how far I am away from home, and from anyone who can help me.

Chapter Thirty-Six

It's painfully bright, like looking into the sun, and even when I turn to the side, blinking, a kaleidoscope of colours burst across my vision. I reach out a hand as I stagger sideways, knuckles scraping against brick. A car door opens, and footsteps come towards me. I try to look up, to see who it is, but the lights are still angled straight at me. I lift a hand to shield my eyes, just in time to see a dark figure block out the light. Fear short-circuits the fight or flight reflex. Not here. Not like this.

'We've got to go.'

The figure speaks, voice cutting through the cotton wool that seems to fill my head.

'Wha...Davey? Is that you?'

'Yes it's me, and we've got to go. Come on, get in.'

He guides me around to the passenger side, before running back around to hop back in himself. We jerk away from the curb thanks to a heavy foot on the accelerator, and I'm pressed back into my seat as we negotiate the quiet residential streets in a style more suited to *Grand Theft Auto*. I'm trying to make sense of this, but the suddenness, the pace of it, short-circuits me for a few seconds. I see Davey look across, worry etched into every line on his face.

'What the...' is all I can manage.

'They're here Maggie. Whoever they are, I'm pretty sure they're here.'

It's as if someone has shut off a valve deep inside, breath catching, pressure building in her chest. I squirm around in my seat, realising I haven't put my belt on yet, but that's the least of my worries. I crane my neck to look behind, but see only shadows and silhouettes.

'What the hell?' I say as we burst out onto the main road. 'How? Where did you see them?'

'Came out looking for you, and figured you must have gone back to the car,' he says, punching it through an amber light, shooting towards West Monkseaton station. 'Figured it'd be quicker to drive around looking for you than wander round the streets. I was just about to start it up when I saw them. Car pulled up on the corner of the field, by Redheugh Road, and a bloke jumped out, headed off over the field the way we'd gone to Mam's. Two more blokes in the car drove off towards their street.'

My hand shoots to my mouth. 'We have to warn them.'

'Already done. I rang Moya and spun her a line about owing money to some bad blokes and they were coming around to collect. She's calling the police now.'

'The police?' My voice rises an octave. 'They're part of this, Davey.'

'Different force. They can't all be,' he says. 'And besides, if they are, we're all screwed anyway. I called Gregor as well. He's sending a couple of his lads over from Earsdon. They'll be there before the coppers will.'

'We have to go back,' I say stubbornly.

'We go back now, and this is all over tonight,' he says. 'This way, there's nothing for them to find. Even if those fellas stick around, I told the 999 operator I saw a gun. They'll be there before you know it.'

We take the Foxhunters roundabout fast enough that I feel sandwiched against the door, and take a winding route through the streets of Whitley Bay, Davey glancing in his mirror what seems like every ten seconds.

'How did they find me?' I say, as much to myself as anyone.

'Fuck knows,' Davey says, but there's something about his tone, and when I look across he focuses on the road, doesn't meet my eye. I wait him out, and he folds faster than a novice poker player.

'Look, Mags,' he pauses, clears his throat. 'There's something I should probably tell you. Well, I say tell you, I probably shouldn't say too much, but seeing as we're joined at the hip at the moment. You asked what me and Gregor were talking about. It's ...' He's clearly not comfortable sharing, and I wonder just how bad this is going to be. 'He asked me to do something for him a few weeks back. I won't get into what, but it's pissed some people off. We're talking the kind you don't even want to know your name, never mind what you've done.'

'Worse than Gregor?'

He holds out one hand, palm down, waggles it as if to say it's a close-run thing.

'Let's say they're from a rival company. Anyway, the point is, those men back there, thinking about it, they could just as easily be here for me.'

There's almost no room left in my head to squeeze in this new variable.

'You couldn't have told me this earlier? After I poured my heart out to you about people trying to kill me, you couldn't even drop it in like *ooh what a coincidence, me too*?'

'What, you want us to bond over life-threatening situations now?' he says with a half-laugh that I can't tell whether it's sarcastic or whether he's actually making a joke right now. The fact that the line he supposedly spun Moya could be bang on the money is not lost on me.

'What did you do, Davey?'

He chews on his bottom lip, choosing his words carefully.

'I'm not like you, Sis,' he says with a shake of the head. 'Wish to God I was, but I was never gonna be anything other than what I am. Working with Gregor, it's what I know. I'm hardly going to get much else with my record, am I?'

'Davey.'

I reach over, covering his hand with mine, willing him to feel the lack of judgement. This tie that binds him to Gregor, it's toxic. I'd hoped it would have severed itself over the years, but there's way too much of that stupid macho bullshit respect going on between them. As long as my brother has himself hitched to Gregor Price, I only see things trending one way. Davey doesn't know the half of it, though. There's a nuclear option that would drive a wedge so deep even a coal miner couldn't reach it. No guarantees of what that does to us. To me and my brother. A problem for another day.

Chapter Thirty-Seven

'You're sure this is the right place?'

I stare at the sweep of the street. Percy Gardens is a street I've driven past so many times as a child, every time we went into Tynemouth, but never ventured into. Where the Sea Banks road follows the coastline, Percy Gardens sweeps a lazy mirrored arc inland, the two making a giant coastal ellipse. The communal gardens that fill the space between the two, give it the look on Google Maps of a giant green eye. Gateposts at either end serve to ward off would-be tourists from parking outside the row of Victorian homes that look out over the ruins of Tynemouth Castle and Priory. Any one of these could buy you at least two houses in most parts of the North East. More if you shopped around.

Davey smiles and nods, cruising in past the sandstone pillars. 'Yep, this is the place.'

'This where he lives now then is it?' I eye up the place we've just pulled up outside.

'It's one of his, yeah.'

'One?' I raise an eyebrow. 'And they say that crime doesn't pay.'

'Bit of advice, Sis. Gregor was a pussycat in school compared to how he can be now, if you don't know how to play him. Too many comments like that, and we'll be heading back out before the first nosy neighbour's curtain has twitched.'

'I'm not stupid, Davey. I know Gregor doesn't exactly earn his money doing odd jobs for old ladies.' A look that passes between us, one that acknowledges Davey isn't too far removed from Gregor in earning his keep.

'I'm just trying to help,' he says, holding his hands up.

'This is big, Davey. Huge. Bigger than you, me and Gregor combined. I just need to know what I'm walking into.'

'You trust me?' he says, short and to the point as they pull up outside a property with a lawn so manicured, I wonder if it's artificial.

'You know I do,' I say, shaking my head. 'It's just …'

'Then trust me when I say you have nothing to worry about. But a man like Gregor doesn't dish out favours lightly, and he's going to want to know why I've called one in.'

'That's just it, though, Davey. He can't know what this is about. You can't tell him. You have to promise me. There's way too much at stake here.'

'Alright, alright,' he says, as they climb out. 'He gets too nosy, you let me do the talking.'

The footpath is black stone, grey slate diamonds inlaid at intervals. Through the front window, a huge modern-style chandelier dropping down from an impossibly high ceiling. An expensive-looking painting hangs over a grey marble fireplace. Everything about this place screams privilege. Davey brushes past me, rapping his knuckles against the heavy wooden door.

When it opens, I'm cast back twenty years to the school playground. Gregor Price has well and truly grown into his frame, but the eyes remain unchanged. Dark pools that bore into me.

'Bang on time, Davey. That's good, I've only got five minutes. Ten tops. Got to go see a man about a dog.'

Even though he was born and raised here, Price has the faintest of Scottish burrs that creeps in if you know what you're looking for, courtesy of his father.

'Maggie,' he says stepping out of the doorway, and coming to where I stand behind Davey. 'Long time.'

'Long time, Gregor,' I agree, thinking what a shame it is it couldn't have been longer. 'You live here now?'

He slots hands into pockets, looks back over his shoulder with a smile. 'What, this little old thing?' He stops short of actually answering the question, though. 'Enough about me, though; you want to tell me what you need my help with?' he says, gesturing over his shoulder with a thumb. 'Davey here was a little sketchy on the detail.'

'I'd rather not,' I say, quiet but firm.

'Still as stubborn as your brother then?'

I know he's doing me a favour, but I can't help myself. There's history here. Stuff that even Davey doesn't know about. Especially not Davey. He'd lose his shit if he found out, but if Price is half as bad as Davey says, that might not end well for Davey, so I just hold his stare, and my tongue. Price glances down at his feet, back up at me, then across to Davey, but says nothing.

I can practically feel the weight of Davey's stare, and wonder if I've cost him anything by Price getting involved. Price breaks the tension with a smile that looks all wrong for his face, too forced.

'Well don't just stand there, come on in.'

An awkward three count passes, and he stands aside to emphasise the welcome. We go to walk past him, but Price puts a hand on Davey's arm.

'I need to pop back out for a bit. Quick word before you go in?'

He gestures back down the path, and I fancy there's a hint of uncertainty in Davey's eye, but he throws me a reassuring smile.

'You wait inside, Sis. With you in a minute.'

I hesitate on the step, realising how little I truly know about my baby brother these days, and the people he spends his time with. Visits back home have been sporadic at best, for a while. Dad's constant grumblings about getting a real job haven't exactly made it a happy return whenever I've headed back, and I have used that, and the very work he hates as an excuse to maintain a healthy distance.

'See you around, Maggie,' Price says, re-enforcing my dismissal by ushering Davey back down the path towards the road.

Both backs turn and I can't make out what's being said, but when Davey glances back, his face tells me that he's not 100 per cent happy with what he has just heard. Gregor's fixed smile barely wavers, as he flicks a final look her way, then walks along the street, climbing into an electric blue Maserati, and disappearing through the far entrance.

My mind strays back a few decades, to when Gregor had a soft spot for me. He hadn't been short of attention, but he'd ignored it, for a while at least, to chase after me. My friends had been shocked when I knocked him back. Even then, though, before he was out of his teens, the cruel streak had been there to see. Not an attractive trait. Not a decision I regret. He's not even half the man Grant was.

Davey watches him go for a beat, then heads up the path to join me.

'Everything okay?'

'Hmm? Oh, yeah, all good,' he replies, but I know that tone. Whatever has been said, it's lurking not too far behind his eyes, but I know not to push.

We head into a hallway straight out of a show home. Our footsteps clack off marble flooring, and Davey heads straight for the staircase. Has he been here before? I follow him up two flights of stairs, and wonder if we're about to casually wander into someone's bedroom, when what I see, stops me in my tracks. Davey has stepped out onto an open-air terrace, and I see a man sitting cross-legged on an L-shaped couch, phone screen glowing in the gloom beside him.

That's not what captures my attention, though. Beyond the glass panels that act as a barrier, the full moon dangles over King Edward's Bay like a bauble in the fading light, ruined stacks of the old Priory silhouetted on the headland like rows of broken teeth. The light from the moon makes the North Sea shimmer like crinkled tinfoil. It's moments like this that remind me of the love I still have for my native North East. Years spent living away, but the umbilical cord has never truly been cut.

Davey wanders over to the man on the couch. Can't be older than twenty, couple of years more at a push. Baggy grey joggers. V-neck matching sweater, cut low enough to see man-cleavage earned through too many hours at the gym. After a brief hushed conversation, the man gets up and disappears back inside. Davey wanders over towards the front of the house that looks out over the sea. I join him and we lean against the rail in silence. When Davey talks again, he keeps his voice low, looking out over the bay.

'He's not all bad you know. Gregor, I mean. Don't get me wrong, he doesn't take any shit, but he's a good fella. Looks out for his own.'

'What was that about?' I ask him. 'Downstairs. You didn't look overly happy when he left.'

'Ah, it's nothing.'

'Didn't look like nothing,' I counter.

'Nothing you need to worry about,' he says, draining half his bottle in a series of long gulps. 'Besides, you've got plenty to deal with yourself without fretting over my shite.'

'As long as the shite you do for Gregor doesn't end you up back inside.'

He shoots a look that says he's not stupid, but all I can think of is the two years he served. The impact it had on the rest of the family. Mam and Dad are of a generation that keeps its dirty laundry hidden away in the depths of the basket. This was splashed across the front page of the *Chronicle*, in no small part thanks to Davey's links to Gregor. Hit the family out of nowhere like a drunk driver skidding on black ice. They all knew Gregor wasn't exactly above board, but everyone turned a blind eye. Still do. Dad in particular. I push the thought out of my mind. I love Dad but he's always had his favourite. I've known where I sit in that pecking order for a long time.

I start to plan out how to get Layt on board. He wasn't exactly leaping to my aid on the phone. I get it to an extent, if he's an invisible man to those chasing me. But he's lost people too. They have to count. By extension, he was good enough for Grant, so I'll follow this thread to wherever it leads, but right now, feels like I'm already in the last chance saloon. If this doesn't work, I might see Grant again sooner than I imagine. I glance at Davey. Just hope I don't take him along with me for the ride.

Chapter Thirty-Eight

Six men sit in silence as the van purrs along the motorway. In the passenger seat, Declan Clay checks his watch. Little over an hour to go. If his intel is correct, this will all be wrapped up by midnight, and everyone can calm the fuck down. By everyone, he means Osgood. Since Clay came on board, he has always reported direct to Osgood. He may not like the man on a personal level, but he respects the work the company does, what they stand for.

His team have been with him for over ten years now. Handpicked to a man. Tried and tested on more occasions than he can count when they were serving their country. That didn't stop when he brought them on board. He trusts them with his life, but not with the truth behind what they fight for now, what they protect. Of those in the van, only he knows the truth of what HELIX is, and what has been done in its name to protect its secrets.

It isn't that he doesn't trust them, but some things like this are need-to-know, and they can work just fine without the detail. They in turn have enough trust and respect for him that they don't question. They follow orders, his orders. Osgood may pay the wages, but it's Clay that they follow into no-man's land every time he asks. They're as close to family as he has.

The current situation, Maggie Brewer, her husband, Christopher bloody Xiang. It's as close as they've come to a true threat. Clay is confident. Knows he's dealing with amateurs, but the scale of fallout that would follow if this house of cards ever came tumbling down is almost unimaginable. The things that have been done in the name of the greater good, in the name of HELIX. There are many who he's sure would understand, who would say what they'd done was right. That the end justifies the means.

There's another chunk of society, though, the growing tide of wokeism. Those who could never understand what true sacrifice is, or make the kind of decisions that keep a country safe. Ones that flirt with lines of legality, often venturing far beyond. These people who would have murderers and rapists walk free because some stupid bastard in a lab hadn't followed protocol when handling a sample.

What he does goes beyond just a job for him. It's a calling. A vocation. He pursues it with a single-minded purpose. The system was broken. HELIX fixed it. Simple as that. Too late for many, including his own mother, dead at the hands of a man who should have been behind bars many times over, but who instead had strangled Sally Clay as a five-year-old Declan and his baby brother lay sleeping twenty feet down the corridor.

His mother's killer was Clay's loyalty bonus of sorts. A gift from Dr Alston Myers a few months after Clay came on board to lead the security team. The man had dropped off the map, living on the streets for years, before Myers served him up on a silver platter, courtesy of HELIX when the man's DNA appeared as part of a more recent investigation. Clay had found the man two days later, and taken his time, making sure the man knew exactly who was dishing out the justice he had evaded for years. He had been Clay's first, out of uniform at least. He's lost count since then. Seemed a bit crass to try and keep score. Besides, it's quality, not quantity, and the way he works, the dark places he's willing to go to, is what has built his reputation. He knows he's one of the best that money can buy. No trumpet blowing, just a fact. Another year or so at what they're paying, and he can probably retire. Unlikely, though. That'd be like asking a shark to swim just for pleasure, not for prey.

But it's the gift of his mother's killer that binds him to this job more than the pay ever could. The reason why he's is more aligned to Myers than Osgood of the two.

Clay glances in the rear-view mirror, at the faces shrouded in shadow, then back at the clock again. Feels the anticipation building. One thing still niggles, worming its way around his subconscious. On Xiang's screen when they came for him, there had been a third window, another party to the conversation, that had winked out before Clay could see anything. He had a man working on Xiang's laptop, looking for traces of who it could be, as well as for what had been stolen from them.

His hand strays to the body cam strapped to his chest. Nothing new. He used to wear them on tour out in Afghan. Not for his safety or benefit these days, though. Osgood likes to watch. The man makes out like he's a cut above, but he insists on footage, even when things get … graphic. Clay shakes his head softly at the thought. Monsters come in all shapes and sizes. At least he recognised what he was. Didn't hide behind a thousand-pound suit and a five-grand smile like Osgood. The ones who don't see the darkness in themselves, they can be the worst of them all.

Chapter Thirty-Nine

'Oi oi,' a voice booms down below somewhere in the house.

No mistaking who it is. Gregor's back, but he's not alone judging by the footsteps coming up the stairs. Seconds later, Gregor marches out onto the terrace, three other men close behind. The first two could be brothers, stocky with the same ski-slope noses. The third is more bean pole, all go-go-gadget limbs.

It's the face of the person sandwiched between the muscles for hire that sends a current through my body, snapping me to attention. Layt.

'Found this lad loitering by the door. Reckons he knows you, Maggie.'

Layt looks like a petrified kid cornered by playground bullies as he's jostled across to the sofa.

'Take a seat, fella,' Gregor says with a smile about as warm as the waves that crash in the distance as he directs Layt to the sofa.

'What the fuck is this, Maggie? Who the hell are these guys? What have you done?'

'Layt, I had no idea they were going to be here. You have to trust me. I—'

'Trust you?' he says with a sneer. 'Only person I trust is me, and after being stupid enough to come here I don't even think I should trust myself anymore.'

'You best watch your mouth boy.'

Gregor drifts over to Layt. Doesn't touch him. Doesn't have to. His presence is enough to strip several shades of colour from Layt's face, leaving it pale as the moon-light. Gregor settles into the sofa, legs lolling apart as if the wider the spread, the more manly the pose. A king holding court.

'Now, which of my house guests wants to tell me what the fuck is going on here?'

I shake my head determinedly. 'I appreciate the use of the house Gregor, I really do, but it's personal.'

'Personal? You mean like the kind of stuff you only tell close friends?' he says, looking from Davey back to me again. 'We're all friends here, right?'

His words are friendly enough, but the undercurrent that runs through them feels far from it. To say my brain is fried is an understatement. Whichever way I look at it, I'm backed into a corner. As if it's not bad enough that the people who killed my husband are hunting me down, now I've potentially got Gregor rooting round, looking to see if it's anything he can leverage to his advantage no doubt.

Layt stands a few feet from Gregor, eyes darting around, but the only way out is either down the stairs or over the railings. The way he looks at me when his gaze lands, feels like the chances of him helping are long gone. The temperature has dropped a few degrees, and I can't help but shiver as the breeze whistles past me, hint of Scandinavian chill carried across the North Sea.

'I need a word with him first,' I say gesturing at Layt.

Gregor's stare smoulders with the heat of a man not used to being told what to do. Seconds tick past until he plasters an over-the-top smile on his face.

'Mi casa, su casa,' he says finally. How does he manage to make everything sound like a threat?

I give Layt what I hope is a reassuring smile, and gesture towards the front of the roof terrace. He doesn't need asking twice.

'Who the hell is that?' he hisses when we're both leaning against the rail.

'They work with my brother, Davey, the one in the leather jacket,' I reply. 'It was meant to be just a loan of a house. If I'd known Gregor was here, I'd have suggested somewhere else. Anywhere else.'

'Really?' Layt says, oozing sarcasm. 'He seems such a lovely guy. What have you told him?'

'Nothing,' I answer quickly, then correct myself. 'Not Gregor anyway. I've told Davey some of it.'

'So why is he here, this Gregor fella?'

'Honestly, I wish I knew.' My breath fogs the air. 'We all went to school together. Davey works for him now, but the sooner we can ditch him the better. We need to be careful how we do it, though; he's a bad man, Layt. The worst.'

'Worse than the ones already after us?'

'Just let me do the talking,' I say. 'I need to give him something, or he's that bloody stubborn he'll keep us up here all night. I'll find a way to send him packing and then we can talk properly and find a way out of this for us.'

'You keep saying that like I'm in the crosshairs, but as far as I know they still don't know I exist.'

'If you're so sure of that then why are you even here?'

'What do you mean?'

'If they're not even looking for you, why would you come here to find out how I tracked you down?' I ask. 'You're either just as scared as me, or you care enough to want to make someone pay for Christopher and Paul. Either way, you're in just as deep as me.'

'Are you going to tell me how you found me at least?'

'Student Services at Northumbria,' I say. 'They called your dad and he gave your mobile number.'

He shakes his head at the simplicity of it. 'Wanker,' he mutters. 'Surprised he even knows it.'

That last part speaks to something deeper that the nosy part of me wants to probe, something he alluded to when he first told me about Cosgrove. Now's not the time, though. Instead I lead him back over towards Gregor and Davey, and I stand in front of the pair with my arms folded, Layt a half step behind me. I stop short of telling the truth, the whole truth and nothing but the truth.

'It's to do with my husband, Grant. He was killed little over a fortnight ago, and I believe this guy can help me find out who is responsible.'

'What is he, some kind of private eye?'

'No,' I say, shaking my head. 'He's a computer whizz. I need him to help me find some information.'

'Who do you think did it then?' Gregor asks, blunt as a five-year-old. 'Who killed your husband?'

'I'd rather not say.'

'What, you worried I'll sort them out for you?' he says with the arrogance of a man who has had many of those conversations. The type where the other party doesn't tend to walk away unscathed, if at all, if rumour is to be believed. Gregor has been a big fish in a small pond for so long, I'm not sure he'd even recognise the threat of a bigger predator if it came along.

'No,' I say, trying not to get drawn into it.

'What then?'

His sheer stubbornness punches a hole in my resolve.

'You're a bad man, Gregor,' I snap, 'but there are bigger and badder out there. This is just something I need to sort out myself.'

He studies me for a second then lets out what sounds like a forced laugh.

'Sweetheart, if they're badder than me, the only thing you're going to sort out is a whole lot of shit for yourself, not to mention your brother here.'

'This isn't your fight,' I'm almost shouting now. To hell with trying to tiptoe around him. 'He was my husband, not yours. This is my fight, not yours.'

Gregor sucks in air through his teeth. 'No, Maggie, you know what, the more I'm hearing, this is becoming more and more my fight. You're hiding in my house from men you say even I should be afraid of, so you're going to tell me exactly what I've waded into here, warts and all.'

I feel my cheeks redden with anger, the dislike for Gregor I've kept bottled up for years, starts to bubble its way towards the surface, all the hotter and angrier for having history. I take a deep breath, knowing he won't be fobbed off, but unwilling to share. The best lies are sandwiched between two truths, and finally I settle on a version I hope is palatable.

'It's something Grant was working on. The people who killed him, they thought he'd stolen something from them.'

'And, had he?'

'Not that I've seen.'

'That's not a no.'

'I don't even know what it is. Jesus, Gregor, if you don't want to help then I'll just leave now.'

'Alright, alright' he says holding his hands up. 'I just thought if you knew why they wanted you, there might be a deal to be done.'

One to help me, or to serve his own interests, I wonder. Men like Gregor don't help people out of the goodness of their hearts. He'd see this as accruing a favour from me no doubt. Maybe one from Davey too. Could that be to do with the chat they'd had earlier? The thought of Davey putting himself in Gregor's debt for me makes my stomach churn like I've swallowed a hamster on a wheel.

The way Gregor looks at me now makes my skin crawl, like a kid studying an ant in a magnifying glass right before tilting it to catch the sun. Hard to tell if he'll let it lie, but for now I feel myself relax ever so slightly in my seat.

'So what do you need then?' he asks looking past me, towards Layt. 'A computer? Fetch this lad the laptop from the kitchen will you?' he asks one of his men. 'Might as well fetch me a beer while you're there.'

Meathead number one hasn't taken more than a few steps towards the door that leads back downstairs when a chime sounds from downstairs.

'We expecting anyone else?' Gregor asks his men.

From the look on their faces it's pretty clear it's a no.

'Pop and see who it is, then tell them to fuck off,' he says to one of the men, who jumps up, scowling, and heads for the stairs.

The guy opens the door, and as he steps through it, I hear a coughing noise from inside. Two short barks. The guy appears to stagger, bumping against the door frame. I watch as he puts a palm to his chest, the other hand gripping the bannister. Another cough, and he leans back onto the door frame. I squint against the glow of the patio lights, shuffling to the edge of my seat, making to get up and check on him seeing as the others don't seem to care.

I'm literally inches off the fabric when I see him start to slide down, back pressed against the open door. The absurdity of it all freezes me in a half-squat position, not wanting to sit back down, struggling to make sense of what I'm seeing. As his backside thuds onto the floor, his body does a quarter twist towards me.

A cluster of dark patches bloom on his light grey sweater. The hand he'd pressed to his chest falls open, fingers outstretched towards me, stained crimson, glistening as if he's slapped it on a freshly painted wall. The sight of blood unlocks my paralysis, and the scream that slips out sounds like it's coming from far away. In my head are a thousand voices shouting the same thing. They're here.

Chapter Forty

Everything seems to happen at once. My scream triggering the men around me into action. Gregor and Davey move almost in tandem, pistols appearing like sleight of hand, crouching low, moving either side of the door. I jerk backwards, as if propelled by the force of my reaction, pinballing off Layt, and bumping into the edge of the sofa.

Gregor's remaining men produce guns of their own, moving towards the door, and I have the surreal notion that any time now, a director will yell to cut, so ridiculous is the explosion of action. Gregor reaches the downed man first, angles his gun around so it points down the stairs, and fires blind. Three shots, deafeningly loud, amplified by the narrow staircase. Before the echoes have dispersed, I see Gregor reach across, grab the slumped figure by the wrist, and pull.

The younger man's body topples like a puppet, deadweight to the floor, and even with Gregor's not inconsiderable strength, movement is merely inches with each heave. The leg Gregor is holding jerks, and I wonder if the guy is still conscious. A second later, my brain catches up with what my eyes are seeing, Tufts of denim fluff up as bullets smack into his legs, a series of coughs punctuated by meaty thuds. Supressed shots. Another scream escapes me, although less panic, more instinct.

I look around, see Layt behind me, his eyes pools of wide-eyed terror, desperately seeking another way out besides that staircase. Davey adds his muscle, grabbing the other arm of the man who is surely dead by now, while Gregor's men follow his lead of blasting shots down unseen, not risking poking heads around the corner. The limp body is hauled clear, and Davey rolls him into his back, looking desperately for some sign that saving him had been worth the risk, but the look on his face tells me all I need to know.

Gregor barks something at his men, but my ears still ring like someone has struck a gong. I see them take up a position either side of the door. Davey moves towards me, shouting something, but it's as if someone has pressed the slo-mo button. Nothing makes sense. Is this HELIX, or part of the local problem Davey has mentioned? If it's HELIX, how the hell have they found me here, at a house I've never been to before tonight?

Davey grabs me by the wrist, dragging me towards the front of the house. I see Gregor scrabbling around on the floor, grabbing a phone. More shots ring out from the hired help.

'We've gotta get out of here, Sis.'

I almost laugh at the stupidity of his words, as if any other option was even up for discussion. Everything feels heavy, slow, like I'm trying to run in the shallow end of a swimming pool. He wraps an arm around my waist, guiding me away from the door, and I grab Layt by the wrist, towing him behind me.

As we make our way to the rear of the building, there's a few seconds of silence, surreal bearing in mind what the last twenty have seen, and in that space, I hear a voice. Loud, but not a shout. Firm and confident, Irish accent.

'We're here for Maggie Brewer. Send her down and we leave before this gets any worse.'

'It's gonna get a whole lot worse in a few minutes when the rest of my crew get here,' Gregor shouts back. 'You piss off before that, and I might even forget that you've killed one of my men.'

'Two by my count,' the voice replies.

'Fuck,' Davey mutters, confirming where my mind was already going – the guy who'd disappeared downstairs when we first arrived.

'Maggie Brewer,' the voice doesn't wait for a reply. 'One time offer. You have ten seconds.'

I look to Gregor, see something in his expression I'm not sure I like. Something that doesn't convince me he isn't open to the offer that's just been made. Davey tugs at me, and my knees bump into something hard, forcing me to break eye contact with Gregor, hope that he has a shred of decency left in him. It's the rear wall that runs around the perimeter of the roof terrace, three feet high, rungs of a ladder poking over it by another foot.

'You two go,' Davey says, 'I'll be right behind you.'

Part of me wants to protest, to tell him to lead the way, but I'm still in a state of shock, cogs not quite meshed in my own head, and I allow myself to be shepherded towards the edge. Davey puts a hand on the ladder, where the struts arch over, bending back into the wall, but snatches it back a second later, shaking it like it's been dipped in scalding water. Sharp inhale of breath, and I see him lean forwards, as if to inspect the metal. Instead, though, he picks up a plant pot. Looks like he's balancing it on the edge near the ladder. What the hell is he playing at?

The pot explodes in a cloud of clay shrapnel, and he turns, heading back towards Gregor, yanking me back with some force.

'Davey, where are we going?'

'Can't use it. They've got someone at the back.'

His words are way too loud seeing as I'm only feet away, but I realise it's for Gregor's benefit. We breeze past him, my hand still holding Layt's, dragging him along like a stubborn toddler, and he keeps slowing, staring at the body on the floor.

'Stop gawping, and move,' I snap at him, tugging his arm hard, and it seems to cut through the paralysing panic plastered on his face.

I'm breathing hard now, as I hear the voice floating upstairs, counting to ten, like a kid getting ready to come and find his mates.

'Five, six...'

'Last chance dickheads,' Gregor shouts, gesturing to us to head for the front, backing away to join us as we pass him, leaving his two men guarding the door against an unknown number downstairs. There's no ladder here, least not one I can see, as we reach the glass panelled barrier.

'Seven ... Eight ...' the voice continues, with all the nonchalance of a bingo caller.

'Shit.' The shout comes from behind them, loud, panicked, and I turn to see what's happening. The two by the door are moving away from it, fast. I see a small black object rattle off the open door, and settle just over the threshold. So much for a ten count.

It's like a lightning strike. The noise is a thunderclap, rolling across the roof terrace, battering already befuddled senses. The flash brighter than a thousand paparazzi sears across my eyes, making me wince. I blink, feeling shockwaves roll across me. The image of the doorway is stamped in my vision when I blink. Hands grab me, pulling me back to the barrier.

'Him first,' I shout, nodding at Layt, but Gregor ignores me, arms grabbing at my waist hoisting me over.'

'Use the guttering,' he says. 'Get to the next roof over. Move, move!'

Seconds later I'm scaling the single-pane barriers, hands grasping at the rail, as a sense of weightlessness hits me. Gregor watches me go, before shoving Layt forward to follow, then swinging a leg over himself. I try to look back, to see where Davey is, but in doing so, I take in the scale of the drop. My stomach swoops like I'm on a rollercoaster, and I feel the tug of gravity, teasing me over the edge. No time to dawdle or dwell, as Gregor is over now, shooing us both along.

The plastic guttering under my feet feels flimsy, and I force myself to focus on the pattern of slate tiles in front me as I make the short traverse across to where the neighbouring terrace starts. Layt is practically pressed up against me, Gregor tight behind him, blocking my view of anything back on the rooftop terrace. It's out of line of sight now. I switch my focus to the line of slate rooves stretching away to my right.

I throw a leg over the rail, practically collapsing onto the terrace as I do. A cracking noise, followed by a yelp, snaps me back up to my feet. Layt's face is lower than it should be, almost level with the railing, and I realise with horror that something must have happened to the guttering. He's trying to pull himself back up, but only one hand is hooked over the edge.

'Maggie, help!'

My hands shoot out and grab his wrist, leaning back with all my weight, and he heaves up, flopping over the edge, collapsing like a marathon runner at the finish line. I spin around, trying the handle of the patio-style doors that lead inside, and mercifully feel it turn. Who needs to lock up three storey's high, right?

There's a step down into a small boxy bedroom, and I leap inside, out of sight, out of the firing line. Layt is right behind me, and I wait for Gregor to appear but the door frame is just a dark patch of night sky, a portal to seal off before anything else follows us from the rooftop next door. I poke my head out, and see Gregor eyeing up an eight-foot gap where the gutter has fallen away. Might as well be eighty from the look on his face.

He glances down, then behind, back to the roof, flinching at the zip-zip of supressed shots. For a crazy slice of a second, I wonder how much better a place the world would be if I do nothing. Just leave him there and walk away. Layt grabs my shoulder.

'We have to get out of here,' he urges. 'Maggie! Now!'

'Wait,' I say, twisting away from him, looking around for something, anything that can help. If I leave now I'm no better than Gregor. The bed. I can use the blanket for him to grab onto. I bunch one corner in my fist, wrapping a double loop around my arm.

'Grab my waist,' I say, heading back outside, then a second time, louder, when he looks baffled. 'Grab my waist, I'm going to throw him this to grab.'

The sheet spills out over the railing, flapping like a flag.

'I won't be able to pull you up,' I tell Gregor. 'But if you can reach it, we can hold it while you climb up it.'

He looks for a second like I've asked him to just step off the roof, but one glance back at what's now a silent roof top is all the motivation he needs. I've barely got time to shout at Layt to grab hold of me when Gregor launches towards the dangling sheet. I grip the sheet with both hands but the shock of his weight jerking me forwards

makes me gasp out loud. Even with Layt's arms squeezing around my waist, and my foot braced flat against one
of the rails, it feels like my arms are about to pop out of
their sockets. If Layt's grip slips, I'll catapult over the top
and race Gregor to the bottom.

Jesus this man is heavy. He starts to climb, one hand
over the other. I grit my teeth, lean back, feeling the tug-
tug-tug as his weight shifts, hear Layt grunt behind me,
his clasped hands clamped around my midriff, making it
harder to breathe. Feels like an eternity, but can only be
a few seconds later when one hand, then a second grasps
the bottom of a rail

A wide-eyed, sweating Gregor throws a leg up, toes
finding purchase on the edge of the ledge. He heaves
himself up and clambers up and over the railing, spilling onto the terrace past me and the relief when I let go
of the sheet is a glorious thing. He's up like a Jack-in-
the-box, lurching inside, opening the bedroom door.

'Gregor,' I shout after him. 'What about Davey?'

'We have to move,' is all he says in reply.

'I'm not leaving him,' I say.

'Your funeral,' Gregor snaps.

The funeral comment flashes Grant to mind. If these
men catch us, it could be mine next. If I die, the world
will continue to believe he's a murderer. For that lie to
die, I need to live.

I hear the faintest hint of a siren from somewhere
down below, and as Gregor charges downstairs, Layt
following close behind him, the significance of the
shots I'd heard, and the fact that they've stopped,
sinks in. If Davey had been following, he'd be across
by now, or shouting for me to come back. The fact he's
doing neither can only mean one thing, and the loss

lances through my heart like an ice-pick, but I can't stop, or I'll end up captured, or worse, and everything, all of this – Grant, Davey, Rose – would have been for nothing.

Chapter Forty-One

Clay hurls the flashbang as his count hits eight. If the men up there are expecting him to run the full ten count, then they're amateurs. This isn't Marquis of fucking Queensbury. No prizes for sportsmanship. He turns away, counting off the seconds, fingers in ears to avoid the disorientated tinnitus-like ringing that comes with these. Sees his men do the same.

The stairwell and terrace beyond are lit up as if by a lightning strike. A blink and you'll miss it explosion of light, followed by a single sharp report as the sound rips back down to where he hunches. The shockwave of sound is like a starter's pistol, and he's taking the steps two at a time before the wispy smoke of the flashbang has time to dissipate, hot on the heels of one of his men who is marginally quicker. These are the moments he lives for. The uncertainty of what's coming around the corner, charging to meet it regardless. It grates on him that one of the others has stolen the march on him. Something to address after this is wrapped up. Clay is never one to forget the little things.

The roof terrace is around half the size of a tennis court, sofas and chairs scattered between here and the front balcony, and he bursts from the staircase in a low crouch, Heckler & Koch pistol held in a two-handed grip. Quick glance left, scan to the right, clear the front, trust that the two men scaling the ladder at the back have things covered.

Six feet to his right lies a body. Clay recognises the grouped shots in the man's chest, three points of a triangle. At his two o'clock one of his men glides forward, gun trained on an L-shaped sofa. Clay stoops to grab an upturned bottle from the floor, tossing it up and over the left-hand side, moving right as it arcs towards the base of the couch, landing a foot short on the hard-tiled floor. The crack of glass is surprisingly loud bearing in mind what's preceded it. Has the desired effect, and Clay sees the young man rise from his hiding place, his own gun held at arms-length, squeezing off three rapid shots at the debris. He barely has time to realise his mistake, eyes flicking to Clay, as the Irishman drills a single silenced shot into his Adam's apple.

Clay sees a spray of red spring from the entry would, speckling the ground like dark rain. The man staggers back a few paces, dropping his gun in a futile grab at his throat. The gurgling noise he makes is louder than the second shot that drops him, centre mass to the chest. There's a time and place for dicking around with head-shots like Hollywood would have you believe.

He looks across at his own man, sees him realise that without Clay's intervention he would have strayed into the concealed man's field of fire. Accepts the nod of thanks he gets. Clay sees two more of his men a few yards behind him. They reach the top as the young man stops twitching, and fan out just as a second man emerges from behind a chair to his left. He manages to squeeze off two shots before Clay sights him. A grunt to Clay's right suggests the round found a home, but he doesn't stop to even check. Two of his own to the man's chest, and he falls like a rag doll. Three down. Where the hell is the woman?

Shots from the front of the terrace, over by the glass barriers that face out to the sea, and Clay moves on instincts. He changes tack, angles off left, narrowly avoiding one of his team lying on the ground, clutching his abdomen. He hadn't expected her to be alone, but he hadn't bargained for walking into a house full of randoms, almost as well armed as his team. The remaining pair of his team take up a position off right, crouching behind a sofa that almost certainly won't stop a round. He needs to end this fast. Their shots might be silenced, but those of the men helping Maggie Brewer aren't. A clock started running the second the first bullet left an unsuppressed barrel, a race to wrap up before a neighbour calls the police, if they haven't already.

The front is a glass-panelled barrier, chest high, nowhere to hide. So where had the shots come from? Clay risks a look over the top. Split second glance, nothing more, and another round zings past him, way too close for comfort. He presses his back against that of the sofa, seeing a head peek over the rear edge. One of his two, hard to say which in this light. A slender silencer is balanced on the ledge and aiming beyond him.

'Doesn't have to be your fight my friend,' he shouts. We need to talk to Mrs Brewer and we'll leave you be. She has something we need.'

Only answer that comes is a volley of five shots, two of which rip through the fabric, exiting inches from his head. It's all the help his man on the rear ledge needs. Muzzle flash has allowed him to adjust his aim, and Clay hears a whistling of shots overhead, whipping past him. A cacophony of crashes, glass shattering, a yelp of pain.

Clay pauses a beat, finger is locked on the trigger, half an ounce from pulling if any fire comes his way, but the rooftop is eerily silent save for footsteps. The two panels furthest left have disappeared, save for jagged shards clinging to the metal frame. No sign of the shooter.

Then Clay sees it, or more importantly them. Two sets of fingers curled over the edge. He motions for his men to hold their fire. He keeps his gun trained on whoever it is. Somewhere in the distance, sirens wail, no way of knowing for sure if they're coming here. No chance he's sticking around to find out, but he does have time for a little bit of fun. He squats down when he gets near the edge, seeing a man's panicked face looking up at him. It's her brother, hands wrapped around guttering that's already groaning at his weight. Two hands means no gun.

Quick check behind confirms that both his men at the rear have joined him on the rooftop. He squats down, scanning the street below. A solitary car winds its way along the coast. By one of the streetlights, a couple walking a tiny dog, one of them pacing, the other holding the lead. Clay squints, seeing a phone held to the man's ear. Could be he's calling a friend, but Clay isn't paid to take chances. He looks down as he speaks.

'Where's your sister, David?'

Stephenson's face is an interesting mix of fear and fury. Not the first time Clay has looked into the eyes of a beaten man, struggling to accept the inevitable.

'She doesn't have to die, David,' he says softly. 'Neither do you. Where is she?'

He sees the lie slide straight past, not landing.

'Go fuck yourself.'

Saliva speckles Stephenson's lips, eyes flickering from Clay, to his own tenuous grip, and back again. Fingertips slipping, moving millimetres. Clay isn't a merciful man, but he's not done with Davey just yet. He shoots an arm out, grabbing the younger man's wrist, wrapping the crook of his own elbow around one of the metal railings as an anchor. He leans back, just enough to lift him up a few inches, sees colour return to knuckles as the pressure of holding his own bodyweight is released.

'Was she here with you, David? Or did you drop her off on your way?'

He sees confusion give way to horror, as Davey reads between the lines, realising it's been him they've tracked, not his sister. The sound of sirens grows marginally louder. A minute away, not much more, maybe less.

'I usually like to take my time, David, but sounds like we're due company. Last time I'll ask. Where is she? You don't answer, and she'll not be the only sister I look for if you catch my drift.'

That one lands like a sledgehammer, triggering Davey into action. He jerks the arm Clay is holding towards him, trying to dislodge his tormentor. Tugs twice, a third time. He's heavy enough that Clay feels the railing bite hard into his arm, but it's simple physics. Davey can't generate the force he needs from this position. The greater risk is that he simply pulls himself out of Clay's grasp. The Irishman grits his teeth, fingers digging into the wrist. It holds. Just.

'Shame,' Clay says, blowing out a breath. 'I like a fella with a bit spirit, but time is a ticking.' He locks eyes with Davey, holds the stare despite the faintest flicker of blue by the entrance to the street. 'I don't make idle threats, David. I'll tell Moya and Julie you said hello.'

He holds it just long enough to see the anguish in Davey's eyes, winks at him, releases his grip, and lets gravity do the rest.

Chapter Forty-Two

I feel like I'm suffocating. As if the very air I'm breathing has mass and weight, clogging up my airways as I work overtime to draw breath. Gregor hustles ahead of us down a tight staircase. This place has a very different feel to next door, none of the more modern style, more original features. Feels a much smaller space, and I soon understand why.

We burst into a living room, mercifully unoccupied, breeze through that, and into a stairwell that appears to wind its way down several floors. Not a house like next door, a series of flats. I glance back up as we spiral downwards. Won't take anyone long to realise we're not hiding on the roof terrace, and you don't have to be a genius to work out there aren't many options as to where we might have fled.

Layt keeps glancing back at me, like he's seeking reassurance that I'm not leaving him with Gregor. I almost lose my footing twice, but eventually skitter down the last flight into a tiled hallway, footsteps amplified by high ceilings, any attempt at stealth out the window. Whether it's thick brick Victorian construction, or self-preservation after hearing gunshots, no nosy neighbours have shown their faces.

The three of us stop by unspoken agreement and stare at the door. I reach for the handle, but Gregor hisses at me.

'Wait!'

He moves to the door, squinting through the peep hole. I lean against the wall, back flat against cool plaster. It's all I can do to avoid sliding to the floor. I press my palms against the wall, close my eyes, focusing on my breathing. After a five count, Gregor turns the handle, opening inches, peering out. A few seconds pass, the three of us breathing hard, as much from the adrenaline as exertion.

I feel a tug at my wrist, eyes fluttering open, and see that he's wrenched the door open. We burst out into night, the only two streetlights working not doing much to illuminate the road, shrouded by the dark cloak of cloud that's snuck in since I arrived.

'This way,' Gregor barks, and propels first me, then Layt along the path and out onto the road.

We head towards the northern exit, and despite the pace Gregor's forcing, I risk a glance back up at the house. Despite the darkness I can make out the railings. No sign of anyone watching, or tracking our escape. Maybe they're doing a room to room in Gregor's place, expecting to find me cowering behind a curtain. As we reach the gate and round the corner, I glance again. Can't help escape the feeling of eyes on me, but the street is quiet as a deserted film set. A flicker of blue plays across the buildings furthest away, accompanied by the increasing pitch of sirens.

Gregor picks up pace, and I pump my arms, running to keep up. Up ahead, light spills out of the Grand Hotel, washing the pavement with a golden glow that I instantly feel drawn to. To my surprise, Gregor, does a quick check over his right shoulder, and angles across the road.

'Wait! Where are you going?' Layt asks.

Comes out as a breathy shout, desperate.

'Beach.'

'What? But that's…we have to hide,' Layt gasps. 'What about that hotel? We can hide in there.'

Gregor slows, turning to face us, backpedalling as he hits the start of the downslope that leads to Crusoe's café, and Longsands beach.

'First place I'd look. Coppers are there now. Should slow 'em down, but we have to keep moving.'

He sets off at a pace again down the hill, leaving the two of us stumbling a few steps after him, torn between Layt's idea of safety, and the terror of being alone. One last glance up at the brightly lit sanctuary of the Grand Hotel, and I grab Layt's hand again, making the choice for him. Have to keep him close. Can't let him strike out alone. Gregor's only fifty yards ahead, but the night starts to swallow him, and I sprint on unsteady legs into the darkness, with a man I've hated for years for the part he played on the night of the fight that sent my brother to prison. Almost as much as I hate myself for letting it happen. The familiar voice in my head whispers how I can never tell Davey. Another one drowns it out now, teasing me with the notion that I couldn't now even if I wanted to. That I dragged him into this, let him down on that rooftop, just like I let him down years ago. He only got five years back then. Tonight's sentence is permanent.

Chapter Forty-Three

Osgood listens, feels the bile threatening to rise in his throat. He has got his own way for so very long now, that he can't remember any other way. Tremendous wealth and privilege will do that for you, but this, this is starting to feel like a runaway train heading for King's Cross, no brakes and accelerating with every mile.

As Clay talks him through the latest developments, he starts to question whether the Irishman really is the man for the job. Wouldn't say that to his face, though. The man is dangerous at best, at worst, downright unhinged. A necessary evil, a man who has done what needed to be done for years now, to protect what Osgood has built. Truth be told, others who came before him laid the foundations, but Osgood is the one who has taken IQ and HELIX to another level entirely. Made it more than the passion project it started out life as. He is the one who monetised it, using the millions of DNA snapshots that live in the servers beneath this very building to drive ground-breaking research that has been flipped into a billion-dollar business.

There's a darker side to it too, though, that's just as much his doing. One that has leveraged the very data HELIX holds to his, and the company's benefit, although not in a way he'll ever admit outside these four walls.

The only man who knows HELIX's dark secrets as well as he does sits opposite him now. A man without whom HELIX would not exist today. Dr Alston Myers reminds him of Mr Magoo from the cartoons his father used to let him watch, on the odd occasion he was allowed the TV on. Shiny dome of a head, myopic eyes magnified by lenses the Hubble Space telescope could put to good use. What he lacks in stature, Myers makes up for in intellect, in reputation. Couldn't hold his own in a fist fight, but Osgood has seen him verbally batter men into submission. Rumour has it his IQ is somewhere approaching one sixty, Einstein territory.

'So, what do you propose now?' Osgood asks when Clay has finished speaking.

'If she had what Cosgrove stole, she would have used it by now' he says without hesitation.

'What then? We just leave her be? You're willing to bet everything on a hunch?' Osgood asks, not sure he likes where Clay is going with this.

'I don't do hunches,' Clay says. 'I'm not saying we stop looking. She's a loose end until we find her. I'm just saying in my professional opinion, she's not as big a risk as you think. You said you've upgraded the security, fixed the weak spot Cosgrove used?'

'We have!' Osgood says tersely. 'When in your *professional* opinion, do you think you can make her no longer a loose end?' Emphasis on the professional, trying to drill home the need to be just that, do his job and preferably not to sound like he enjoys it quite as much as Osgood suspects.

'Couple of days. Week tops. Someone of her background hasn't got the resources or the network to last longer than that.'

'However long it takes Mr Clay. That's what you get paid for.'

Statement of fact, but it doubles as a reminder of the pecking order. Osgood ends the call, collecting his thoughts, before addressing Dr Myers.

'She got away.'

Myers strokes his beard, something Osgood has seen him do a hundred times. Some might see it as an exaggerated affectation, but Osgood knows it's more of a means to gather his thoughts, choose words carefully.

'How did she get past Clay?'

'Seems she had help. Quite a bit of it from the sounds of what they ran into. Clay took care of most of them, but the woman escaped. Climbed across a roof and into the next-door property, but by the time they realised, the police were there, and they had to slip away.'

'What will he do now?'

Osgood shrugs. 'She still has family. He'll be paying them a visit.'

'And what about our...lost property?'

'We'll get it back, you have my word. Everything that Cosgrove took.'

'You're still sure it was him?'

'You're not?'

'I recruited Paul myself. He was exceptional in his field, but even that wouldn't get him past the kind of security we have.'

'He and Xiang have been taken care of. Our problem is almost solved.'

'Almost,' says Myers, shuffling to the edge of his seat, a precursor to rising. He's knocking on the door of eighty, but still has something of a bounce in his step. 'One of the most double-edged words in the English language. I almost didn't get funding for HELIX all those years ago, until one man stood up to be counted. A word like almost has the thinnest of margins between success and failure. I fell on the right side of that line. See that this doesn't land on the other. Such a pity if we have to call a meeting of The Six to fix this.'

The doctor pushes up to his feet, and Osgood rises to match him. He tolerates Myers and his little speeches because of what he's given to the company, what he's made possible with his genius, but it's been a long time since the company needed him, really needed him. He's not a young man anymore, and if anything were to happen to him, Osgood's world would keep on turning.

Myers walks slowly out of the office, and Osgood sinks back into his seat. The doctor's threats of The Six rolls off him like raindrops off an umbrella. The Six, of which he and Myers make up a third, are all powerful men. Each of them helped lay the groundwork to create HELIX back in the day, but they're little more than relics now. Anachronisms. Figureheads from a different era, wielding as much power in real terms as the Royal Family do in the running of the country.

He can't imagine them pulling any rabbits out of hats that could hurt him, but he's nothing if not cautious. He has planned, insulated himself in ways they can't imagine. Between Clay's insolence, and Myers' intellectual snobbery, it's as if people are starting to turn on each other. If it comes down to last man standing, there'll only be one winner, and that'll be Osgood.

When this is all wrapped up, and Maggie Brewer is but a distant memory, the time has come to shrug off the dusty remnants of what HELIX began as, along with everyone involved, and take this onwards, to its next evolution. Whatever Maggie Brewer thinks she knows, it's just a fraction of what he plans next. A move to eclipse everything and everyone that has come before him.

Chapter Forty-Four

By the time Gregor's man picks us up, my teeth are chattering. The jog along the beach, a half mile to the safety of shadows at the far end, has left me with wet shoes, sea spray soaking my jeans, and a chill that seems to run right through my core. Layt hasn't said a word since we hit the sand. He looks practically catatonic.

I accept the towels that the driver hands me, wrapping one around Layt, and another around myself like a cloak, and shuffle into the back seat on autopilot. If Grant's loss was a body blow, then Davey is the shot that sends me crashing to the canvas. I squeeze my eyes shut as we pull away, seeing the rooftop scene as a series of stills. Davey pushing me towards the railings, look of desperation in his eyes. How can I ever face my family again?

Gregor slides into the passenger seat in front, barking orders into a phone.

'Change of plans. Percy Gardens is no go. We'll meet you at the place near St Peter's Basin ... Yeah the one we used last time with the Scottish thing. Make a stop on the way and pick up Manny and Karl. Make sure they're carrying ... What? No, he didn't make it.'

When he says that last part, the hard edge drops from his voice, a glimmer of vulnerability, but it snaps back into place within seconds.

'Oh aye, we'll even the fucking score. Don't you worry about that.'

He ends the call as they pull away from the curb, leaving his seatbelt off so he can twist around. I sense this rather than see it, as I stare down into the footwell. My head is still spinning, trying to grasp what's happened. Yet another narrow escape for me to add to a growing list. It's as if they're toying with me, cat with mouse, seeing how much collateral damage they can inflict before they finally take me.

When I don't hear him turn back around, I finally raise my gaze to meet his. There's a mix of suspicion and concern, but he doesn't speak immediately. Just studies me. An uncomfortable few seconds tick past, neither of us saying a word, until finally he slips back into his seat, stretching the belt across.

'We're going somewhere safe,' he says eventually, talking over his shoulder rather than twisting back around. 'And when we get there, I'll send someone around to keep an eye on your folks' house in case those fuckers look for you there.'

'Thank you,' I say, so quietly, I'm not even sure if he heard.

'Don't thank me yet. You've not heard the rest. You might not like it, but this is how it's going to be.'

I'm exhausted. The kind of tired that makes your limbs feel like they're stuffed with magnets, and stuck to an even larger one under your seat. It was a chore to get in the car, and it feels like I'm not getting out any time soon. So tired. Too tired to snap at him, whatever he says.

'I said I'd do this for Davey, and damned if I'm going back on my word after what just happened, but I'm not doing it blind anymore. Once we're safe, you two are going to tell me every last detail of who the fuck just shot up my rooftop and why.'

I exhale pure relief. I was starting to wonder if Gregor would slink into the background, leave me to fend for myself. Short lived, though, as he carries on talking.

'And when I say every detail, I mean the director's cut, and if I think you're holding back on me, putting me and my men's lives at more risk than it already is, then you'll be on your own.'

'What? No, I just need—'

'You need to take a look around, realise I'm telling, not asking.'

'Gregor, this isn't something you want to be mixed up in,' I try, feeling stress levels start to spike.

'Too bloody right I don't, yet here I am, balls-deep.' He pulls his seatbelt out a few inches, turning his head to look me in the eye. 'You lost a brother, I lost a mate, plus four other good men. I've got to look their families in the eye and say I'm sorry. Sorry for something that, if I didn't look at Davey like he was my own brother, I'd not have sent any of them up there to help you with whatever bullshit this is. So yeah, I don't want to be mixed up in it, but I'm in it till the ride stops now.'

He faces front again, leaving me speechless and stewing in the back. Feels like I've had my legs taken out from under me, but what else can I do. Can't very well drag Layt out of the car and disappear. Where would I go now, without endangering someone else I care about?

Like it or not, our fate is bound to Gregor's, for now at least. There is a flip side of course. Protection, in the short term at least. The men he has at his disposal. The morally questionable choices he'll make if he has to.

I look over at Layt now, and consider for the first time the possibility that he has nothing new to share with me. No magic bullet to call off their dogs, let alone lift the curtain on the whole thing. Now's not the time, though. I need to figure out a way to speak to him without eavesdroppers.

Gregor falls into easy conversation with their driver. All very vanilla, though. Saying plenty without really saying anything. St Peter's Basin is less than twenty minutes away, and I use the time to try and plan out my conversation with Layt.

He has seen HELIX with his own eyes, or on his own screen at least. More than anyone outside the organisation, he's the one who might be able to show me where to shine a torch on it, explain how he got inside in the first place. Maybe even do it again. I try not to elevate him to the position of knight on white charger just yet, and another thought worms its way to the front. If he's already in possession of all the same info Xiang was, with the skills to evade their cyber security, why hasn't he done something about it already? Cosgrove was a friend, as was Xiang, both dead now at the hands of the very people chasing me, who would likely kill him too given half a chance, and yet he hasn't pushed any kind of nuclear button. Why not? Has he got another agenda I know nothing about? Either way, I need to know what he knows, regardless of whether I feel I can trust him or not. I remind myself that Grant had put his faith in Layt and Christopher, and that has to be enough for me too until Layt gives me a reason to think otherwise. Besides, what better options do I have right now?

I'm bumped out of my reverie as we come to a sharp stop, making me tilt forward, leaning into the belt. Not St Peter's Basin, least not the side of it I knew. Nestled down by the Tyne, it's a city commuter's dream. View over the river and marina, small clump of houses and flats just a short hop from the city centre. The place they've pulled up outside is a warehouse. Double-storeyed brick, topped off with a faded grey crown of corrugated metal.

Both men are up and out before the engine has had a chance to stop ticking over. Gregor opens my door for me, stands back and waits like a low-budget chauffeur. I climb out, scanning the street both ways, but fancy it wouldn't see much footfall on a busy day, let alone at this time of night. When Layt climbs out, there's a cornered animal glint in his eye, like he might bolt off into the darkness.

The warehouse is one of a matching pair, set back from the road, fenced off by dull spiky steel fencing. Only one other car parked outside, and no signs of life anywhere else I can make out.

I see Gregor do a similar scan of the surroundings. The gun by his side jiggles as he taps the trigger guard with his fingers, shaking the weapon like he's got a slight tremor.

'What is this place?' I ask.

Gregor grunts what I take as an acknowledgement, but makes no move to head inside. A razor thin bar of light drawn across the bottom of the battered roller door is the only hint we're not alone. Gregor lets his driver slide past him, all the time scanning for unseen threats. Puts me even more on edge just watching him, half-expecting him to whip his gun up and start taking pot-shots at shadows at any moment.

The grumble and squeak of the roller door is magnified by the silence. Sounds like it's not been oiled since flares were in fashion first time around. Makes my already twitchy heart skip a beat. In the relative silence of the night, it's like the grinding of tectonic plates.

Light spills out, pooling by my feet, as the gap widens with glacial speed, revealing the interior inch by inch. Gregor doesn't wait, stooping under the still-rising door. I share a glance with Layt, gaze out at the darkness that surrounds us, then walk into the brightly lit warehouse, hoping Gregor stays true to his word. Hoping I won't regret not taking my chances in the shadows.

Chapter Forty-Five

Gregor doesn't speak, he just heads over to a door set in the back wall. The room we follow him into isn't any more luxurious than the warehouse itself. Minimal is the watchword, single desk, one chair behind it, three more fanned out around the front. Four faces turn to face us.

'Give us the room, will you lads?' Gregor says, fixing his eyes on the main attraction, and the three troop out, closing the door behind them. They file out leaving just the three of us. Gregor gestures to the seats, but when Layt and I slump into them, Gregor stays standing.

'The floor's yours, Maggie,' he says, arms folded.

Pointless stalling, but I need to figure out how to drip feed Gregor just enough, then find a way to get Layt alone.

'I'm so sorry about all this,' I say to Layt, gesturing around the room. 'This isn't what I wanted.'

All I get is a silent glare in return.

'Are you alright?' I ask, my words sounding so inadequate in the circumstances.

'Just peachy,' he says, with a grin that screams sarcasm. 'You?'

He might look twenty, but he's playing the part of a stroppy teenager to a tee.

'Look, Layt, I didn't ask to get dragged into this, but what you and your friends stumbled upon, it's … well, it's huge. These people, the ones who killed my husband and

Dr Xiang, they came after me again tonight. My brother was helping me, and they ...'

I swallow hard. It's as if the words have hooks that catch in my throat. Can't let myself grieve, not yet. If I don't talk Layt round, I might never get the chance to.

'Too many people have been hurt already,' I say finally. 'People we both cared about. We can't let that be for nothing.'

A chink in his armour, eyes softening as I share my loss, and I move to press home the advantage.

'They're not going to stop Layt. They're going to keep on coming till they find us. You, me, anyone that stands in their way.'

A buzzing from behind. Gregor's phone. I watch him deliberate whether to take it or not, but after a second and third set of vibrations, he moves towards the door.

'Back in two,' and he bustles out, phone to his ear.

I wait for the door to close behind him before I continue.

'He's a friend of my brothers. Not a nice guy, but he's kept us safe so far. I won't let them hurt you Layt, I need you.'

'Need me? For what?'

'To stop them,' I get right to it. No sense beating around the bush. 'You've found a way in once. If we can get back in, get proof of what they're doing, we can blow it all wide open.' I lean forward in my chair. 'Think about it, if the whole world sees proof, then it's not just two nut jobs peddling a conspiracy theory, is it?'

'Yeah, I got in,' he says, 'and look how that turned out. 'They've never seen me. Don't even know my name. Why would I stick my head back up and stick two fingers at them now?'

He sits back, arms folded, the tiniest of head shakes. His body language clear as a flashing neon sign. Not interested.

'Because you know if I can find you they will. Might not be today or tomorrow, but do you really want to be looking over your shoulder the rest of your life? They'll have Chris's computer. They'll see a third email address on the Zoom invite. You really think they won't tear the town up till they find who it belongs to?'

No answer. He just stares off to the side, aiming for bored, but a tap-tap-tap of his heel against the floor gives him away.

'Why do you do what you do?' I ask, trying a different route.

The shift takes him by surprise. 'Hmm? What you mean?'

'You're a bright kid. Dare say you could use what you know to land yourself a good job, but instead you use it to do things like sneak past HELIX firewalls. Why?'

'Kills time when there's nothing on TV.'

'Isn't it about exposing secrets? The kind that nobody else can find. The kind that people hide for a very good reason.'

He huffs out a loud breath, like he's impatient, better places to be.

'They won't quit, Layt, and they won't stop. They'll come after you, your family, just like they came after mine, unless we do something about it. If there's anyone you care about, do it for them, not me. I just need help getting the proof, and I guarantee every newspaper and TV station in the country will fall over themselves to run it. I can't do this without you, Layt.'

I rest back in my chair now, letting the words sink in. The notion that doing nothing could see him lose more than just a friend. I see his teeth working away at his lower lip. Again, the slightest of head shakes, like he's telling himself off for something he hasn't done yet.

'I don't even know if I could do it again,' he says finally. 'I had Paul's laptop, and his access got me part way in for starters. Besides, they know we were in there. There's no way they haven't cut off his access and changed their protocols since then.'

'You're saying it can't be done?'

'I'm saying I don't know.'

'But you'll try?'

'Not here,' he says firmly, 'not with these dickheads around.'

'Gregor's a …' I stop short of saying friend. 'He's on our side.'

'Yours maybe. Not mine. You get me out of here, and I'll help you.'

'Get you out? You make it sound like a jailbreak.'

''Cos those little angels are out there just guarding the door to protect us,' he says with a sneer.

'What? No, they're—'

I don't get a chance to finish my sentence as Gregor breezes back in, and there's something in his expression that gives me pause. I narrow my eyes, trying to get a read. Then he goes and throws a curveball that lights up my world.

'Maggie, it's Davey. He's alive.'

Chapter Forty-Six

They had arrived in two cars, so it's a tight squeeze with six bodies shoe-horned inside the BMW X6. Three sit in the back, a fourth laid across their laps. Tinted windows shield them from prying eyes, but the only ones Declan Clay are concerned about are front and centre.

Clay can still see the Audi he arrived in, parked five doors down from the house they've just exited via the rear fire escape ladders. Might go unnoticed, might not. Depends how nosy the neighbours are when the police come knocking. Nothing in there to trace back to him either way. More of an inconvenience

He raises the Carl Zeiss Victory binoculars, adjusting the focus a fraction. Watches blue light flicker in waves across the front of neighbouring buildings, and feels the first prickle of real irritation. He has no issues being up against a worthy adversary, in fact he thrives on it. Makes it all the sweeter when he comes out on top, as he invariably does. This woman, though, is an amateur in every sense. They should have had her back at her apartment in Manchester, and they'd missed her by less than an hour at her editor's. Her luck will run out soon enough, but in the meantime, it's chipping away at the thin veneer of civility he maintains. When he has his time with her, he'll draw it out. Make it last, even if she gives him the information he needs up front.

No conversation in the back seat, the only sound is laboured breathing from the man who was clipped by a round on the roof. Tore a furrow of flesh along his bicep, but it isn't as if Clay can just swing by an A&E. The patch-up will have to make do until the job is finished.

Up ahead, he sees officers start knocking on doors. They'll be a while yet, but he's patient. They'll do what they have to, but eventually they'll leave, and when they do, he'll do what they'll least expect, and sneak back inside for a look around. There had been a moment, a fraction before Davey had started to fall, where his eyes had flicked right. Barely enough time with the first police car turning into the street, for Clay to lean out over the edge and spot the broken glass on the next terrace over. She'd been there. He was sure of it. Something or someone had drawn her to that house, and he needed to know who, or what that had been.

The presence of armed men on the rooftop intrigues him. That suggests one thing. Criminals of some sort. Who else would be tooled up like that? Criminals he can work with. Criminals can be bought. Once he knows who owns the place, he'll follow that thread as far as it leads.

He'd made a promise to Davey Stephenson that he'd pay a visit to the other two sisters. If he had a way of contacting Maggie, he'd make good on that promise tonight. See if she places her own safety over their suffering. Without a means to let her know, though, that's not a productive option just yet.

There is someone else. Another ally of hers, down in Harrogate. One who hasn't had the pleasure of seeing how persuasive Clay can be. One who he suspects may have a means by which to get her a message that her sisters need her. It's a bit of a trek, and he's just working through logistics and timings in his head, when the fluorescent blur of an ambulance whizzes past, taking the turn into Percy Gardens at speed.

Only reason they charge in like the cavalry now is if someone is still alive. He knows for certain that nobody on the terrace had a pulse when he left, checked them himself. That only leaves one option. The brother. Jesus, that man must have fallen fifty feet onto gravel and pavement. No, Clay corrects himself. There was shrubbery, a tree even, on one side as they'd entered. Could that have broken his fall?

The why isn't important. The fact he might have survived adds another variable back in the mix. Clay mutters orders over his shoulder, and one of the men slips out, crossing the street, disappearing into a back lane. He'll take care of a second pass at the house once the police have left. Clay has a different move in mind now.

Less than five minutes pass before the ambulance noses out again, blues blazing but minus the siren, exiting the far end of the street. He starts the car, peeling away from the curb, decision made. If her brother is alive, she'll be drawn to him like a moth to a flame, and he'll be there when she is, to witness the family reunion. Then he'll visit her sisters after that. What's the point of making promises if you don't keep them? By that point, the job will be done, though, and it won't be business, just pure pleasure.

Chapter Forty-Seven

'If you don't take me I'll walk out of here now and hitch a lift there myself,' I say, trying to push past Gregor.

'You don't think they'll figure that out too?' he says, grabbing me by the shoulders. 'Those men who tried to kill us. That's what I'd do if I was them. Wait till you rock up with a bunch of grapes and some Lucozade, and bundle you in a van outside A&E. You think that's what Davey would want?'

'Don't give me that clichéd bullshit,' I snap, wriggling out of his grasp. 'I can't just sit here while he's in there. What if I don't go and he...'

I can't bring myself to finish. Can't give voice to what I thought had already been his fate. Too much loss in such a short space already. Please God, I offer a silent prayer, please don't take him too.

'Okay, okay, how about this? Let me send a couple of my lads to check in on him first, make sure there's nobody waiting for you. Then as long as it's clear, I'll drive you there myself. Meantime, you two,' he waves a hand towards Layt, 'figure out what you need to figure out.'

I glare at him for a few seconds, not wanting to step down, but struggle to fault his logic.

'You might not like me Maggie, and probably with good reason, but like I said, whoever these fuckers are, as far as they're concerned, I've helped you, so I'm with you. I need them coming after me like I need a hole in the head. Bad for business, so if you reckon you and super geek here can fix this, then it's in my interests to keep you safe till you can, and I'm nothing if not a selfish bastard.'

I tell myself again that I don't owe him anything, that accepting more help doesn't put me in any kind of debt. And he's right to be wary of visiting Davey straightaway. They probably wouldn't let anyone see him while they treated him anyway, not even family. I force myself not to think of how badly hurt he might be.

Instead I look back at Layt, remembering his ask in exchange for helping me. To get out of here.

'Alright,' I say finally. 'We'll do it your way.'

Gregor puffs out a loud breath, nodding, and calls to someone I can't see, to find out what hospital he's at. Up at Cramlington most likely, the nearest A&E. Something else occurs to me, and I look at him accusingly.

'How do you know he's alive?'

Gregor just stares for a few seconds before replying. 'People like to tell me things,' he says with a shrug.

The obvious inference hits me square between the eyes. 'Someone in the police?'

The question slides off him like water off a brolly, but the evasion tells its own tale. 'I've got some other business I need to sort while we wait. You two stay here till we know it's safe. Once we do, I'll come back, you'll fill me in on whatever this shit is, and I'll take you to see him, okay? You need anything in the meantime. Food? Drink?'

'How about a laptop?' Layt asks.

Gregor gives him a funny look, as if he's just remembered he's there, then nods.

'There's one in the top drawer,' he says, pointing at the desk.

'Suppose Wi-Fi is too much to ask?' There's the sullen teenage undertone again.

'Oh yeah 'cos we're a regular office here.' Gregor wrinkles up his nose, like Layt has just asked him for a back massage.

Layt ignores him, already pulling the laptop out of the drawer, powering it up, wiggling fingers in anticipation. He pulls out an iPhone. Someone calls for Gregor from out in the warehouse, and he scowls, but disappears through the door. Whatever it is, it's important enough to Gregor to make him forget his promise to sit in on my time with Layt. That could change any minute. Time is of the essence.

'How much can you do with no internet?' I ask.

'This'll do for now,' he says, tapping and swiping at the screen in equal measures. 'I can just use this as a hotspot, connect through a VPN and see where we get to.'

He must clock my blank look, and he obliges by translating.

'Hotspot,' he says pointing at the phone. 'The laptop connects through my phone signal, and VPN is a virtual private network. Means it won't give away who we are or more importantly, where we are.'

'You can hack back in from here then?' I ask, feeling a flutter of excitement.

He shakes his head and pops that particular balloon. 'Not without the code I wrote last time round. That's the beauty of it. It's literally a unique key, the only thing that mirrors the code I left behind inside HELIX. One-time thing. That's what makes it so secure. Even I couldn't replicate it, because only the code at the HELIX end knows what it's looking for before it'll open up the door again.'

'And that was on Paul's laptop?'

Layt nods, a grunt of satisfaction as he lays the phone on the desk beside the laptop. It's like watching a meta-morphosis with high-speed scrubbing. Gone is the cagey demeanour, the tightness around his jawline, moody aura. He has come alive, fingers flying over the keyboard like a concert pianist.

'Yep, which they've probably ground into more pieces than a jigsaw by now. If we had that, it'd be closer to a fair fight. Couldn't download anything from HELIX, but I did save screenshots of a few hundred records on there. Last time I spoke to Paul said he had made a copy of the folder, given it to your husband. That had everything in, including my code. So, unless you know where your hubby might have stashed it ...'

His voice trails off, eyes locked on to a pop-up window with reams of text scrolling down it. He talks at a hun-dred miles an hour, words gushing out like water, but a few of those catch at the front of my mind. Grant had a copy. Dawns on me that he was far better at keeping secrets than I thought.

'You're sure?'

'Mmm-hmm. Told me a few days before he disappeared.'

'They could already have it,' I say, 'They had him for long enough in the police car before he died.'

I try and fail to stop my mind wandering to what that ride must have been like. What they might have done to him to get him to part with information. That's if he was conscious of course.

'Nah,' Layt says, looking up. 'They had that, they wouldn't be coming at you so hard. Like I said, without that, you're just a reporter stirring up shit to sell copy, and that's if you'd be allowed to print it with zero proof.'

'So it's still out there somewhere to find?'

A half-smile creases across his cheeks. 'So is the proof of who killed JFK, but we're not likely to find that anytime soon either.'

There's something in the flippant way he slings his attempts at humour my way, chipping the edge off my excitement at the thought they might be getting somewhere.

'This isn't a bloody joke,' I snap. 'If there's something out there that can help us, we should try and find it.'

'They were in your place, right? Chances are it looks like half a dozen tramps have squatted in it by the time they finished taking it apart. If it was there, they would have found it.'

Scenes of domestic carnage flicker to mind. Drawers emptied, possessions lying discarded on the floor like the wake of a tornado. Photos, mementoes of a life with Grant, as shattered as my life feels right now.

'Besides,' he continues, 'when they hit Chris's place, that Irish fella asked him where it was. Wouldn't be doing that if they'd already got it from your hubby.'

The mention of the Irishman throws me back an hour. Blink and I'm back on the rooftop. A voice, assured, but calm, floating upstairs and out onto the terrace.

We need to talk to Mrs Brewer and we'll leave you be. She has something we need.

The voice. The same one I'd heard over Zoom, placid as an undisturbed lake.

We just want what's ours.

It hits me like a freight train. Why had I not made the connection earlier? The man who killed Xiang, he was there tonight. He's the one who tried to kill me. Nearly killed Davey. Still might if his injuries are bad enough. Layt's voice snaps me back into the room.

'Right, here's where we start,' he says, shifting the screen round a few degrees to give me a better view. 'I started doing some digging yesterday. If we start from Luminosity, they're a subsidiary of Gentech, who are owned by another company called GLK, and so on and so forth. It's like corporate musical chairs. Company director names are different for each. I'm assuming none of them are familiar?'

I scan the info on screen, nothing jumping out, and shake my head.

'Then we take a tour outside the UK. The next few are incorporated in the Caymans and the British Virgin Islands. No public listing for shareholders. Names listed there are directors for hire, so meaningless really. It's like playing six degrees of separation, but we're already eight steps away.'

Xiang had likened it to a spider's web, and I'm beginning to see why. Whoever is at the root of this, isn't just covering tracks. They're burying them under a rain forest's worth of paperwork.

'Does it end anywhere?' I ask.

He shakes his head, says nothing.

'So how does this help us then?'

'You've not spotted it, have you?' he says, raising an eyebrow.

'Spotted what?'

'I spent ages to get to the end of it, but who owns it is a trick question. There is no end. It's a fucking circle.'

'Gah,' I groan. 'Will you stop with all this riddle shit and just tell me what you found?'

'Alright, jeez.'

He flicks between a half-dozen open windows, scaling sizes so they're all visible at the same time.

'You get fifteen companies deep, and Luminosity pops up again.'

'I don't understand,' I say, furrowed frown popping across my forehead.

'They own a chunk of the previous company. It's all one big incestuous circle. You're missing the small print, though.'

He slides the cursor across a line on each open window, and a slash of yellow appears across each. I lean in, peering at a name I don't recognise. Marshall, Watson, Parker & Assoc.

'Who are they?' I ask. 'Looks like solicitors or accountants.'

'Bingo with door number one,' says Layt. 'They're a minority shareholder on every single company. Could be that's who set them all up, or just a casual investor, right?'

'Right.'

'Wrong. Not that you'd know from seeing this.' He waves a hand across the screen. 'But if you sent them an email posing as a rival firm, threatening to sue them for malpractice, with an attachment that contains the particulars, one they open, and activate another little piece of code that some genius might have written...'

He rolls his eyes upwards, mouth twisting into an innocent pout to emphasise his own glory. Almost enough to make me smile. Almost.

'Alright, you're a smart-arse. What did you find?'

He basks for a beat, then puts me out of my misery.

'After a stroll through their servers, turns out that Mr Marshall, Mr Parker, and Ms Watson all sit on the board of a not-for-profit called IQ. They promote access to healthcare in developing countries, crisis areas, war zones. Also, on that board, are two names that stand out.

First one is Dr Alston Myers. He used to be the Deputy Chief Medical Officer for England back in the eighties and nineties. Now he's the Head of R&D at IQ, the parent company.'

'And the second name?' I ask cautiously, unsure of the significance of what I'm hearing.

'You've heard people use the phrase "follow the money"?' he asks. Rhetorical, as he carries on without waiting for an answer. 'Well, the second name is the money. That stroll through the servers, it shows the same person has financed the set-up of every single one of those companies. That, and he ploughed a shit load into Luminosity when it first kicked off. We're talking GDP of a small country money.'

'Who is it?'

'You ever hear of a guy called Osgood? Francis Osgood?'

Chapter Forty-Eight

People believe too much of what they see on TV these days. The action thriller where someone, hero or bad guy, strolls into a hospital, slips into a locker room, swipes a set of scrubs or a white coat, and poses as a doctor to do what they need to do.

The reality of it is that in most large hospitals there's just as much risk of it going pear-shaped, and not worth the risk. Too many people, too many cameras. Clay prefers to style it out, be bold. With the resources at his disposal, he can be pretty much anyone he wants to be. They pull into the car park at Northumbria Specialist Emergency Care Hospital. It's a modern building, looks like a series of pods stitched together. An awning stretches across the front like twin tent peaks. A&Es are rarely quiet, and this one is no exception. No uniforms milling about, or patrol cars parked up, though.

He slips a card holder from the glove box, slides an ID card out and transfers it to his jacket. Tells his men to wait here. This isn't the time for direct action. Not yet anyway. Outside, a mixed cast of characters as he approaches. A young lad in a full leg cast, puffing away in his wheelchair on an e-cig, clouds of sweet-smelling vapour swirling around him. A man with his arm around a heavily pregnant woman, helping her through the over-sized revolving doors. Even one chap in a hospital gown, roll-up dangling from his bottom lip, looking like he's ready to abscond.

None of them even glance at him as he strolls past them, into the stuffy waiting area. Standing room only, with a line snaking back from the reception desk. Clay scans the room. Spots a nurse coming out of a gift shop to his right, with coffee to go. Less of a spectacle than busting his way to the front of a queue of walking wounded.

'Excuse me, Miss,' he says, wearing a shy smile designed to disarm, sliding the ID from his jacket pocket. 'Hope you can help. My name is Detective Inspector Laughlin, I'm with the National Crime Agency. I'm here to check on a patient that came in a little while ago. David Stephenson? If you could point me in the direction of someone who can help, I'd be much obliged.'

He turns up the accent a notch, holding the ID out still for her to inspect. Sees the initial stiffness in her expression melt a touch as she does.

'Why don't you come with me, I'll see what we can do.'

They skirt the edge of the crowd, and slip through a side door. The nurse sticks her head through a hatch to the side, and after a quick conversation he can't quite make out, turns to him and smiles.

'Mr Stephenson is here,' she confirms. 'Had quite a nasty fall. Broke two ribs, left arm, and a nasty concussion. He's also got what we think may be a gunshot wound. Sliced a nice groove into the side of his chest, but no bullet. Either way, there's a couple of officers here keeping an eye on him. I can take you through if you like?'

He ignores the question for now. 'Are any of his family here yet?'

She shakes her head. 'Not yet, but one of the officers said they're on their way. Would you like me to show you through?'

'I've got to check back in with my boss first,' he says, another warm smile to keep up appearances, tilting his head back towards the doors. 'Where will I find him when I'm done?'

She points off to her left, at a set of double doors. 'Just come through there. If you don't see me, ask one of the others for Marian. That's me,' she says, tapping her own ID badge, flashing a bright smile of her own.

He thanks her, and moves back towards the main entrance. Slim chance Stephenson might talk to the police, but it'll be the word of a concussed, medicated suspect in a multiple shooting. Without the proof that is still floating out there somewhere, it's ramblings and rumour. That sparks a secondary train of thought. The information Cosgrove stole, that he'd admitted passing to Grant Brewer after some not so gentle per-suasion, it's still an unknown variable. Clay's guess is that Maggie doesn't have it. She would have tried to use it by now. The editor, Rose, she would have been a perfect person for Maggie to share with, to get it out in the public domain. After Clay had finished with Rose, she'd had no dark corners left to hide secrets in.

No, Maggie doesn't have it, or if she does, she doesn't know it. They took the Brewers' flat apart with foren-sic efficiency. Nothing on the laptop, email accounts, no USB sticks or memory cards. No safety deposit boxes in either name. No secondary property. Clay makes a note to send a team back for a second pass. He and his men are good, but in most systems, human error is always the weak point. There's a spread of pos-sibilities that will all need checking, houses of family or friends where he could have secreted something. The newspaper office maybe. Nowhere is out of reach for him, but it all adds time. Time that Osgood doesn't want to give.

Clay has worked for many different bosses. He's served Queen and country. Been commanded by some of the hardest men he's ever met. Osgood falls well short in those stakes, but Clay is under no illusion how dangerous a man his current paymaster can be. That kind of money, power and influence makes people like him feel above consequence, but no amount of money will save Osgood, if Clay can't finish the job. His boss would do well to remember that.

The casual whim on which he ordered the execution of Oliver Hermannson, a serving police officer, makes Clay twitchy. He has a number of go-bags stashed, money syphoned into off-shore accounts, that he could disappear tonight if he wanted. What keeps him here, for now at least, is the chase. There's no pursuit quite like that of hunting down another human being. If Osgood loses the plot, goes for some kind of nuclear option, Clay's only decision will be whether or not he teaches his boss some manners before he vanishes

He takes up a spot just inside the main doors, facing out towards the car park, head bent over his phone, letting his eyes flick up each time footsteps approach. Five faces burned into his mind. Parents. Two sisters. Remaining brother. Whoever arrives, he's sent reinforcements to their houses to carry out a thorough search while they're pre-occupied here.

Davey Stephenson is a loose end, though. Regardless of what he knows or doesn't know, he's seen Clay's face. Only for seconds and under a not inconsiderable amount of stress, but he's the only man outside Clay's own team who has seen Clay at work and lived to tell the tale. At some point in proceedings, he will have to be taken care of. Not yet, though. For now, he serves a purpose. The cheese in Clay's trap.

With injuries like the nurse described, unlikely Stephenson will leave here tonight. Even if he's taken into custody, there are always ways to reach people. If Maggie comes to see him, it'll be in the next twenty-four hours.

It's just over quarter of an hour later when he sees familiar faces. You've got to love a good old-fashioned Catholic family, falling over themselves to get to his bedside. Reminds him of his own mother, not around anymore God rest her soul, but she loved a good tragedy according to his auntie who raised him after his mother died. The children flank their parents like Secret Service, Moya and Julie either side, Freddie bringing up the rear.

Head down as they pass, not that there's any danger of being recognised. Clay hits send on a group WhatsApp. If the data has been stashed anywhere in their houses, he'll have it within the hour. Maggie won't be forgotten about, but he can afford to take his time then. Make her feel like she's slipped the net. As if she has a shot at getting clear of this.

Clay glances back up, sees the family reach the queue. Watches as Freddie barges forwards, pushing his way towards the receptionist, as if the others are just here for the hell of it. The two sisters hook arms into their parents, pulling in close. Clay's gaze flicks between them. Which one will he start with when the time comes. Eenie, meenie, miney … He settles on Moya. No reason, other than she's angled to face more towards him. No matter, Julie will get her turn too. They all will. Even if Moya gives him everything he needs. Can't be sure no copies have been made, passed on to God knows who and where. With something this important there is no margin for error. Clay hasn't got this far in life without being cautious, and isn't about to start now. By the time he finishes, there'll not be a Stephenson left standing.

Chapter Forty-Nine

Francis Osgood. The name is vaguely familiar, but I can't recall the context no matter how fast the hamster in my brain turns his wheel.

'He was a career politician. Part of the Government back in the nineties. He was Home Secretary for a bit. He got a load of grief for sending in the SAS to that cult who took hostages.'

Vaguely rings a bell, but I'm fuzzy on the detail.

'Doesn't matter,' says Layt, shaking his head. 'Anyway, that's not all he hits the headlines for if you google him.' He opens a fresh window, doing just that, clicking into images.

A stern-faced man, Osgood I assume, pictured from a distance. He's dressed all in black, walking out of a church with his arm around a young boy. Osgood is broad shouldered, short, neat centre parting, and something of a thousand yards stare.

'This was taken at his wife's funeral,' says Layt, flicking through a dozen more images faster than I can take them in. 'She was murdered back in ninety-five. Her family comes from money. I'm talking old money, like industrial revolution money, so not like he ever had to work. One of those who does it 'cos he wants to. Dropped out of politics not long after she died.'

'And what, you think he's the one behind all this?'

Layt shrugs. 'He's the one who paid for it all, so unless he just likes throwing cash around, he's a dead cert to at least be part of it in my book, if not the top dude himself.'

'Could be just a generous investor?'

'Could be,' Layt echoes, but his face couldn't disagree more.

'Is he alive still?' I ask. 'He looks easily in his forties in that pic, and it was taken over thirty years ago.'

'He's in his seventies now. Lives down near Oxford. Became a bit of a philanthropist. Set up a trust in his wife's name and funds all sorts of community projects.'

'What happened to his wife?' I ask softly, strings of my own grief being plucked by another's loss.

'Strangled by a burglar. Osgood was in London for a few days and some guy broke in. They even looked at Osgood for it to start with. Rumours of an affair. Said he had a window, that he could have made the trip back, killed her, and been back in Westminster for Prime Minister's questions before anyone even knew he'd gone.'

'But he didn't do it?' I shake my head, even though I know people are capable of this and much worse.

'Nah, turns out he'd been with a constituent around the same time she was killed. When they came forward he was off the hook. Took a few years before they caught the guy who did it. Anyway, we're getting off track. Without him, without his money, HELIX doesn't exist.'

'I don't get it, though,' I counter. 'Why would one man want to do this? I'd get it if he was still in politics, but wouldn't he have stayed in Government, used it somehow?'

'What if that's exactly why he left Government?' Layt says. 'Get himself out of the public eye, and build this thing. Who's to say he isn't still part of that world behind the scenes? Think about it, something like this goes in front of Parliament to sign off, people would lose their shit. There was enough kick-off over prisoners' human rights if we try and take away their ability to vote, think about what people would say when they find out they've all been catalogued. But you do it behind closed doors, privately funded, who's to know?'

'So this has all been one massive long-term plan, and you think he's pulling strings on behalf of the Government? To what end? All this just to lock up a few more criminals? If that's the case, there might be as many agree with that as disagree.'

Layt pushes away from the laptop for the first time since he started tapping away at the keys.

'I spent ages on this before Chris brought you in,' he says, folding his arms. 'Took some doing, even for me, but I know what it's all about now. Oldest motive in the book. Money.'

'I don't understand,' I say. 'I thought you said Osgood was already rich?'

Layt rolls his eyes. ''Cos of course, rich people hate getting richer.' He chuckles, shaking his head like I'm missing something so obvious. 'Osgood was a millionaire before he became an MP, but IQ has made him a billionaire.'

'But how does having a bunch of DNA stored away make him billions?'

'Here,' says Layt, tapping a finger at the screen. 'Check out Luminosity's market value. All told, once you know how it's all stitched together, Osgood owns just short of 80 per cent.'

I lean in, eyes popping wide with surprise as I read an article that values the company around the twenty billion mark, largely down to patents on a long list of drugs and treatments they've pioneered over the last few decades.

'Wow,' is all I can manage.

'How far would you go to protect that?'

It's monopoly money. A licence to print cash if what Layt is saying is true, and I don't doubt it. A hundred more questions batter away, demanding answers. Where do I even start?

'So, Osgood does this on behalf of the Government, who let him make his billions in exchange for what?' I try to tease the knots out of what feels like mental spaghetti jumbled in my head. 'A cut of the proceeds? Bragging rights that a British company leads the way? What if it's what Christopher suggested. A means to access millions of samples to speed up research. End justifies the means?'

'Nothing justifies what he's done.' Layt's voice rises an octave.

'I didn't mean who they've killed. I meant the lives they save with their research.'

'Pretty sure the last people to use that excuse wore grey uniforms and shouted *Sieg Heil.*'

'Jesus, Layt, I'm not on their side, I'm just trying to make sense of this, same as you,' I snap back at him. I'm tired of spats like this. We're meant to be working towards a common purpose, and he seems to delight in scoring childish points.

'More I think about it, the more I'm sure I'm right,' he says, running his tongue across his teeth. 'Think about it. How would you go about it? Where would you even start? Not as if you can set up like a blood dona-tion drive and get people walking in off the street. You'd need infrastructure, resources, staff. They might make billions, but it must have cost millions, tens of millions easy, to set up and run.'

He counts them off on his fingers, leaves them stand-ing to attention, looking at me like I'm supposed to pick up from his cue with more of the same. A faint sound from behind makes me whip my head around. Gregor has left the door open a foot or so. I see a flash of a face trying hard to look like he wasn't paying attention. One of Gregor's men. Briefest of eye contacts, and he's gone, footsteps fading to nothing.

'Is that not a weak point in your theory, though?' I ask. 'How many people would you need to pull it together, keep it running? The wider the circle, the bigger the risk.'

'I haven't got as far as the how yet,' he says. 'Need more time, and preferably better equipment than this shit. And I need that code. I can have another pop without it, but chances are they'll have doubled up on everything since I last snuck past the firewalls. They'll be looking for me this time too.'

A few seconds of silence stretch out, and when Layt renews his attack on the keyboard, I rub at tired eyes, lean back in my chair, and wonder when I'll next get the chance to crawl under a warm duvet. Feels like I'm running on fumes, and not sure how long it can carry on before my body pulls the ripcord and forces me to take a break.

I leave him to it, and push the door all the way open. Voices off to the right. One of them is Gregor's. The other I see is the man whose face had appeared at the door. Whatever's being said, it's not going down well. Can't shake the feeling my presence here isn't welcomed by all from the look he gives me.

Gregor spots me, finishes the one-sided conversation with a few terse muttered words I can't make out, punctuated by a hard stare at his man that could curdle milk. He crosses to join me.

'Everything alright in there? You get what you need?'

Even though he saved my life earlier, I still can't bring myself to entirely trust him with everything I know. I know him too well of old for that. I know if I stall or stonewall, it'll only provoke him, so I aim for what I hope is a convincing middle ground.

'He's working on it. Whoever is after us is hiding behind a load of shell companies.'

'So no names yet?'

I shake my head, forcing myself to keep eye contact, hoping it looks earnest enough to sell it. He seems to let that soak in, before nodding thoughtfully.

'Got something for you,' he says, reaching into his pocket, pulling out an older model iPhone.

'I already bought a new phone yesterday,' I say, arms folded across my chest.

He laughs. 'I'm not giving it to you to keep. You might want to call that number, though.'

I peer at the screen as he holds it up. A number I don't recognise. 'Who is it?' I ask as I take it from him.

'Just ring the bloody number,' he says, and pulls out a cigarette with his free hand.

I hit the screen to dial, and watch him as I raise it to my ear. Both corners of his mouth twitch up as if tugged by invisible string. Three rings and it connects. I recognise the voice, even just from the one-word greeting. It's enough to make tears pop in both eyes.

Chapter Fifty

'Hello?'

'Freddie? Is that you?'

'Maggie?' My older brother's usually gruff voice is a few notes higher with worry. 'Where are you? Are you okay?'

'Davey?' I ask, ignoring the question about my own safety. 'How bad is he?'

Deep sigh on the other end. 'He's pretty banged up' Freddie admits. 'Not life-threatening, thank God. Lucky sod is the only man I know who could take a swan dive from a three-storey house and come off better than the shrubbery he landed on.'

Freddie rattles off the list of injuries, and I feel snakes squirm in my stomach at the thought of my baby brother covered in a patchwork of bandages and plaster cast.

'What the hell is going on, Mags?' he asks when he's done. 'What's he got into now, and how has he managed to pull you into it? I heard about your editor. The police are saying some Manchester coppers want to speak to you about that.'

'Are the police there now Freddie?' I ask, half expecting to hear officers breathing down the phone.

'No,' he says. 'I mean they're here, at the hospital, but I've popped into the loo to take this.'

'How did you know it would be me calling?'

'Some bloke said he works for Gregor caught Moya when she popped to the toilet. Slipped her this phone, and said you'd be in touch.'

Explains why I didn't recognise it. Not Freddie's usual phone.

'Someone killed Grant,' I say, 'for a story he was writing, and now they're trying to stop me from running with it. Davey was helping me try and fix things, so go easy on him. This isn't his fault.'

'Makes a change,' Freddie gives the obvious tired comeback. He has always tried to hide it, but I suspect Freddie sees our baby brother as a burden more often than he'd like.

'Will you tell him I'm sorry?'

Emotion swells my chest like a set of bellows, and I have to bite down hard on my lip to keep it in check.

'Where are you Maggie? Let me come get you and we can go to the police and sort this out together.'

'It's not that simple,' I say sadly. 'These are powerful people. They're making me out to be something I'm not, and I think the police are part of it. At least some of them, anyway.'

'Jesus, Maggie, what the hell?'

'Look, I've got to go', I say, even though all I want is to keep talking, to lose myself in the banality of family gossip. Just a breath or two worth of normality. Not possible, though. Every second on the phone is time I could be spending with Layt, straightening out the kinks in the story, tracing back to source until we find a weakness.

'Maggie, wait!' He sounds just as desperate to keep me on the line. All I hear for a few seconds is him breathing. 'Look, keep this number. Don't call me on mine in case someone's listening in. You're the best of a bad bunch and if you tell me you haven't done anything wrong, I believe you. Anything I can do, just call, yeah?'

I promise I will, even though I'm not sure I can bring myself to ask anything of anyone outside of Gregor and Layt. Enough people have been hurt, killed even. The fact I didn't know the ones on the rooftop doesn't make the heavy feeling in my stomach subside. Everything that's flowed since finding Grant's phone has been impacted by my choices. If I hadn't suspected him of having an affair, Rose would still be alive. Davey would be at home.

I shake my head, trying to reset. Can't start thinking like that. This isn't my fault. I end the call, look over at Gregor and nod my thanks. Footsteps follow me as I head back into the room, and I sense him right up behind me as I go back through the door. Just one set of steps, though. Whatever is going on with him and his other business tonight, it's left outside of this room, for now.

All I get from Layt is a flick of the eyes, then he's back in the zone, fingers practically blurring, flitting between windows, his cursor spewing out lines of what I assume is code.

'What's the score, Rain Man?' Gregor smirks at his own joke, but Layt doesn't react, giving him the same silent treatment as he gave me.

'With this machine, not much different from when you left the room. Need my own kit to crack it. That or something similar.'

'Shops are shut, kid. You'll have to make do.'

The young hacker stops abruptly, pushes the laptop away six inches and cracks his knuckles. 'I can't "make do",' he says, air quotes for emphasis, 'any more than you could make do with a water pistol instead of a real gun. You want me to work, give me real tools.'

Gregor looks to me as if to say can you believe this kid. I incline my head, wisps of an idea forming. One that cuts Gregor out.

'We can't do what he does, Gregor.'

'Look mate, you let me pop home, I'll crack on from there, and we'll get done a lot faster.'

Shake of the head from Gregor. 'I'll send one of the lads to pick up whatever you need.'

'They don't know what they're doing, man. You send them, they'll probably bring back my PlayStation.'

'Come on, Gregor,' I implore. 'He's no danger to you. He's only here to help me. Let us borrow a car, I'll go with him and get it. We can be back here in an hour. Give you a chance to focus on your other stuff.'

I nod towards the door, see his eyes narrowing, looking for angles being worked.

'For crying out loud, I'm the one they want. You're safer away from me if anything. Whatever you've got going on out there with this business rival of yours,' I say, loosely disguised sarcasm in that term, 'you don't want to be fighting on two fronts. Whatever promise you made Davey, you owe him more than that, and you know it.'

There it is, the elephant in the room that only he and I know exists, but my point lands home and lands hard. It's a risk playing this card so forcefully, but I'm out of options. Can't have him knowing the full truth of what he's stumbled into.

'Okay,' he says eventually, 'but you take Ash out there along for the ride, you know, a little protection for you, a little insurance for me.'

I start to protest, but the look he flashes leaves little room for interpretation. It's not a negotiation. Ash, it turns out, is the guy I'd seen him giving the dressing down to outside. As Gregor tells him what's happening, he nods his head, but the rest of his face is at odds with that acceptance, not happy about what he's being ordered to do, but in no position to argue.

Gregor walks them to a car that hadn't been there when they arrived. A silver Audi saloon. Ash climbs in, muttering something about being a 'fucking taxi driver', and Layt trudges across, sliding into the back seat. Gregor makes as if to shepherd me towards the passenger side front, but I stop by the other rear door. My own tiny passive-aggressive protest at being chaperoned.

'Straight back here mind,' he warns. 'Wouldn't do to get caught in the open when I'm not there to look out for you.'

He closes the door behind me, trudging back into the depths of the warehouse. Ash starts the engine, but instead of driving off, he starts looking around like he's lost something.

I stare at the descending roller door, and it's like a glitch in the matrix, mirror image of my arrival, only this time with Gregor's feet visible. It closes with a concertinaed clunk, draping the car in darkness.

'Left my fucking phone,' Ash mutters, and he's up and out of the car, slamming the door behind him, storming across to the side door.

I'm nervous enough about dealing with Gregor, let alone the pissed-off hired help. There's no telling how Gregor will react if he's backed into a corner again like they were back on the rooftop. He has form for putting himself first. Crossing whatever lines serve his purpose. Capable of carrying out violent acts. With doing what it takes to get what he wants. That's what worries me – not knowing exactly what that is. To hear him, it's an honour amongst thieves thing. A promise to Davey, but

I can't bring myself to trust him, not after all the water that's passed under that particular bridge.

Beside me, Layt fires off replies to a barrage of texts that have come in while his phone was confiscated. Outside, the shadows seem to seep towards us in the stillness. Can't escape the feeling that something, or someone is rushing towards us unseen. Closing in. Claustrophobic. Wrapping iron fingers around my chest, squeezing.

I move the instant the thought hits me, before I can talk myself out of it. Out the door, quick-timing it around to the driver's side, sliding into Ash's seat.

'Maggie?' Layt's voice from behind me. 'What are you doing?'

I slam the door and pull away, tugging at the seatbelt as I swing the car back around towards the road.

'Maggie, what the fuck?'

'He won't let us go, Layt,' I talk over my shoulder. 'Not anytime soon anyway. He's a control freak, and if we can't be the ones deciding what to do, then what's the point?'

'He has men, though, and guns.'

'And he's holed up in a warehouse like Custer's last stand. Didn't help him back on that rooftop, did it? We do this. You and me. We don't need him.'

'Like I have a choice,' he says, and I'm not sure if he's smiling of scowling in the darkness.

We wind our way towards the town centre, heading towards the Tyne Bridge. Of all the pieces swirling around my head, I have the inescapable feeling that some of them belong together, but they're fragments, wispy shapes, like strangers in the mist.

One step at a time. And right now, that step is to take a ride with a stroppy hacker, in a car belonging to a man who I hold responsible for my brother's lost five years in prison. The absurdity of it all is almost enough to squeeze out a nervous laugh, but I swallow it down, staring at the sweeping twin arcs of the Tyne and Millennium bridges off to my left as they roll down Walker Road. Over the bridge that crosses the Ouseburn, and my mind sticks like an ant in treacle on one recurring thought. If this doesn't work, if Layt can't get back inside HELIX, where else can I run?

The rocking motion of the car is like a lullaby. My eyelids weigh a ton. If only I had time to rest. Tired, so tired.

Chapter Fifty-One

Ten minutes out according to the satnav. Layt's face is a ghostly glow in the rear-view lit by his phone. He pauses, frowning like he's contemplating something complex.

'Listen,' he begins. 'Just wanted to say, I'm sorry, you know, for being a bit of a dick back there. And for you losing your husband.'

It's the most serious and sombre I've seen him, and it has the effect for a few seconds of stripping away the kid-like exterior.

'Thank you,' is all I can manage.

'I mean, that must be pretty rough losing your soul-mate any time, but the way this has gone down, it's so messed up, man.'

'Sorry for your friend too,' I say, returning the olive branch.

We settle back into silence. I stare out of the window, mesmerised by the blurry trail of lights whizzing past in the northbound lanes. Sitting still for this long, feels like the past few days is catching up. Everything's a little foggy, fragments of thought floating free. My still-heavy eyes begin to close by the millimetre. I open the window, cold air slapping me awake, and that's when it slots into place.

I sit bolt upright. Such a sudden movement that I see Layt flinch.

'You alright?' he asks.

'I think I know,' I say.

'Know what?'
'I think I know where it is.'
'Where what is?'
'The proof. I think I know where Grant hid the proof.'

Chapter Fifty-Two

The street we pull into is eerily deserted. A wash of black shadows coats the pavements. Rows of trees stand sentry either side, flanking a road with only a handful of cars parked along it, most houses having driveways big enough to accommodate three or four. All detached. Set back from the road. Nobody on this street needs to shop in the reduced section, she thinks.

'Which one's yours?' I ask.

'Next one on the left.'

'Wow,' I say, wondering if my own flat would fit inside this place twice or even three times over. 'I'm in the wrong line of work.'

Layt shakes his head. 'My dad's place.' Then adds, 'He's a barrister,' as if explanation was needed. Dad's place, not parents'. No mother on the scene, I wonder.

'Will he be in?'

'Nah. Dad spends most of the week in London. The lady from the uni was lucky to catch him before he left earlier. S'just me here during the week usually.'

Neither of us speak as we pull into the driveway. Dark windows stare back, unblinking eyes in the overcast night.

We head to the door and I follow Layt into the hallway as he flicks the lights on. Inside, it's the definition of minimalist. Small single-frame prints on each wall. Little in the way of an attempt to dress the living room up from what I can see. Makes me wonder how long it's just been him and his dad.

251

'Kitchen's that way,' Layt points down the hall. 'Help yourself if you want a drink or a snack. I'm heading upstairs to make a start. Can't stay here too long, though.'

'You think we're not safe here?' I ask.

'You're the one who keeps telling me how easy it was to find me,' he says with a grin. 'Why take the risk?'

'Where have you got in mind?'

My mind flicks to family. To my own and to Izzy, but to ask them is to put them in danger.

'I've got a few mates who won't mind a gatecrash, for a bit anyway.'

He disappears upstairs without another word, and I head through into the kitchen. The sandwich I grabbed with Davey feels like a lifetime ago, but the thought of food makes my stomach do somersaults, so I settle for a glass of water, and head upstairs.

I'm not sure what I expected to see, but the room is surprisingly normal. Cream walls free of any trappings. Two bookcases against one wall, full and with piles spilling out onto the floor too. Mainly crime fiction. Some names I've heard of, local authors like LJ Ross, Howard Linskey and Mari Hannah, others new to me. A desk is wedged into the gap between them. Underneath I see three PC towers, lights glowing, same number of monitors on his desk like a set-up from *The Matrix,* plus a laptop off to one side.

Layt is lost in a world I can't begin to understand, boxes scattered across each monitor, lines of what I assume is code cascading down, lists of files, and God only knows what else.

'What's the plan then?' I ask him.

'I'm going back in through the law firm. They represent every company on that list we ran through before. Might be a route in that way. If I can follow the money upstream, see where it's coming from and going to, I might be able to figure out how HELIX was put together.'

I perch on the edge of his bed, feeling about as much use as a chocolate fireguard.

'You're sure about your next move while I do this then. You really think you know where Grant hid the data?'

'It's the only thing that makes sense,' I say. 'If I'm wrong, then I'm all out of ideas. We'll know soon enough anyway. I'll wait till morning then check it out.'

Layt's fingers resume their tap-dance across the keyboard. I grab the nearest book but give in after a few pages. None of it can penetrate the cloud of questions I still have about this whole debacle. If Osgood is behind all of this, how did Grant get in his radar? Without Gregor to help, how can I check in on Davey without running the risk of being caught, either by the police, or the Irishman?

I toss the book on the bed, and wander across to the window. An inky inch of darkness separates the curtains and I peer out onto the street.

'When's your dad back?' I ask, staring through the ghost of my face reflected back at me.

'Friday.'

'Can I ask about your mam?'

'Lives up in Northumberland with her new fella.'

I'm debating whether to pry and ask if he sees her much when two sets of lights sweep up the road at pace, pulling up hard onto the curb beside our car. Dark figures spill out, two peel off and peer through the windows, another four by my count start to scan the houses. Thank God I parked on the curb, not the drive. Might buy us a few seconds while they decide which house to try. There's one face I recognise as street lights wash over it. Ash. The man whose car I stole to get us here.

'Layt!' My voice is a strangled whisper. I shrink back from the window. Gregor's men are outside. What do we do?'

His head whips around, fingers frozen in place over the keyboard.

'You're sure it's them? Not the Irishman?'

I nod. 'Ash, the one who was meant to drive us here, he's there. How the hell did they find us?'

Layt moves fast as he talks, grabbing his laptop, a bunch of cables and what looks like a portable hard drive, scooping them into a rucksack.

'Dunno. Some kind of tracker on the car probably. There's another way out. Follow me,' and he disappears out into the hallway.

No time for more questions. I tuck in behind him, bracing myself for the crash of a door being kicked in as we head into the bathroom. He snaps open the large single pane window, and gestures for me to go first. Below, a dark grey felt roof stretches out. There's enough of a chill in the air tonight to see my breath as I use the toilet as a step stool, easing myself through the frame, taking care with the trailing leg to not catch the small shaving mirror perched on the ledge. Only four feet to the roof, and tips of trellis poke up from one edge, corners like a jagged row of wooden teeth.

I pause, scanning the shadowy tree line at the end of a garden that could easily accommodate another house the same size. See a darker patch of shadow dead centre, a gate set into the fence. Each breath out fogs the air, like smoke signals to my invisible pursuers.

'Here, watch me,' Layt says, squeezing past. He turns, lowers one leg over the edge till his toes find the wall. I pull the window closed behind me. Anything to buy an extra second. I half-expect to see an outline against opaque glass, my name shouted, a face appearing. Nothing. Not yet. I don't think Gregor would hurt me, but can't say the same for Ash. Might get handsy for being made to look a fool with the car. Here's hoping we don't have to find out.

I copy Layt, a slow careful descent, nerves jangling with worry that the trellis won't take my weight, that it'll splinter, but it holds, and I drop the last few feet, landing with a solid but soft thud. The back gate is secured by a rusty bolt, that scrapes like nails on chalkboard as he slides it free. From somewhere inside the house I hear a hammering, like angry fists pummelling the door. The sound is a starter's pistol, and we're off through the gate, pausing only to close it behind me, before setting off at a jog across half a mile of fields and scrub. How often has Layt used this route to sneak out himself, I wonder?

Streetlights glow beyond the far tree-line, but the only noises I hear are my own heavy breathing and our legs swishing through grass that paints damp strokes across my calves and shins. No drone of traffic, at least not a consistent one. Twice I hear an engine growl and fade. By the time we reach the trees, I'm breathing hard, as much from nerves as effort. A glance back over the field, no movement in the shadows.

'You okay?' Layt asks. 'I don't think they've followed us.'

'I'm fine,' I say, hoping I sound more confident than I feel. 'I have to go tonight, though. Find what Grant hid. Can't risk waiting around to get scooped up by Gregor, or worse.'

'In case you didn't notice, we just lost our wheels.'

'Where's that friend you mentioned? Are they close by?'

'Uh-uh, they live in Wallsend. I can ring 'em, though. Get them to come and get us.'

'Come and get you,' I say, hating myself already for the choices I'm about to make.

'Me? What about you? You haven't even said where you're going never mind how you're going to get there.'

He's sounding pissed off at me for being vague, but if we go our separate ways, I can't risk him knowing where I'm headed. Can't take the chance in case he gets picked up and pumped for information. Gregor doesn't take rejection well; and the Irishman, something tells me he can be persuasive in all the worst ways.

'Better if you don't, least not till I've checked it out. If it doesn't work out, no sense us both being caught.'

He looks far from convinced, but agrees to call his friend to come pick him up. I've got a ride of my own in mind. One I just hope I don't regret calling.

Chapter Fifty-Three

Thirty minutes since Layt disappeared to meet his friend. I've opted to stay in the shadows of the trees by the main road. Last thing Gregor's men will expect me to do is hunker down and stay put. That's what I hope anyway.

Headlights flicker off to my right, and a low rumble announces a new vehicle. I shrink back behind the largest of the nearby trees, barely feeling the cold bark rasping against my palms. It comes closer, and takes on a lower tone as if slowing down. I risk a peek, relief washing over me as I see the familiar car approaching. Last glance over my shoulder, then I pop out of my hiding place, double-timing it down the short slope, into the familiar arms of my big brother. One of the last people I want to involve, but one of the very few I can trust to help me right now.

'Freddie,' is all I manage, as he folds me into a hug.

I'm making him part of a big gamble. Huge, but at this stage there's almost more to gain than there is left to lose. Almost.

Chapter Fifty-Four

By the time I finish my story, we're pulling into Wetherby Services on the A1, and Freddie's wearing the kind of stunned expression of a guy who has just found out he was adopted. I want to ask him what he's thinking, but sense he needs a few seconds more to process what he's just had thrown at him.

'Jesus,' he says after a pause. 'That's ... it's almost too much to get your head around, you know? That something like that could operate right under our noses, and nobody is any the wiser.'

'We're still figuring that part out,' I say. 'How it works, I mean. How they get the samples in the first place.'

'You say we. This is you and this Layt kid?'

'Yep. He's the one who figured out that it's Francis Osgood's money behind it. He needs the code he wrote to unlock some backdoor that he left inside HELIX, though. Without that we don't get inside, and we can't get proof. Without proof,' I shrug, 'best case I get arrested for a murder I didn't commit. Worst case, I end up on a slab myself.'

'And you really think they can do that? Set you up, I mean?'

'It's what they did to Grant,' I say. 'Made it look like he killed Paul Cosgrove by planting his DNA at the scene. They've tried to kill me twice in the last twenty-four hours, Freddie. They're not going to stop.' I lapse into silence for a ten count. 'Thank you for coming, by the way.

Wasn't sure you would, or that I should even ask you to, but thank you.'

'I nearly didn't,' he admits. 'The police at the hospital, they told us about that man who died, they said you were there, and that you were a "person of interest".' He takes one hand off the wheel to frame the last few words with an air quote. 'I'm just a teacher, Maggie, I've got Joan and the kids to think about. I can't get mixed up in this.'

'Then why did you?' I ask, instantly regretting the words. Freddie has always been the most principled of all of us. Least likely to keep a fiver if he found it on the street.

'Davey begged me. That, and he swore that you hadn't done anything wrong, that once I knew the details, I'd want to do it anyway.'

'And?'

'And what?'

'Do you want to help still?'

'Honestly? No. Not because I don't believe you, but people are dying, Maggie. But...'

'But...?'

'But I'm sat here with Crimestoppers most wanted woman in my passenger seat, so that kind of seals in my position, you know?'

First hint of a smile as I look across. He pulls into a parking space and turns to face me and it broadens into a full, if nervous one.

'Assuming you're right then, that you manage to find this proof, what then?' he asks.

'I find someone who'll report it,' I say, knowing deep down that doing that doesn't guarantee my safety. If Osgood is coming for me now when I haven't actually hurt him yet, he'll double down when his back is against the wall. A man of his power and resources will surround me with a wall of lawyers.

'Your paper?'

'Maybe. Maybe bigger though, one of the nationals. I don't care which, as long as someone runs it. Problem is I don't know how much influence Osgood has, whether he's got enough clout with any of them to squash it, so I'm thinking hedge our bets. Send it out to every-one. Doesn't bother me how many run it, as long as someone does.'

We lapse into silence for a moment, and I feel the tired-ness seeping into my brain, fogging my thoughts. Deep breath in, out through the nose.

'What will you say to Joan about where you've been?'

'I'll let you know when I figure that out,' he says. 'Far as she's concerned, I'm at the hospital all night. I think your next ride has arrived,' he says, gesturing across the car park.

Across the way, a door opens, light illuminating the interior, and shadows dance across Izzy's face. God only knows what I'm about to walk into, or whether I should even be involving her, but I can't do this alone, and it can't be Freddie. Davey needs family by his bedside.

I lean over, hug Freddie for the longest time, then hop out, and head to Izzy. If I look back, I might talk myself out of this, and I have to keep moving. If I stop too long, I might as well hand myself over to the Irishman.

Izzy climbs out to meet me by her bumper, pulling me in for the tightest of hugs.

'Thank you for this,' she says as we pull back, and climb inside her car.

'For what?' I ask.

'For letting me help clear his name, and fix whatever this shit is you're in,' she says and sweeps out of the car park. I hold up a hand to Freddie, smiling as we pass, and see him return it, but the look on his face is nothing but worry.

'He'd be so proud of you,' Izzy says as we rejoin the motorway, and again I feel closer to him just by having her here. Maybe that's why I've let her help, although the thought of anything happening to her is just as terrifying as if I'd let Freddie stay. I need him back at the hospital with Davey though.

I say nothing, just reach across and squeeze her hand as I think through how tonight might play out. These past forty-eight hours have proved that any plans can get derailed at a moment's notice, but I can't let doubt creep in. I have to believe that I can come out the other side, just like I have to believe that my husband is not capable of murder. Evidence be damned. To allow any other thought to exist is to give weight to Osgood's lies.

'You going to tell me where we're headed exactly then?' Izzy asks.

I stare out at the twin lanes illuminated in the headlights, stretching out before us. Picture how we'll wind our way across the moors and down across the other side of the country. Many of the features of the land aren't visible this time of night, but the journey is comfortingly familiar.

'Home,' I say. 'We're going home.'

Chapter Fifty-Five

Clay is alone for the first time in days, his men deployed nearby, waiting for him to give them the go-ahead to move in on their target. He may be the only person in the vehicle, but his is not the only voice.

'What the fuck do you mean he's alive?'

Osgood's face is turning an unhealthy shade of salmon pink, a pot about to boil over. Coming to you live in all his HD glory via FaceTime.

'He won't help the police, sir.'

'What makes you so sure?'

'The house we hit them at, it's owned by a local gang leader by the name of Gregor Price. Stephenson's boss. These people don't talk to police.'

'He's seen you though? He can identify you?'

'He can,' Clay replies, 'but he won't.'

'You're taking care of it?'

Clay doesn't reply. Just inclines his head.

'Have we heard anything back from our other friends in blue?'

'They're still classing her as a person of interest for Rose Evans as well as Xiang,' says Clay. 'My contact tells me they've drawn a blank with her phone. She's either switched it off or isn't using it. I'm expecting a call back soon, though. I've asked them to look at numbers that called the brother going back twenty-four hours before he took a swan dive off the roof. She had to have contacted him somehow. We get that number, we find her.'

'I want this closing down for good,' Osgood snaps. The angrier he gets, the more he reminds Clay of a petulant child. 'And I mean today.'

It's a little after one in the morning. Twenty-three hours should be more than enough, especially with what he has planned.

'It'll be done,' he says.

'You mentioned a police contact; not Detective Hermannson, I presume?'

Clay shakes his head.

'That's taken care of then?'

'You want details?'

'No, no, of course not. I trust you.'

If you trust me, thinks Clay, why not let me do the job without constantly telling me how it should be done? He says none of this, just gives a terse smile, and hopes the conversation is at an end. He's itching to get back to the task at hand, so moves to close it down.

'If there's nothing else then, Mr Osgood?'

Clay gives him a whole second before he taps the button to end the call. Small acts of defiance bring a smile to his face. He looks out of the window now, studying the house two doors down. There hasn't been a single person or car come past him in the twenty minutes since he parked up, but he's taking no chances, reaching up and pulling his hood up to cover his head. The balaclava can wait until he's almost at the door. He taps out a short text to the team WhatsApp group.

Alpha team two-minute warning.

A second message on the same thread.

> Bravo team – sitrep?

Seconds later, he sees the replies pop in. Thumbs up emojis from Alpha. Bravo team confirm sixty minutes out from secondary target.

> Roger that both

He climbs out, takes care closing the door in the relative silence. Easing it in, pushing rather than swinging it closed. Rubber-soled-boots sound muted against cold concrete, and Clay strides towards the house, pulling down the brim of his balaclava as he rounds the garden gate. He knocks on the door with one hand, holding an ID badge up to the spy hole with the other. It's late, but he knows nobody inside will be asleep. A faint glow that edges the curtains in the front window back that up. That, and he watched the owner of the house arrive home not half an hour ago.

A dark smudge appears behind the glass pane, pausing in the middle of the door to study what he's holding. It opens, slowly, and the face that appears looks exhausted, pensive. Confusion crinkles across her face. He sees her questioning why the face on the police issue ID she has just seen is dressed like a burglar, hood casting shadows across his eyes. The clock in his head has only seconds left of the two minutes. If she runs, the rear is covered. He hopes she'll try. It's the small pleasures in life. He smiles, seeing fear spread across her face like ripples on a pond.

'Good evening, Moya,' he says softly. Less is more. Why shout when a whispered word, controlled menace, lands so much better, and Clay has a gift for just that. 'We need to talk about Maggie.'

Chapter Fifty-Six

I try my best to doze, but when I start to drift, I see a horrific highlight reel. Davey lying broken on the ground like a chick fallen out of its nest. Grant lying limply on the back seat of a car, hair matted with blood. I jerk back awake to the drone of tyres on road, Izzy's fingers reaching across to stroke my hair.

'Shhh,' she coos. 'You're okay, you're safe.'

I blink owlishly, staring at the tail-lights ahead. The shadowy ribbon of the M62 motorway stretches out before us, winding its way across the moors. Up ahead in the darkness, Stott Hall Farm lies sandwiched between two carriageways like a nut waiting to be cracked.

'What will you do if you find it?' she asks. 'This proof?'

'Honestly,' I say, picturing Hermannson, wondering how deep this corruption could run, 'I think the only way is to get the story out there for everyone to read. I figure if it's not a secret anymore, then they've got nothing left to protect.'

The silence that follows sits heavy. Am I being too naive? Too optimistic? There's just as much chance that they'll still hunt me down out of spite, but I can't let myself think like that.

'You know, in a fucked-up kind of way, this could be it for you. The story, I mean.'

'How do you mean?'

'I mean who better to write Grant's story than his wife?'

It's not like I haven't thought of that myself, but it doesn't stop me doubling down on the self-doubt.

'We'll see.'

'Nah,' she says. 'Don't you do that. What you're going through right now, shitty doesn't even cover it, but don't start doubting yourself.'

'I mean, I want to,' I say, 'but that's not how it works. The paper will decide who writes it.'

'Then you write it yourself before they can,' Izzy says. 'Post it on fucking Facebook for all I care, but you write it, and tell everyone what they did to Grant. To you.'

I smile, feeling a little of her fire spark some life into me.

'I'll try.'

'That's my girl,' she says, grinning as she glances over at me. 'Whatever you write, it'll be from the heart. Not even your dad will be able to turn his nose up at it.'

'You've met my dad, right?' I say, twisting my face into pretend confusion.

That gets a chuckle from both of us, and after a beat, Izzy sighs.

'He'd be so fucking proud of you, you know,' she echoes her earlier words. 'You were his world.' The soft edges disappear a second later, replaced by something infinitely harder. All cold edges and malice that ignites something deep inside me as she speaks.

'Now let's go and rip the curtain down and show the world who those bastards really are.'

Chapter Fifty-Seven

It's a strange feeling as we wait near the end of my street. Not quite one of returning home, more of a former one. Somewhere I no longer feel safe, unable to scrub away the memories of yesterday's close call.

Conversation has slowed to a trickle these past twenty minutes, Izzy's idea to hang back, observe, see if anyone is watching. Sum total of life in my street so far has consisted of a taxi pulling up four doors down, drunken couple whose names escape me spilling out, and an urban fox, cautious, warily padding across the street, disappearing into a hedgerow.

No sign of life tonight, curtains drawn just as I'd left them last night. Door closed. I lick my lips for the hundredth time, seeing patches of moving shadow everywhere I look, but I know it's just the wind ruffling through the trees, whipping up leaves like snow in a globe. There's a nervous energy in the car, crackling across my shoulders and down my spine. Even the air feels charged, buzzing with anticipation.

'Let me go,' says Izzy, and I love her as much in that moment as I do my own sisters, seeing the nervous bob of her leg as she offers to walk into the lion's den for me.

'You've done enough already Izzy,' I say, laying a hand on her leg to steady her. 'I'll be fine. I need to do this.'

Bless her, she looks equal parts relieved and worried at being stood down.

'Honestly, it's fine. Speaking of which, might as well give it a go. Not seen any reason not to.'

Izzy slowly nods, chewing on a ragged corner of thumbnail. 'And you really think it could be here?'

I shake my head. 'Not for certain, but it's something that makes sense. Something Grant told Layt. We'll soon see.'

I lean over, hug Izzy, then I'm up and out before she can say another word. As quiet as it looks, I won't risk just waltzing up to the front door. Instead I head in the opposite direction, angling down the cut that leads to a tight back lane. Easy to pick the back gate out thanks to sepia-toned street-lighting. A lamp-post stands right beside mine, and I wheel a neighbour's recycling bin across, haul myself up to the top of a seven-foot wall with the help of a lamp-post tucked in by my neighbours' garage, a route I've taken twice when I've forgotten my key.

Up, over and drop down into my own yard, not quite nailing the landing, staggering against my own bin with an empty thud that sounds thunderous in the silence of the street, sending my heart racing. I stand stock still in the shadowy corner for a ten count, then when I'm satisfied I'm the only person casting one here, I trot over to the back door. I reach under the window ledge, fingers feeling their way into the hole underneath, brushing against cold metal of the spare key.

The sound of it rasping home into the lock sets my teeth on edge. Soft push down on the handle, telling myself to breathe, just breathe. The door swings open into a utility room, usual appliances in the corner, but my mouth drops open at the state of the place. It'd be a shorter list to say what hadn't been pulled out, thrown, torn, trampled.

My fear starts to fizzle with anger around the edges, at the invasion of privacy, the disregard for my possessions that I'm sure will await me in the other rooms.

Sure enough, every room tells a similar tale. One of controlled aggression, desperation to find what they're looking for, which I can relate to. I've been building it up in my own head as a golden ticket, a passport back to a normal life, but what would be normal about it? Grant will still have been stolen away. Rose will still be dead. Davey will still be lying battered in a hospital bed. Christ, I hope he makes a full recovery, or I'll spend a lifetime doing penance for his hurt.

I stop in the kitchen, listening, seeing if the flat gives up any clues to whether anybody is lying in wait. Nothing, No creaky floorboards, no hushed conversations in other rooms. I stare at a spot on the wall, close my eyes, blotting out everything, as I soak in the silence. A few seconds more, then I shake myself loose of the trance, satisfied I'm alone, but still pick my way across the kitchen slowly and deliberately.

Packets of food have been emptied out in their frenzied attempt to find whatever proof exists. Pile of flour like a mini Vesuvius, an opened and emptied bag of Doritos propped against the microwave. A rolling pin discarded under the small two-seater table. I crouch down, pick it up, feeling marginally more comfortable now I can feel the heft of it, and I'm armed.

Out into the hallway, and along towards the living room. What I'm here for isn't actually in the flat itself. If it's here at all, it's out front. This, I hope, might just be enough to have saved it from the whirlwind that passed through here. What if they found it anyway? What if I've guessed this all wrong? Can't allow these thoughts oxygen just yet, and I move across to the bay window, stepping around sofa cushions that lie like an obstacle course across the carpet.

I press my face against the angle of wall, peering out at the thin strip of garden visible without opening the curtains. It's a peephole-style view that's helped me avoid Jehovah's Witnesses and door-to-door salesmen in the past. I haven't turned on a single light since I came in, so my night vision is pretty well adjusted, and I huff out a sigh of relief when I spot it exactly where it should be. Of course, if anyone is watching the flat, the moment I step outside, I'll be in the crosshairs, but at least this way, I won't be penned in. Always an option to retreat the way I came. That, plus Izzy knows that if anyone starts running towards the house, she's to sit tight and wait for me to re-emerge from the lane. The spot we chose isn't boxed in and sits on the corner of the next street along, so she can gun the engine and choose one of three escape routes.

I walk slowly along the hallway, jaw tightening at the ruthlessness of my pursuers. Empty spots on the walls where photo frames should hang. Every one of them lies on the floor, backs opened, pictures scattered. Images of holidays, birthdays, even one from our honeymoon, litter the floor like oversized confetti. By the time I reach the door, both fists are balled up tight, and I picture driving them into Francis Osgood's face.

What comes next is the risky part. A low hedge across the front provides a hint of cover, but I can't do anything about the fact the door will be open, a dead giveaway that someone's home. Worry about what you can change, I tell myself, not what you can't. I reach out to the handle, twisting the lock open, fingers curling around cool metal, staying there as I take three deep breaths, in through the nose, out through the mouth. Showtime.

I only open it halfway, just enough to exit at a crouch and pull it almost closed again behind me. Keeping low, I duck-walk across the postage-stamp-sized lawn, to the solitary tree in the corner by the hedge. More of a sapling really, a cherry tree that Julie had bought as a moving-in present for us. Tucked up against the base of it, exactly where it should be, a garden gnome sits on the obligatory red toadstool, fishing rod in hand, with a now dirty-grey scaled fish dangling from his line.

I grab it and retrace my steps, all the time bracing for a shout, or worse, but nothing comes. Back inside, I straighten up, closing the door behind me, realise I've been holding my breath for most of the return leg. One hand clutches the gnome, the other presses against my chest, feeling the *thud-thud* base notes of my heart. There's little time to waste, but I need a moment. Looking down the trail of defilement those bastards left, I'm pretty sure I'll never feel safe here again, and that seems to sink a heavy stone deep in my stomach. Here, the home I shared with Grant, stuffed with happy memories, feels like part of my past already.

I push away from the door, heading back to the kitchen, fighting the urge to check if I'm right, or if this has all been a needless risk, a wasted trip. The voice inside my head is screaming at me to get the hell out, and that's exactly what I intend to do, but the urge becomes a physical need.

I study the gnome that reminds me of Grant in so many ways, not least of all because he had it specially cast to look like him. What I had dismissed as the weirdest gift ever, had also been hiding a diamond solitaire, or more precisely the fish had. Everything about the proposal had been Grant to a tee. Wisecracks about my being his 'sole-mate' with a picture of me sellotaped to the fish, a compliment in his eyes, telling me I was a catch. Wasn't until I saw the metallic edge and tiny brass hinges along the fish's dorsal fin, that I realised it was as much a Trojan horse as a fish.

I run a finger along the seam now, hands trembling with a mash-up of nerves and excitement. The urge to get the hell out of here borders on a physical force, shoving between shoulder blades, but I have to look. Have to know if I'm right, if something will finally swing in my favour, however marginally. I set the gnome on the counter, angling the face away so I don't have to look at a mini-Grant. Taking the fish by the tail between forefinger and thumb, I click the clasp open, watching to see what falls out, listening for a clattering sound that never comes.

Fault lines zigzag through what's left of my hope, a fragile thing, ready to splinter and crack. Has to be here. It's the only thing that makes sense. Fingers fumble with the edges, slipping into the grooves inside the now splayed open fish. Brushing something other than a smooth surface. I crouch over the bench, flip it around, angling towards what little moonlight streams through the kitchen window. There, in the belly of the fish, like Jonah in the whale, a tiny package is taped to the inside. I go to peel it off, but freeze at a sound that echoes down the hallway. The sound of a handle being tried, of a door opening hard and fast. They're here.

Chapter Fifty-Eight

I straighten up, bolt upright like a meercat. The realisation that I've forgotten to lock the door behind me is a starter's pistol, and I dart towards the kitchen. Even as I move, the cacophony of sound draws closer, combination of a voice and heavy footsteps thumping off laminate.

'Police. Mrs Brewer, if you're in here, stay where you are.'

Somewhere in my brain, I register that it's a single set of steps. Can't be more than a few feet away from the kitchen door. I tug at the fishing line and it parts with a pop. In one fluid movement, I turn and throw the gnome, aiming for the centre of the still-empty doorframe. I reach one hand behind me, groping for the door back out to the yard, as I watch a mini-gnomified version of my husband turn end over end, reaching the doorway just as a young uniformed constable appears. There's barely time for surprise to register, hands rising to protect his face, but not making it above chest height, before the gnome clatters against his collarbone. It shatters, head shooting off into the hallway, body ricocheting up, jagged edge tracing a thin red line across his cheek. The unexpectedness of it is enough to make the officer stagger into the frame, head hitting the edge with a solid thunk.

Hardly a decisive blow, but stuns him enough to buy me a valuable few seconds. I wrench the door open, fish clutched in one hand, and sprint towards the corner

I entered from. The distance can't be more than twenty yards, but my chest burns as if I'm finishing a marathon

'Stop!' Comes the shout again. 'Police, stop!'

Clenching the fish tight enough I worry it might break, I vault up onto the bin, feeling it rock under the momentum, bump hard against the wall, but it stays upright. I reach up the final few feet, looping arms around the top of the brick wall, and haul myself up. Hard to make out the noise of my pursuer now above my ragged breathing, and I'm swinging a trailing leg over when the fingers grasp my ankle.

The shock of it is enough to make me cry out, and I kick back like a donkey, trying to shake it, but it holds fast. I can't let him pull me back down. If I fall back into the yard, I'm done, and the chance to clear Grant's name right along with me. The thought of it is like mainlining a fresh shot of adrenaline.

I risk a glance back, looking for a target to aim the next kick at. Realise it's a double-handed grip. The officer's face is lit by the nearby lamp-post, startlingly close up now, determination scored into every line across his forehead. Readying to lean back, put all his bodyweight into it, not just the arms.

Then it just goes slack. Everything. His face, his grip. The release of all pressure from his side means I almost catapult over the wall, nail on my ring finger scraping across stone, pain shooting through fingertips as a chunk of brick nearby seems to explode. A noise, not from the officer, from somewhere back towards the house. My brain translates. Same sound as the rooftop at Tynemouth. Silenced gunshot.

The officer is falling back now, look of confusion, turning side on, grunting as they seem to jerk to one side.

I see a shadowy figure standing over by the back door, arms outstretched. Something slams into brick by my head, where I lay horizontal atop the wall, and splinters sting my cheek. I shift my weight, rolling, not worrying about finding a better grip, and both legs swing around and over the edge, arcing around, until my own body-weight drags me down into the back lane. The zip of another shot rips past the spot my head was an instant earlier.

I land awkwardly, left ankle partly folding inwards, but not buckling, and end up on all fours. Only for a split sec-ond though, before survival instinct kicks in, and I push up and set off down the lane. The officer's face flashes to mind as I pump my arms, feeling the itch across my shoulder blades of the next bullet incoming. My feelings about the police have yo-yoed these past few days, but this officer was there to take me in, not hurt me. Pretty bloody obvious from what I've just witnessed that they're not all working with or for Osgood, or that poor sod back there wouldn't be getting used for target practice.

Whoever the shooter is, has to be Osgood's man. The fact that they'll kill is bad enough, but the ease with which they have just gunned down an officer of the law adds wings to my escape, and I fly down the fifty-foot stretch, feet slapping against damp concrete. No time to glance back. No sense of whether they'd crested the wall yet. As I skid around the corner that leads back to the main road, footsteps pound pavement closer than I imagined possible, as if they'd dropped out of thin air close behind.

I hit the main road, turn right and curse. It's a move borne out of habit, but one that takes me the wrong way. Away from where Izzy is parked up and waiting.

I instinctively glance behind, as a dark-clad figure bursts from the back lane, long-barrelled gun whipping up and down as he pumps his arms in pursuit. I dart left between two parked cars, desperate to put anything between the two of us, frantically looking around for an alternative that keeps me out of the line of fire.

Another glance. He's followed suit, raising his gun. I angle right, aiming to cut between two cars, but as I make my move, pain explodes in my hip, spinning me round, cartwheeling to the tarmac. I touch a hand to the source of pain. No blood. Above me, a car wing mirror dangles like a pendulum, and I am out of time.

The man in black is only ten feet away now. I push up on to my elbows, trying to scoot backwards in a reverse sniper. I see his face now as he draws closer, scanning the street for witnesses before he finishes the job presumably. Not features I recognise, but then again why would I? Nothing distinguishing about him. Just a hard face with harder edges. No emotion. All business. I edge back another few feet, into the gap between the two cars, knowing it's futile, instinctive.

I clutch the fish to my chest, like Mam does with rosary beads, except this won't offer the salvation I had hoped. The sharp edge of the tail bites into my thumb as I grip it, and I wonder if it's the last thing I'll feel.

Six feet now, barrel of his gun starting to rise. His eyes flick to my prize, squinting to make sense it. The corners of his mouth twitch. Clearly, he had expected something that looked a little more high-tech. The arc of the barrel sweeps up past my feet, and it's around my knees when I hear it. A sound from somewhere off to the left. He hears it too, and whatever it is, it's enough to draw his attention for a split second. As he turns his head, it's like someone has flicked a light switch, and he's bathed in a supernova glow.

I watch as he swings the gun away from me, switching to a two-handed grip, barrel jerking up twice to signify the two shots he gets off before a larger shape blurs past, and he simply isn't there anymore.

Chapter Fifty-Nine

It's a blink and you miss it moment, then he's back with a sickening thump like a sack of wet laundry, limbs at the kind of angles a child twists its toys into. The shock of it squeezes out a squeal, as I push back, bumping up against the curb. One hand flying to my mouth, breath coming heavy, and I sit like that for a three count, staring at him, waiting for him to move, to twitch even, but he just lies there, stretched across the road like a speedbump. I'm thankful that relative darkness has returned so I don't have to see his injuries, and use the nearest car bumper to pull myself up, stuffing the tiny fish into my pocket.

Izzy is out of her car, running towards me, face set in a grim expression. She takes my face in both hands.

'Are you okay?' she stammers. 'Did he hurt you? Are you okay?'

I look past her, at the still-slumbering street around them. Defies belief that the past sixty seconds happened without so much as a curtain twitching.

'No, I'm … I mean no, I'm not hurt. I … Izzy, are you okay?'

The way she's frowning, you'd think I'd asked her in German or French. Her hands drop, finding mine, holding them tight.

'Me? I'm fine, I thought he …'

Izzy's gaze flicks over to the body on the ground, the man she has just mown down. I see her eyes widen, as if just realising what's happened, what she's done.

'Is he ...'

She can't bring himself to finish the sentence.

'I don't know, but he was going to kill me, Izzy. You saved my life.' Over Izzy's shoulder, five doors down, a flash of light at a window. 'But we have to get out of here.'

Izzy is still staring at the man, lips parting, furrows like canyons across his brow. I feel the tremor in her hands, and know she's in danger of unravelling. I let go of both hands, taking her face between my palms, mirroring her gesture of seconds ago.

'Izzy, we need to leave.'

A second curtain is pulled back, only two doors away this time.

'Now!' I bark the order at her, the urgency and strength in my voice bursting the bubble of shock.

I drop one hand, gripping the other more tightly and tow her along in my wake towards the car. Without thinking I move to the driver's side, ignoring her protests of me not being insured.

I glance in my wing mirror, seeing the dark lump of my would-be attacker on the road behind us. Glow of light in my peripheral vision, and I twist around to see an outline standing in a doorway behind us, two doors along from mine. Can't make out the face, but I've spoken with Mr Harbottle dozens of times. He won't know this car, but he'll recognise me if he comes any closer.

I stamp on the accelerator, Izzy's door not quite closed, and we tear off down the street, irony not lost on me that of all that's happened, leaving the scene of a hit and run is the first actual crime I've committed. Whoever that is lying on the road, they made their choices as surely as they're forcing me to make mine.

As I wrench the wheel to take the first corner, an image pops to mind. The slack surprise in the policeman's face in my back yard. They can't have been part of this, not to have been gunned down like that. Just someone doing their job. Someone's son, brother, husband. I can't run away from that.

'You have to call 999,' I say to Izzy. 'That man, he shot someone else in my yard. A policeman. We have to send help.'

'What? Oh, yes, of course,' Izzy mumbles, picking up her phone from the cupholder.

'Not with that,' I snap, 'use this one.'

I hand her the burner phone Gregor gave me. When Izzy has finished giving the operator the address, I hold my hand out, eyes still on the road. She complies on autopilot, not even thinking to end the call. I buzz my window down, and with a flick of the wrist, frisbee the handset out into the night. Izzy stares after it, open-mouthed, and I wonder if she's regretting taking my call yet.

'He was going to kill me, Izzy,' I say again. 'You saved me. That counts for something. Everything. He's part of the organisation that killed Grant.'

She nods meekly at first, but I can see that getting through to her. Helping rationalise what she's done. Give her a sense of justice being delivered. We drive in silence for another few minutes, before she thinks to ask the obvious question. 'Did you find what you were looking for?'

I nod. 'I think so. Here, take a look.'

I stuff a hand in my pocket, pulling out the fish and passing it to Izzy. As much as I want to look myself, the need to put distance between us and what happened back there is stronger.

I steal glances across every other second. See Izzy peel back thin black strips of electrician's tape from the edges. She holds up a small square object between thumb and forefinger, an opaque plastic case of some kind, sealed shut with some kind of cellophane-style wrapping, weather-proofing no doubt. Takes Izzy a full minute to unpick the edges, peel it back and pop it open.

Inside, a micro-SD memory card. Izzy lays it on one palm, holding it towards me.

'So this is what all the fuss is about,' she says. 'And this is proof of everything you've told me?'

Just seeing it makes me feel a little giddy, like a kid who's just found the last Easter egg with nothing left to do now but tuck in. Almost laughable that everything that's happened can be fixed with something the size of a postage stamp. Whether it's shock or exhaustion, laugh is exactly what I want to do.

'Either that, or it's Grant's porn stash,' I say, biting my bottom lip to swallow a chuckle.

Izzy looks across at me, twisting her face. 'Euuww!' she says, but it's quickly followed by a laugh that I can't help but join in with. We ride that wave for a few seconds more, then settle into an easy silence. She'll need more time to wrap her head around this, I know that. How much time we'll have is another matter entirely. My thoughts turn back to the memory card. I need to get it to Layt as soon as possible.

'Here, take this,' I pass my remaining phone over to Izzy. 'Can you sync it up to the car's Bluetooth for me?'

She does as she's told, and a minute later, a ringing tone echoes through the car. Eight rings and cuts to an automated voicemail. I try again, same result. A third time, the robotic voice kicking in again, every word a fresh pinprick into my dwindling bubble of enthusiasm. What if something has happened to him? Without him, I haven't the first clue where to start with any code that's on here. If Izzy picks up on my sinking mood she doesn't say. I grip the wheel tight enough to blanche knuckles, and stare out over the dented bonnet at the road ahead as we head back to the North East, and could swear the sky is still getting darker.

Chapter Sixty

For the first time since he started this particular job, Clay feels a spurt of anger, not at Maggie Brewer or Osgood, but at himself for only leaving one man on the Brewer's flat. One of his police contacts had delivered the news a few minutes ago. Clay had taken it in calmly, outwardly at least, but inside he seethes with waves of a fury that will need an outlet, and soon.

One thing it has convinced him of, is that she has what he needs. Why else would she stick her head back into the lion's mouth and go back to the very flat she had fled from? What could be worth that risk other than to retrieve what Grant Brewer had stolen? The evidence that could shine a light on HELIX harsh enough to make it wither and die.

His new prize possessions are feet away in the body of his van, bound and gagged. Not only Moya Stephenson, but her sister Julie as well, no doubt regretting popping in for a cuppa after dropping her off following their hospital visit. The absence of the older brother, Freddie, bothers him. Clay's man who stayed behind at A&E has yet to spot him. A problem for another time.

The decision had already been made to step this up a notch, but even that now seems to fall short of the mark. From this vantage point he watches as the roller door creaks up for the third time since he arrived. Clay watches through binoculars as two men hurry out, hustling into a four by four, and speed away. Sees Gregor

Price pacing back and forth inside the warehouse. He has two teams currently in the field, the one with him now, and the second, Bravo team, too far away to be useful right now, dispatched to fix another piece of the puzzle in place.

Only two cars remain out front of the property now, and the man he positioned in the treeline has reported seeing only three more faces besides Price's in there, allowing for the two recent departures. Four glorified thugs. Bullies who just haven't met a bigger bully, yet. Clay is confident they could sweep through the building with little risk, but a second option begins to take shape.

Maggie Brewer and her husband, they got into this mess because of their principles, little chance of talking them out of their misguided crusade for truth. Men like Price, from the intel Clay has seen, are open to other forms of persuasion, and Clay can be as persuasive as they come. He has already had his contact email him through chapter and verse on Price. His legitimate, and not so legitimate businesses, plus who he has trampled on to climb the hill he now sits atop. He sits for a moment, lets the pieces slot into place, like a game of mental *Tetris*, before whispering hushed instructions to his team.

Two minutes later, he stands close enough that he could reach out and scratch the rust off the warehouse door. This goes one of two ways in his experience, and he's prepared for either. His knuckles rap out a rhythm that ripples the roller door a touch. Someone must be standing close, as seconds later, it starts to rise. Clay lets his hands dangle by his side, open, no visible threat.

The man that greets him looks like an extra from *Geordie Shore*. Too much product on his hair, teeth whiter than his trainers, and a low-cut, tight-fit v-neck T-shirt to show off the gym bod. Wanna-be gangster, Clay thinks, a dozen ways he could incapacitate the man stepping out to meet him. Instead he flashes a charming smile, and keeps it civil.

'I'd like to speak to Mr Price please.'

'And who the fuck might you be?'

'I'm the man asking to speak to your boss.'

'Yeah, well he's not in.'

'I think he'll be interested in what I have to say.'

'He's too busy to bother with the likes of you, now piss off.'

'Which is it?'

'Which is what?

'Is he not here, or is he too busy?'

'You better piss off, I'm not warning you again.'

Clay senses the changes in the man. Slight shift of weight onto balls of the feet, fingers starting to curl into fists. Ready to make good on any and all threats. Clay sees it playing out in his head, frame by frame. It'll take seconds and his pulse won't even top sixty.

'That you playing nice with the neighbours again, Sean?'

Price appears in a doorway towards the rear, hands in pockets, the easy confidence of a man who is used to being the Alpha in the room.

'He was just leaving, Mr Price,' says the man he now knows as Sean, keeping his eyes on Clay.

Price looks mildly amused, like a spectator wondering which dog to bet on.

'Mr Price,' Clay calls over Sean's shoulder. 'My name is Mr Clay. I have a proposal I'd like to discuss with you on behalf of my employer.'

285

'And who might that be?' Price asks.

'Not at liberty to say just yet,' Clay does his best to look apologetic. 'But I know a businessman like you isn't one to walk away from a good opportunity.'

'And just what exactly do you think you know about me?' he asks, eyes narrowing in suspicion.

'I know you're having a difference of opinion with one of your business rivals at the moment. We would be happy to help you resolve that.'

'Sorry, mate, don't know what you mean.'

Clay shrugs. 'As you wish. I'm sure your competition will say the same when I make them the same offer.'

All hint of amusement is gone from Gregor's face now, and he walks slowly over towards where Clay stands stopping ten feet short.

'I'd be careful who I make offers like that to if I were you.'

He stares at Clay, eyes boring holes, looking for a flinch, but the Irishman has faced down far more dangerous men than Gregor Price, and simply waits him out.

'Sean,' says Price finally, 'I think it's time our friend here pissed off after all.'

'You heard the boss. Time to piss off.'

A cruel glint fires up in Sean's eyes, a bully being given the green light to do what he loves. Smiling, he moves to close the gap. His left hand comes up reaching out to grab Clay's shoulder. Clay whips his right arm around clockwise, up and over, then pulls tight into his side, pinning the arm. His left shoots out, landing a backhanded chop to the Adam's apple. He releases the trapped arm, and Sean staggers backwards, clutching at his throat, eyes bulging, making a noise somewhere between a wheeze and a saw as he struggles to breathe.

Clay takes a step back, letting both arms fall by his sides again, just as Gregor reaches behind him, whipping out a pistol from his waistband, taking three quick strides towards Clay.

'Try that with me,' he snarls, stopping just out of reach. Not quite as stupid as his man then, Clay thinks.

'Five minutes, Mr Price. That's all I need, and it could work out very well for you.'

'You've got five seconds to tell me why I shouldn't put a fucking bullet through your head.'

'Oh, I can think of a few,' says Clay, nodding towards Price's chest.

Price holds his gaze, trying to work out the Irishman's play. Clay gives a little raise of the eyebrows, tilting his head, inviting a look. Price takes a couple of steps back, buying himself more time if he needs it, and glances down.

The three red dots swarm across his heart like mosquitoes jostling for position, flickering millimetres left and right.

'What the fuck is this?' Price murmurs, looking back at Clay.

'This is option B,' Clay says, very matter of fact. 'I'd strongly advise taking option A.'

Silence hangs heavy as seconds tick by, Price scanning the darkness of the treeline, chances of spotting anyone in this light practically zero. The gun barrel sags an inch, then another, and finally drops to Price's side.

Behind him, two more men come bustling in from a hidden room off to one side, late to the party, and Price extends his free hand behind him to settle things down.

'Five minutes,' he nods, and turns to head back into his office.

'Here's fine,' says Clay.

Price huffs out a loud breath, looks down at his feet, then shrugs, stashing the gun, holding his palms out. 'Your turn now,' he says, looking down at the dots. 'Call it a goodwill gesture.'

Clay nods, holds up one hand, thumb and forefinger pinched into an 'okay' sign, and the three dots wink out like snuffed candles.

'What exactly is it you think you can help with?'

Clay spots a pair of metal chairs, folded and propped against the wall. He picks them up, setting them ten feet apart, takes the one closest to the door, inviting Price to join him.

'My sources tell me your rival organisation blames you for the untimely demise of a few of their associates.'

'Yeah, well what can I say, they're misinformed.'

'Whether you did or didn't, doesn't bother me either way.'

'You've got four and half minutes left, no matter who you've got out there,' Price nods beyond him at the darkness. 'What's your point?'

'My point is that your life, your business, would be much easier if this rival firm ran into trouble.'

'And what, you can make that happen? You a copper?' There's an edge to Price's voice. No love lost for obvious reasons.

'Me?' Clay places a hand on his chest. 'God, no, but let's just say my employer has the means to make that happen. Maybe even make it look like what happened to his people was the work of somebody on his side.'

Price studies him with suspicion. 'And hypothetically, if you did that for me, what would I be doing for you?'

And there it is. The hook is in. 'Not much,' says Clay. 'Maybe just even share a little information.'

'Such as?'

'Such as the whereabouts of Maggie Brewer.'

He sees Price's eyes widen. Sees him shift forward in his seat ready to explode.

'You? On the roof in Tynemouth, the accent, that was you.'

Statement, not a question. Price is up out of his seat and reaching behind him in the same movement. His men pile forward too, but this was never going to be a fair fight. A twin *zip-zip* as bullets tear through the air, both men crumpling face first onto concrete. Clay has his own weapon out before Price's is halfway up.

'Now might be a good time to point out that just because there are no dots dancing over you, doesn't mean you'd have time to reach your gun, let alone pull the trigger. It's very important we speak with Mrs Brewer.'

If looks could kill, Clay would be twitching on the ground by now. Price may be mad, but he is no fool. Arms move out to the sides, jaw clenched tight, working like he's chewing gristle, but he lowers slowly back into his seat.

'If you can help me find her, my employer will make sure your problem with your rivals goes away. We'll also compensate you for the unfortunate loss of your men. Shall we say five grand a head?'

Price looks incredulous, glancing either side at the bodies, then at Sean who has dragged himself across to the wall, chest heaving as he still struggles to suck in air through his damaged throat. Clay sees the change in his face, to a more calculating expression.

'Make it ten grand a piece in Bitcoin, and I need to see it before we talk anymore.'

Got to love a criminal. Far easier to deal with under these circumstances, quicker to spot the upside and work their own angle. Clay pretends to mull it over before nodding. Small fry if it gets him to Maggie Brewer.

'Deal. You have account details?'

Clay walks across and reads them off Price's phone, tapping in the transaction details in the other. His finger hovers above send.

'Just to be clear, if you try to get out of our deal, or go back in any way, I think the position is fairly clear, yes?'

Price nods grimly, and Clay taps the screen.

'Now, Mrs Brewer?'

'She was here,' he admits. 'Last night, but she went off on her own, over Durham way.'

'Why Durham?'

'They needed some computer gear.'

'You have an address?'

Price nods, looking a little sheepish. 'I do. We went there but the place was empty.'

Clay feels the first prickle of irritation. 'You expect me to walk away happy that this is what I've bought for my money?'

'She's a fucking journalist,' Price says. 'You think whatever she's into that she isn't going to need more help? Who'd you think she'll turn to?' he taps a finger at his chest.

'Really? You think she ran away from you because she trusts you, and she'll come back for more,' Clay says, mind racing ahead to his next move, now this hasn't panned out. Deal with Price, then take his phone. Should be able to log in and retrieve the Bitcoin.

Price shrugs. 'Maybe, maybe not. Doesn't matter. But what she will do, is get in touch with her brother again.

Davey, the one you chucked off the roof. Soon as she does, Bob's your uncle.'

'I don't follow.'

'Two of them have been thick as thieves. Wouldn't tell me anything, even though I put my fucking neck on the line for them, so I made sure I can find out next time she calls.'

'How so?'

'Davey's phone was knackered after what happened, so I replaced it with one of mine, 'cept this one's cloned, so I see everything, hear everything. Soon as I know, you know.'

Price fixes him with a used car salesman's grin, knowing what he's selling isn't what was advertised.

Clay considers this for a moment, deciding to add a little incentive. 'Twenty-four hours,' he says. 'You get me a location by then, or you won't be around to spend that money. Am I clear?'

Price licks his lips, any semblance of bravado has left the building for now, realising he's painted himself into a corner. He nods, and Clay pushes up to his feet, pulling out a pen, scrawling a number on a scrap of paper from his pocket, and handing it to Price.

'Look forward to hearing from you,' he says, and turns before Price can reply. He's just past the threshold when he stops, turns, and fixes Price with an inquisitive look.

'You said *they*. Who's *they*?'

'Hmm?'

'You said they needed computer gear.'

'Oh, aye, Maggie's mate. Layt Brown.'

'Who is he?'

Price stands up, smoothing out creases from his shirt. 'Just some kid. Some kind of computer whizz. One of those hackers, you know.'

'Your man is with him now?'

Price looks bashful again. 'He's disappeared as well.'

Jesus, thinks Clay. As tricky as it's been to track her down, Price had her and her friend, and let them both slip away. You pay peanuts, you get monkeys. All the same though, this is the most interesting development yet. So, she's teamed up with a hacker? Is this a friend of hers, or of Xiang's? His mind wanders back to the laptop screen at Xiang's house. To the third window he had seen pop like a bubble before he could get close enough to read a name. This is it, he thinks, this is the true source of their leak, working side by side with Maggie Brewer. Find one, find them both.

'I'll take that Durham address after all.'

Chapter Sixty-One

We're just passing the sign for Wetherby Services heading back north on the A1 when a ringing snaps me out of my trance. A glance across shows Izzy still napping. It's a number, not a name, and I click a button on the wheel to answer, but wait for whoever's calling to speak first.

After a few seconds, I hear a welcome voice, 'Hello? Maggie?'

'Layt!' Relief washes over me like cool surf racing up the sand. 'I was worried, I thought—'

'Nah, I'm fine. Sorry about not answering earlier. Phone died, and had to get a lift to a twenty-four-hour Tesco for a charger. How'd it go anyway? You find it?'

'I think so,' I say, describing what I've found, skimming over details of what happened during and after the find, as much to keep Izzy's name out of the picture as to spare Layt.

'Won't take too long to check when I see it,' he says, 'speaking of which, where are you now?'

Although we're travelling north at a rate of knots, I still haven't decided where exactly I'm heading, where it's safe to regroup.

'Just coming past Wetherby. Where are you? I'll come to you.'

'I've got a better idea,' says Layt. 'Can you meet me at Durham train station?'

'I...um... I suppose so. You taking a trip?'

'We both are.'

'What are you not telling me?'

'I'll explain when I see you,' says Layt. 'Safer than over the phone. We'll have time to talk before the train, then we can catch some sleep on the way down.'

'Way down where?'

'Oxford. Oh, and you might want to grab a couple of coffees on your way here.'

'What's in Oxford?'

'Not what. Who?'

A memory of a prior conversation flits to mind, even as he tells me.

'Francis Osgood.'

Chapter Sixty-Two

Despite the early hour, the faces staring back at Osgood from the on-screen gallery look as alert as if they're midway through an ordinary day's work. That, despite them all being well into their seventies and beyond. Four faces on screen, one more in the room. Dr Alston Myers sits off to one side, staring at the screen rather than Osgood.

'I can assure you gentlemen, I've just spoken to Mr Clay, and he has assurances from a third party that Mrs Brewer will be found and secured within hours.'

'You'll excuse me if I don't sound convinced,' says the face top left of his screen. General Arthur Samson, former Chief of the Defence Staff is a man who has spent decades giving orders, not accepting the kind of vague bullshit Osgood is peddling. 'Tonight's events have changed things somewhat.'

Osgood glares across at Dr Myers. Samson is the one who called this meeting, but he wonders if Myers has been whispering in his ear.

'I think I speak for us all when I say that we're not against making the tough decisions when they're called for. God knows we've made enough over the years. This is different though. The policeman who was shot, his father is a rather vocal Trade Union leader, and someone who would not be particularly sympathetic to our cause.'

'I understand that Arthur, but—'

'If you'll allow me to finish,' he says in clipped tones. 'Clay's man on the ground, quite literally on the ground. What is the risk he leads back to us?'

'None,' says Osgood, wishing he felt as confident as he sounded. 'Clay picks his team carefully. They're as elite as they come, with rock solid identities.'

'But not quite elite enough to handle one female reporter,' says another of the men, former Surgeon General, Nicholas Harper, long-time friend of Osgood's father. The other two men, both former national heads of respective military branches, grunt their approval of the quip. Former First Sea Lord, James Flemming, and former Air Chief Marshall, Benjamin Tarsett. All four men have been part of HELIX since its inception, way before Osgood took over the reins.

'Where is Clay now, and what is his next move. Be specific.'

Osgood squirms at the schoolteacher tone, but keeps an outwardly placid expression. 'The man who helped Mrs Brewer get away last night, he's working with us now.'

'Just like that?' Harper's face creases with sceptical concern.

'Clay can be quite persuasive. Let's just say he made him an offer that was in his interests to accept.'

'And what, he's just going to deliver her tied up in a neat bow?' asks Benjamin Tarsett.

'Something like that, yes.' Osgood glares back, aiming for a 'back the hell off' vibe, but doubts it will pierce the armour of entitlement that these men were born into.

'And if he doesn't?' Harper chimes back in. 'Say we don't find her in time and she has what we think she has. Run us through worst case.'

Osgood shrugs. If they want the Doomsday scenario, so be it. 'Worst case, from what we pieced together she has several hundred records downloaded from HELIX, ones that can hurt us, show when and how we gathered them. We'll have some of the media onside to spin things our way, but worst case, Luminosity plc buckles under the weight of litigation, so we lose our cash cow. None of you are directly implicated as such, but the when and how it started, won't take Sherlock Holmes to draw a reasonable inference of the level of influence it took to bring this to bear to begin with.'

'If it gets to that, we won't be the only ones getting dragged down with it,' grumbles Flemming.

'Gentlemen, gentlemen,' Dr Myers interjects. 'I'm sure it won't come to that, but if it does, do we honestly think that the contribution we've made to the world will suddenly be overlooked? That doctors will stop prescribing our treatments, our products, because of this?' He shakes his head, leaning forwards and steepling his fingers. 'No, what we've achieved is nothing short of a miracle these past decades. The lives we've saved, the impact we've had on so many over and above that.'

Osgood sees a quadrant of nodding heads. Hates the fact that Myers holds more sway over these men than he does. The status quo between himself and the good doctor has always been an uneasy one. He can't help think that Myers would throw him under the proverbial bus if it suited his purposes, and not look back.

'Look at it this way,' Myers continues. 'We live in a world where presidents get away with inciting violence in their own capital, where people and companies reinvent themselves all the time with the right spin applied. What we do will enrage and excite in equal measures.'

He leans back into his seat now. 'Would it be preferable for us to stay in the background? Of course, but for every great advancement in human history, someone has to take risks. Would any of you choose differently if you could turn back the clock?'

Unanimous shaking of heads. Osgood starts to shake his without thinking, stops himself, not because he disagrees, but because it annoys him that Myers is the one whose 'once more unto the breach' is getting through to them.

'We could guarantee everyone's safety if we just cut the cord,' says Nicholas Harper. 'Shut the whole thing down.'

Myers shakes his head. 'Our structure is such that we each have more layers of protection than those brave men you have all sent into battle over the years. What you're suggesting is a nuclear option that would be nigh on impossible to walk back.'

For once, Osgood and Myers are in complete accord, even if not for the same reasons. He and Myers are privy to parts of HELIX that not even the other members of The Six on screen are aware of. Elements they have leveraged for their own personal gain. But it runs deeper than that. There are levels that even Myers doesn't know of. Plans for the future of HELIX that will turn billions into trillions. Becoming a truly global operation, sold to anyone willing to pay the going rate, one that will be steeper than Everest. Governments, or private institutions. The who doesn't matter to him. Burning all of this to the ground in a private bonfire to save the reputation of four retired old farts is not an option.

'I didn't get woken up at this ungodly hour to sit and chew the fat till sunrise,' says Tarsett. 'I say we give Clay until midnight tonight. Just shy of twenty hours by my count. If we're no further forward, then my vote will be to pull the plug. It's not like we need the money for God's sake. I'm not risking spending what time I have left in a bloody prison cell.'

Osgood steps in before the pessimistic tone catches on. 'Of course, Ben, whatever we need to do, we need to be unanimous, and none of us want that. Something of this magnitude should be discussed face-to-face. Let's not let the grass grow under our feet. If Mr Clay is no further forward by five p.m., I suggest you all come to HQ as my guests, and we hash this out over dinner. It's been too long. I'll get Antonio in to cook for us in the boardroom, and I'll book you all into the Westerbury.'

They haven't all been in the same room for over six months, and the lure of Osgood's private chef, coupled with an overnighter at one of the most exclusive hotels in the country, seems to halt the decline in mood, all heads nodding save for Myers. The doctor gives him a look like a kid trying to work out a magician's secrets, but settles for a tight-lipped smile.

Osgood agrees to send a company chopper to each of them if it comes to that, and they end the call, no further forward, but a little less disgruntled.

'I presume you're free to join us this evening, Alston?' he asks when the connection is severed.

'Wouldn't miss it,' Myers says, then cocks his head slightly to one side. 'Unlike you to be so hospitable. I thought you couldn't bear them all together in one room.'

Osgood had said as much in a fit of frustration the last time that had occurred.

'Desperate times, and all that,' he says with a forced smile.

'Of course, you and I have a little more to lose than our four esteemed colleagues,' says Myers. 'If they knew the full extent to which HELIX has grown, how we've used it to remove a few ... obstacles, they may not be quite so understanding.'

Osgood studies the older man now, trying and failing to read where his head is at.

'I do sincerely hope that's not some kind of veiled threat, Alston. We're on the same team here.'

'Of course we are,' says Myers with a tip of the head. 'I'm just as much your man as I was your father's.'

The mention of his father niggles Osgood. The two men have had something of a complicated relationship, his father raising him after his mother was murdered when he was only ten years old. As a former government minister, his dad spent weekdays at Westminster, and weekends working out how to be a single parent. Wasn't that the old man was absent, more like neither could speak the other's language when it came to express grief.

A man with a reputation like his dad casts a longer shadow than Big Ben. Despite everything he has achieved himself, in some people's eyes he'll always just be 'Frank's boy', and he can't help the speck of resentment towards the old man any time it comes up. He's made his mark on the world every bit as much as his dad, maybe even more so in his own humble opinion.

'What do you think they would say, Alston? If it all comes out?'

'They? The rest of The Six you mean?'

'No, I mean everyone. The world at large,' he says, leaning back into the soft leather chair. 'Do you think they'd judge us or thank us?'

Myers ponders on it for a few seconds then shrugs. 'At this point I don't suppose it really matters. No matter how many HELIX has saved, there'll be just as many up in arms about how we did what we did, that they'll look right past the good we've done. I think the more important question is would you make the same choices if you had a do-over?'

Osgood doesn't believe in fate, only actions and outcomes. He is where he is because he has made the hard calls that others shirk from. Some that have destroyed livelihoods, others have literally destroyed lives. But when Myers asked the question, there wasn't even a heartbeat of hesitation before an answer flashed to mind.

'Not a thing,' he says.

'Then what do you care if they judge you?' Myers stands, arthritic knees popping like firecrackers. 'Anyway, if you'll excuse me, I've got work to do,' he says, flashing an enigmatic smile, then hobbling out of the boardroom, and disappears down the hall.

Osgood lets out a long slow breath. He's a careful man, with a platoon of lawyers, homes in several countries with no extradition treaty, and more money squirrelled away in offshore accounts that he could spend in a dozen lifetimes. He has no real concerns about getting out if he needs to. What worries him is the exposure it would bring. The kind of people that would become his enemies if everything came to light. People whose lives and loved ones he has manipulated using HELIX, ruined and worse. The kind of people who don't respect treaties, or care about any laws. The kind who he would be constantly looking over his shoulder for, even with someone like Clay watching his back.

The undercurrent of panic he's picking up from The Six is a worry. Truth be told he outgrew those old fools years ago. Any power they think they wield today is a mere ghost of the weight they could throw about back in the day. They would do well to remember that before they get any fanciful notions about telling him how to steer the ship. He has played out multiple worst-case scenarios in his head, including some or all of The Six going rogue, or worse still going public.

If they do, it'll be the last mistake they ever make. There's no line Osgood won't cross to protect what's his. They might arrive in helicopters, but if they try and shut him down, they'll leave in body bags.

Chapter Sixty-Three

It's approaching eight a.m. by the time I turn into the long winding road that leads up to the station. Izzy woke up as we left the A1, but hasn't had much to say. Layt had signed off by telling me to meet him at the underpass that runs under the station. As I round the corner, I spy a lone figure sitting on the steps, head bowed over a glowing phone screen. The dimly lit oval of the underpass looks like a gloomy cave in this light. I pull over to the side, and kill the engine.

Izzy stares out the window at Layt. 'This is the kid who's going to fix this then?'

'He's older than he looks, and yeah. He's the one who broke in and uncovered this in the first place.'

Even after everything we've been through since she picked me up from Wetherby Services, everything she's seen and learned, she looks far from convinced, but settles for a slow, accepting nod.

'What will you do now?' I ask her.

She looks lost for a second, the night's events towering over the notion of doing anything more mundane, then pats the dashboard. 'I need to get the car booked in for a facelift.'

Luckily, the impact had been bang in the centre, so both headlights are unbroken, but the bumper is cracked, and the bonnet creased. Won't be cheap, but insurance should cover it.

I pop my seatbelt, lean across and she turns into the hug. We cling to each other for the longest few seconds. As I let go, I whisper into her ear.

'Love you, Sis.'

Looks for a split second like she's filling up, but she swallows it down. 'Promise me if this doesn't work, whatever it is you're trying, that you'll call me. We can figure out another way. They can't have every copper in the country in their pocket. We could try someone local to me.'

'I'll do that if you promise me you'll stay somewhere else tonight. Anywhere but home.'

She frowns. 'You really think they'd come after me?'

'I think there's nothing they wouldn't do.'

A few seconds of heavy silence, then she nods.

One more hug for the road, then I climb out, watching as Izzy's car disappears down the hill, and turn to Layt with a tired smile.

'Forgot the coffee,' I say, holding up the memory card. 'Got this though.'

He shakes his head, hint of a smile as he stands. 'No coffee? You're dead to me.'

I walk around the railings that divide us, and we trudge up the stairs into the station. The waiting room is packed, people hiding from the sharp bite of the breeze, so we opt for a quiet spot on a bench down the far end of the platform.

'Nice dent in your ride,' he says casually. 'You hit a hedgehog on the way back up?'

That gets a tired chuckle, and I take one more glance around, making sure we're alone. I hold up the tiny card like an offering, and as he takes it, I start to talk him through the Manchester trip in full, blow by blow. When I'm finished, he shakes his head.

'Lucky they only had one guy there.'

I nod agreement. 'Guess they figured I probably wouldn't be stupid enough to go back.'

'You checked the news yet,' he asks. 'If a copper got hurt, they'll be coming just as hard as Osgood.'

Please let him just be hurt, I think. I know it's not my fault, whether they're injured or dead, but that won't stop me from adding another weight into the emotional basket I'm lugging around.

Layt pulls up a browser window on his iPhone, scans for a second then tilts so I can see.

Police were called to an incident on Lapwing Road just outside of Manchester in the early hours of this morning. What looks like a burglary gone wrong, left one man dead, and a police officer fighting for his life. A police spokesperson said they would like to talk to the driver of a dark saloon car that neighbours saw driving away, but refuse to be drawn on speculation that there could be a link to the recent murder of prominent research scientist, Dr Christopher Xiang. Dr Xiang was found dead just days ago at his flat. Police would still like to speak to Maggie Brewer, a journalist at the Manchester Standard, *who may have been the last person to see Dr Xiang alive, and is a resident of Lapwing Road.*

My attacker is dead. I assumed as much, but seeing it in print makes it real. The officer is alive. That's one thing at least, but this story isn't on the local Manchester news page. It's national. That thought tramples all over any relief I felt that the policeman isn't dead. Makes me do another nervous sweep over both shoulders. If Mam and Dad didn't know anything before, they probably will now.

'Relax,' says Layt. 'Most people have either got headphones on or they're lost in their laptops. They haven't released your picture, that's something.'

I'm a million miles away, making a series of pessimistic mental 'what if' leaps. What if Freddie's car or Izzy's gets picked up on the ANPR cameras they use? What if the contents of the drive are damaged, or not enough to prove what HELIX is? What if there's no way to link the pile of broken bones and torn flesh on the road to HELIX? That makes him just a random pedestrian, and that makes Izzy a murderer.

'Maggie,' Layt says, snapping his fingers. 'We're close now. With what I found out while you were away, plus this,' he holds the card up, 'we've got a fighting chance.'

'Even if we *can* prove it?' I say, as a fresh wave of tiredness soaks into every muscle, 'What then? There's no guarantee we'll be safe while any investigation takes place.'

'Trust me, with what I know now, we won't just prove it,' he says, with an energy I wish I could tap into. 'We're gonna blow the fucking roof off.'

Chapter Sixty-Four

'HELIX goes back to the nineties,' he says, tucking one leg under the other, turning sideways on the bench to face me, 'but there's not as much of an electronic trail when you go that far back. The law firm, that Marshall Watson Parker bunch, they're as knee deep in it as the rest. With the kind of money I'm talking, you'd think they'd have better security, but then again, it's me we're talking about, so probably wouldn't have saved them anyway.'

I see it for the attempt to lighten the tone that it is. 'Course. Goes without saying.'

'So get this, the lawyers have funnelled money from IQ, through a dozen different trusts, who in turn have passed it on to some rather interesting people. All the cutting-edge shit that Chris was into, the regulations around it are a little vague and sketchy. There's the "thou shalt not clone a human" stance, but after that, a lot of it is shades of grey. There are a few groups that advise the Government on it, like Genetic Testing Network and the Human Genetics Commission, and the main body is the Medicines and Healthcare Products Regulatory Agency. Just so happens that a number of prominent members of each of these lovely groups, had "donations",' he says making air quotes, 'from IQ via the law firm, right around the time they were voting on certain matters that allowed Luminosity to crack on with work that's led to some of their biggest discoveries and patents.'

'They're buying their way around red tape?' I ask.

'That's about the size of it, and with HELIX to dip into for subjects, they've got the biggest testing pool to fish in.'

'So it really does boil down to money then?' I say. 'Greed.'

'Gets worse,' Layt says, any hint of earlier humour has evaporated. 'That's how I think they've built HELIX too. They've bought it.'

'How do you mean? Who from? How do you buy millions of people's DNA?'

'There were shedloads more payments to people and companies, running into the millions. Only had time to check a sample, but a few stood out. Companies that are part of that whole spider web of corporations we talked about. Some of which handle waste disposal. Medical waste.'

'I don't follow?'

'IQ indirectly owns a series of companies that handle medical waste disposal for the NHS. That includes sharps disposal. Needles that doctors have used to dish out vaccinations and the like. Every one they do, it comes with a batch number and bar code. Has for years, and they have to dispose of each one by sealing it in a separate bag before they drop it in the bin.'

'You're saying that IQ have been stealing these and taking samples from them?'

'Not stealing,' he says with a shrug. 'They've got the contracts to get rid of them, but what they do with them between collection and disposal is another matter.'

'But that would still take years,' I say. 'I can't even begin to imagine how many people you'd need to do that.'

'They've had years,' he says simply. 'Around thirty to be precise from when IQ was set up. Think about it, percentage take-up on childhood vaccinations is around the mid-nineties. They've been dishing out MMR since the seventies, so they might even have been at it for longer, and that's before we even start talking about the COVID vaccine they rolled out a few years back. We never said HELIX has 100 per cent coverage, but that's a pretty strong foundation to build on, don't you think? And if they can do that, who's to say what other ways they've thought of?'

'Oh my God.'

My head is already swimming with tiredness. The deeper we dig, the more layers we expose, and now it turns out this stretches back decades.

'We've got fifteen minutes before the train. Let's see what we've got here,' Layt says, sliding a laptop out of his overstuffed rucksack.

He powers up, clicking the SD card into a slot on the side. I watch as a window pops into view, list of files streaming across the screen as Layt scrolls through, unsure what I'm expecting to see. He double clicks on a sub-folder, opens the only file inside, and rubs his hands together.

'Jackpot.'

'That's the code you talked about?'

He nods. 'Yep. Only problem is the Wi-Fi on the trains is crap. I'll see what I can do with it on the way down, but might have to find a Starbucks or something like that when we get down.'

'You still haven't said exactly what you've got in mind? Shouldn't we be staying as far away from him as we can?'

'That's exactly why we're going after Francis Osgood.'

'Won't that be more dangerous, though?'

'What have you done since we first met?'

'I've … well I've been on the run, I guess.'

'Exactly,' he says with a snap of his fingers. 'They're gonna be chasing shadows up north, while we head down south and make old Francis an offer he can't refuse.'

'Which is?'

'To keep his legacy intact. That's what this is all about, don't you see? This whole fucking thing is a memorial to his wife. Like I already told you they couldn't find her killer back then, not for years, but that's gotta be what it's about. I mean why else would you drop out of being the PM's right-hand man, unless it was for a bigger prize? Don't forget this isn't just about money, it's about power, and if this goes public he risks losing both of them, and his family name, gets dragged through the mud.'

'Won't he be protected, though?'

'Remember on the Zoom call with Chris, I told you your husband wasn't the only one?'

'Yeah.'

'When we broke in there, I managed to decrypt a few hundred records before Paul got jumpy. Not just DNA profiles. We're talking names, dates of birth, addresses, the works. I've got a nifty programme I wrote. I call it the Ferret. You feed that kind of shit in, it trawls a load of databases and pulls in what it can find. Had hits on twelve. News articles. A dozen people who are all serving time as we speak. Couple of which are, or were, quite outspoken about the kind of genetic research Luminosity specialises in. One was a Lib Dem MP who'd voted against some key pieces of legislation around genetics, another was a Bishop in the Church of England who spent more time on his soapbox than Donald Trump about his stolen election. The MP, Julian Pitt, went down for GBH, Bishop

Cartwright was for a hit and run. Want to guess what kind of evidence they were both convicted on?

I'm so caught up in the narrative Layt is spinning that his question takes me by surprise. Takes a second or two for my tired brain to whirr into action.

'I'm assuming DNA?'

'Got it in one. Both adamant they were innocent. Denied any involvement, but DNA doesn't lie. Unless of course—'

'You have a sample you can plant, or a database you can doctor,' I finish it for him.

'Quite the coincidence that people who oppose them get cut down to size with what it is they're opposing, don't you think? The others are interesting but in a different way. Look here,' he says, clicking away so fast it sounds like Morse code, selection of new windows popping on screen. Each has the same set of fields in it: names, addresses, none of which she recognises.

'These two,' he taps a pair of names, 'are part of a family that run a big chunk of Glasgow. Got sent down for armed robbery based on DNA evidence. And this one,' tapping a third, 'has links to an organised crime outfit down in London. What if those three people were all emailed an anonymous copy of evidence that suggested their DNA had been illegally sampled, stored and potentially used in evidence against them?'

'Are you saying they didn't do those things?'

'What? No. I don't know. They don't exactly sound like choirboys, so there's every chance they did, but wouldn't that stop them from appealing, or from wanting to have a word with the person whose company might have helped them out there? There's no amount of lawyers Osgood can throw at these kinds of people that'll stop them.'

'And how exactly do we get close enough to Osgood to have any kind of conversation with him?' I ask. 'The moment he sees me, what's to stop him and his hired help from just shooting me on the spot?'

'They won't if it's public enough,' says Layt. 'And I can set up a new address and have an email scheduled to go out with everything we've got attached, if we don't log back in and stop it. You know, like an insurance policy. I'd offer to do it myself, but as far as I know, they don't know who I am yet, if they even know I exist at all. The longer they don't know you've got help, the more of an edge we've got.'

A thought forces its way through the mental sludge clogging up my mind.

'Wait a minute; before, you mentioned he'll care about his legacy?'

'Yeah, I don't know why that didn't click earlier, but now we've got proof of the financial side of—'

'But you said he'd jump at the chance to save it.'

'Wouldn't you if you were him?'

'People have died. My husband has died. He doesn't get to save it Layt, any of it.'

The idea of taking on Osgood terrifies me, makes my rational mind freeze over with indecision, but lurking beneath that, the slow-simmering fury at the thought of Grant's death being for nothing, no meaning and with no consequence.

I've been happy to take his steer when it comes to the data, the proof we need, but this is a bridge too far, and I push up to my feet. Off to my right, a low hum, growing louder, sliding up through the decibels as the train approaches.

'If we're going down there to shake his hand and ask to call it a draw, you can do that on your own. I'll finish this myself some other way.'

Even as I say it, the thought terrifies me. Starting over, no proof, no allies, least not outside my own family, but I'll do it, for Grant, for Christopher Xiang, and for anyone else whose lives IQ has ruined. Occurs to me that this definition now includes me. I don't give him a chance to retort, and turn on my heel, striding off down the platform.

'Maggie, wait, I didn't mean—'

The rest of his sentence is swallowed by the roar of a train, not stopping, just passing through. I watch it whistle past, disappearing around the bend and out of sight. No more clue where it's destination might be than I have of my own.

Chapter Sixty-Five

Layt catches up with me just short of the exit, rucksack slung over one shoulder, laptop tucked under his arm.

'Maggie, listen to me. I—'

'You're going to miss your train, Layt.'

'You've got the wrong end of the stick,' he says, moving to stand in front of me, blocking the doorway.

'Which part? The bit where we let him get away with murder, or the bit where he continues to make billions of pounds from stealing people's DNA?'

'Both,' he says, side-stepping in sync as I try to slide past him. 'I said he'll want to save his legacy. I never said we'd let him.'

I stop, eyeing him up like a suspicious snake-oil salesman.

'But you said—'

'You never let me finish. All we need is for him to believe it, even just a tiny bit. But sitting down and having the talk with him gets us the cherry on top of the cake.'

'In what way?' I fold my arms across my chest, no longer looking for a way out, but still far from convinced.

'We do exactly what I said. We set up a time-delay mail that goes to every major paper as our back-up threat. We play to his ego. We tell him we understand why he did what he did, that we see the good in it, and that we'll keep quiet in return for calling off the dogs, plus a slice of the pie.'

'You think he'll pay us off?'

'Why not? He's done it with everyone else,' Layt shrugs. 'But that's not important. What we need is him offering to, or at least talking about it.'

'We're going to record him?'

'Exactly. He can put a spin on anything else we publish, the money funnelled through solicitors, allegations about HELIX, but we get him admitting it, and that's the iceberg that takes down the *Titanic*.'

'You've got a plan for how we do this I presume?'

Layt taps his head. 'All makes sense up here. I'll talk you through it on the train. Speaking of which.' He nods over my shoulder just as a set of carriages grind to a halt, station announcer's voice echoing around me.

'It'll work, Maggie,' he says, and the earnest look he gives me chips through my resolve.

We hop on board as the station guard blows their whistle, and it's as if Layt has booked out a private carriage for us – Coach D is designated the quiet one, and we settle into a four-seater table mid-way along. The journey to Oxford should take around five hours, via King's Cross, over to Paddington, then bouncing back up to our eventual destination.

I wonder where Izzy is now. Whether she's keeping her promise to lay low until I call her. Thinking of her promise to me reminds me of my own. Not just to her, but to myself. To Grant. The promise to tell his story. I'm about to walk into the lion's den, but what if I don't walk out?

I open the mail app on my phone, feeling a prick of panic as I stare at the blank page, wondering if I can really do this justice. Echoes of Izzy's voice goad me on, and when I start, it's a slow burn. My mind whirring like a hard drive, riffling through the worst week of my life.

Slowly but surely, sentences start to appear. Faltering at first, but then they begin to flow, like water from a burst dam. Everything I've been bottling up. All my fears, feelings and fury pour out onto the page. My thumbs begin to ache but I power through. It'll need a lot of polish before it's published, but every paragraph, every word, brings with it a sense of purpose, a creative catharsis. A feeling that in telling Grant's tale, I'm grabbing a future with both hands. One I haven't opened myself up to until now.

It takes me an hour to get the bones of it down. A quick google gives me the news desk addresses for all the major outlets, and I add them into the recipients list. I open up the send options, choosing a time twenty-four hours from now. I hit send to activate the time delay, then delete the mail app from my phone. If the meeting with Osgood goes south, there'll be no trace of it for them to find before it lands in editors' inboxes, the deadly spark that'll burn it all to the ground. If I walk away from this, I can always cancel the mail, tidy up the article, and decide what to do with it then. Either way, this stops being a secret.

A tiny voice chimes up in my head, telling me this is an insurance policy against any curveball Layt might throw as well. I have to believe he's 100 per cent with me, but I've still only known him a matter of days. Who's to say he won't buckle under any pressure that Osgood and his people might bring to bear.

I lay my phone down on the table. Layt is still tapping away at his keyboard but it's as if the effort of capturing everything has drained my battery. I manage to keep my eyes open long enough for the guard to come and check our tickets. The last thing I see as my head presses against the cool glass is Layt, hunched over his laptop, and the clickety-clack base notes of the train entwines with the lighter drum beat of fingers on keyboard, dragging me down into a mercifully dreamless sleep.

Chapter Sixty-Six

Waking up feels like wading through treacle, slow, consciousness oozing back in, squinting as the late morning sunshine streams into slowly opening eyes. I feel a gentle tug at my shoulder. See Layt reaching over the table, doing his best to wake me gently.

'King's Cross in ten minutes,' he says as I stretch, blinking away the last of the power nap. Only a few hours when it feels like a full twenty-four is needed, but I feel surprisingly alert for it. My mind flashes to Mam and the urge to call her is all-consuming. I wonder what she might have heard by now. What she must think of me, of my radio silence?

A quick glance around shows the carriage half-full, most wearing a variation on a theme, commuters destined for a day at a desk. The seat next to Layt is occupied too. A large man squeezed between the armrests, gut wedged against the table like a jelly in a mould waiting to set. The laptop is shut, anything on the memory card hidden from prying eyes, and I wonder how much time Layt had to work before the fat man poached his personal space.

We shuffle off the train with the rest of the herd. I'm itching to ask him, and try my best to get that across in a glance when our eyes meet. Tiny shake of the head. I remember his comment about train Wi-Fi, and when he suggests a coffee at Leon to pass the time before our connection, I understand it's still a work in progress. I let him pay for a pair of latte's, each with an extra shot of espresso, and we slide into a seat in the corner. He gets right down to it, jumping on the Wi-Fi, muttering about his VPN, IP address, speaking fluent acronym. Under normal circumstances, I would surf the web, browse Facebook and Instagram, but thoughts of HELIX and Osgood are all encompassing. All the permutations that could see this go pear-shaped.

After the longest two minutes of my life, spent catching then avoiding eye contact with other customers, I excuse myself, and head out into the body of the station. High above, the elegantly curving roof undulates, a rippling cloak of glass, hypnotic if you stare long enough. I move away from the centre, where clumps of people stand staring at the departures board, waiting for their platform, rooted to the spot like rows of terracotta warriors. Sunlight streams in through the south exit, and a gust of cool winter air splashes across my face like a wake-up call.

Before parting ways with Freddie, I made sure I saved both his, Izzy's and Davey's numbers in my own burner phone. Mindful of Freddie's late-night taxi duties, I opt to let him sleep, calling Davey first to see how he is, wondering as I do, whether he'll even be allowed his phone on the ward.

'Well, well. If it isn't Britain's most wanted,' he says, sounding half-asleep. Just woken up or just drugged up? I lean back against the wall, closing my eyes, savouring a moment in the eye rather than the storm.

'How's my favourite hypochondriac?'

'Ah, it's just a flesh wound,' he says, and I smile, corners of my mouth stretching into full beam for the first time in a long time.

I listen as he recounts what he remembers of the rooftop, and his subsequent trip to the hospital. There's still an officer stationed outside his room, but they've not charged him with anything yet. I take my turn after that, and when I'm finished, he whistles out a loud breath.

'Jeez, Sis, busy night, eh?'

'Nah, pretty standard,' I say, feeling that little bit lighter just talking to him.

'So this kid, he's the real deal then?'

'Yep. He's the one who cracked them first time round. He's the only one I know who has a hope of doing it again.'

'And what then?'

I'm about to talk him through Layt's plan, when two British Transport police officers round the corner. They're chatting with one another, but two sets of eyes scan the sea of faces. Looking for anything, or anyone in particular I wonder? I push off the wall, turning my back to them.

'Gotta go, Davey. Call you later, yeah?'

His tinny voice is still chattering away as I end the call. I raise it back to my ear, pretending to continue the conversation, tensed and waiting for a hand on my shoulder that never comes. The pair stroll past, and don't give me so much as a second glance. All the same, I don't feel safe out here anymore, and head back inside to join Layt.

He grunts an acknowledgement as I slide back into my seat, but his fingers don't stop typing. I try my best to find distractions, flicking through a discarded copy of the *Metro*, left behind by another customer, losing myself as best I can in what's going on in other people's lives, desperate to leave my own behind for a while.

Forty-five minutes of the hour that we have before we need to leave for Paddington passes with painful slowness. I'm about to get up and stretch my legs to risk a call to Freddie, when Layt slides back in his seat, muttering under his breath.

'Fuck me.'

'What? What is it? Are you in?'

He shakes his head, and I worry for a minute that it's all been a wasted effort.

'I'm in, but it's worse than we thought, Maggie.'

'Worse? How can it possibly be worse?'

It's already grown in my head over the past few days like a cancerous tumour, out of control, choking the life out of everything it touches. What else could there be to make it worse. He has to be exaggerating.

We're cutting it fine for our connecting train so we set off for Paddington, joining throngs of people pouring down into the Underground. Timing is nigh on perfect, a Tube train pulling in just as we reach the platform, and once we're on board, he starts talking. I listen, symphony of sound around me, roaring from an open window as we power into a tunnel, until I'm forced to agree with him. It's worse. So much worse.

Chapter Sixty-Seven

Gregor Price has made a career out of self-interest, making money off the misfortune of others. Drugs mainly, with a sprinkling of other sources of income as and when they present. This is no different, he tells himself. He knows Maggie of old, sure, but what other option does he have? If it's a straight choice between himself and her, sentimentality goes out the window. Davey will go berserk if he finds out, and when he loses his shit, it's best to stand back out of reach. His temper is the sort that takes seconds to ignite, days to ice over. Best make sure he doesn't find out then.

He fishes out the scrap of paper from his pocket, taps the number into his phone and clears his throat as it rings.

'Hello.'

The quiet voice unnerves him in a way he can't explain. 'It's me,' he says, then adds, 'Price.'

'Mr Price, calling with good news I hope, for both our sakes?'

'Something like that, yeah.'

'You have a location?'

'Not a location, a number. She made a call to check on Davey. Have you got a pen, and I'll read it out?'

He doesn't mention that the call was actually a couple of hours ago, his way of reconciling what he's doing. This way he can say he gave her a fighting chance, and still hit the Irishman's deadline. Self-preservation to the bitter end.

'Text it over,' says Clay.

Price had already considered that, preferring to call, speak to the man, satisfy himself that they're all square.

'Will do. So we're all good?'

'You've kept your end, I'll keep mine,' comes the reply. 'Of course, if it turns out you haven't, then our next chat might not be as friendly as our first.'

Price is glad Clay isn't here to see the bemused look on his face. If that first chat had been friendly, he never wants to experience an unfriendly one. His natural instinct is to posture, to meet threat with threat, but he can't escape the feeling of a former big fish now dropped in the ocean with the real predators. He promises himself that when this is over, he'll make discreet enquiries about Clay, decide if it's something he should pursue further down the line from a position of strength, not an in the moment knee jerk.

'I'll send it now.'

The line cuts out before he has a chance to say anything else. Arrogant fucker. Now he's off the line, Price's natural need to be the Alpha reasserts itself, telling him he can handle this however it plays out. He briefly flirts with the notion of playing both sides, but dismisses it as fast as it occurs. If anything happens to Maggie, Davey might well be a handful, but he's one man. Something tells him the Irishman is a far more dangerous enemy. He'd take a mad haymaker-throwing Geordie, over the kind of ice-cool menace Clay brings to the party. The quiet ones are always the worst. Besides, it isn't as if this is the first time he'll have kept secrets from Davey.

The last one landed Davey inside for two years. Only two other people know about it. One has been taken care of already. The other is Maggie Brewer. Sentimentality aside, if this plays out Clay's way, maybe there's an upside for him after all. He slides the phone back into his pocket. Que sera, sera.

Chapter Sixty-Eight

The Circle line Tube ride to Paddington is one of the most eye-opening journeys in my life. Nothing to do with the surroundings, commuters or stations that blur past. Just when I thought I was at the bottom of the rabbit hole, Layt's revelations reveal layers beneath the layers.

'The code worked a treat,' he begins. 'I'd have struggled to get in any time soon without it. They'd popped a few extra measures in place, but it was the equivalent of having a mate inside opening the door for you. Got me straight back in. You could spend years going through the data in there. I mean in terms of size, we're talking the Mount Everest of databases. Zetta bytes of the stuff. We're on a clock though, so I went for the two I mentioned earlier first.'

'The Bishop and the MP?'

'Yep. Chapter and verse on the pair of them. Full DNA profile, the where and when collected. That in itself is a violation of the Human Tissues Act, but anyway, each file has a full audit trail on. Where and when sampled and sequenced, a user ID, so some underpaid lab tech. Who knows whether they're NDA'd, or maybe they just think they're processing genuine samples?'

He's talking low and fast at a hundred miles an hour, angling his body towards the door on the far side of the carriage to reduce the chances of his words carrying.

'But as well as that, there's a file history. Who's accessed it, when, any edits, that type of thing. Part of that, though, includes outgoing transfers, and both have an entry against that. Both were sent to the same place, and this is the part that'll blow your fucking mind.'

He stops talking abruptly as the doors open at Baker Street, incoming passengers jostling past outgoing, in the kind of rugby scrum you only see on the Tube, too many people heads down, off in their own little worlds. The wait is excruciating, ten times worse than if Jeremy Clarkson has just asked whether that's my final answer in the Millionaire chair. It serves to intensify the claustrophobia I always feel on the Tube the sense of carriage walls closing in, collapsing in like tinfoil.

By the time we pull away again, I'm acutely aware of my vest top underneath my sweater blotting against my back. The outside world, and all its fresh air, can't come soon enough.

'So get this,' he picks up where he left off. 'Both records were sent from HELIX, direct to the National DNA Database.'

He pauses, watching for a reaction that clearly doesn't come as quickly as he hoped, so he jumps back in. 'They literally planted the results in there, so when the coppers ran samples they found, they got hits first time.'

'Surely, the police can spot they're fakes though?' I lean in, keeping my voice low, closer to his ear.

'They've got that covered. I only had a chance to scan the coding in the background, but from what I saw, it's a two-way handshake.'

'What do you mean?'

'I mean that the request to compare against the national database triggered an anonymous ping to HELIX, which cross-referenced that with its own inventory, converted into a different format, presumably how it needs to look on the national side, then slides the record across. Here's the thing though, there's nothing in that outgoing transfer about the person taking the sample. The version they send back, claims it was taken at a completely different time and place, by whichever police force is local to them.'

'The police are in on it after all then. All of them.' I say, weight of my words squeezing my temples, bringing with it a sense of tightness behind the eyes, early of an epic headache.

'I don't think so,' Layt says as we pull into Edgware Road, platform surprisingly quiet, enough that there's no pause in conversation this time. 'I only had time to google both officers who it says secured the samples, but neither turned up any hits as part of the coverage of the cases. Can't explain that at the minute, but if I have more time, I can check the names against personnel records.'

'Sorry, you can what? Are you talking about hacking into police records?'

He looks amused. ''Cos of course, getting caught doing that would be the biggest of our worries right now.'

Any other time, I would be flabbergasted at the casual reference to breaking these kinds of laws, let alone have any part in it, but he makes it sound like just an average day at the office.

'Don't worry, I know how to cover my tracks. Besides, they've never caught me when I've been in before.'

I open my mouth to ask him what he means by that, but stop. Best stay on track rather than get lost down yet another surreal tangent.

'You want my professional opinion?' he asks, making it sound as credible as a doctor or lawyer. 'They've got the means to collect and clone DNA. Could go one of two ways. Either they plant that at a crime scene, and have some kind of algorithm scuttling between the two databases that makes sure the corresponding sample gets inserted in the national database with the name they need when the police run their checks, and bingo. Instant ID confirmed. Either that, or the police do a search for a sample that has no matches, and HELIX gives these guys, whoever they are, the option of choosing who they claim that sample belongs to by inserting fake records. Either way, DNA is never wrong, not in court. Slam dunk.'

He finishes just as they pull into Paddington, and we wait till last to exit. Even though I've left the swaying carriages, the ground feels anything but firm under my feet.

How do you beat someone who can literally manufacture your guilt from thin air? What Layt is proposing is so convoluted, so serpentine, it's making me queasy. Focus on Grant. Focus on Rose, I tell myself. Don't let this smother you.

We ascend the escalator from the Tube onto the main railway station concourse.

'Will it stretch any deeper do you think?' I ask. 'Every time I think I've got my head around it, it doubles in size. It's like David and Goliath.'

'Exactly,' says Layt, flashing a smile that suggests supreme confidence. 'So let's go and find a fucking big stone to sling.'

Chapter Sixty-Nine

Declan Clay is starting to have a begrudging respect for Maggie Brewer. Not that it'll buy her any leeway when he finally catches up with her. Not only has she escaped what he'd considered to be as good as a sealed room on the rooftop, she'd also taken one of his men off the board permanently in Manchester. Now, she's managed to disappear like a fart in the wind, yet again.

Reports from the incident at her flat, filtered through his police contact, were inconclusive as to why she'd been there, but he knew. Why else would she risk going back? Whatever Grant had been in possession of, he has to presume she now has. He doesn't know specifics, just that Osgood says it's enough to sink them all. He's never seen his boss's anxiety spike like it has this past week or so. Having her new number doesn't give him a location, not yet anyway. He'll feed it in via his contact, but these things take time, and patience. Both in short supply. Time to apply some not so gentle pressure.

Clay gets out of the van. They've come to a disused patch of land down by the river, not far from Price's warehouse. A pitstop for now, while one of his men is off procuring more suitable premises for the next phase of his plan. Somewhere away from prying eyes.

The loss of his man in Manchester takes his core team down to seven now, plus himself, but he has a mental black book of names he can call on from his military days, men who never stood a chance of a normal life after what they have done and seen. Men who need this kind of work to still find meaning on civvy street. Two of them have been dispatched to the Durham address for Layt Brown. If Price tries to cross him, he'll remove the trumped-up little gangster from whatever regional two-bit pecking order he thinks he's top of, without so much as a glance in the rear-view mirror.

Down to more immediate business. He taps on the window of the car next to him, stooping to mutter instructions for the occupants. Lookout duty, nothing more. Doesn't expect things will get too out of control just yet, but pays to be careful. Quick check both ways. To his left, a five-storeyed block of flats. To his right, the quayside path stretches alongside the river. From this perspective, the Tyne Bridge looks trapped inside the arc of the closer Millennium Bridge. On the south bank, the Sage building squats, curving glass canopy glinting in the sunshine.

Clay opens up the back door of the van and hops inside. Three pairs of eyes greet him. Two of those sets are terrified, and he drinks it in. His own man gives a half-smirk of a greeting from his position, sat on a wooden box over a wheel arch. Moya and Julie Stephenson sit at the far end. Both have wrists and ankles pinned by cable ties. Matching rags stuffed in mouths and held in place with tape. Clay takes a seat on the opposite wheel arch to his man.

'These ladies behaving, Laurie?'

'Good as gold,' Laurie replies, scouse accent so thick you could do with subtitles at times.

'Good, good,' Clay flashes the sisters a smile. 'I do apologise about the accommodation ladies, but you've your sister Maggie to thank for this. Anyway, here's what's going to happen. Your sister has something that doesn't belong to her, and you're going to help persuade her to give it back. Let's give her quick tinkle, shall we?'

Clay pulls out his phone, calling the number Price gave him, selecting video call, and points the camera at Moya and Julie. It's as if the camera carries a charge. Both flinch as he taps the screen to adjust focus in the dim light of the windowless interior, nostrils flaring as they hyperventilate into their gags.

The message that pops up says call failed. Checks his phone, but it has full 5G signal. He tries a second time, same result. Third, fourth. Something must change in his face, harden as the call refuses to connect. Julie Stephenson turns into her sister, burying her face in Moya's shoulder. Both women are breathing hard through their noses. Their fear is a palpable thing, as if Clay can literally reach out and scoop a handful.

He tries a normal phone call this time. Same result. Her phone is either switched off, or somewhere out of signal. Clay weighs up his options. Decides on a simple voicemail.

'Mrs Brewer. So sorry we didn't manage to have a chat last night in Tynemouth. I'd really appreciate a call when you get a moment though. Got to go now, but I'll say hi to your sisters for you.'

Discreet enough that if the phone has fallen into other hands, the words mean little. To Maggie, though, each one will be a sharp stab with a cattle prod, poking her up out of whatever hole she's hunkering down in. Clay ends the call, walks closer to the women, squatting down just out of kicking range in case he's misjudged their fear.

'Don't worry, ladies. She doesn't strike me as the sort who would let her family suffer, so you'll get to see your sister soon enough. I'll let you in on a little secret, though,' he says, leaning a touch closer, voice dropping to a whisper. 'You're going to suffer anyway, whether she turns up or not.'

Clay watches both intently. Eyes widening, straining against cable ties that truss them up like chickens. He drinks in the muted screams, noise soaked up by their gags, reminding himself again that it's the small pleasures in life.

Chapter Seventy

'What do we do if he's not there?' I ask.

'The older we get, the more creatures of habit we become,' says Layt. 'According to his credit card statements, he's eaten lunch at the Oxford Golf Club every Wednesday as far back as I can see, even around the same time.'

'You've hacked his bank accounts?' Oxford is only minutes away, and the carriage we're in is far from crowded. The nearest person sits a good ten feet away, but I'm still worried my voice will carry.

Layt frowns. 'What? Oh, no, haven't had time for that, but I'm already inside the solicitor's servers, so I just did the same to the accountants they have on record for him. Bounced them a mail from the solicitor's account, and once they opened that it let me slide right in. They have email copies of his statements from his tax returns.'

'Remind me never to get on the wrong side of you,' I say. 'What then? I just stroll up to him on the tee box and say, "Excuse me Mr Osgood, please stop trying to kill me"?'

Layt looks at me, eyebrows raised. 'Actually, yeah, something along those lines. Although not on the course. I'm thinking we collar him in the car park. More people around. Like I said, for people like him, reputation is like trading stock. They'll do anything they can to avoid it going into freefall. When they finish a game, everyone generally sticks their clubs back in the car first, changes their shoes, and then they hit the club house. We catch him then.'

I give him half a grin. 'Didn't have you pegged as the golfing type.'

'My dad,' says Layt. 'Tried to get me into it. Yet another one chalked up in the "Why my son disappoints me" column. Used to make me caddy for him when he played with his friends.'

The mention of friends draws the smallest of sneers from him, and I feel a pang of pity, not for the first time. This young man, so talented in many ways, but sounds like he has just as complicated a relationship with his dad as my own.

'How do we record him then? I can't see him just spilling his guts in the car park.'

Layt shakes his head. 'Me neither. My guess is he'll ask you to hop in the car, drive somewhere else. That or try and arrange to meet you somewhere later. He tries either of those, you stand your ground. Can't give him time to call in the cavalry. Here, let me see your phone.'

I pass him the burner I bought at the service station a lifetime ago. Not exactly top of the range, but it has served its purpose. He traces a finger across app icons, shaking his head.

'Tell you what, use mine. Yours doesn't have any kind of voice memo or Dictaphone app.'

He passes me his handset, tossing mine onto the seat beside him, and shows me how to use it, adding my fingerprint so I can unlock it if needed.

'It'll keep recording even when the screen goes into standby. If you have the top of your bag open, microphone end pointing upwards, it should pick up everything just fine.'

The train guard's voice crackles over the PA system, giving us a two-minute-warning our stop is approaching, so we make a move to the vestibule, watching as the station slides into view. There's a chilled bite in the air as we hop out onto the platform, and I follow Layt's lead, ambling through the ticket barriers, and wait our turn in the taxi rank.

'Where will you be when I'm chatting to him?' I ask.

'I'll be literally a few minutes away up the road. Gonna offer the cabbie a few quid extra to wait for you in case we need a quick exit, so if anything spooks you, just turn around and head back out the gate and jump in. I'm just going to be in a Costa a half mile away. Need their Wi-Fi to finish something I started on the train. Don't worry if he spots the phone either. It auto-uploads to the cloud, so even if he makes a grab for it, it's all backed up.'

'He's in his seventies. Do you really think he's going to get physical himself when he has men to do that for him?'

'I'm just trying to cover all the bases,' Layt says, and I can feel the nerves coming off him in waves, even though it's me who'll be walking in there to confront Osgood. Talking through it now, I feel unnaturally calm. Maybe it's because there's an end in sight, however improbable; maybe it's because I'm not alone. Layt's sense of purpose is rubbing off on me, and I'm happy to ride the wave of confidence, however fleeting it might be. Happy to trust in his plan. In him.

A taxi glides to a halt in front of us, and we hop in, Layt haggling from the start about the extra time they need. He offers an extra ten pounds, the driver asks for twenty, and Layt pretends to huff and puff, but accepts, knowing he was already willing to pay. This will buy us half an hour of the engine running while I go inside. Anything bad that's going to happen, chances are it'd be far quicker than that.

It's only a fifteen-minute ride, and we use the time to lean in close, agree my approach. No danger of the cabbie eavesdropping, Eminem's greatest hits pumping through the car's speakers.

'I've been thinking about what you said,' I start. 'About his legacy. I'm thinking the best way is to try and come across like a true believer. Tell him I agree with what he's done, that I admire him for his work. You know the saying, keep your friends close—'

'And your enemies closer,' Layt nods. 'Like it!'

'Then I go with what you suggested, that I don't want to tear this down, that all I want is to walk away. Tell him I'm happy to hand over what I have, but that I need some assurances.'

'Spot on. If you can get him talking about why he started it in the first place, that'd be amazing. Gauge the mood, but might be worth asking him about his wife.'

I nod, feeling tension twist end over end in my gut, like it's a tangible thing skewered on a spit. We slow to a stop by the Costa on Cowley Road, and Layt gives my hand a quick squeeze before he jumps out.

'You got this,' he says, flashing a smile that fills his face but doesn't seem to reach his eyes. 'Here's some extra cash in case you need to buy more time.' He nods towards the oblivious driver, and I return the squeeze, watching him disappear into the coffee shop, wondering if I'll ever see him again.

Chapter Seventy-One

The golf course is less than a mile away, and the driver turns the music down a touch, tapping his watch to show the time, and how much of his I've bought for my money. The entrance and clubhouse look low-key and quite plain. Not the car park rammed with Range Rovers against a backdrop of pristine palatial buildings I'd expected.

Layt had made a call earlier, posing as a friend of Osgood's, asking if he was already in a four-ball, and whether the tee-off time either side of his was free. From that, an educated guess had him finishing anytime now. I pull out Layt's phone, taking another glance at the pictures they found of Osgood online, committing his features to memory.

He puts me in mind of Ian McKellen, albeit with a narrower nose, and dark-brown eyes in place of the actor's pale blue. The face of a murderer, or at least one who has ordered them. I make a beeline for the far end of the car park, figuring that gives me a vantage point to cover the entire area. I've already decided if anyone challenges me, I'm going to hit them with the truth of waiting to see Osgood, but hope that won't be necessary.

I prop myself against the trunk of a large oak tree, and check off the world's slowest minute on my watch. Five more follow, only a handful of people making their way in or out during them, none of them looking vaguely like Osgood. I'm almost ten minutes in, nerves starting to fizz in my gut like Alka-Seltzer, when I see him.

Osgood appears from behind the clubhouse, lost in conversation with two other men. Just the three of them, no security detail, no men in shades watching the perimeter. I scan the area, worried that I've missed something, that I'll hear shouts and pounding feet any second, but the three men just keep walking, bags slung over shoulders, splitting only by degrees to head to their respective cars. His is a good twenty yards clear of his nearest partner's, and before I can think too deeply about it, I'm moving, tapping the phone screen to start recording, closing the gap. Fifteen yards, ten.

He must sense me approaching, because he looks up when I'm five yards away, but there's no recognition there, no hostility, not even surprise. Only a tiny raise of the eyebrows as I come to a halt beside the rear door of his Lexus SUV.

'Mr Osgood?'

It's not that he looks older than the pictures, just more tired. Frayed around the edges, and a touch slimmer, as if any round edges have been filed away.

'Sorry, do we know one another?'

'I'm Maggie Brewer. Grant Brewer's wife.'

I stare at him, watching for a reaction, but there's nothing, not even at a micro level to suggest the names ring a bell.

'I'm sorry,' he says, hefting his clubs into the boot. 'You have me at a disadvantage. You know me, but your name doesn't ring a bell. Have we met?'

No time to waste. I can see one of the other men glancing their way.

'I need to speak to you about HELIX, Mr Osgood.'

That does get a response. Not much, just a slight crinkling around the eyes, but there nonetheless.

'Who did you say you were again?'

'Maggie Brewer. I'm the one you and your men have been chasing.'

'Men?' he laughs, looking around the car park. 'What men?'

'The same ones who killed my husband, and Dr Xiang, for what they knew.'

'And what exactly did they know?'

'About HELIX,' I say simply. 'About what you've built.'

'Frank,' a voice comes from over to their right, one of Osgood's golf buddies. 'You coming in?'

'I'll follow you in,' Osgood calls, eyes not leaving me. 'Order me a coffee, would you?'

I glance up in time to see both men disappear around the clubhouse corner, leaving the two of us alone.

'And what is it you want, Mrs Brewer?'

'I want my life back. I want to not be looking over my shoulder.'

'I wish I could help you, Mrs Brewer, but I'm afraid I don't know what you're talking about. Now, if you'll excuse me.'

Osgood pushes a button inside his boot, and the door begins to close. He doesn't wait for it, turning away towards the clubhouse, leaving me open-mouthed. Takes me a few seconds to regain my composure.

'I have proof,' I call after him.

Do I imagine it or does he slow, slight hitch in his step at my words? He doesn't stop though, so I call out again. 'Proof of what it is, what it does. Proof of how you've abused it to send innocent people to jail.'

He stops, turns around, walks slowly back towards me. 'What is it you think you have proof of, Mrs Brewer?'

'I know about Bishop Cartwright, and the Union man, Richard Judd. I know they were framed because they stood against you, against what you built, and why you built it.'

'And what exactly do you think I built?' he asks, coming closer still, just feet away now.

This man who once had the ear of the Prime Minister, who has had a hand on the rudder that steers the country. Even now, at his age, I can feel the force of his personality. He's sharp as a tack as well, not admitting anything, answering questions with questions. This isn't going how I planned it in my head. Come on, I scold myself. I've done a hundred interviews with people just as famous in their respective fields, for the paper. Know I need to build rapport, work my way in.

'Something amazing,' I force myself to say. 'Something brave. I'm sorry, I'm not coming across very well here. I don't want to make waves. This isn't about a story. This is about me getting mixed up in something I'd rather not have, and I wanted to tell you to your face, that if you can forget about me, I can forget about you, like this never happened.'

'What exactly do you think I've done to you?' Osgood asks, looking and sounding genuinely curious.

He glances around the car park again. It's a sure sign in my eyes that he doesn't want anyone within earshot. I ignore his question, heart pounding, not so much as laying my cards on the table as throwing them.

'As much as I admire what you've built, I have proof of the bribes and false convictions that happened along the way, and if I have to use them to get my life back I will, but I'd rather come to an arrangement.'

'Mrs Brewer, if that's what your proof is telling you, then you've been misinformed. HELIX is ...' he stops himself, and I worry for a moment that he's pulling himself back from the brink. 'It's none of those things. I've always wondered if anyone would ever catch wind of it, but let me assure you, it only exists for good, not for any of those things you're alleging. Least it was when I was at the helm, but I can promise you—'

'Wait, what do you mean, when you were at the helm? You're the CEO at IQ still.'

He smiles, a genuine warm expression that has likely won plenty of votes over the years. Osgood shakes his head.

'I stepped down a while back now, God, it must be coming up ten years.'

'I don't understand. Companies House still has you listed. I checked. Francis Matthew Osgood. Are you saying that's out of date?'

'No, he says, 'That's right, but there's more than one of us.'

I open my mouth to speak, but it's as if my brain has powered down. He's not making any sense.

'My son,' he says. 'He's a third-generation Francis Matthew. It's a family thing. He hates the Francis part though so he goes by his middle name. He's been calling the shots at IQ since I stepped down.'

Blind-sided. Again.

Chapter Seventy-Two

'I don't know exactly what this proof is you say you have, but I'm sure it's all some kind of misunderstanding,' Osgood says. 'I can call Matthew and have this all straightened out.'

'Wait, so you're telling me you've had nothing to do with IQ or HELIX for almost a decade?'

'Not directly, no. I had a health scare back then. Heart attack. Ended up with five stents for my trouble,' he says, patting his chest. 'So I handed over to Matthew on doctor's orders. He still asks for the occasional bit of advice, but apart from that, he steers the ship. Now, I know you said you lost your husband recently, but if you're going to start repeating these allegations anywhere other than a car park, you'd better have a good lawyer on retainer.'

'He was murdered,' I say softly.

'Beg your pardon?'

'I didn't lose him,' I say, hint of venom in my voice. 'He was murdered.'

Osgood isn't easy to read. He sounds convincing, but he was a politician for a long time. Comes with the territory. If what he's saying is true, it doesn't change the play. It's still about legacy, just depends how much sway father holds over son, assuming that is, that Osgood senior is as distanced from all this as he claims.

'He was murdered because he uncovered the truth behind HELIX. That it's not just being used to line your family pockets, but that somebody, your son I assume seeing as he's steering the ship,' I sling his own phrase back at him with interest, 'had him killed to keep him quiet. Him and two of your own scientists, because IQ has been buying its way through regulations and red tape for years, using what you've built to put people behind bars, or worse, if they get in your way. You're telling me you know nothing about this? Whatever.' I say holding up my hands. 'But everything I've told you is a fact, and we have documented proof of it. So you need to call your son, and tell him to sod off and leave me be, 'cos if anything happens to me, everything gets emailed to every major paper in the country.'

I'm panting by the time I finish spitting it all out. Anger, fear, frustration, all of it channelled into my words. His eyes are fixed on mine, a hard, flat stare that carries an actual weight to it. A couple of seconds tick by, a Mexican standoff in suburban Oxford. I'm about to tell him again that he needs to call his son, when my phone goes. Not mine as such, but Layt's. I'm puzzled for a moment as to why my own name flashes across the screen, then realise it has to be Layt calling from my handset.

'Do you need to take that?' he asks.

I'm paralysed by indecision for a few seconds, but Layt knows I'm likely mid-conversation, and the worry as to why he's calling wins out. I take a half turn away as I answer, but keep Osgood in my peripheral vision.

'I'm kind of in the middle of something,' I half-whisper. 'Is everything alright?'

He sounds as if someone has pressed the fast-forward button, like there's some kind of pressure forcing the words out at a pace. I listen to a hastily delivered monologue, trying to keep a neutral expression, but what he's telling me feels like the equivalent of hosing gasoline over an already roaring fire. I promise to call him the moment I leave the club, end the call, and turn back to face Osgood, heart thumping out a double-time rhythm.

'Look, why don't you come inside for a coffee, and whatever you think you know, we can sit down and talk this through. I'm sorry about your husband, but what-ever this is, you've got it all back to front. HELIX saves lives, not takes them. Taking this public now can only hurt people.'

I nod, not trusting myself to speak as I process what Layt has shared. He gestures towards the club, and he's covered half the distance before I move to join him. Again, not how I saw this panning out. But he does seem so genuine. Plus if this is true about his son, I might be talking to the wrong man entirely. The information Layt has armed me with now is nothing short of dropping a depth charge into a puddle if I'm not careful. Best to hear what he has to say first, then ruin his life afterwards.

Chapter Seventy-Three

Osgood grabs his coffee from his golfing buddy, orders one for me, then leads me to the far end of the large open-plan lounge. Not private in the true sense, but nobody within fifty feet.

'You've made some pretty strong allegations, Mrs Brewer. This proof you say you have; can I see it?'

I open an app Layt has showed me, copies of emails, accounts, payments, all converted to PDF's. I lay the handset on the table, facing towards him and flick through, watching his face as I do. It's a struggle to read him, his face about as expressive as an Easter Island statue. Finally, when I stop scrolling he sits back in his chair, crosses one leg over the other, and sips at coffee in a cup tattooed with the club crest. Everything about him oozes control.

'Most of what you've shown me is easily faked,' he says finally. 'Assuming I believed a word of what you're selling here, what is it you think I can do to help you?'

'You can choose to believe me or not, Mr Osgood, but in the last week I've lost my husband, almost lost my brother, been shot at, had people I know hurt, killed even, and all because of what you built. If your son is in charge now, maybe he's the man I need to speak to, but either I get my life back, or I swear to God, I'll burn it all to the ground. You spent a career in politics, spinning stories to get people's support. You look at me and tell me, do I look like I'm lying?'

He says nothing, just stares at me over his cup.

'I'll be honest, I don't even care who publishes. Even if it's only the *Sunday Sport*, as long as it gets out there. Now, if you're telling me you've no knowledge of this, then surely you should want to get to the bottom of this too. I mean you built something...' I pause, hoping he takes it as me just searching for the right words, in reality, psyching myself up to praise the institution that killed my husband. 'Something incredible. I mean, how many lives are better for having had treatment that's stemmed from HELIX-inspired research? But that's not the main part is it? Not for you?'

Another pause, wanting to soften the tone, strike a chord that taps into the reason I think he started all of this decades ago.

'I read about your wife. About what happened to her. How they didn't catch the man who did it, at least not back then. If you'd asked me a couple of weeks ago, I'd have said I can't even imagine what you went through. Now though, after Grant was ...' I feel tears threatening to pop in both eyes, taking a deep breath to steady myself. 'Since he was killed, it's like this constant sense of a gaping hole next to me, like someone's cut him out of a photo, you know?'

Osgood lays down his cup, resting hands palms down on the armrests. His mouth is a tight line, dark eyes like burnt treacle fixed on me.

'HELIX has helped so many, not just the medical side, though. The idea that so many people have been punished thanks to what you built, that might have otherwise got away with it, like Ossie Reynolds, that's something you can be proud of.'

The false praise sticks in my throat, but the mention of his wife's killer hit home, sinking its barbs in deep.

'Took too long for that man to get his comeuppance,' he says. 'Wondered what he would look like every damn day of it. When it came to it, he wasn't some hideous-looking monster. Just a scruffy bum looking to score some easy cash to shoot up his arm.' Osgood is looking off to one side now, not at me or the lounge but at a thirty-year-old memory.

'But they caught him in the end, thanks to HELIX.'

Osgood nods. 'God only knows what other crimes he committed by the time he was arrested. Might never have been stopped if it wasn't for HELIX.'

'End justifies the means,' I agree. 'But someone, and I'm not saying it's your son, has twisted what you built. Warped it into something darker, something way beyond anything you'd dreamed. People have been targeted, Mr Osgood. Sent down for crimes they didn't commit, just because they opposed some of the more extreme types of research IQ wanted to invest in. That's a fact.'

Osgood shakes his head. 'That's an awful lot of maybes and what-ifs,' he says. 'HELIX doesn't just point a random finger. Without a sample on the police side, there's nothing to match against in HELIX.'

'We have audit trails, copies of change logs where their samples were linked to crimes they swear they didn't commit. Samples that your records show were used to generate additional genetic material for research purposes. Material that couldn't be accounted for at a later date, and could have been left at a scene, knowing it was guaranteed a hit when police ran it against the national database.'

Osgood sits forward now, jaw muscles clenching. 'Now you listen here, HELIX was set up by a handful of the finest scientific minds in the world at the time. It's been looked after by more of the same over the years. They're not a bunch of criminals looking to make a fast buck. These are doctors, professors, men of science. There are fail-safes built in to stop anyone tampering, and I can tell you now that nothing like that happened on my watch, nor would it happen on Matthew's. Now I suggest we sort this out once and for all before you go spouting this nonsense to someone who's stupid enough to print it. I'm calling my son, and whatever threat you think you're under from IQ, we can straighten this out.'

He starts to root around in his jacket pocket for his phone.

'I don't think that's a good idea, Mr Osgood.'

'And I don't think it's a good idea to let lies go unchecked,' he says, nostalgia evaporating, replaced by irritation. 'Whoever has fed you this rubbish needs to stop playing on the emotions of a recently widowed woman. I'm sure we can come to an arrangement as you put it, a donation to your husband's favourite charity, that type of thing. Of course, we can just pass it to you and trust that you'll make sure it gets to where it needs to be.'

He flashes a self-satisfied smirk as he pulls his phone out. I force myself not to glance down at my bag, where the phone sits passively recording the lot. What's on there isn't everything I had hoped for. No admission of guilt as such, but confirmation that HELIX exists, and that he is its creator. Time to light the fuse Layt has just given me, and see how big the blast radius is.

'Before you do, Mr Osgood, there's something else you should know.'

'What is it?' he snaps, clearly past the limits of whatever patience he'd had.

'It's a lie, all of it.'

'So you admit it?' he says, triumphant gleam in his eyes.

'No, not what I've told you today. That's true, all of it. No, I mean HELIX is a lie. It's all built on one huge lie.'

His face colours now, anger flowing into puffed-out pink cheeks. 'I built it to honour my wife,' he says through gritted teeth. 'I built it because no matter how much money we had, I couldn't buy justice, at least not in the right way, so I built HELIX instead. Now you dare to try and drag that, and her memory, into the mud with some crackpot conspiracy theory? I think you'd better leave. Now.'

I'm losing him. He's gone from listening, to humouring, is shifting now to disbelieving anger. I blurt out the last piece as he rises to his feet.

'Your wife's killer, his DNA was uploaded in HELIX by the same person who uploaded the two others I mentioned. One single sample, not a mass upload from a load of used needles. Almost everyone else, millions, were put there in huge batches. Not these ones.'

Osgood's mouth twists into a snarl, ready to repeat his order no doubt, when something changes. A look of mild confusion creeps over him.

'That doesn't make any sense,' he says, soft shake of the head. 'Only time we ever did singles or smaller numbers was when we added the staff in. Who uploaded them?'

'It was a doctor,' I say. 'Dr Alston Myers.'

Chapter Seventy-Four

Myers knows Matthew Osgood is unravelling. He's always known the man could be unstable in the right circumstances, but these past few weeks, it's been like someone has tugged a loose thread on a jumper, and now there's more yarn than clothing left. Myers doesn't fully trust him. Hasn't for some time. Matthew isn't half the man his father is, or at least was when he was still a regular sight around these parts. Since the invite was extended to The Six, Osgood has been noticeably absent. Myers can't help but think whatever he's planning, it won't end well, and he needs to make sure that calmer heads prevail. He for one stands to lose a lot more than just money if things fall apart.

Myers ambles along the corridor to his office, nodding to the handful of staff he sees along the way. Gone are the days when he could move much faster. Two hip surgeries, and a love of fine food has hobbled him to the point where he feels his age the moment he sits up in bed these days.

If he'd led any other life, he would have retired years ago to somewhere a damn sight warmer than Milton Keynes. But his work is his life. He's joked in the past that he'll die in his lab, but these days it feels more and more a possibility. The thought that one woman could bring this crashing down is enough to churn his insides on spin cycle. He has sacrificed way too much over the years, personally and professionally, to let that happen.

It's never been about the money or power for Myers. It's about pushing boundaries. For that to happen, secrets need to stay buried. His have layers that not even Osgood is aware of. Ones that if a light was shone on them, could bring it all crashing down like a house of cards in a category five hurricane.

The rate at which this is spinning out of control makes him nervous about waiting until Osgood's five p.m. deadline, let alone midnight. No, this needs halting in its tracks now. Just like a basic chemical reaction, add an accelerant, stand back and watch things on fast forward.

HELIX houses over sixty million records, but only a handful are of enough concern for him to have an alert that flags any access. Ossie Reynolds is one such record. Myers glances at his phone again as he opens the door to his office, lowering himself into his well-worn chair. The notification that came through tells him just that the file was opened, and when. Should have told him who, but that field is worryingly blank. An outsider then, and that can only be Maggie Brewer. Anyone else, for it to happen right at this exact moment, the odds are astronomical.

Myers is about to make the call to a number only he and Osgood possess, but his phone lights up before he can. A familiar name, but another coincidence that grates against his growing sense of unease. He isn't aware he's holding his breath until the screen winks off again, call unanswered. He hasn't spoken to Frank Osgood in months. Osgood senior isn't a man you ignore, but there's somebody else he needs to speak to first, before calling back.

Declan Clay answers on the second ring.

'Well, if it isn't the good doctor. To what do I owe the pleasure?'

'Do you know where she is yet?'

'Straight to the point,' Clay says. 'Not yet, but it'll be done by end of today.'

'Not that I doubt your abilities, Mr Clay, but there's been a change of plans.'

'Oh, how so?'

'I need you to bring the sisters here. When you track her down, she needs to come here, or somewhere nearby anyway. I need to speak to her personally, to understand how she and her husband compromised our firewalls.'

There's a pause, Clay is no fool, and the holes in Myers' logic are big enough to drive a bus through.

'Safer if you let me do that from a distance,' he says. 'Also, not really your area of expertise.'

'It needs to be here,' Myers presses his case. 'It's not enough that she admits it, I need to know how, and the architecture of HELIX is my area of expertise.'

Another pause. 'And Mr Osgood is on board with this change I presume?'

'Mr Osgood is a little distracted at the moment,' Myers admits. 'He's not seeing the bigger picture. It's up to the likes of you and me to fix this. I know you're a practical man, Mr Clay, so let me put it in plain terms. We pay you and your team well for the work you do, and you do it exceptionally well, even if you might not like who you do it for at times, am I right?'

At times, Clay's disdain for Matthew Osgood has been about as subtle as a bat across the head, the seconds of silence that follows his question confirming this.

'If you do as I ask, you'll have enough money that you never have to take orders from him again, or anyone else for that matter, if you don't want to. Assuming it stays between us that is.'

'Well, we wouldn't want to stress Mr Osgood out any more than he already is, would we? Of course, depends on what kind of number we're talking here.'

Clay is already a hired hand, and everyone has a price. Myers gives him a number, large by any ordinary estimation, knowing Clay will ask for more, but thanks to IQ, Myers is rich beyond most people's dreams. This is a drop in the ocean compared to what he stands to lose.

The Irishman does indeed barter, asking for 50 per cent extra, and they settle on thirty, although Myers would have paid asking price if Clay had dug his heels in. He agrees to pay 20 per cent now, balance on delivery.

'You have somewhere private we can meet?' Myers asks.

'I'll text you the address,' says Clay. 'Meet you there in four hours. If all goes to plan, won't just be Maggie Brewer you get to chat with.'

Clay explains about her helper, a young man he believes is the brains behind the actual breach. That it may not just be Maggie who turns up to a meeting.

'Well, we'll cross that bridge when we come to it,' Myers says, all the while thinking he'll happily throw Maggie and her friend off the very same bridge. 'I'll have the funds over to you in the next hour.'

Myers takes a moment before making his next call. Closes his eyes, centres himself, reminds himself that what he's built, everything he's done, it's not just a job; it's a calling. One he's already sacrificed so much for. The lines he's crossed in the name of progress. Legal, moral, ethical. What's a few more cracked eggs when the omelette is already made?

He taps to return Osgood's call. Hears the click after only a couple of rings, and forces a smile, hoping it'll make him sound more relaxed, less forced.

'Frank! Long time no speak.'

'Alston, it's been too long,' Osgood sounds a little quiet, but Myers forces himself to stop overanalysing.

'How are you keeping, Frank? Still isn't the same here without you.'

'I'm … good. Getting more golf in than I have in decades. You? No sign of retiring yet?'

'Ah you know me,' Myers cracks out the favourite cliché, 'they'll have to carry me out of there in a box.'

A sprinkling of polite laughter at both ends of the line.

'Ah, anyway, reason for my call is I was thinking of swinging by and seeing Matthew. I thought I'd buy you a late lunch.'

'Lunch? Today? Ah, I'm afraid it's not a good time.' Myers feels a prickle of perspiration. 'I'll be in the lab all day.'

'You've got any one of a dozen young brains who can handle that for you,' Osgood says, in a tone Myers remembers well over the years. 'I've booked us a table at the Westerbury for four p.m. See you there.'

Myers starts to stammer another excuse but he's talking to a dead line. Obstinate bastard that he is, Osgood always gets the last word. Always has in the forty-plus years the two have known each other. Myers knows if he isn't there, Osgood will most likely rock up at the lab in person. Today of all days, he needs this like a hole in the head.

He checks his watch. A little after two p.m. Time to meet and shoot the breeze with Frank, then be ready to meet Clay. Myers places his phone face down on his desk. Closing his eyes once more, feeling the weight of every single one of his seventy-eight years. Maybe he should walk away after this. Enjoy the fruits of his labour while he still can. But for him to do that, Maggie Brewer and her sisters will have to be silenced, permanently. Not a part of this he enjoys, but on his own set of scales, worth the sacrifice.

Chapter Seventy-Five

'There hasn't been a day that I don't miss Catriona,' Francis Osgood says, and I see the damp sheen in his eyes at the mention of his wife's name. 'You'd think with who I am, who I was at the time, that they'd not have given up, kept looking.'

'They just stopped?' I ask.

'Not for a while, but yes, after a few months, the updates weren't as regular. Other cases took priority, and she just ... she just didn't matter as much to them. Then, it didn't matter who I was, or how much money I had, I was ... helpless.'

'I'm sorry,' I offer a token apology. 'That must have been awful.'

'Matthew barely spoke for a year after it happened. Took hours of counselling to get back to any sense of normality, but something like this, it never goes away. It's like an echo, you know. Everywhere around you. The way people act around you, little things in the house that belonged to her. Then about six months after it happened, I had a conversation that changed everything.'

'How do you mean?'

'Everything I'm about to tell you is off the record. You print a word of it, and I'll deny it before you have time to say "defamation".'

I nod, not stupid enough to argue back and cut short what he's about to share.

'I was approached by Alston Myers. He was a senior member of staff on the Chief Medical Officer's team at the time. He and I had clashed a year or so before, funnily enough over the kind of cutting-edge work IQ has been sponsoring for years now. DNA was still largely an unknown quantity as far as policing went, and what he'd proposed was a mandatory database. We're talking a good ten years or more before the national one was founded. I'd voted against it, and made sure plenty of others did too. Just didn't feel right, you know. Of course, that was before Catriona. Things looked a little different after that.'

'So, he asked you to support him again?'

'Not publicly. There had been far too much noise in Westminster the first time around. No, what he proposed was more of a private venture for the public good. He would provide the scientific know-how, plus a carefully selected staff. I would provide the funds, and use my connections to help build it.'

'Where do you even start with something that huge?' I ask, fascinated to finally hear it confirmed, the very organisation that's torn my life apart.

'Started out as a military thing. Back then the combined size was over quarter of a million across Army, Navy and Air Force. When he pitched it that second time, he was knocking on an open door. The inner circle was kept small. I called in favours with the Heads of the Armed Forces branches to gather samples as part of routine check-ups. Part of the pitch was the promise of research into the genetics of a perfect soldier. That plus some genuine cutting-edge medical research. He painted such a pure picture to bait me, that I found it hard to say no. The chance to make sure that no family ever had to

357

go through what mine did. The work that Alston got to do on top of that was the cherry on the cake, but what I did, I did for my wife and son.'

'When you called him just there, how did he sound?'

'Nervous,' Osgood nods.

'My um, associate,' I choose my words carefully, no point in giving away freebies. 'He took a look at Mr Reynolds's background. He'd spent quite a few years on the streets, in and out of shelters. Wasn't registered with a GP. He'd never served in the Forces. How do you suppose Dr Myers ended up with his sample?'

My mind is racing away with the possibilities, but I need to get Osgood to align of his own accord. He can't feel coerced or fed a line. The deeper I lead him into this rabbit hole, the more convinced his reactions have me that while he may be part of the HELIX inner circle, he hasn't been part of whatever arm of it is hunting me.

Osgood's frown is deep, like furrows ploughed in a field. 'That is something I'll be sure to ask him in person.'

'Would someone of his standing usually upload anything?'

'No,' he admits. 'That would be unusual.'

'And for the man who convinced you to finance HELIX, to be the one linked to your wife's killer,' I shake my head, chewing on my lip, 'I mean, what are the odds of that?'

'What exactly are you insinuating? That Alston somehow set this Reynolds up?'

'That'd be something you'd have to ask him in person,' I say, reflecting his own words back at him, 'but I know it'd be a pretty big leap of faith if that was me, to think that the two aren't linked.'

'I've known him for over forty years all told,' Osgood says, but I see from the pained expression it's more of a reflex comment. 'I'll put it to him. I owe him that much.'

There's a sadness to him now, not just his words, but scored into the lines of his face. A man slowly allowing himself to come to terms with the idea that he's been used, exploited by someone he trusted.

'You mentioned it started with the Forces,' I ask. Worth seeing what else I can get him to confirm while the doubt is seeping in. 'How on earth did you manage to build the rest of it without anyone knowing?'

His reply sounds distracted. 'Alston used his influence to change how the NHS track vaccinations, and dispose of sharps. Every single one is barcoded, and once given, they're sealed in a pouch for disposal. MMR has been given out since the seventies, so that was easy to piggyback on. By the time I handed over to Matthew, we already had over eighty per cent coverage. I'd imagine once COVID hit and more or less everyone was vaccinated, it'll be high nineties now. We don't actually need everybody's,' he says, looking almost apologetic. 'If you have brothers or sisters in there, they'd show as a familial hit. We had teams of lab assistants at different locations, working around the clock, thinking they were sequencing anonymous voluntary samples for military use. All covered by the Official Secrets Act of course.'

His golfing buddies have long since disappeared, leaving just the two of us behind.

'You said that the only time smaller batches were uploaded were when the staff had theirs done?'

'Alston's idea. Everyone had to be all in, offer their own up in exchange for a place on his team. Something about making them part of it, more invested I suppose.'

I take a deep breath, then toss the final piece of information Layt shared. A grenade with the pin already pulled. I watch as it hits home, burying deep like shrapnel. See the change on Osgood's face, cycling through disbelief, settling on something more like grim determination, right where I need him.

Chapter Seventy-Six

Food is a passion of his, and the restaurant at the Westerbury is one of Alston Myers' favourite places to eat. Today though, as he follows the waiter to their table, it feels strange, unfamiliar even. He's fifteen minutes early, but Francis Osgood has beaten him here, and he can't shake the feeling that Osgood is eyeing him up like an entrée. As he approaches, Osgood stands, smooths down his tie, and offers a hand.

'Alston, how the devil are you?'

Seems a warm-enough greeting, genuine smile. 'I'm good, Frank,' he says, going for the more familiar address. 'So lovely to see you again.'

They take their seats, exchange pleasantries, and Osgood pushes a glass of red across the table towards him. They settle into an easy rhythm. Safe topics. How they're both not as young as they once were, whether the new chef, still saddled with the tag after two years, has lived up to expectations, and how the current PM couldn't govern his way out of a cul-de-sac. Myers drains his glass quickly, gratefully accepting a second, feeling its warmth start to melt the tension from his neck and shoulders. Just this one more, he promises himself, just to steady the ship.

He starts to swirl the dark cherry-coloured liquid around his glass when Osgood drops in the most casual of conversational bombs.

'I had an interesting chat today,' he says, refreshing his own glass. 'Someone asking me about Ossie Reynolds, if you can believe that after all these years.'

'Here's to his continued incarceration,' Myers raises his in toast, feeling the first whispers of doubt creeping into his comfortable glow.

'Funny thing is, this person I spoke to, they don't think he should have been put there in the first place.'

Myers screws up his face in shared outrage. 'That's ridiculous. We know how sound that conviction was – is, even,' he corrects himself. 'Who the hell have you been talking to?' he asks, only noticing now, that Osgood didn't return the toast.

'They've asked me to keep that between the two of us for now, but I must confess, it's more than a little troubling.'

'What about the evidence against him?' Myers protests. 'They literally found his skin under her fingernails.'

Osgood nods, as if considering this for the first time. 'They found skin, yes.'

'Well then, whoever this is, Frank, tell them to scuttle off back under their rock and stop raking up old memories.'

'Do you know the most interesting thing, though,' he says, tapping a finger idly against the base of his glass. 'They mentioned a name. The person who had uploaded Reynolds into HELIX. Very bizarre, done as a one off.'

Myers bites down on his tongue. Knows what's coming but fights to keep a neutral expression. Takes another sip.

'The name they gave was yours, Alston.'

He does his best to work through the expected emotions. Shock, denial, outrage. All the while, conscious of Osgood's constant scrutiny.

'Where are they getting this from?' he blusters. 'I mean, it's possible, I've not done many compared to the sampling teams, but we've all mucked in at one time or another, especially back in the early days.'

'Perhaps,' Osgood concedes, 'but then again, this isn't just any old sample, is it?'

'Well, no, obviously, but—'

'We've done good work over the years, Alston. I mean, on top of the medical side of things. All those people who would have walked away scot-free if HELIX hadn't provided a match. Even now, I still believe what we did was right, that it needed doing no matter how distasteful some might view it as. What are the odds, though, of all the millions of samples, that you of all people handled my wife's killer's, and in a single transaction at that?'

It's only a few seconds of silence, but Myers can feel the weight of every one of them, draped heavy across the table like a wet blanket. This conversation has always been a possibility, one he's played out in his mind, but now it's here he's temporarily tongue-tied. When he eventually speaks, it rings overly jovial in his own ears.

'Pretty huge I'd say. I mean, wow, what are the odds indeed? Might have a better chance with a lottery ticket.'

'Wouldn't it have occurred to you to mention it at the time?'

'Huh? No, well, of course, I would have if I'd known, even just to say what a crazy coincidence it was.'

'And you didn't know?'

'Of course not! I'd have said if I did.'

'You know, I think back to those early days. Back when we knew it worked, but we were still surprised at just how well. You remember?'

'I do,' Myers nods, feeling one foot back on firmer ground.

'I remember the data we used to feed back to the other members of The Six. Validation of us having made the tough choices.'

'They were a tough crowd to please outside of their own self-interest,' he admits.

'I remember us poring over them. Thing is Alston, that data included every name of every subject we fed to the police. A list that included Ossie Reynolds. I remember seeing him on there, clear as if it were yesterday. I remember you were there that day, telling me you were so proud that what we'd built had helped catch him. Now are you still telling me you don't remember?'

'I … ahm … I don't know what you want me to say, Frank. I don't. Honest to God, I don't. I mean look at me, I'm nearly eighty. Sometimes I can't remember what I had for breakfast,' he says, knowing they both see it for the lie that it is.

Osgood nods, hard to read what he's thinking. There are a hundred places Myers would rather be than here, now, with Frank. Already his mind is racing ahead. Has to be Maggie Brewer Frank has spoken with. He'll know for sure if Clay does his job. Only question then will be what she's shared with Frank apart from suspicions.

'I know we've been through a lot together, Alston. Worked with some powerful people, all of whom have their own agendas. Some of which I've not always seen eye to eye with. I might be retired, but I'm still a good man to have in your corner. If there's anything you need to tell me, anyone who has maybe put pressure on you, maybe someone who needed Reynolds adding to HELIX at the right moment, now would be the time.'

Myers shakes his head, giving Osgood a look as if he'd just suggested they strip and streak through the restaurant.

'Frank, you have my word, whoever is feeding you this, I don't know what they're talking about. Look, if it makes you happy, I'll gladly log on when I get back in and see what I can see on Reynolds's file. See if it's been compromised in any way.'

Osgood smiles warmly, nodding graciously. 'That'd be appreciated.'

'Speaking of which,' Myers tips his glass up, 'I really should get going. I'll give you a call, though.'

Osgood rises, shaking hands again. 'You sure you can't stay for a bite?'

'I'd love to, but you know how it is. These youngsters have a tendency to make more cock-ups when the grown-ups aren't there to supervise.'

Myers picks his way through tables, back towards the door. Can't help a last glance over at Frank before he disappears from view. Nothing he said gave an ounce of credence to Frank's insinuations. Everything is fine, he tells himself. One more day then this will be over. Normality restored.

Why is it then, that Frank looks oddly satisfied? As if he got exactly what he came for?

Chapter Seventy-Seven

'What did he say?' Layt asks as I end the call.

'He met with him. Said he was about as jumpy as a kangaroo on steroids.'

'He said that?'

I shrug. 'I may have paraphrased. He said it was all a bit uncomfortable, but he did what we talked about. Should know for sure in a few hours.'

'Wow, that fast?'

'He still has plenty of sway there apparently.'

'You still think he's on the level?'

I nod. 'How he sounded there, the look on his face when I told him what you'd found out. Yeah, I think it's worked its way deep enough that he has to know for sure now.'

He had looked angry. I don't think he could fake that kind of angry. Not shouty sweary anger. More of a cold, barely contained fury.

'Not one to be too pessimistic, but I still say we move on. If there's even a tiny chance he comes down on the wrong side of this, this'll be their new starting point for finding us.'

I've joined him in Costa. Safety in numbers, but more prying eyes and ears.

'Okay, lets head back to the station. We can decide where when we get there. Oh, let me check in with Davey first, see how he's doing.'

I hold my hand out for my handset back, the other offering him his in return. He looks at it, something inscrutable about his expression. A pause that doesn't belong, before he reaches into his pocket and makes the trade.

'Maggie, look, there's something I need to tell you.'

'Sounds serious,' I say, curiosity piqued.

'While you were away, there was a message came through. A voicemail, and a text actually, from a number not a name. Text said the offer on the voicemail had an expiration of one hour, and I, well I didn't know for sure how long you'd be, so I had a listen.'

I give him a quizzical look, seeing the very same text in my inbox, cryptic as *The Times* crossword. I flick to the calls list, see the last dialled one for voicemail and click to listen.

The voice makes my skin crawl. Soft, sibilant. Settling over me the way a spider steps onto its web. At the mention of my sisters, the next breath catches in my throat. I swipe frantically to my short contacts list, call Davey and glare at Layt as it rings.

'You knew about this since I got back,' I hiss. 'If anything's happened to them—' Davey's voice cuts in before I can finish.

'Mags, thank God you're still okay.'

'Davey – Moya and Julie, I think they're in danger.'

He pauses a beat, and I know then that I'm too late. I listen as he lays out what little they know. Last seen leaving the hospital together. Dad had been round earlier to see Moya. Found the door open, and signs of a struggle. Julie's car was still outside. Too early for police to get involved.

'He's got them, Davey. The Irishman from the roof at Tynemouth.'

'I'll fucking kill him if I get my hands on him,' he snarls, but I hear the strain in his voice. Body still recovering.

An even more horrific thought seeps into my mind. If they've taken my sisters, Mam and Dad are surely in danger too.

'What if they come for Mam and Dad next?' I ask him. 'Or you again?'

'Speak to Gregor,' Davey says, 'Get him to bring in reinforcements and keep an eye on everyone.'

I debate not telling him I've done a runner, but best he hears it from me.

'Jesus, Maggie, why? He can protect you.'

'I don't trust him, Davey. He was looking for an angle, some way he can profit from this, just like he always does.'

'Maggie, I know you and he have never got on, but it's not like you're spoiled for choice here. He promised me he'd take care of you, and I trust him. Please, call him, if not for your sake then do it for me.'

'I don't know, Davey.'

I know what he doesn't. That his belief in Gregor is built on foundations no sturdier than those underpinning Francis Osgood's trust in his former organisation right now. Not for the first time, I toy with ripping off the plaster, telling him why I, and he, should never trust Gregor. Too much going on to get into this now, and I tuck it away for another time.

'If not him, then what other option have you got?'

'Only one,' I say feeling the shiver slink down the kinks in my spine. 'I need to call the Irishman.'

Chapter Seventy-Eight

'I was beginning to wonder if something had happened to you,' Clay says, and I can picture that half-smirk of his, the one I saw right before he blew Christopher Xiang's head across my screen.

'I want to see my sisters.' I cut to the chase, determined I won't let him catch a whiff of the fear that surrounds me like an aura.

'Then we're aligned,' he says. 'Lovely ladies. They've been perfect guests. They're keen to see you too.'

'Where are they? I want to speak to them.'

The line goes quiet, and I'm wondering if he's hung up when I hear a sound that makes my heart sing. Moya swearing.

'Watch where you're putting your hands you pervy bastard.'

She sounds a million miles away at first, but then all of a sudden, she's right there, voice so clear it's like I can reach out and touch her.

'Mags? Mags? Is that you?'

'Moya,' I gasp, nodding even though she can't see me. 'Are you okay? Have they hurt you? Is Julie with you?' Questions tumble out and there's a hitch in my breath that I do my best to dampen down. I need to sound strong for her.

'I'm okay,' she says, sounding far from it. Far quieter than she was when she berated her captors just now. 'We both are. What about you?'

I smile through rapidly filling eyes. Ever the big sister, more worried about me than her own safety.

'I'm fine. I'm going to fix this, Moya, I promise. I'm going to—'

She cuts across me. 'Do what you need to, but don't you dare tell these pricks where you are. You hear me. We'll be fine. Don't you dare.'

There's a series of grunts and curses, and I can't avoid the picture popping to mind of Moya manhandled.

'My brother is going to snap you in half,' I hear her yell.

'Your brother's been taken care of,' a response comes from a voice I don't recognise.

The thought of Davey in a hospital bed lights a fire in my belly. One fierce enough to burn it all to the ground – Clay, Osgood, the whole bloody lot of them.

'Moya!' I yell into the phone. 'Moya, can you hear me? If you can hear me, I'm going to fix this.'

But there's no reply. She's not there anymore. The next voice I hear is Clay.

'Put her back on,' I say with far more steel in my voice than I feel.

'No.'

'Put Julie on then,' I snap. 'You want me to play ball, let me speak to her as well.'

'Maggie, Maggie, this isn't like Hollywood where we pretend you've got any real bargaining power. Just boils down to what matters more to you. Seeing them again in one piece as opposed to many, or chasing after this pipedream story of yours? And I'm gonna need an answer before we finish this call or I'll choose for you.'

Lose–lose. Give him what he wants and Grant died for nothing. Don't, and my sisters go the same way. I've seen him work now. Know he isn't one to bluff. It's no real choice, and I give the only answer I can.

'What do I have to do?'

'That's my girl. I knew you'd see sense. Let's start by getting yourself down to Milton Keynes by tomorrow morning.'

'I can do that,' I say, wondering if I'll hear back from Osgood by then, or if it'll all be over by the time he tries to reach me.

'I'll text you an address,' Clay continues. 'Oh, and Maggie, like I said, this isn't Hollywood, so I don't need to ask you not to call the police, or do anything stupid now, do I?'

'I'll be there.'

'That's my girl,' he says again, paternalistic yet patronising. 'Feel free to bring your little friend too. Be lovely to meet him too.'

'My ... my friend?'

'Layt, isn't it? Say hi from me.'

With that, the line goes dead. I stare across at Layt, anger still simmering, and take more pleasure than I should telling him about his invite to the party.

'Fuck!' is all he can manage, then regroups. 'I'm sorry, Maggie, I just didn't want to throw you off your game while you were with Osgood.'

'Throw me off? We're talking about my sisters here. God only knows what he'll do to them. What he might have done already.'

'You know it's a one-way ticket if we meet him, right?'

'What else can I do?'

'He's not going to let any of us walk away from this, Maggie. Not you, not me and not your sisters.'

'I know,' she says softly. 'But I still have to go.'

'No, you don't,' he says, reaching over to take her hand in his. '*We* do.'

Chapter Seventy-Nine

On the outskirts of Milton Keynes, the surface of Willen Lake is practically a mirror, the gentlest of breezes dragging the occasional finger across. I check my watch. Twenty minutes until the allotted meeting time.

'Any sign?'

Layt's voice comes through the Air Pod in my right ear as if he's inches away.

'Not yet,' I reply, strolling past an open grassy expanse to my right. Google Maps showed it as Willen maze. No hedges though, more like work paths, like outlines of Inca ruins. A hundred metres or so ahead, the path cuts right at ninety degrees to the water, and I see a white pagoda, raised sandstone base and walkway, flanked by stone lions. The park is eerily quiet, but then again it is a weekday morning, rest of the world at work, chugging along in the daily routines, while I struggle to find a way back to mine.

I picture Mam and Dad, sat by the phone back home. Desperate for news about their three girls. Dozens of unanswered questions battering them from all sides. I only hope when this is over, they understand why I've made the choices I have. Why this is the only way to clear Grant's name. To get us all out from under it.

Layt and I have spent all night in a twenty-four-hour McDonald's, drinking coffee, trying to second-guess all the ways this could go pear-shaped. There's no amount of prep that guarantees we all walk away from this intact, but what other choice do we have? We're opting for a variation on a previous theme, Layt listening in and recording via an open Skype call via his laptop, tucked away out of sight in the Community Centre on the edge of the woods that surround the park.

As I draw closer, I see a solitary figure studying the gold statue inset into the pagoda. Even from this distance I know it isn't the Irishman. Wrong height, noticeably wider around the waist. Looks like grey hair poking out from underneath a flat cap too. Plenty of time for whoever it is to have their moment and leave. I turn a slow three-sixty as I reach the foot of the steps. Two couples at opposite ends of the lake, strolling arm in arm, a frustrated fisherman leaning forwards in his chair by the water's edge, shooing away a family of ducks from his pitch, a couple of other people in the distance, but too far away to make out anything about them. As I set foot on the first step, the man turns to face me.

'Mrs Brewer.'

He's not asking. This man knows exactly who I am. What the hell is going on?

'Who are you?'

'I'm the man Mr Clay works for,' he says, 'Please.' He extends a hand like he's about to help me board a boat.

Of the few players I know in this game, he's too old to be Osgood's son, so I take a wild guess.

'Dr Myers?'

His face crinkles into a smile, the sort you'd expect from a kind old grandfather. He inclines his head in acknowledgement. 'Clever girl.'

What is with these idiots and their condescension, I wonder? Half a dozen more steps and I'm up level with him.

'You're wondering where Mr Clay is?' he says, answering before I can. 'Close by, with your sisters. I thought it would be far more pleasant for us to chat here first though. We can go to them soon enough.' He stands, hands clasped behind his back, studying me. 'I must say, you've given us quite the run around.'

He sounds impressed, but I don't react or respond, still scanning the treeline.

'They're quite safe, I assure you. You've done the right thing by meeting me. I wanted a chance to talk plainly, off the record, though,' he says, tapping a finger to his nose, smiling like they've just shared an in-joke. 'What we do, it wouldn't be appreciated or understood by everyone if word got out.'

'If people knew you'd stolen their DNA you mean?' I ask, as innocently as if enquiring after his health.

'He who is not courageous enough to take risks will accomplish nothing in life.'

I try my best to look unimpressed, unflustered. 'Who's that meant to be? Plato, Einstein?'

'Muhammad Ali actually. All I'm saying is the risks we took were considerable, and I know not everyone will agree, but ask those whose health has improved due to treatments we have pioneered. Ask families who had years longer with loved ones because of what we did. Could you look any one of them in the eye and tell them they did not deserve that? That they should have let people they love suffer longer, die sooner, all because some people would not want their DNA being used for the good of others? Conviction rates have never been this high since records began. Less than three per cent of murders go unsolved now thanks to what I helped build. Are you telling me you'd swap that to preserve someone's right to privacy?'

Never mind Francis Osgood, Alston Myers should be a politician. He phrases his arguments in such a way as to make disagreeing with him unpalatable.

'That's not the point though, is it,' I counter. 'You could have asked. Should have asked. Given people a choice at least.'

'Did you know only four per cent of eligible people donate blood?' he asks. 'Just because people can do good, doesn't mean they will.'

'That doesn't make it right,' I say, hating that there's a hint of logic in what he says.

'If people like me don't take considered risks, people like you die. It's that simple,' he says, strolling past her to the edge of the walkway, gazing out at the lake. 'A doctor called Nicholas Stern, back in the early 1900s, inserted a cancerous lymph node under his skin to prove it wasn't infectious. A little extreme I'll grant you, but without risks, we'd still be in the Stone Age.'

'Except you don't take the same risks as everyone else, do you, Dr Myers?'

A narrowing of eyes, friendly mask slipping for a second. 'What do you mean by that?'

'I mean that you don't appear in HELIX, do you?'

'What? Don't be ridiculous. Of course, I do. We all do.'

'You forget, we've had a browse around. Had a chance to have a look at a few records in particular. Ossie Reynolds for one. You remember him? You added him yourself.'

'That's no secret,' he says. 'Anyone with access can see that.'

'Can they see the hidden change logs, though?' I ask. 'The ones that your admin access shows. The ones that include a command to overwrite the entry in the national database with your version. Why would you need to do that I wonder?'

'This isn't about me, this is much bigger—' he starts but I cut him off.

'It is about you, though. It's about why you needed to make sure he was caught. It's why you don't appear in HELIX.'

'I hoped we could talk this through,' he says. 'Come to an understanding that lets everyone walk away, but I can see now I should have listened to Mr Clay, done this his way. Don't say I didn't try. He has men close by. If you run, it'll only make things worse for your sisters.'

I don't believe for a second that he ever had any intention of a peaceful resolution. See him reach into his jacket pocket, pulling out a phone. Time to pull the pin.

'I know it was you,' I blurt out. 'Who killed Catriona Osgood.'

It's more a series of twitches than an expression, half-turning his head as if he's been slapped, but he quickly recovers. 'Enough of this madness,' he says, but there's a rawness to his voice, like he's hoarse from shouting. He must have tapped to make a call, because he speaks again, but not to me. 'Mr Clay, would you join us now, please?'

At the mention of his name, I go on high alert, eyes flicking back down the path, across to the treeline. At first, nothing. Then a cluster of dark shapes move, detaching themselves from shadows. Moving across the open ground at a trot. Five figures.

'Shit,' I mutter under my breath, then to Myers, 'It's not madness though, is it,' I say, words gushing out now. 'You couldn't be part of the database, because one of the first names to flag would have been yours. You killed her. Why, I don't know, but you killed her and framed Ossie

Reynolds, overwrote the sample they took at the scene, your sample with his, and watched him go down.'

'I really wish it didn't have to happen like this,' Myers says with what sounds like genuine regret.

'You were a match in HELIX then, and you're a match in HELIX now,' she's a shade below a shout now.

Behind his thick rimmed glasses, his eyes sparkle with mischief. 'Risk and sacrifice, Mrs Brewer. Without mine, HELIX would never have existed. I did what I had to do, made my choices. I've lived them for thirty years, which is more than you'll be able to say for you and your sisters. But if, as you say, I'm not in there how could I be a match for anything?'

'You weren't in there,' she agrees, checking her watch, 'at least not until around half an hour ago.'

'What? That's ... have you lost your mind? No matter, this conversation is over. You can chat with Mr Clay from here.'

'She means you're in there now.'

A familiar voice from the path to the east. Its sound is like a ripcord, snapping me out of my growing panic, reminding me I hold more cards now than I have in the past forty-eight hours.

'Frank.'

It comes out as a confused gasp. Myers sounds short of breath, and I watch him take two steps back, resting against the stone surround of the pagoda.

'Alston,' Osgood, nods a greeting. 'Now would be a good time to call off your boys there,' he says, gesturing to the men who've picked up pace, fifty metres out now.

Myers swallows, does his best to square back his shoulders, regain a hint of composure. 'Why would I do that Frank?'

'Because it's over, Alston. You're done.'

'Done? What? Please tell me you don't believe this nonsense, Frank?'

'I didn't until yesterday afternoon.'

'What? Frank, how can you say that, after everything we've built, everything we've achieved?'

'Because she's right, Alston. Now, please, gentlemen.'

He appears to speak the last few words to nobody in particular, but I see movement off to his right, and down by the lake. The two couples who had been out for an afternoon stroll were now approaching, coats open, handguns drawn, closing the gap. One branched off to cover Myers, the other three fan right to intercept the approaching men, who pull guns of their own. Not all though. There's one who isn't armed. A face that should be safe over a mile away. Layt is eggshell white, looking like he might faint any minute.

The final face takes me a second, but only till I clock those eyes. The same ones that stared at me through a webcam after killing Christopher Xiang. The Irishman. Any doubt evaporates when he speaks.

'Figured if we're having a party, we need to make sure everyone's invited,' Clay says, and every soft syllable is like nails on a blackboard.

'Sorry, Maggie,' Layt stammers.

Poor kid just looks like he needs a hug.

'Frank, what the hell is this,' Myers protests, but it's weaker now, borderline pleading.

'This is me honouring my wife's memory,' he says, slow walk to close the gap between him and Myers. 'When Mrs Brewer came to me, told me about how you'd twisted what we built into ...' he searches for the words, pained expression like he's passing wind, 'exactly what I was afraid of all those years ago when I voted against the genetics bill the first time around. Back before you took her from me.'

'I would never—'

'Save it, Alston. I know it was you. Earlier, at the West-erbury. The glass you drank out of. I called in a favour at your lab from one of the old techs that knows me from way back. He rushed it through for me, uploaded it, and what do you know? It pinged as a duplicate for an exist-ing record. The one for Ossie Reynolds. The same DNA that was found under Catriona's nails. DNA is never wrong, Alston. You taught me that.'

It's like watching a balloon deflate. Myers gives up any previous attempt to posture up, instead sagging back against the stone surround.

'She wasn't meant to get hurt,' he says after a beat.

'Dr Myers,' Clay chimes in, edging a few steps for-wards. 'Let's not be too hasty and say anything we might regret, shall we?'

'My work is my life, Frank, you know that. I had such big dreams back then. Dreams you helped bring to life. You just ... needed the right motivation.'

'Motivation,' Osgood breathes out. 'Motivation?' Louder now, rising to a roar as he advances on Myers. 'By God I'll give you motivation.'

He grabs Myers by the lapels, swinging him around, pushing him up against the pagoda.

'It was an accident, I swear.'

'Tell me then, Alston. Tell me how you *accidentally* killed my wife?'

'Dr Myers,' Clay tries again. 'Why don't we call Mr Osgood, and see if we can't straighten this all out?' He's walking slowly towards the pagoda still, hands out and open.

'Stay where you are,' one of Osgood's men yells, pistol trained on Clay's centre mass.

'Who's this, Frank? You got your own team now?'

'Short-term loan thanks to one of our friends in The Six,' he says. 'They won't be attending Matthew's little meeting later anymore, by the way. And no need to call my son. I'm the only Osgood that matters here today.'

'She was having an affair,' Myers says weakly. 'With one of your staff. I saw them together when I came to your house to try and persuade you to change your mind after the vote. Didn't realise you were still in Westminster that day. I waited until he left, then confronted her. Said if she didn't convince you to vote my way, I'd tell you about the affair. She said I was a peeping Tom, called me disgusting, said she'd report me as a prowler, and that you'd make sure I never worked anywhere worthwhile ever again. Started laughing, saying I'd be lucky to teach science at a primary school when you were done with me. Something just snapped, and I ... next thing I know, I'd grabbed her, and ...'

Words slow to a dribble, and he can't meet Osgood's stare anymore. When he turns his head, Maggie could swear she sees tears.

'I'm sorry, Frank, I tried to make it up to you, I tried—'

'You tried to ... don't you see,' Osgood leans to one side so he can look him in the eye again. 'Everything, all of it, from that point on, has been a lie.'

He sounds choked up now, thirty years of what he deemed good work, crumbling like wave-battered cliffs.

'Not all of it,' Myers tries to salvage the smallest inch. 'The work we did, the lives our treatments saved—'

'Bought by blood money,' Osgood counters. 'Mine to start with, then company money to buy votes when they were needed. Whenever anyone threatened to vote the way I should have. And if they couldn't be bought, you set them up.'

'N-n-no, that wasn't my idea, that was ...'

He clams up, stopping short of naming names, but doesn't take Sherlock Holmes to work out he means Frank's son, Matthew.

Clay sighs, takes another few steps forward. He's close enough to reach out and touch the stone lion now if he wanted.

'I wouldn't advise it, son,' says Osgood, giving him the briefest of glances.

'Back,' one of Osgood's men barks at him. 'Step back.'

'Ah what are you gonna do?' he asks softy. 'Shoot an unarmed man in the back? I won't make any trouble. Here you go.'

He slowly raises both hands, clasping them behind his head, lacing fingers together. There's something about the calm cockiness that makes my scalp itch.

The man covering Clay with the pistol switches to a one-handed grip, moving closer, grabbing one of Clay's hands, presumably to secure him just like his team.

I don't think I've ever seen someone move so fast. Nothing wasted, smooth, flowing like water. As soon as the hand touches Clay, he's whirling around, dropping into a half-crouch. Hammering a fist into the man's groin, reaching up to grab the wrist of the gun hand as he doubles over, stripping it from nerveless fingers. Osgood's men aren't reacting fast enough. Clay is still moving as the man crumples to the ground, sprinting the few metres to the side, jamming his newly acquired weapon into Layt. I feel an arm snake around my waist and see to my horror that one of Clay's men has used the confusion to dart behind me. Both he and Clay swing

Layt and I around, positioning us as shields, guns to our heads.

'Stand 'em down, Frank,' Clay says, usual softness on his voice replaced with something akin to excitement. 'Stand 'em down and we all head home and put our feet up.'

'This isn't your fight,' Osgood tells him. 'You're just the hired help.'

That gets a laugh. 'That's exactly why it's my fight,' he says. 'You're not exactly gonna give me a nice review on Trustpilot if I don't do my job are you?'

'Last chance,' says Osgood. 'This is between me and him,' he nods towards Myers, 'and my son it seems.'

'Your son will pay me a damn sight more than you will to make sure this goes the right way,' says Clay, 'and that starts with her.' As he says it, he shifts his aim inches to the left, and I find myself staring down the small, unblinking eye of a gun barrel. 'Where is it, Maggie, the proof you went back to your flat for?'

'It's somewhere safe,' I say recoiling as the gun barrel strokes the skin by my temple. 'You hurt any of us and you'll never get your hands on it.'

'Oh, how very Hollywood,' Clay says, looking genuinely amused. 'Then this must be the part where I say maybe, maybe not, but Layt here won't be alive to see it either way.'

Layt's legs look about to buckle, abject terror plastered across his face.

'Now I'll ask again, where is it?'

From the corner of my eye, Osgood's men take baby steps, trying to change the angles, but Clay and his man counter with moves of their own. How the hell this ends peacefully is anyone's guess, but with quite literally a gun to my head, I can only see one way out of the cul-de-sac.

'It's in my pocket,' I say finally. I move my hand down at a snail's pace.

'See now, how hard was that?' Clay says. 'Now pass it to my man there, nice and slow.'

When I slide it out, I grip it like my life depends on it, feeling the sharp edge of the tail dig into my fingers. For the first time since waking up in the hotel room that night, my world seems to stop the tailspin. I'm so fucking sick of being told what to do. Of being done to. Forced to run, to hide.

Clay cocks his head to one side, expecting a USB stick, puzzled as to what he's seeing. His face has the same effect on the man behind me, and he shifts his gun hand as he peers around me to see what I'm holding, moving the barrel off to the side a few inches. The other hand holding my arm relaxes a touch.

I clutch harder, the spines on the tail sending pain pulsing through my hand. Pain turns to anger. Anger to action. I wrench my arm away, wheeling around, ducking inches in case he manages to bring the pistol back around. The metallic edge of the tail whistles around in a short arc, snagging as if in slo-mo in the man's neck.

I see it all in full technicolour. Flap of skin opening like the corner of a juice carton. A pulse of red shooting out. Momentum sends me in a graceless pirouette, pulling him around blocking me, in some part at least, from Clay. I stumble to one knee, flinching as something hard strikes my leg.

His gun has landed barrel first on my kneecap as both of his hands scrabble to find a grip on the ceramic fish.

The weapon clatters onto the ground and I scoop it up, aware of shouting going on from all sides.

The man is swaying, like a tree about to be felled. Beyond him, for the first time since he popped onto my Zoom screen, Clay looks surprised. Rattled even. But it disappears just as fast, replaced with a look that oozes controlled anger. I raise the gun, hand shaking like a leaf in the breeze, and point it towards him. He sneers and presses the barrel of his own till it bites into the flesh on Layt's head, hard enough to make Layt cry out in pain.

'You'll probably miss us both,' Clay says, 'but I won't miss him. Now drop the fucking gun, or I drop your boy, then you.'

'You do that, they'll kill you,' I say, stepping back from Clay's man, now lying on his back making a noise like he's choking on a chip. There's blood on my hand. His blood. My face feels wet too but I daren't do anything except keep the gun focused on Clay. He's right, of course. No way can I shoot for fear of hitting Layt, but what else can I do?

Around me, voices scream at Clay to drop the gun, but it's all just white noise. My world reduces to Clay and Layt. Nothing else matters. They're close enough that I see his cheeks wet with tears. See him swallow hard. Eyes begging me to save him. If only I knew how.

'They're going to shoot me anyway,' Clay says. 'Or try at least. Here's what's going to happen. Playtime's over. You've got till the count of five to give me what I want, then I'm pulling the trigger.'

I know he's not bluffing, so why has this sense of calm draped over me like I've stepped into the eye of the storm? Quick flick of the eyes to one side and I see the panic on Myers' face as things look set to spiral further away from his picture-perfect ending.

I look into Clay's eyes, icy pools of blue. Sense that he's readying the last ounce of pressure on the trigger. The original SD card he craves so much sits snugly inside the novelty fish case that dangles from the neck of the man I've just killed. The irony of me finally becoming the murderer they've tried to frame me as.

'If you've laid a finger on my sisters—'

'No more talking, just counting.'

I lock eyes with Layt as he finally speaks.

'Remember the rooftop, Maggie.' I see Layt holding three fingers by his side, out of sight of Clay.

What's he on about? My finger trembles against the trigger.

'Was it you who killed Rose?'

'Five …'

'Did you set Grant up?'

'Four …'

'Was it you?' I ask. 'Who threw Davey off that roof?'

'Three …'

'Remember the ten count,' Layt shouts, and as his last finger curls up, I understand. In that same moment, Layt kicks back, heel meeting shin, and jerks his head away to the right.

Clay hadn't finished his count back in Tynemouth. Time to play by his rules. Layt's sudden move distracts him, but the speed of his recovery is insane. He ignores Layt, ignores any pain from the kick to his shin. Starts swinging his gun towards me.

I point and pull. Once. Twice. The third time, the zip of the bullet coming back at me is an angry mosquito. I close my eyes, bracing for impact, and all I see is Grant.

Chapter Eighty

When I open my eyes, the first thing I see are Clay's, but something has changed. A mash-up of surprise and confusion spreads out from them, like ripples on a pond. The arm holding his gun is bobbing downwards, an inch at a time, as if lowered by a puppeteer. Two red blotches bloom on his shirt. One high in his chest, the other lower down off-centre above his belly button.

I keep the gun pointed towards him, even as men rush in, closing their hands over me, over the weapon, peeling my fingers gently back. Two of them have advanced on Clay, weapons trained on him. I suck in a series of breaths, and it's as if Clay and I are synced up. Each one I take, his arm sags lower, knees buckle, sinking to the ground. His mouth twitches, forming shapes with no sound, and a second later, he keels over. I stay rooted to the spot as those pale eyes that have haunted my last forty-eight hours close for the last time.

'Maggie,' Layt calls to me as he gets up from where he fell. 'Maggie, are you alright. Tell me you're okay?'

'I'm fine,' I say, sounding and feeling flat, massive adrenaline crash hitting home, and Layt lurches towards me. We practically collapse into one another, clinging tight. Another arm drapes across my shoulder as my own knees start to tremble. Frank Osgood.

'It's okay,' he says softly. 'It's done.'

I let Layt hold me there, face angled so I can still see Clay's body, readying myself for the eyes to pop open again, but he's no more alive than the stone lions by the fountain.

Footsteps behind us make me flinch, and I peel apart from Layt as another four men pound across the grass towards us, dressed similar to Clay's men.

'It's okay,' Osgood reassures me. 'They're with me.' I watch as two of them make a beeline for Myers, the other pair moving to help their colleagues with Clay's remaining men.

My head is vibrating like a rung bell, and I'm just getting my legs back under me when Frank Osgood squeezes my shoulder.

'Maggie. Someone else to see you. Two someone's, actually.'

From the south end of the lake, four more figures emerge from the tree-line. Two are kitted out the same as the other men, but two are unmistakably female.

'They had them in a van over by the Buddhist temple,' Osgood says.

Before he's halfway through his sentence, I'm out of the blocks like a sprinter, running to them. Moya and Julie break away, streaking across the grass towards me. We come together in a collision of tears, hugging so tight it threatens to cut off circulation. This is all that matters, everything else can wait.

Chapter Eighty-One

Matthew Osgood paces past the plate glass windows for the hundredth time. Myers. Clay. Every member of the fucking Six. None of them are returning his calls. His irritation levels have risen to those of a dumped teenager blocked by their ex. It's a wonder he hasn't worn a groove in the carpet.

Hundreds of feet below him, football fields of servers, the beating heart of HELIX. Millions of souls, essence captured, held captive till called upon. After today, a new start. Clear the decks. Double down on cyber-security, deal with the others, Myers included. Time for The Six to become The One.

His father and Myers think they've scaled the heights, but it's just the foothills. Thanks to the post-COVID UK border controls, two-minute rapid tests for every man, woman and child entering or leaving the UK, he has added thirty-million plus to his stash in the last year alone. Initial talks with a number of interested foreign powers have progressed better than he could have hoped for. The money they're willing to pay for their own versions of HELIX is set to dwarf what they make from IQ. Fuck Gates, Musk and Bezos. This time next year, he'll be looking down on all of them.

The ping of an elevator cuts through his daydream. Doors slide open, but it's not a face he's expecting, today of all days.

'What are you doing here?'

'Son. We need to talk.'

He just stares as his father strides in like he still owns the place. Well, technically, he does, having retained the controlling interest in the hive of companies that make up the layers around IQ, despite Matthew having been in the CEO seat for a good few years now.

'It's not a good time, Dad,' he stammers, hating the way his father's presence rattles him, even now. The old bastard still casts the longest of shadows. 'I'm kind of in the middle of something.'

'Not anymore you aren't.'

'What ... I ... what do you mean?'

'I mean it's over, Matty.'

The use of his childhood name throws him even more. His father has never been the sentimental type, but it catapults him back twenty-some years, to the first few years when it had been just the two of them. Two against the world.

'What's over?'

Of course, there's only one thing he could be referring to, but for the life of him, Matthew can't grasp how his dad could possibly know about any of it, so playing dumb is still the best option. Only one.

'Maggie Brewer. She's safe. I have what she had, or a copy at least. It's more than enough to sink all of us without a trace.'

'Wait, you have it?' Even as he says it, he curses himself for the indirect admission of guilt. 'How?'

Shake of the head from Dad. 'Doesn't matter. What matters is this is going to need a bigger clean up than Chernobyl, and you can't be the man to do it.'

'Like hell I'm not. Since I took over, I've—'

'Since you took over, you've warped everything I built,' his father snaps. 'HELIX was built in a moral no-man's land, but you changed all that the moment you used it to manipulate things to suit your own ends.'

'I did what I had to do. You would have done the same.'

'No!' Crack of a palm on the table echoes like a gunshot. 'What I created was done with pure motives. None of this ... this shady backroom crap you've pulled. People's lives have been ruined, for God's sake. HELIX was made to punish the guilty, not to take care of arguments you can't win.'

'I did what I had to,' he repeats, sounding like a stubborn five-year-old. 'And if you think you can just waltz back in here and push me out, I'll fight you. The others will stand with me, Myers and the others in The Six.'

'The Six won't stand in the same room as you after today, let alone beside you,' his dad says. 'Not if they value their own freedom. I've made sure of that. And as for Alston...'

It's as if someone has flicked a dimmer switch on the glare of his father's righteous indignation. He gestures to the seat beside him.

'Sit, please. There's something else we need to talk about. Something more important.'

Matthew screws up his face in disbelief. First the old man waltzes in laying down the law, looking to strip away his livelihood, and now he changes tack, as if HELIX is nothing more than a pet passion project in a garage.

'Please, Matthew.'

He's a ticking timebomb of pent-up frustration, ready to do pretty much anything to avoid being sucked back into his father's shadow, but something in his dad's eyes draws him in, guides him to the seat.

'The other reason it has to be me that takes care of this,' he says, leaning forward, taking Matthew's hands in his, which throws him off balance even more. 'It's a lie, Matty. All of it, right from the start.'

'Eh? What's a lie?'

He listens as his dad tells him about how HELIX really came to be. About Alston Myers, and about what really happened to his mum. Matthew is so transfixed by what he's hearing, he doesn't even think to pull his hands free to wipe the tears as his dad tells him how Myers strangled her, and called it a risk in the name of science. When his dad has finished, he lets go of Matthew's hands, pulling him into a hug, and they just sit like that for a time. Father and son, mourning their loss for a second time.

Chapter Eighty-Two

My footsteps echo as I make my way across the raised wooden stage. As I make my way across to the microphone, it's as if all the air is sucked out of the room. I fix my eyes ahead. Can't look into the crowd. Not yet.

Eight days since I buried my husband. Countless hours staring at sheets of paper with lines scratched through paragraphs. A dozen scrapped versions of what I want to say. But as I reach the raised wooden lectern, a cocktail of grief and anger at the reason I'm here, towards Osgood and Myers, wipes the words from my mind.

I place the folded piece of paper on a flat surface and smooth out the creases with a palm. When I finally allow myself to glance up, there's a sea of faces, from God only knows how many newspapers, but the only ones I actually want to see are sat off to the side of the stage with me. Mam, Moya and Julie. I swear Mam has aged these past few weeks. If things had gone differently she could have been left with only Freddie by her side, after I managed to drag most of my siblings into the crosshairs.

For the longest heartbeat I feel a flash forward of the pain I could have caused her, and it's almost enough to crush me like a car in a compactor.

Shutters whirr from the rows of expectant lenses at the front. The same press who happily held Grant up as a murderer, are here in droves to hear what really happened.

But all I can talk about is the tip of the iceberg. So much has to remain hidden, courtesy of a reluctant deal with Frank Osgood. Then it dawns on me, the reason I'm here, the words I have to say. And as I open my mouth to speak, it's as if unseen hands tap away at a keyboard, sentences unfurling in my mind. I'm not here to give a statement to the press. I'm here to tell the story of the man I love.

'My husband would have loved to see me standing here today. I hate public speaking. He'd have been the first to heckle me. And I wouldn't have had it any other way.'

My throat already feels raw from the effort of keeping any kind of game face on. Julie and Moya bookend Mam. They sit shoulder to shoulder with her, like minders. Both of them give an encouraging nod when I glance their way that cranks up the pressure in the dam holding back my tears.

'Grant was kind, caring, thoughtful and the worst karaoke singer I've ever had the misfortune to hear.'

Sympathetic laughter ripples through the room.

'He was also someone who believed in doing what's right. In telling the stories that needed to be told, no matter what the cost. He was a good man, and unfortunately for him, and for me, it cost him his life.'

Each sentence is a step out onto emotionally thin ice, never knowing when it might crack.

'The police have asked me not to comment on what that story is as it's part of an ongoing investigation into the murders of Rose Evans, Paul Cosgrove and Christopher Xiang. Suffice to say, Grant died trying to make the world a better place, even though he leaves it a poorer one for not being in it anymore. All charges against him and me have been dropped, and I'd appreciate it if everyone here can respect that.'

The lies blended in between the facts make me feel like a fraud. Have to remind myself of the ripple effect of coming clean. How would the press react to the truth, the whole truth and nothing but? It'd be a feeding frenzy. Might make me feel better, but, as much as I hate to say it, there's a degree of sense in what Osgood is proposing. It's more dangerous unleashed than bottled up. Too many cases would be thrown open for review, too many bad people getting their freedom back to do more bad things.

'I couldn't save him, but I can save his reputation.'

I barely make it to the end of the sentence, when the first sob escapes. I grip the lectern so tight I fancy I can snap the sides off. I do my best to swallow down the sickly sense of sorrow that threatens to spill out and swamp me. I try and force out the next words, but they just won't come. That's when I feel it. The arms around my shoulders.

I turn to see Mam on one side, Moya and Julie on the other. Their strength flows into me, giving the tears permission to come without shame. But with them comes certainty. The knowledge that whatever life throws at me, this family is unbreakable. A rock against which all that other shit will shatter and turn to dust.

I surprise myself at how clear my voice sounds in spite of the tears.

'There are still those out there who say no smoke without fire. That Grant and I somehow played a role in the tragic deaths of Rose, Paul and Christopher. To them I say this. He was ten times the human being of any of you, and if everyone could be a little bit more like him, the world would be a better place. And that's what I intend to do, in my own small way by continuing his work and his legacy at the *Manchester Standard.*'

The shutter clicks have slowed, faces solemn, and I wonder how they'll report this tomorrow. Will it be a faithful account of what I've said, or will it be littered with speculation and 'sources say' style teasers.

'Each of you here can do your part by just telling the truth of what I'm saying. By not continuing your pointless speculations for the sake of shifting a few copies or racking up views. But how many of you are brave enough to settle for that?'

For a few heartbeats there is blessed silence. The slightest of squeezes from Mam. If only I could click my heels and be in her house with a cup of tea now.

'Now if you'll excuse me, my family and I have somewhere to be,' I say, slipping my hand into Mam's.

We walk off stage to a chorus of questions, and I leave every last one in the room. No encore here today. Far more important places to be right now. Everything else can wait in line.

Chapter Eighty-Three

'And you're sure he's got the clout to make it happen?' Davey asks, sceptical to the last. 'He might try and double cross us.'

Even though he's in a private room now, we're still talking in stage whispers, never sure if footsteps passing outside might be about to burst in.

I shake my head. 'He knows I still have enough to sink the whole thing if I go public. Once the doc signs you off, you're free to go.'

'Don't suppose I can hang on to his number for next time I'm in bother as well, can I?' he asks hopefully.

'Best not push it,' I say.

'So this is the kid who saved your arse then?', and I remember that I didn't get a chance to do a proper intro back on the rooftop before Clay stormed the place.

'Yep, this is Layton,' I say, quickly correcting myself, 'Layt.'

'Doesn't look like much,' Davey says, looking between them, cheeky smile flickering to life. 'But anyone who does right by you, is alright by me.'

'You're the first bloke I've ever met that fell that far without a parachute and lived,' Layt says, and the three of us crease into genuine, relieved smiles.

'So, you're not going to then,' Davey asks. 'Go public I mean? You really think you can just let sleeping dogs lie?'

The size of the sigh speaks volumes as to how difficult a decision this has been. Still is. I lock eyes with Izzy where she sits in the chair beside me, as I shake my head. She was furious when I first told her, but she understands now.

'HELIX has helped convict thousands of people over the years, and from what we've seen, there are only a handful where it's been misused, and only by a small group of people. If we go public, there's a chance every single conviction will be overturned. A hell of a lot of bad people would be out there, doing the same again, or worse maybe. Couldn't have that on my conscience.'

'What about the doctor? What happens with him?'

'Myers is going down for Christopher, Rose and Paul Cosgrove's murders.'

'Am I missing something?' Davey asks.

'Too many questions asked if they try and send him down for Catriona Osgood, about how the DNA got cocked up. Besides, thanks to Frank Osgood, a sample of the doctor's DNA has been found at all three scenes now,' I say with a double eyebrow raise.

'Couldn't happen to a nicer bloke, except that Clay fella. Shame he's not around to get any proper justice,' Layt chips in.

'Oh, I dunno,' Davey shrugs. 'I'm quite happy with him where he is to be honest.'

'You and me both,' I agree. 'One good thing to come out of this, though. Osgood said he'll have Xiang's Alzheimer's findings reviewed. Try and pick up where he left off if they can. That, plus a promise that every single HELIX conviction will be reviewed behind the scenes. He's asked me and Layt to be part of it to make sure it's done properly.'

'Going to work for him?' Davey puffs out his cheeks. 'Didn't see that one coming. You sure that's what you want?

What's to say they won't just pick up where they left off once you finish and swan off?'

I look at Layt, catch his wink and smile.

'Layt here has installed a second back door. One that gives us sight of anything that comes in or out of HELIX. They try and do it again, this lets us block it before it happens.'

Davey laughs. Starts as a chuckle, then rises until it's a bellow to rival Brian Blessed. 'Anyone ever tell you that you'd make a bloody good criminal? The pair of you.'

'Don't need to come and work with you anyway. I start my new job in two weeks.'

'New job?' Davey asks. 'You leaving the paper then?'

I shake my head. 'Turns out Osgood knows the owner of the *Standard*. He's called in a favour and looks like I'm going to get a crack at the real stories after all. They're giving me Grant's job, well on a six-month trial anyway.'

Davey grabs my hand, wincing through his smile that takes over his whole face.

'Trial my arse,' he says. 'That's the job you were born to do.'

I feel arms wrap around me from behind, and twist my head to see Izzy latched on. This part is a surprise I'd been saving, even from her.

'He'd be so bloody proud,' she says, echoes of her earlier words from the car journey. 'I'm so bloody proud of you as well.'

I relax into her squeezing arms and smile, swallowing hard.

'Well,' I say finally, 'it was either that or come and work with you, Davey, and I'd only show you up.'

His laughter is contagious, and the four of us ride the wave, until silence finally settles again.

'I'll put in a word with Gregor for you,' Davey says, and from the look on his face, I'm not entirely convinced he's joking. The mention of his name, though, is a trigger, and I shoot a glance first Layt's way, then Izzy's.

'I'd best head off,' he says, grabbing his rucksack. 'Call you tomorrow, Maggie.'

'Hey,' Davey calls after him as he reaches the door. Layt turns, waiting for another wisecrack, but instead, he gets sincerity. 'Thanks, man, for having her back when I couldn't. I owe you.'

Layt smiles, nods. 'Enjoyed every minute of it,' and steps out into the corridor.

Izzy moves in for one more squeeze from me, followed by a gentler one for Davey, then follows Layt out.

I stare after her for a few seconds, psyching myself up for a conversation he's not going to want to hear.

'Davey, about Gregor, there's something you need to know.'

'Oh, you've got your serious face on. Is this where you tell me I should stop hanging round with him and get a proper job at Maccy D's or somewhere?'

'He sold us out, Davey. Gave them Layt's name. My new mobile number. Even had your phone rigged to track my calls to you.'

'What?' he screws his face up. 'Don't be daft, man. Gregor's not like that. He's not on the straight and narrow, but he's had my back for years. He promised he'd watch out for you, and in my world, that means something.'

Enough of this stupid fucking boys' club-style loyalty where it hasn't been earned. 'He hasn't though. Had your back for years I mean. He's the reason ...'

I stop myself before I spit out the rest. It's clear from his face that he won't let it lie, though.

'Reason? What for?'

'Nothing.'

'Oh no you don't. He's a mate, Mags, and we've been through a lot of shit together. You've never liked him, but that doesn't mean you can slag him off for no reason.'

It's a conversation that's been over a decade in the making, but the last few days have sapped my tolerance for bullshit to absolute zero.

'He's the reason you spent two years inside,' I say calmly.

Davey looks at her blankly. 'What the fuck's that supposed to mean?'

'I mean the guy you put in hospital that night, the one you thought had grabbed my backside, he was just stepping in to help me. Gregor's the one who grabbed hold of me.'

'Wait, what? That makes no sense. He said—'

'Yeah, I know what he said. That he'd seen it, stepped in to help his mate's little sister, but that's a lie. Look him in the eye and ask him yourself.'

'If that's a lie,' he says narrowing his eyes, 'then why didn't you say something? Why did you let it happen?'

I feel the tears threatening to pop now, and swallow hard. 'Because you were already in the back of the police van. He said if I kept quiet, he'd fix it. Call in a favour and get you out. Then when I realised it was too late after they charged you, he said he'd call in different kinds of favours if I came clean. The kind that would make all of our lives difficult if he went down. Mine, Mam's, Dad's, everyone's.'

'No ...' he says, slowly shaking his head. 'No, I don't believe it, he wouldn't—'

'Why do you think I left for Manchester not long after you got out?' I ask. 'Couldn't bring myself to look at either of you. Look at me now, though, Davey,' I say, fixing him with an earnest stare. 'After all we've been through, look at me and tell me if you think I'm lying.'

Only takes a few seconds for him to start nodding. 'I'll kill him,' he growls. 'I'll fucking kill him.'

'You do that, and you'll be back in, only for longer this time,' I say, stabbing a finger towards the ground. 'We all need you here.' Another heavy swallow. 'I need you here. Promise me.'

The struggle is a physical battle on his face, tearing him between what he's hard-wired to do, and family loyalty. Rages on for what feels like an eternity, but in the end, he grits his teeth, nods. Might not be the last time I have to persuade him, but for now, family trumps everything.

Chapter Eighty-Four

As I step through the double doors into the car park, I close my eyes, pausing by the ticket machine. Suck in a long deep lungful. Feel my bed calling to me even from this distance. I've taken up Moya's offer of the spare room for a few days, at least until Davey gets out. After that, who knows?

It's a kind of purgatory, a half-way house. Stuck between my Manchester flat where every breath I draw sucks in memories of Grant, of what happened, and here in the North East, steeped in just as much sorrow, parts of my past I can't imagine facing up to again. Not yet at least.

I see him before he clocks me. On his own, fiddling with his key-fob to lock the car before he heads inside. Personally, I have always thought I take after Mam more, but there's no mistaking the Stephenson nose, a marginally more petite version gracing my face, but Dad's is true to the original template I've seen on old family photos, going back as far as my great grandfather.

I wait by the curb as he finishes faffing and crosses over, spotting me when he's halfway. He's aged these past three or four years in particular, but I could swear there are fresh lines since I saw him last at his house.

'Maggie, I thought you'd be back at Moya's by now.'

I shake my head. 'Not yet. Just wanted to make sure Davey was okay.'

There's an awkward silence, familiar though. Small talk has never been his strong point, and I've had enough short sharp conversations with him over the years to not want to draw them out.

'I'd better head anyway, she's expecting me.'

I step to the side to move past, but Dad shoots out a hand to stop me.

'Listen, Maggie, I ...' he stops, looking lost for words.

'It's fine Dad, I'm okay.'

'No, it's not that, although I'm glad you are,' he says, smiling weakly. Takes a deep breath, reminding me of my own build-up to a serious chat with Davey. 'Davey, he told me ... well he told me what happened. All of it.'

Maggie looks at him like he's lost the plot. 'What do you mean, "all of it"?'

'Everything,' he says. 'About the DNA, what happened to Grant, to him, and what they tried to do to you.'

'He had no right,' I snap. 'I'll bloody kill him.'

'No, please, he was just—'

'He was just stupid. This is dangerous stuff still, Dad. You say anything to anyone and this could hurt a lot of people.'

'What? No, I would never ...' Another deep breath. 'I might be getting on a bit, but I don't think that's why he told me.'

'Come on then, why did he?'

'You and I have never ... well we've clashed quite a bit, over all sorts. Boyfriends, careers, you name it.'

Here we go, I think. Time for a good old-fashioned pep talk. Maybe this one will be extra-special even by his standards. Along the lines of what a great opportunity it could be for a fresh start. Maybe even move back here and get a real job.

'What you did,' Dad says nodding, 'I knew you were strong, but never knew just how strong. Facing up to these people like that, standing your ground ... I know we haven't always seen eye to eye, but what you did ... you're the bravest person I know, Maggie, and even if I can't tell anyone else about it, and whatever you do from here, I just wanted to tell you how proud I am.'

Did not see that coming. It slips under my defences, squeezing my heart, and I can't swallow these tears back down. Nor can he, and he pulls me in close.

'I might struggle saying it at times, but I do love you, sweetheart.'

If the proud comment caught me unawares, this one is the knockout punch. I squeeze him back so hard I fear he might crack like porcelain. Family wins, I tell myself again. Always family.

Acknowledgments

If you've read this far, I'm hoping you'll indulge me a little longer. I'll come on to the much-needed 'thank you's in a moment, but wanted to share with you a little bit about how this book came to be first, because it very nearly didn't make it to the bookshelves. The reason I want to share this is linked to one of the most common questions I get asked at an event: what advice would I give to aspiring authors? Apart from to just get a first draft finished no matter how rough, my go-to is to talk about the need to be resilient, and not be put off by rejection. It's such a subjective industry, and you story just needs to find the right person at the right time.

The Missing Hour is the book that got me my agent, David Headley. When it first went out on submission back in 2021, I got the nicest rejections ever, saying that as much as they loved the writing and the concept, they just couldn't see where it would fit in their list right then. I was obviously disappointed, but went back to the drawing board, and wrote Seven Days, which found a home with Hodder, and somehow even snuck onto the Sunday Times's Bestseller List. When it came to book two of that contract, I still believed The Missing Hour was good enough to see the light of day, and we shared with my editor. Turns out this was that right time, right story, right person, and so here we are, at the end of a book that grabbed its second chance with both hands. The point of sharing this is that, like it or not, rejection has been a

407

part of most writer's lives at some point, so don't give up. If the story is good enough, you'll find a way to make it heard.

Speaking of the quality of a story, what you've just read is a far more polished version than that first draft I finished years ago. Just like this book, I've had a second lease of life as an author, and that started when my agent, David Headley, read a rough draft of this book back in 2021 and decided to take a punt on me. His advice and counsel are worth their weight in gold, and there's nobody I'd rather have in my corner.

My editor at Hodder, Phoebe Morgan, is one of the best in the business, and my books are all the better for having her on the case. Alainna, Jake and Andy over at Team Hodder have kept me on track and helped me navigate the murky waters of events, edits and everything in between, so a huge thanks to them too.

Big shout out to the booksellers who bridge that gap between authors and readers. Rebecca and the team at Goldsboro, Helen and the team at Forum Books, Adele at The Bound, and Fiona Sharp at Waterstones Durham to name but a few. Then there are the librarians, like Clare Pepper in North Tyneside, who I can't thank enough for how passionately you help promote my books to the local communities.

Writing has helped me find my tribe in the form of a few WhatsApp groups of my peers and friends that keep me sane from book to book. The New Criminal Minds group - pincers up people! The Circle of Trust - are legends, one and all. And my Northern Crime Syndicate crew, helping me fly the flag for Northern writers - our Whose Crime Is It Anyway events are some of the most fun I've ever done.

Acknowledgments

The fact you've bought a copy of this book gets you a thank you as well - yes you, reading this now. Without you folks I wouldn't have a job, so thanks for all the books you buy and reviews you leave. Of the thousands of stories you could have picked up, thanks for giving mine a go, and I hope you enjoyed it enough to pick up the next one, or dip into my back catalogue.

When I was promoting my last book, I ran a competition for readers to be a named character in the next one. Big thanks to all who entered, but there can only be one winner, and that is Paul Cosgrove, all the way over in the USA via North East England - thanks for buying a copy of Seven Days, Paul!

No acknowledgments are complete without a tip of the hat to the family that support and encourage me every step of the way: My in-laws, the Sage's, for all moving North and letting Nic marry a Geordie; my parents, Margaret and Bob, who filled my childhood with so many books that writing them now feels like it was always inevitable; and last but by no means least, my wife and kids - Nic, Lucy, Jake and Lily. The best parts of my life are the stories I get to make with you guys every day together as a family.

The Instant *Sunday Times* Bestseller

SEVEN DAYS

Your father is on death row.
You have seven days to save him.
But do you want to?

Read on for an extract of *Seven Days*,
Robert Rutherford's gripping,
high-octane debut thriller

HODDER &
STOUGHTON

Prologue

FLORIDA, 2011

Manny knows that the only way that he walks out of here is if the other guy doesn't. He sees it in the other man's face. A look he's worn himself more times than he cares to remember. Lips drawn into a thin line, narrowing of the eyes. That singular focus that comes with knowing there's only one outcome.

He reaches into the pocket of his jeans for the switch-blade, fingers closing around the handle. The first time he registers that something is wrong is when he flicks his wrist to open the blade. There's a clumsiness to it, like he's a bottle of whiskey deep, relying on sheer muscle memory.

'You walk outta here now, or you'll never walk again,' he shouts at the man, even though he's only six feet away.

No answer. Something glints by the man's side, making Manny's eyes flick down. Just for a second, but it's long enough. The man doesn't so much move as flow towards him. Manny hadn't bothered to turn the kitchen light on, so the dark shape that lunges at him might as well be shadow.

Manny stabs, aiming at the guy's face, but even as he does so, he feels the sluggishness of his efforts. Might as well have concrete flowing in his veins. It's like everything's on slo-mo, for him at least. Not so much his attacker. The man leans to one side, stepping in to slap a palm against Manny's knife hand. The blade slices through the spot where the man's head should have been. Manny tries to reverse the blade, bring it arcing back down, but it's like his head is pumped full of cotton wool, and his hand won't obey fast enough.

The man's hand snakes around Manny's neck, pulling his head down as he slams a knee up and under his ribs, driving the air out with such a force that Manny hears a wet snapping sound before the pain lances through his side. He drops like he's been shot by a sniper. Tries to howl in pain, but can't even draw breath. It's like he's suffocating. Takes a few seconds to realise that the weird gargling noise is coming from him.

One hand clutches his side, the other goes to slash with the switchblade, but there's no strength in his fingers and the knife tumbles harmlessly to the floor. The man swings a foot at it, sending it skittering away out of sight. The pain in Manny's side is a fluid thing. The first flash was hot and white, but already it's being swept away by adrenaline, morphing into something else, a dull ache, throbbing with a drum beat all of its own.

His head feels like an over-shaken snow globe. This isn't a fight he's going to win with his fists. Not unless he can buy a little time to recover.

'Look man,' he rasps, squinting up at the man staring down at him. 'Whatever this is, I'm sure we can work something out.'

The words come out in ones and twos rather than complete sentences as he tries desperately to catch his breath.

He knows that face. Has seen it recently, but can't quite place it. Disgruntled customer, maybe? Manny usually cuts a little of this, and a little of that into his product before he sells it on. Sometimes baby formula, sometimes a little creatine. Could be he'd just been heavy-handed with his extra ingredients, and the dude had a shitty high.

'Look, I don't usually do refunds,' he wheezes, forcing a smile. 'But I can make an exception.'

The man squats down a foot away. Manny tries to rise up onto one elbow, but it's like pushing up through treacle. He feels the man put a hand on his chest.

In through the nose, out through the mouth. Manny lies back, repeats the mantra, desperately trying to find a rhythm, but his breathing is like a misfiring motor. He notices a warmness for the first time. At first, he thinks it's just from the exertion, but it's spreading outwards across his whole body. Like he's being wrapped in a warm blanket. The harder he fights it, the deeper he sinks, as if the carpet is swallowing him up. Manny goes to speak again as the man leans in close.

'Let's . . . look man, I just wanna . . .'

Words run together, jumbled, borderline incoherent.

The eyes that bore into his might as well be glass marbles for all the emotion they contain. Manny's head feels heavy, like it's made of stone, but he manages to force his gaze down to the man's hand, remembering that it had been holding something that twinkled in the light.

It's more ice pick than blade. Four inches of steel tapering to an impossibly fine point. Manny wills himself to reach up, slap it out of the man's hand. Can't be more than twelve inches from his face, but might as well be twelve miles. It's as if someone or something has short-circuited his brain, stopping any orders it sends to his body.

The man studies him for a moment, then flicks the pick around with practised ease, until it's pointing at Manny's left eye.

'You've got to pay what you owe, Manny. I'm here to collect.'

Chapter One

Monday – Seven days to go

Pain sears through Alice's foot as her toes connect with the heavy wooden chair leg. The words sneak out through gritted teeth before she can stop them.

'Bloody hell!'

She doesn't even need to see the disapproving look on her mum's face to know it's there. What qualifies as swearing is a long-time bone of contention. A battle she knows she'll never win. Even so, she cringes inwardly at the apology that follows on autopilot.

She pivots, Mum's arm still round her shoulder, and lowers her into the armchair.

'You get yourself away,' Mum says, even before Alice can straighten up.

It comes out sounding more like *your-shelf*. Even now, four years on from the stroke, there are markers it laid down. Mum jokes that it makes her sound like Sean Connery, but the bravado is just behind closed doors to a safe audience of Alice and her younger sister, Fiona. With anyone else, if you know where to look, the self-conscious tells are there. The way she digs one thumbnail into the edge of the other, worrying at it.

More than once Mum's drawn blood, as if the pain will keep her sharp.

'Plenty of time, Mum,' Alice says, even though she needs to leave in five minutes, tops. She reaches down, easing her mum forwards a few inches to slide an extra cushion behind her back for support.

'Shona'll be here soon,' Mum says shooing her away with one hand. 'Go on, away you go.'

These morning exchanges are regular as clockwork, part of the fabric of Alice's life. Feel borderline scripted at times. She loves her mum, although there are layers to it. Some of them best left alone for everyone's sake. Her carer, Shona, has patience that goes on for days. Enough that it makes Alice feel lacking in that department at times.

'Fiona says she'll swing by this afternoon,' Alice says, smoothing out the creases in her skirt. 'I'll pop in on my way back home later.'

'I'll be fine,' her mum says, a little terse even by her standards.

Alice wishes she had her mum's confidence. Too many times to count she's popped in to find a trail of destruction where Mum has tried to reclaim her independence. Doctors have said she'll likely never regain the full use of her left foot or right arm, both victims of the stroke that nearly killed her. It's enough that she warrants Shona being here five days a week, with Alice and Fiona covering the weekend shifts. Doesn't stop Mum making a cup of tea with her one good hand. Getting it back to her seat intact is another matter entirely.

It's an endless see-saw of emotions for Alice. There are days where she wishes her mum had gone into the assisted living facility the doctors had suggested, for both their sakes. Others where the mere thought of it makes her feel like a candidate for world's worst daughter. God knows it would be the easier option, for her at least. It isn't as if this is their childhood home, stacked with memories that she wants to cling on to. That house is four thousand miles across the Atlantic, and most of the memories there are ones she's happy to forget.

Alice bends down, planting a kiss on her mum's forehead.

'See you later, Mum.'

Alice grabs her bag as she heads out into the hallway. She hears the soft purr of her phone vibrating somewhere in the depths, and rummages around until her fingers close around it.

'Just leaving now,' she says, tucking it under her chin, bag in one hand, the other pulling the door closed.

'Your house, your mum's, or did you stop somewhere else last night?'

The playful insinuation is enough that Alice can picture the twinkle in Moira Wilkinson's eye as she asks the question.

'I'll take the fifth amendment on that one.'

'You're not in the good old US of A now, counsellor,' Moira says, swapping out what Alice thinks of as her posh Geordie accent for a butchered American one.

Ever since she came home from the States four years ago, Moira has never let her forget the lingering accent she brought back with her. It's long gone now, unless she's speaking to one of her friends back in New York, but that doesn't stop her assistant from poking fun when it's just the two of them. Moira's been at the firm since Alice was in nappies, and that kind of tenure buys you a level of tolerance in certain circles.

'I'm just getting in the car now,' Alice says, heels clacking as she walks down the street towards her car. 'Be with you in half an hour. Remind me who my first meeting is with?'

'Mr and Mrs Williams at nine-thirty,' Moira says without missing a beat, 'but you might want to get an extra shot of espresso on your way. Fiona's here, insisting on jumping the queue.'

Alice's brow creases at the mention of her little sister. Since the twins came along, Fiona has lived her life by their routine to a level of precision that would put a drill sergeant to shame. Quick check of the watch shows it's a few minutes after eight. Why the hell is her sister at her office instead of shovelling breakfast into a pair of four-year-olds?

'What does she want?'

'Beats me,' Moira says. 'I told her to call you instead, but she said she'd rather wait. Whatever it is, she's going to owe you a new carpet the way she's pacing.'

Alice thanks Moira for the advance warning and heads out into early morning Whitley Bay traffic. Seagulls drift overhead, circling in search for scraps. The faint hint of salty sea air drifts through the open car window. Pale October sunshine sneaking through gaps in the clouds is just for show, not warmth. Alice smiles to herself, savouring these little pieces of the jigsaw that make up her home town. Worlds apart from the melting pot of her old life in New York City.

She forgot to ask Moira if Fiona's alone, or whether Jake and Lily are there with her. For a split second she has an image of the pair of them scribbling pictures of stickmen on the walls of her office. It'd almost be worth it to see Moira's reaction. She makes her usual resolution to pop round and see the kids more. Somehow, she has acquired the mantle of cool Auntie Alice, even though she feels like she barely gets to see them between work and looking after her mum.

The journey to Newcastle is death by a thousand traffic jams. Alice joins the treacle-slow procession of commuters that crawls along the Cradlewell bypass. She can't help but people-watch as they inch along. Everything from full-blown car karaoke to stoic silence as people get their game faces on for another day in the office.

Hers is a stone's throw from the river, and as she winds down towards the Quayside, the dull green curve of the Tyne bridge arcs over the water like a raised eyebrow. The water beneath is millpond calm, barely flowing.

A flash of light on the south bank catches her eye where early morning sunlight glints off the Sage concert hall. It crouches on top of the riverbank, a giant collage of glass and steel. It's all so different from the Newcastle of her childhood. One she can only remember in snatches. She was nine when her life was uprooted, transplanted from northern nirvana to the muggy humidity of her father's home town of Orlando, Florida.

All Dad's doing. A fresh start he'd said. A homecoming, for him at least. Painting pictures of sunshine and theme parks. The truth was a little more tarnished. Always was where Dad was involved. Something he was happy to bend into a shape that suited. Is he still there, she wonders? Shacked up with *her*, while the mother of his children spends her days trapped in a body that did its level best to throw in the towel four years ago.

Alice hasn't spoken to him since she was twenty-one. The same day her mum finally kicked him out fourteen years ago. He tried an olive branch a couple of times in the months that followed, but the stubbornness she has inherited from him wouldn't let her accept his half-hearted apologies.

It's almost ten to nine by the time she parks up and walks through the doors of Shaw, Finnie and Co, tucked away behind the Crown Court. As soon as she sets foot inside, she sees Moira making a beeline for her, like a sprinter from the blocks, albeit far more elegant. Moira dresses to impress, with a seemingly never-ending procession of outfits. Alice has joked that she only wears them once then throws them away. Fact of the matter is, Moira isn't here for the money. Her husband Steven works Monday to Friday at a London hedge fund. She could walk out the door now and never work another day in her life, but that's just not how she's wired.

'I've made up a nine o'clock for you, so she'll have to be quick,' Moira says with a wry smile.

Alice can't help but smile at how protective Moira gets, even if the opposition is her own sister instead of another solicitor.

'Everything okay with your mum?' Moira asks, voice softening. She lost her own not long after Alice joined the firm. She's never one to overshare, but Alice remembers her talking about how hard it was at the time to juggle her own life, while helping her mum towards the end of hers.

'She's on good form,' Alice says, flashing a practised smile.

'I'll leave you to it,' says Moira after the briefest of pauses.

Alice watches her go, then looks down the length of the building towards her own office. An opaque strip runs through the middle of the glass wall, like a layer of buttercream in a cake. Floating above it, the top of Fiona's head bobs backwards and forwards like a brunette iceberg as she walks back and forth.

Alice puffs out her cheeks as she heads towards the door, half expecting to see two pairs of four-year-old legs running along the length of her office, but when she opens the door, it's just Fiona. Her sister is cut from a different cloth. Four inches shorter than Alice's five six. Dark hair a far cry from Alice's own sandy curls, which she's wearing scraped back.

Her sister stops pacing when she sees her. There's something about her expression that troubles Alice. Something she can't quite read.

'Morning,' she says, trying to inject a level of cheeriness she doesn't feel. 'To what do I owe the pleasure?'

'You might want to sit down,' Fiona says after a beat, with a look that speaks of nothing good to follow.

'What's up? Are the kids okay?' Alice asks, hearing a note of panic in her own voice.

'What? Oh, yeah, they're fine. It's nothing to do with the kids.'

'Where are they?'

'With Trevor, but that's not why I'm here.'

The corners of Alice's mouth turn down at the mention of the kids' dad and Fiona's on-off boyfriend, like she's just sniffed sour milk. Back playing part-time parent by the sounds of it. She sees Fiona clock her reaction, but for once, her sister doesn't bite.

'Why are you here then?'

Fiona slips into a seat beside Alice's desk, gesturing for her to do the same. Alice sighs at the theatrics of whatever this is. She shrugs, then slides past Fiona. Fine, she thinks. She'll play the game until Fiona is ready to get whatever it is off her chest.

Alice lets her bag slide off her shoulder and drop by her feet, then leans back into her seat.

'I've got a nine o'clock,' she says, glancing at her watch to emphasise the point.

'They're going to kill him in seven days,' Fiona's words fall out at a hundred miles an hour.

'What?' Alice says, forehead folding into a spider's web of confused creases. 'What are you talking about? Who's going to kill who?'

'Dad. They're going to kill Dad.'